WHAT YOU SEE

WHAT YOU SEE

HILLY BARMBY

This edition produced in Great Britain in 2025

by Hobeck Books Limited, 24 Brookside Business Park, Stone, Staffordshire ST15 0RZ

www.hobeck.net

A CIP catalogue for this book is available from the British Library.

ISBN 978-1-915-817-74-7 (pbk)

ISBN 978-1-915-817-73-0 (ebook)

Cover design by Jayne Mapp Design

Printed and bound in Great Britain

Are you a thriller seeker?

Hobeck Books is an independent publisher of crime, thrillers and suspense fiction and we have one aim – to bring you the books you want to read.

For more details about our books, our authors and our plans, plus the chance to download free novellas, sign up for our newsletter at **www.hobeck.net**.

You can also find us on Twitter **@hobeckbooks** or on Facebook **www.facebook.com/hobeckbooks10**.

To my mum and dad (who have both passed on), as they never wanted me to let go of my dreams and told me to do whatever I wanted in life. I did, but I wish they were here to see it.

And to my partner, Malk, who is always so supportive, even when I am boring him senseless with all my angst and worries.

And finally, thanks to our hounds, Lara and Daisy. Lara has helped me write all my books, but I must admit her spelling is a@T*ro-sh%us!sz.

Prologue

IF YOU ARE A TWIN, are you always 'you'?

Stepping out through the automatic doors at Málaga airport was like walking into a furnace. The other passengers who'd been on Tilda's flight were immensely pleased and crowing 'heatwave', though the intense light and boiling air made her queasy. Maybe that bottle of wine she'd had mostly to herself last night and the chicken jalfrezi hadn't been such a good idea.

Baseball cap pulled down low, she squinted out at the pick-up area, where the English tourists were consulting maps or waving down taxis, their voices raucous. Did she look the part? Was she being 'Haitch' enough? Certainly, the hangover was genuine. Tilda briefly wondered why Haitch's agent, Damian, hadn't escorted her on the plane. If 'Haitch' was such precious cargo, surely, he'd ensure she arrived on time, especially with her track record.

The Spanish, who were either returning home or heading out, navigated it all cheerfully, herding small children and wheeling trolleys piled with suitcases with alacrity and a lot of amiable shouting. Cars were bumper to bumper, and some were bibbing, and there seemed to be a lot of scary activity concerning parking spaces.

'Haitch!'

For one tiny moment, Tilda forgot who she was supposed to be and looked around her as if expecting Haitch herself to spring out of the shadowy interior.

She spotted Damian waving at her. Bugger! Nearly blown it at the first hurdle. *Concentrate.*

'I'm Haitch, I'm Haitch, I'm Haitch,' she mumbled under her breath.

PART I
The Twins

ONE

Haitch

Saturday 11th June – four days previously

THE STRIDENT MUSIC reverberating around her room made Haitch wince: The Sex Pistols 'Anarchy in the UK'. Whatever had induced her to choose that particular ringtone was beyond her. The drunkard's choice. The White Lightning of ringtones. Surfacing took a long time, as if she was at the bottom of a deep well that was slowly filling, pushing her steadily towards the lip and the light. The phone ceased its wail.

Oh, dear God! She couldn't bear to open her eyes. Was this a hangover? Because she could deal with that. The tingling in her nose and the fullness of her sinuses, coupled with the pounding across the top of her skull and the hot, flushed cheeks stretched tautly; well, that wasn't good. The phone rang again, and Haitch made a fumbling grab for it. She could just make out her agent's blurry name on the tiny screen: Damian Montgomery.

'Oh, bollocks.'

Sliding the bar across, she let him speak first.

'You haven't forgotten where you're meant to be on Thursday, have you, my sweetheart?' His voice was clipped, a bit posh. Haitch reckoned he put it on and was really from Essex.

Haitch lay for a bit in a stupor. 'What? What's happening Thursday?'

'You're going to that crucially important party, remember? The one that could send your career out into space. The one where you're supposed to be impressing a potential patron?'

'What day is it today?'

'For fuck's sake, Haitch. You really need to get a grip. You're not Russell Brand, you know.'

'Had him. I think.'

'Is there anyone left on this planet that you haven't?'

'Only you, my darling boy.'

Haitch could hear the rustle of his silk suit as he moved. The sound exuded exasperation. He was fidgeting.

Damian's voice hardened as though it'd been dunked in a vat of liquid nitrogen. 'Haitch. You're going to be on that bloody plane Thursday morning, or I will bloody kill you.'

'Okay, don't get your sweet panties in a twist.' How the hell was she going to tell him she was ill. Could she front it out?

'What's wrong with your voice? You sound like you've smoked forty packets of cigarettes every day for the last week.' Good. He'd pre-empted her.

'Listen, Damian. I think I've got the lurgy—'

'No, no, no. You listen, Haitch. I've set this up for you. Eighty thousand quid in the offing. Just think about that. If you're not on that plane, I'm not going to be a happy bunny.'

'I feel terrible—'

'If you make me come round to your place and drag you out by the scruff of your neck, I'll do it. Remember, you lent me your spare key?'

Giving him her spare key had seemed a good idea at the time, but now she wasn't so sure.

'I'll be on it.'

'That's my girl, and yes, you will be on it.' A pause. 'Haitch? When was the last time you saw your brother-in-law?' There was an underlying threat in his voice.

'What?'

'Sam, wasn't it?'

'Yeah, but—'

'Have you spoken to him? Told him about this party?'

'Fuck, no.' Scrambled egg brains weren't helping her think. 'I saw him at the gallery. That time with you.' Oh man, she really didn't want to remember that night.

'Not since? Have you told your sister anything?'

'No. I barely speak to her, and she's definitely not speaking to Sam. You saw what a mess he was.' More like, what a mess she was.

'Okay.'

'Why? What's he got to do with this?' Did she want to know?

'Nothing... just... well, just be on that plane.'

You didn't cross Damian twice. Been there. Done that. But not twice. When the phone went dead, Haitch rubbed her eyes. She stared blearily at the dark smudges on the tips of her fingers. As if she'd trailed them across old ash. Why had he mentioned Sam? That was pretty unnerving. Anything to do with Sam meant bad news. For her. Nausea was bubbling up from deep inside and throwing up over her expensive designer bed linen wasn't an option. The fact that bright sunshine was trying to scrabble, as if it was an unwanted guest, under the heavy curtains must mean that it was daytime. Oh, but the cruel light hurt so much. One naked boob flopped over the top of the plush duvet. She pulled the cover back over herself and sneezed five times in a row so hard it felt as though someone had whacked her over the head with a frying pan.

'Aaargh, you've got to be kidding!'

There was something soft under her head, and she sank back against it. Okay. It took a moment to muster the energy to open her eyes again. She'd managed to make it back to her apartment, although the bit in-between her leaving her flat a couple of days ago and waking up was a bit hazy. Attending parties in her position was all par for the course, and there were always going to be drinks and drugs. Sucking on her teeth, she remembered the bottle of fine Scotch whisky shared with whats-his-name and the dabs of coke with young oojamaflip, but what came after? Memory was patchy at best after sessions like that. Was she alone? The familiar soft 'thing' she was lying on had been known in the past to be another person. Surely the horrendous bout of sneezing would be enough to wake anyone. She carefully inched round. It looked like only a plump pillow was in bed with her. Small mercies, eh?

This wasn't a cold. How the hell was she going to travel to Spain of all places with the bloody flu? Hugging her pillow to her chest, one idea swirled around her head.

'No way, Jose.' But the thought wouldn't go away. Would Tilda do it if she begged and grovelled? Sure, Tilda was in a bad way, but they both were, really. She was hooked on booze and drugs and the sheer buzz of fame, while Tilda, her polar opposite, lived the life of a broken-hearted hermit, imbibing herb tea and eating kale, her only companion being a crazy dog. Who in their right mind calls a scared rescue dog 'Boo' for Christ's sake! Boo! Shit all over everywhere!

Would she do it? Swap places? They'd done it so many times before. So many times... well, she had, hadn't she? Damian's question about Sam triggered memories. If only she could pop the top off her skull as if it was a jam jar and use a bottle brush to clean up the dregs of her mind.

TWO

Matilda

'Tea break.'

Tilda quickly dunked her paintbrush in a glass of water, the soft earth colour swirling like a misty dust-devil. Swishing it out, she sucked the sable hairs into a sharp point. The painting of 'Godfather Death' would have to wait, even if it was for Walker Books.

The chair scraped teeth-jarringly across the bare, painted floorboards of her bedroom as she stood. She stretched, cricking her neck a couple of times. Now doubling as her studio, the cluttered desk was tucked below the window for maximum natural light. It was a tight squeeze as a lot of her possessions were still in boxes, and she had to thrust the chair under the table to get down the side of the bed.

Tilda entered the kitchen next door and shimmied past the oak gate-leg table that could only be opened on one side, or it filled the gap to the sink and made it impassable. Boo, the dog with an impossible amount of fluffy black-and-white fur, followed at her heels, claws clicking rhythmically. Tilda struggled not to think about the sheer amount of space; the gleaming overpriced gadgets sat on expensive worktops she used to have, but this only made it clearer in her mind. All those designer names. All those buttons and knobs to press. So retro, so modern. So many products she'd been conditioned to believe she couldn't survive without. All those things she'd used with Sam. She topped up the white plastic kettle. It had a blue light and cost less than fifteen pounds in Argos. Times had clearly changed, hadn't they? Sam. Did all men want their cake and to eat it, too? The biggest, most cream covered and chocolatey cake that'd ever existed? Or was it just him? *Stop!* Veering off on this tangent again wouldn't do her any good. Not even thirty and already discarded. Unbelievable!

'Fuck you, Sam!'

The dog jumped as Tilda never shouted.

'Sorry, Boo.'

Shaking herself mentally and physically, she stared out the kitchen window as she made her tea. It wasn't bad for a basement. You could almost imagine that it was a house, a house the same as her old one, where you stepped out of patio doors into a garden lovingly planted and tended. Now she had tiny pebbles strewn over a concrete space barely big enough to get a table and two chairs in, befitting a rented flat in Brighton.

Tilda was pouring milk into her mug when the hands-free phone trilled loudly in the hall. It was a bit antiquated, but it was there if she lost her mobile. As she just had. Her hand froze. There were only three individuals on this Earth, as far as she knew, who had her new landline number: her mum, her sister and her lawyer. She didn't want to speak to any of them. Was it too much to ask that they leave her alone? Ignoring it, she placed the milk back in the fridge and added a tip-of-the-spoon of sugar. Stirring her tea, she continued to gaze at the few potted geraniums on the wooden table outside, bursting with thick new leaves and the beginnings of flower buds.

A voice burbled a message, but Tilda chose not to listen, humming something tuneless under her breath. She'd thrown her mobile away. Literally, chucked it into the waves surging up the shingles like a pack of hungry white wolves, and then she'd felt terribly guilty about her eco-footprint. But her lawyer insisted she had at least one point of contact other than her email. Facebook had been shut down. Couldn't bear any more messages of 'support and deepest love', or, more often, 'he's a wanker and you're better off without him'.

Walking back into the hall, something clambered up her spine with tiny sharp claws as she passed the little winking red light on her landline. What now?

Tilda bent down to scratch Boo under her chin. A cross-breed rescue dog, Boo was as mad as a sack of ferrets. Was that because of the abuse she'd suffered or was it an inherent trait? It didn't matter. Boo was Boo. Tilda was Tilda. Although occasionally, she wasn't.

'Fancy a walk, Boo?'

There were times when only movement could shift these uneasy feelings. Boo's answer was a long ham pink tongue and lots of white teeth. Tilda always took that to be a 'yes'. Her hoodie found and zipped, she bent down and clicked on Boo's lead. Boo made her usual wild dash around the tiny porch, bumping against the shoe rack and knocking over the umbrella leaning against the wall. She whined so piteously, it made Tilda feel as though she'd kicked her. It was an effort to physically get the dog outside.

Blowsy, fiery-coloured wildflowers and silvery green low-growing spruce overran the front yard, concrete edges failing to keep them reined in. A spiky holly bush poked through the wall that fronted the three-storey property. She couldn't be arsed to prune it.

There were some days when the three months they'd been

there already felt like years, yet there were other days when it seemed only a few minutes had passed. Time was obviously relative, depending on her current state of mind. Whether she was looking forwards and upwards, to a possible brighter future, or delving back and down to the days of darkness. Remembering him. Counting what she'd lost. And still trying to work out why. A recurring pattern. Maybe she should seek therapy, get someone to rummage through her psyche to discover the reason why the men in her life always left her. Was she strong enough to deal with the answer?

Down Bristol Terrace and left past the ornate front portico of the white-painted church – St John the Baptist's. Good old Salome had the right idea: 'Off with their heads!'

Weaving along the far pavement and across the next main road, she could see the sea. Even now, the sight was entrancing. Anyone brought up in a big city knows the power of seeing the sea. On the estate where she grew up, you were lucky to have a few huddled trees, gouged with initials and phalluses, in a concrete park at the end of the road. Today, the sea was a deep cerulean and calm. Sparkles danced where the sun was shining on it, and blueberry shadows chased each other. Gold-tinged clouds trailing fingers raced across the sky.

Tilda breathed in as deeply as she could and then held her breath, not letting it woosh out, until she thought her lungs might burst. Licking her lips, she savoured that slightly sticky, salty taste before a rankle of annoyance spoiled the moment. What was that damn phone call about? It wouldn't be Sam, now, would it? Begging forgiveness, swearing 'it was all a mistake, Tilly'. Using her special name. Tilly. The only person who called her that. No. Of course not. She hadn't given him her new number. But was she hoping for that? Dear God! Stop thinking about him! Haitch went through men as if they were sweeties, a packet of Revels with myriad flavours to chew on.

She never seemed to get any stuck in her teeth. How did she manage that? Was it the sheer number? So many men that they became blurred and indistinct. A homogenous man-shaped blob. What would it feel like to be so free? Not bothered. Plenty more where that came from. Why couldn't she do that? Shut up now. Leave it.

Boo seemed happy enough to trot up the wide pavement towards the white cliffs that thrust into the sky in the distance. They hadn't walked that far yet. She wondered how many miles it was to them. What were they called? 'Ladies' Fingers'? No, that was a nasty tasting vegetable she'd had in Indian restaurants. Maybe just 'The Fingers'?

A distinctive red-and-cream Brighton bus slowed to a standstill just ahead to allow people off. A couple of teenage girls sauntered towards her, chewing gum, and laughing loudly. One turned as they passed, and she heard her exclaim: 'That's Haitch, isn't it?'

The other girl must have stopped, too. 'Looks like her, kinda.'

A curl of exasperation coiled outwards from the pit of her stomach. Not again. Tilda tugged her hood up over her hair and sped up away from them, Boo now loping by her side.

'Oy?' The voice was high. 'Are you Haitch?'

'Nope,' she shouted over her shoulder. *Bugger!* Was no place safe? But then Brighton was a cosmopolitan city. It was to be expected that she'd be recognised by default, especially as her, or at least Haitch's heavily painted face was plastered all over this month's *Vogue*, headline screaming about her newfound fame. This was one reason why she didn't go into WHSmith anymore. It was too unsettling, and she had to look away. That face might resemble her face, but it wasn't her. It gave her a funny sensation as if she'd got chronic indigestion.

On the way back down St James's Street she tied Boo up to

a signpost and dodged into Superdrug, head down, her hood still pulled low over her head. She would be five minutes, maybe ten tops. She exited to the plaintive baying of Boo.

'Sorry, Boo. It was only a moment. Calm down now. I'm here.' Bending down, she untied the dog, who was now making a truly un-earthly sound that always attracted attention and set your teeth on edge.

The walk back up the high street towards home seemed to take ages. It was getting warmer now, although Tilda resisted the urge to take off the hoodie. Camouflage in the city.

The postman had been since she'd left. Bending to scoop the two letters lying on the floor, she saw the red flashing light from the phone. Would ignoring it make it go away? Tilda shrugged off her jacket. Rummaging inside her bag, she pulled out a shiny box. While Boo sat in companionable silence, watching closely, sprawled across the bathroom floor, Tilda read the instructions on the packet of hair dye she'd just bought.

'I'm not Haitch. I'm me.' Her resentment startled her.

It didn't take too long, and when she'd towel-dried her hair, she examined herself in the bathroom mirror. She smiled to herself. Now chestnut brown waves curled about her shoulders. They suited her. She'd never been the white blonde that Haitch favoured but a few shades darker. Still, being blonde meant there was always the chance of recognition, as shown by today. Bending to stroke Boo, she smiled. 'See Boo? I'm not her, am I?'

Boo bobbed up and licked her chin.

THREE

Haitch

Damian

WHAT WAS IT ABOUT HIM? If she had a façade to hide behind, then he had a forty-foot breeze-block wall with barbed wire and machine-gun turrets perched on top. They met four years ago when he picked her up at her third exhibition in the Brick Lane Gallery – a show entirely of women artists. Haitch knew that her paintings, collages and environmental installations were unique, but that didn't mean that people would appreciate them. She often wondered if her obsession with repetition and pattern was because she was a twin? Influenced by pop art, abstract expressionism, minimalism and surrealism, she managed to weave in feminism and sexuality that obviously enthralled some and frightened the bejesus out of others. This was exactly what she wanted, what she craved. Who wants their work to be 'nice' for God's sake! It had to have a profound effect, or it hadn't worked.

Four years previously

'If people throw up over my art, then I'd be pretty pleased.' That was her opening remark to Damian. 'If they have sex on it, then all the better.'

Eyeing her like a great white shark that was already opening its massive jaws for its first bite, he replied with, 'Better make them waterproof then.'

He took her out for dinner later that night. Lavish and expensive. What she expected from a man such as him. What she hadn't expected was being left on the doorstep of her shared house in Newington Green.

'Not coming in for a coffee?' She couldn't believe she said that. Such a cliché, but what else could she say? *Fancy popping up for a shag?*

Turning at the small wall that fronted the property, he smiled over his shoulder calling out, 'I try not to mix business and pleasure, and although it has most definitely been a pleasure, you are now my business. Goodnight, Haitch.'

That was a first. Going to bed alone. At least Damian paid for it all. It was easy to convince herself that she didn't care, although there was a pit of vipers coiling in her stomach as she switched off the light and pulled up the duvet. Turned down? She had to pretend she meant for him to come in for a coffee and only that. But he'd know that was bullshit. Haitch threw herself round in the bed, kicking off the heavy duvet that was pushing down on her and forcing the air from her lungs. Is this what it felt like to be humiliated? How would she know? She ensured she was always the one dishing it out, never on the receiving end. Okay, she'd fallen at the first hurdle, but she'd get back up. Wasn't that one of her principal qualities? That she never gave up.

So, what was it about him? He had a kind of Roman beauty.

He had deep brown-gold eyes that sucked you into places you didn't want to go. But he was also cold, in the same way as those chiselled busts of Caesar that watched and waited silently in cool, dimly lit museums. He had a dangerous quality, something she couldn't quite put her finger on. She found it seductive. Didn't every girl secretly lust after the bad boy?

As the months drew on, she knew it was bad form to get involved with an agent, especially if things went south. But there were moments when she sensed he was almost about to do or say something that might shatter the fragile balance between them. Maybe at that point, she'd turn him down with a sneer. Maybe? She had to keep telling herself it was probably for the best. Her work started selling, commanding higher prices. Then it turned into a bit of a feeding frenzy. The front cover of *Vogue*, for God's sake. Not bad for a poor girl from an estate in the arse end of London. All this had come about since that fateful meeting with Damian. Best not to blow it. The thing was, the more she reasoned with herself, the more she wanted him. Around and around and around. What a game.

He instinctively knew how to market her, and she realised, somewhat belatedly, that she was little more than a commodity. It wasn't that difficult to reconcile. Her work was out there and sought after. But when it brought in heaps of cash, well, wasn't that a bonus? Not everyone was cut out to be the starving artist in the garret. She'd been there, done that and got the bloody t-shirt.

That phone call to Tilda. Had she done the right thing? She'd never told Damian she was a twin, although he now knew she had a sister, thanks to Sam. She'd promised to give Tilda space. Time to grieve. Would Tilda even agree in the first place? And then be able to impersonate her well enough? What would happen if she got found out? They'd have to say it was another project, that it was all part of the next installation. *Surprise! We're twins!* How would Damian react. She'd crossed him once. Hadn't turned up to an arranged meeting with a client. Too drunk to stand. They'd had words, as they say, which seemed to include a backhander across her face. It wasn't something either one of them was proud about. But that slap, the sudden pain and shock had somehow made her feel more alive, which was strange and confusing. How dirty. No, fucked up! But the arousal she felt, well, possibly, this was a source of entertainment to be explored at a later date.

Brought up by a single, hard-working mum in a council estate, she knew all about kids being beaten. How many of her friends had thought it was just a way of life? It was an everyday occurrence, though neither Haitch nor Tilda had ever been hit. Their mum and dad had used words, not heavy fists to discipline them. Then their dad had died in a car accident. Hit and run. The other driver was under-age, as pissed as a monkey king, joyriding with mates, with no insurance or even a driving licence. He was a friend from school. Was. Did he ever understand what he'd done to them? Two thirteen-year-olds stood by the closed coffin as their dad was not in a state to be seen.

'Sorry,' the boy had said. Sorry didn't cover it.

No holidays or new clothes; they were charity store junkies. They made the best they could of it and never complained. At age sixteen, Haitch had worked Saturdays in the chemist and Tilda in a hairdresser. This was when they'd started to swap. It was only a joke. Got a little tricky on occasions but that was what made it so amusing. The beginning, leading far too fast to the end. Should've seen it coming, but she was too wrapped up in it all. The games. Haitch squirmed from the memories. What a bitch she'd been, but she just couldn't help it. Could she?

FOUR

Matilda

TILDA DIDN'T USUALLY LEAVE the door open to the hall, but tonight, it was as if she had to remind herself that there was a message waiting for her, whether she wanted to receive it or not. The blinking light from the landline cast an eerie shadow on the ceiling, as if a tiny piece of Hell had escaped and was camping out in her living room.

'What do you think, Boo?' Sat on the sofa, she rubbed the dog's muzzle. Boo was stretched out across her lap, belly exposed, one leg in the air, paw floppy. Trusting. Woman's best friend. Well, this woman, anyway. Boo would never knowingly hurt her, and that was the truth of it. Not like some.

'So,' she started again, 'should I listen to it tonight, tomorrow, or should I erase it without listening to it?'

Boo snuffled noisily and tried to lick her chin. This was something she liked to do. Or maybe her moisturiser tasted nice.

Whatever.

'Tomorrow? Funny, that. I think I agree with you.'

When the credits on the film she now couldn't remember the name of were rolling, Tilda stirred and nudged Boo to the floor. Opening the back door to allow Boo her last wee, she put some milk onto boil for her nightly hot chocolate. The 'clicks' and 'clunks' as she locked the door and the security bolts turned in their sockets were satisfying. She was alone here, and Boo was a rubbish guard dog. Sat in bed, sipping her chocolate, Boo on her bean bag bed in the corner, Tilda allowed herself to wonder who had called her and why. Could it wait until morning, or would she simply toss and turn all night?

'Bugger, bugger, bugger!'

Fumbling about for her slippers, she crept into the hall and pressed the play button.

'Hey, Tilda... it's Harriet.' There was a pause. 'I mean Haitch.' Her voice was hoarse for some reason, but still recognisable. 'I know you don't want to hear from me, but I really need to beg a favour. And I know you're probably shouting at the phone right now to leave you alone, and I don't blame you. Listen, I swear I'll make it up to you.' There was a pause. 'Tilda, I'm so sorry, please call me. I need you.'

Shouting at the phone? No, not this time. She was too tired. Tilda shook her head. What did Haitch want now?

Haitch. It was Tilda who'd nicknamed her that when they were really little. Harriet was too much of a mouthful, so she simply called her H. When Harriet had started to have success with her art, that was the name she gave herself. Just Haitch. Like Adele. No need for anything more. Anyway, Harriet didn't fit with the new persona, did it? It was funny how their working-class mother assumed that by giving her girls such aspirational names, that would be enough to elevate them to another class. Instead, in their comprehensive in Hackney, they had been ridiculed and taunted. Poor kids with posh names. Lesson learned. When she'd sat with Sam, and they'd discussed baby names, all the Atticuses, Noahs, Seraphinas and Eugenies were rapidly scribbled off the list. They hadn't got as far as choosing a potential name by the time of the ultimate betrayal and fall from grace. Maybe it was better that way. The loss of an imaginary baby was bad enough, but to have named it beforehand, to have this name inscribed on the heart, that was just torture.

'It's okay, Boo. Everything's okay. Let's go to bed. I'll deal with this in the morning.'

Boo trailed her into the bedroom. Tilda pulled the covers back and climbed in. A new bed, new mattress, so new it didn't even have that comforting body shaped dent. Not even just the one, let alone two. Boo snuffled under Tilda's hand and nudged it.

'You know you're not supposed to be on the bed. It sets a bad precedent.' The nose under her hand was damp and cold. It nudged her again. Tilda rolled over, and the dog leapt in, spun once and lay down. 'Just this time then.'

The heat of Boo brought back the memories of another body, lean and hard, wedged up against her, hand tousling in her hair, fingers questing, warm breath tickling. It was strange how she didn't want to cry in front of Boo. Hadn't the poor dog been traumatised enough in her short life?

'I hate you, Sam.'

Sleep seemed a long time coming.

Sunday 12th June

Sunlight trickled under the bedroom curtains and slid down the wall, sending chocolate fingers of shadows across the canvas wardrobe and a cheap yellowy pine chest of drawers. Boo was half under the covers, snoring gently, with one paw trembling and twitching. Was she dreaming? What do dogs dream of? Chasing rabbits, they say. Did Boo dream of hard hands, shouted incomprehensible words, of endless puppies in cramped and stinky pens? Did she wake fearful and then realise that her life had changed? Unlike Tilda, whose dreams were full of love and light, yet her reality was cold and dark and lonely when she awoke. Again.

She yawned and stretched. 'I've got to speak to Haitch. She'll never leave me alone until I do.'

Pushing Boo from the bed, she retrieved her slippers, wrapped her dressing-gown around her and padded into the kitchen to make a cup of tea. 'What does she need now? I don't think I can cope with anything new, Boo.' Knowing that work would be impossible until she'd found out what Haitch wanted, she took her tea into the living room. Her reflection in the mirror was salt-sore and puffy, seemingly her new normality. Feet up on the sofa, she phoned her sister.

'Haitch? It's me.'

'Oh, thank God. I'm sorry to have to ask this, Tilda, but I need a massive favour, and you're the only one who can do it.'

'Well, no preamble there. Whatever happened to "How are you, Tilda, since your whole world crumbled and fell apart?" Thanks for that.'

'I know how you are. You're having a shit time, so I don't need to ask.'

'Twin intuition?'

'No, stupid. Something to do with your husband being a complete dickhead and running off with his secretary or whoever.'

'Oh!'

'Listen, you told me not to call with platitudes or threats of assassination. This is neither. I'm in a bit of a bind.'

'I'm not up for much right now. I can barely tie my own shoelaces.'

There was a heartbeat of silence. 'Since when do you own anything with shoelaces?'

'Since I became a wife. Since then.' Tilda closed her eyes for a moment. 'A boring wife obviously, with boring clothes, saying boring things, with a boring body—'

'Tilda, I can say with certainty that your body is certainly not boring, considering I have the same one.'

'Maybe you use yours better than I do.'

There was a sharp intake of breath.

Tilda groaned. 'This is why I asked you not to call yet. Still dealing with it all. You sound rough. Too much partying?'

'Normally, yes, but I've actually got the flu.'

'Sorry to hear that. What do you want then?'

Haitch cleared her throat noisily. 'You remember when we used to pretend to be each other all the time?'

The pause was so long that Tilda realised that she was meant to fill in the gap. 'What about it?'

'I need you to pretend to be me.'

'Why? Where will you be?'

'I'll be in bed with the flu. I'm really ill, and I've got to go to this important party that Damian has arranged. I can't go in this state. I just can't.'

'A party? Where?'

'Southern Spain—'

'What? Are you out of your mind? You expect me to fly to Spain and pretend to be you?'

'That's it. It'll be fun.'

'Something that Damian, your scary agent has set up?'

'Lots of fun.'

'Pretend to be Haitch, a famous artist with presumably a load of people that I've never met but who have met you?'

'I think they'll all be strangers.'

Tilda heard the doubt. 'You think, or you know for sure?'

'Um, I think.'

'Not in this lifetime.'

'Tilda?' There was a desperate note to her voice. 'I'll help you. No one will know you're not me. If I don't go, Damian will probably kill me.' There was a horrible bout of coughing, where Haitch made sounds Tilda would rather not hear.

'Harriet! For crying out loud. If I go, he'll definitely kill you. I can't pass myself off as you. I'll balls it all up. It'll be terrible, like a motorway pile-up.'

Haitch's voice was quiet. 'Okay. I understand. But tell me this. What else are you doing at the moment?'

It was as if her sister had kicked her in the gut. 'You mean in my sad and pathetic little life?'

'No... I mean yes. Why not go to a party where the champagne will flow like water, you can wear my expensive grungy designer clothes, and you get to mingle with potential stars and celebrities? My room is in the villa where they're hosting the party. No trying to find a taxi at three in the morning, as we've done so many times before.'

Was it always going to be this way? Subtly or not so subtly manipulated. Always the words. 'I'd prefer to huddle in my flat, thanks all the same.'

'Please think about it. It'll take your mind off your troubles?'

'I've got deadlines too, you know. I may not have my face plastered over glossy magazines, but I've got a set of illustrations for Walker Books I must finish.'

'Walker Books? That's fantastic, Tilda.'

'Yes, it is. While you're off gallivanting all over the place, I'm holding down a job, remember?' Why did Haitch habitually sound so surprised that she was doing well? Like she was the only one who could be a success.

'I get it, and I need to point out that my work is a job, too.' There was a sigh that sounded exasperated. 'At least consider it. Pretty please?'

Tilda sucked on her upper lip. A nervous habit. Maybe she'd been a little hard on Haitch. 'What do I do with Boo? I won't leave her here by herself.' She knew her petulant tone would rub Haitch up the wrong way. Good.

'Bring her up to me.'

'You hate my dog.'

'I know.'

Tilda stared at Boo for a moment. 'I'll call you back.'

<hr>

What the hell?

Surely, she wasn't even going to grace this with another thought? But Haitch was right. She was beginning to atrophy. If she stayed like this any longer, she'd turn into stone. Haitch had said it would only be for a couple of days. The accommodation was in the villa, so, if necessary, she could slope off to bed with a feigned headache or whatever. She knew all her sister's work, had helped with ideas on occasions; the thinking outside the box business was always easier if two heads were working on something, even if they looked exactly the same.

Of the two of them, Haitch had always been the outgoing twin, the one who wanted it all on a huge silver plate, and that's not to say she hadn't worked her *doodangles* off for it. Hungry for fame and fortune. A first degree at The Slade School of Fine Art, followed by an MA with distinction and numerous bursaries and commendations. Damian had spotted her at one of her exhibitions and then he'd pounced. Yes, he'd helped her meteoric rise to fame and fortune, although it appeared he'd also stripped Haitch of all control. Was she jealous? Not really. Tilda had been content to be in her shadow, building her own artistic life of illustrations and stories, tucked in her green belt world of wife and marriage until that was blown apart. Identical in every aspect except personality. But they'd swapped before. And playing the role of Haitch was like having a refreshing breeze blowing through her. Was this her sister controlling her as usual, or had she made this decision on her own?

On the other hand, if Tilda threw off her shackles, she could be free, even for a couple of days. Free of thinking. That could be enough. Hell, she could catch up with her own work when she got back.

The call was brief. 'I'll do it.'

FIVE

Haitch

Wednesday 15th June

PREPARATION WAS vital in a situation as extreme as this, although Haitch found it tough to get out of bed. Apart from being super-glued to the sheet, it felt as though she had a metal cap bolted to her head that was a size too small, and she was sure her face was swollen to twice its normal size in recompense. Her bones ached so much like they were being eaten from the inside out by voracious toothed worms. Was she dying? It took the last of her strength to totter out when she heard the front door slam and Tilda calling her name.

'I'm here—' Tilda sidestepped out of her way. 'Shit, you look awful.' Pulling Boo in behind her, she dropped her small suitcase on the floor, which resounded with a weird clunking sound. 'I wasn't sure if you were blagging me.'

Boo was tugging against the lead and making weird whining sounds.

Haitch rested her forehead against the door jamb. Even though it was cool to the touch, her head still throbbed. 'I told you I'd got flu.' She focused. 'Wow, that new colour suits you. Never pegged us as being brunettes.'

Tilda tugged a lock of hair loose from under her baseball cap and stared at it. 'Too many people thinking I was you.' She waggled her fingers at Haitch. 'No kisses – I don't want this lurgy either.' She indicated with her chin. 'Living room? Can I let Boo off now? She'll go mad for a bit, then she'll calm down.'

'Yep,' said Haitch. She remained leaning against the door. 'Fuck me, but I feel bad.'

Thumping and banging from the living room presumably meant that Boo was acclimatising. At a snail's pace, she crept into the room to find Tilda folding t-shirts and knickers that had been left draped across the plump, ochre-coloured sofa. Boo was now curled in a ball on the floor.

'Sorry, Tilda. That's as far as these tumble-dried clothes have got. After taking them out, I had to spend an hour recuperating on top of them.'

There was a faint twitch to Tilda's mouth. 'Here you go, I've made space. I'll put the kettle on, and then we can talk.'

Haitch sat slowly. Even though it was like sinking into a jar of soft honey, she wondered how she could hurt so much. 'What's in your suitcase? I told you, you didn't need to bring anything bar clean undies and your moisturiser.'

Tilda draped a blanket with a rich geometric design across Haitch's knees. 'I've brought dog food and all Boo's paraphernalia. You're not in a fit state to go out, and I don't want her neglected.'

Haitch eyed the dog, pulling the blanket tightly up around her neck. She'd picked it up in a Moroccan shop in Camden Lock, although she pretended to all her friends to have haggled for it in a souk in Marrakesh.

Smiling up at Tilda, she whispered, 'You're going to make a fabulous mum one day.'

Tilda straightened quickly, her face rigid, and Haitch realised that was probably the wrong thing to say right now.

'You've got to have a husband first, haven't you? And I seem to have lost mine.'

'Mislaid.' Haitch looked down at her lap. 'Anyway, you don't need a man for anything nowadays.'

'Hmmph. So, you keep saying.' Tilda disappeared into the kitchen, Boo a shaggy shadow glued to her heels. Haitch winced at the bang of cupboard doors, water being splashed, the clatter of mugs and spoons. Two more crotchety females to deal with. It was all too much.

As Tilda returned with the tea, she asked, 'Explain to me why you couldn't say no?'

'Damian has a client who is offering a cushty bursary. He might buy a piece of work as well. Maybe more. It's all set up, and Damian made it plain that I was going regardless of how ill I felt. The client's very influential and affluent. Japanese or Asian or something.'

'Good to see you know what's going on. How much is the bursary? I need to know how pressurised I'm going to be.'

'Then I'll only say it's enough to keep me going for quite a bit.'

'Okay. So why this party? Why Spain? Why not a private meet here in London?'

'The client said he wanted to meet me in a social setting first. The party is for a group of us. I presume we're competing against each other for his dosh.'

'Hell. This isn't going to work. I don't know if I can pretend to be you anymore. You've changed so much over the last few years.'

'That's why it'll work. You'll be like the old me. You'll be sober for a start.'

'I thought you said there'd be buckets of champagne?'

'Yes, but you sip demurely while I stick my whole head in. There's a difference.' She had to stop to clear her lungs, grappling for a box of tissues on the side table. Tilda visibly grimaced and shifted further away.

'Listen.' Haitch wiped her mouth and blew her nose as if she was a bad-tempered elephant seal. 'All you have to do is be you, and by default, you'll be me. No one knows I have a twin. We've got different names. Also, I've never mentioned you. We decided to keep our lives separate, remember?'

Tilda screwed her eyes shut as if she needed time to think and couldn't bear to see Haitch watching her. All Haitch had to do was wait and hold herself back from interrupting. Tilda being here was half the battle won. If she pushed too hard, she knew from experience that she might clam up, and that would be that.

Tilda nodded, finally. Only the once. It was enough. 'Okay, but you have to help me choose what I'll be wearing, or I might end up in tweeds and a pearl necklace.'

'That's not even a joke!'

'So, I fly out on Thursday. I'll be met by Damian, then we drive to this place?'

'Yeah. The party is in the evening. Your flight back is the next day, so it's pretty whirlwind.' Another bout of coughing, and Haitch was sure her eyeballs would burst out of her sockets and roll like marbles across the carpet. Oh man, did her throat hurt, as if she'd swallowed a wad of sandpaper, washed down with bleach.

'Do you know who's going to this? Who we'll be up against? Will they all be artists?'

'Damian said none of us would know until we get there. I got the feeling that we're all young or at least up-and-coming in our fields but not quite household names.'

'Your face is plastered all over the front cover of *Vogue*. I think people recognise you now and, by default, me.'

'Yes but no one knew who I was a couple of months ago, did they? This is all recent.' She raised her eyebrows. 'Seems I'm a hit with the younger generation.'

Tilda's eyebrows also rose. 'What? I thought we were the younger generation?'

'Not anymore and that's pretty horrifying.'

'Holy crap. Okay. Will there be loads of us?'

Haitch shrugged. 'That I couldn't say. Which would you prefer?'

'I don't know. You can get lost in a crowd, but then you're Billy No Mates. At least if there are only a few people, you're kind of forced to speak to them.'

'You'll be fine. Remember you're pretending to be me, so any stupid thing you say or do, they'll think it's me. Okay?'

Tilda fiddled with something on her top. A nervous gesture from childhood. 'I have a set of Grimm's illustrations that I've got to finish. I must be back on Friday, or I'm going to be hard-pressed to complete by the deadline.'

'Well, then you'll be pleased to know you won't have to wait in the queue at the airport. I have privileged boarding.'

'Wow, hark at you, Miss Famous.'

'I'm making the most of everything, 'cos I know things don't always last.'

'Talk to me about that.' Tilda snorted. 'I've got my passport—'

'Hang on,' Haitch held out a hand. 'You can't use that; you'll have to use mine. I mean, you're pretending to be me. It'll all be under my name.'

'Oh yeah. Right. Silly me.'

'This gets a little complicated on occasions, doesn't it?'

'Pretty much.' Tilda nodded then her eyes narrowed. 'What

I really need to know is, have you shagged Damian? I don't want to be in a car with him and say completely the wrong thing.'

'Ugh.' Haitch tried to wave her away, but she ached too much to move. 'No, I can truthfully say I haven't done the dirty with him.' *Not yet at least.*

'Why not? What's wrong with him? He's not gay.'

'No, he's not. At least I don't think he is. There's just something... you know?'

'Nope. Like what?'

'Just something.' Haitch turned to face her sister. 'I think if we hooked up, we'd fly so close to the sun, our wings would burn like old whatshisface.'

'You mean it could happen? Interesting.'

'Oh, please do not even think about it. Not with him, not while pretending to be me.'

'That'd make things spicy for you, wouldn't it?' Tilda grinned. Haitch realised that it was the first time in forever that she'd seen her sister smile. Tilda winced as if it had hurt her.

'Oh, shut up!' Haitch pulled the blanket up about her chin. 'I give you free rein over anyone you meet there. Please let me know afterwards, but Damian is out of bounds. Understood?' What if Tilda ignored her and she got something on with Damian? Her heart sped up.

'Sure.' Tilda touched the tip of her tongue to her front teeth. 'But you do like him, don't you?'

Haitch rolled her eyes. 'He's... out... of... bounds.'

Tilda smiled again. 'Maybe he needs to know that you are interested. Leave him to work it all out.'

'He knows. He'd have to be blind and mostly dead not to.' Haitch didn't want to continue with this line of thought. It was too close. 'Can you leave it, Tilda?'

'Why?'

'Because he's married. Right, now I've said it.'

Tilda's face froze. 'What? God! Sorry. I promise I won't do anything to compromise you. Or him.'

Shite! Was she now thinking of Sam? Haitch had to stop any mental pictures of infidelity. 'Thank you. Listen, you'll have to take my phone as it's the one Damian will be expecting you to use. It'll seem odd if you have a new one. I mean if I have a new one.'

'Good point.' Tilda's face hadn't reset properly. Haitch had to keep talking.

'I presume you haven't got one yet, since you made the grand gesture of chucking it away?' She continued, slightly out of breath. 'Great job on being eco-friendly. No good waffling on about recycling and then litter the sea with plastic.'

'Ha! Is that a lecture, Miss "I don't even know where the recycling bins are"?' Tilda made a face at her. 'I picked one up straight after I agreed to do this mad-cap scheme of yours. It's a Samsung Galaxy A25. What's your one?'

'Samsung Galaxy S24. About the same but the camera on this baby is bloody brilliant. You can take some great photos of the place and then I'll feel I went.'

'And you'll know if you're ever asked about it.'

'And that. Good. I thought I'd be phoneless and that would be like having my leg amputated.'

'I'm going to work my way through your wardrobe now,' said Tilda. 'Can you make it upstairs?'

'Yeah, but I might have to stay there. Can your doggy open its own tins of food and use the loo in the bathroom?'

'No.'

'Fuck!'

SIX

Matilda

THEY MAY HAVE both come from an estate, but Haitch certainly wasn't in one now.

SW3. Chelsea. Or at least within spitting distance. Home to artists and musicians: Vivienne Westwood and the likes of the Beatles and the Rolling Stones. Even Kylie had hung out here. No wonder, with the price tags attached. Tilda wasn't envious, though she could appreciate the urbanity of it. Haitch's flat was modern, sleek and beautiful. If you liked that sort of thing. All chrome, white and real solid birch wood. Not even a snifter of veneer. You could fit Tilda's current flat in the kitchen, but she had to remind herself she was only renting in Brighton until the sale of the family home had gone through. The sale of her old life. Shaking her head, she tried to throw the image out of Sam rolling around inside his new floozy, in Tilda's bed that she'd stupidly thought she shared solely with her husband, in the home they'd bought together three years previously. The moral of the tale had to be never visit your mother on a weekday.

Tilda snapped back to what she was doing. Sometimes it was hard to focus on the present. Her mind seemed to be drifting to the past a lot these days, like watching an old movie reel.

Scrabbling through Haitch's wardrobe was a particular delight. Tilda smiled over her shoulder. 'I love your clothes.'

Haitch was crumpled on the bed. 'So do I, luckily.'

That was one thing you could say about Haitch, she did have great style. The milestone of thirty was looming on the horizon for them both. Whereas Tilda managed to look nearly thirty, Haitch's style was still young and trendy, without appearing to be the proverbial mutton. Hoodies and ripped jeans, designer printed t-shirts and heavy-soled buckled boots. Even her dresses seemed to have a retro-punk look, modern but dirty looking, involving grinning skulls, roses and reams of material. Tilda cycled everywhere, and Haitch went down the gym. But even so, blessed with their mother's genes, they could both eat all they wanted and not put on weight. Perhaps they would reach thirty and suddenly turn into blimps?

'What do you think?' Tilda slipped into the clothes that Haitch had picked. 'Is this the look you want for the party?' Strange how changing into Haitch's clothes could make her feel as if she was a more potent, razor-edged version of herself.

'Perfect.' Haitch coughed noisily and grabbed a tissue from a box on her bedside table. Tilda noted it was nearly empty, and the soiled ones were lying in a pyramid shape overflowing the bin. She covered her nose and mouth with her free hand. 'I'll beat you senseless if I get this.' She waved a pair of leggings and a set of boots. 'Can I wear these on the plane?' Tweaking a long t-shirt out, she placed it in front of her. 'This all goes together, doesn't it?'

Haitch nodded. 'Do you want to call for a takeaway? I'm not that hungry, but you can get what you want.'

'Are you sure you're going to be alright?'

'It's only flu. No one dies from the flu.'

Tilda sucked on her teeth. 'Apart from the Spanish flu of 1918, which killed somewhere between fifty to a hundred million people.' She raised her eyebrows. 'Just saying.'

Haitch went even paler. 'You are kidding?

Tilda twirled in front of the mirror. 'No, I'm not kidding, but you'll be fine.'

'Right, you need to stay here. You can't leave me.' Haitch made a strange and discomforting snorkelling sound that made Tilda want to hawk and spit. 'How do you know these things? I mean, didn't we go to the same school?'

'I know these things because I listened in class while you made googly-eyes at all the boys.'

'Someone had to. Don't go. I'm far too young to die.'

Tilda wagged a finger. 'Sleep and drink lots of water—'

'I don't drink water! God knows what it's got in it!'

'You should try it for a change; you might find you like it. Anyway, I've got your job to do.'

'Fuck that. I'll tell Damian I can't go.'

'I'm up for it now. The game is on. I'll go and order dinner, and we'll finish tomorrow.'

'Are you sure I won't die? Promise me?'

'God, you're ridiculous when you're ill. You act like a man with a cold.'

'Okay. I get it. Listen, there's wine in the wine rack. Choose whatever. I might even have a glass.'

Tilda sniffed loudly. 'You can't be that ill if you can consider drinking wine.'

'Hair of the bloody dog, Tilda.'

'Is that dog not bald by now?'

You couldn't beat a curry. But was it such a good idea if you were flying the next day? Tilda thought about it for a moment and then ordered it all regardless. The bottle of wine she chose was a Spanish Rioja, in honour of her destination.

Haitch had a tiny bowl of food but struggled, so Tilda reasoned she must be ill. Neither of them ever turned down good food, possibly a legacy of their upbringing with a frugal Scottish mother.

Haitch waved a hand at Tilda's head.

'Oh no,' Tilda tugged at her hair. 'Don't tell me I have to change it back? I only dyed it to stop people thinking I'm you.'

'No, we can get away with the colour. It's just that it's three inches longer than mine.'

'So? Who will notice?'

'Damian for starters. He was with me when I had that photoshoot for the cover of *Vogue*. He'll notice. Get the scissors.'

'What? Dear God? You will seriously owe me for this.'

Haitch was going to chop off a wedge of her hair? Okay, Haitch was pretty punky, but Tilda had meetings with conservative and old-fashioned editors within the publishing industry. She had to calm down. She could always wear a hat. Returning with a set of kitchen scissors, she sat on a chair in the middle of the bedroom while Haitch hovered around her, a blanket slung around her hunched shoulders. A walking wounded bearing very sharp blades. Tilda tried not to flinch in case she lost a bit of ear. It didn't take long. Hack, hack, hack.

'That's it.' Haitch stumbled back to the bed. 'Now you look more like me.'

Tilda stood and peered at herself in the mirror. It was as if she was morphing. Half Haitch and half her. 'Not bad. I must remember to take your gel and your make-up too.'

'Sure. I won't be needing all that.'

'Haitch?' Tilda perched on the edge of the bed, hopefully

out of range of any rogue sneezes. 'Do you really think I can do this?'

'You'll be fine.'

"You'll be fine."

Lying in bed that night in Haitch's spare bedroom, Tilda thought about these few words that meant so much. Or so little. *You'll be fine.* Closely followed by *you'll get over it.* Really? Haitch had only been trying to help her that awful day, but sometimes you really don't need help like that. Especially from your own twin. How many times had she said that to her? After every boyfriend had disappeared, running at full pelt into the distance. Haitch really didn't get it. And now Sam, who was the air that she breathed, the solid ground under her feet, the blood pumping around her veins, the beat in her heart. She was never going to 'get over it'. Tilda understood that Haitch had never been in love. Properly in love. She'd been in lust countless times, and Tilda wondered if she'd mistaken that for love. It was easy to give up lust and get over it because there would always be more lust in dark places. But not real love. That might come only once for most people. She'd had the man whom she believed to be her soulmate snatched from her, leaving her dangling in space, no sky above, no earth below, in a numbing vacuum bereft of warmth and friendship.

Of course, it was Haitch she'd phoned first. Disbelief and sheer rage vying for the top position. Her chest was so tight that it was as if she'd been crushed by a massive weight.

Wednesday April 6th

'Sam's had an affair.' Her hands were shaking so much, she had trouble holding the phone. This was greeted by silence, and the sound of a breath sucked in. 'Haitch? Did you hear me? Sam's had an affair.'

'What... what?' Haitch sounded equally shocked. 'How do you know this?'

'He told me. I got back from staying over at Mum's.' She tried not to sob. 'And he was in the house... he had a bag packed... and... and he said, he told me that it was over between us.' There was nothing she could do to stop the wrenching spasms wracking her body. 'He's left me, Haitch.' It was more of a wail than actual words.

'Oh, dear God! Tilda, this can't be true. Sam would never leave you.'

'He has. He left this morning. Gone to stay with his brother.'

Tilda let the phone drop to her lap, allowing the grief to wash over her in heavy waves. In the background, she could hear snatches of words and sounds like white noise. Was that Haitch calling to her?

Lifting the phone to her ear, she said, 'I don't know what to do. Tell me what to do, Haitch.'

'I'm coming over right now. I'll be there in half an hour, tops. Are you listening, Tilda? I'll be there as fast as I can.'

Waiting was a nightmare. Swirling thoughts, of things she didn't want to see, imagining stuff she didn't want to imagine. The doorbell ringing and the banging on the front door brought her round. Tottering into the hall, her legs barely able to keep her upright, she opened the door and Haitch practically fell in.

'Holy shit! I'm here, I'm here now.' Haitch gathered her into her arms and held her tight. Tilda could feel her fingernails digging into her ribs. A sister's bear hug. 'Okay,' she said, 'let me in, and I'll make us a cuppa.'

'I think I need something stronger,' Tilda said, as she moved out of the way. Haitch had a holdall with her, which she dropped by the table that housed all their odd-job bits and bobs that was needed as they left the house. Only her stuff remained on it now.

'Come on.'

Haitch put her arm around Tilda's shoulders and led her, as if she was an old blind dog into the spacious living room. Lowering herself into the familiarity and comfort of the sofa, Tilda wiped at her face and looked up at Haitch.

'I don't understand what's happened. I just don't.'

Tilda saw that Haitch looked as shaken as Tilda felt, her face grey.

'He said that he couldn't keep it secret anymore.' Her voice was trembling. 'That he'd met someone else, and he'd realised that it wasn't the same as it used to be... between us. He said it was over and that he was sorry.' Tilda opened her hands and stared at them. 'He said he was sorry. Well, that makes it okay, doesn't it?'

'Did he say who... she was?'

'No. I asked if I knew who this woman was, and he said no. So, I don't have any face to fit with the pictures in my head. If I did, I'd smash her fucking face in.'

'Did he say how long this has been going on?'

'I think it was recent. Not sure if that makes me feel any better, you know? I suppose he hasn't kept it from me for long then. The lying, cheating, deceitful shit.' Tilda raised her head and stared at Haitch. 'Why has this happened? Why wasn't I enough for him? For Christ sake's, why didn't he talk to me about it?'

'Men are shits, Tilda. We both know that.' There was such vehemence in her voice that Tilda reared back.

'Sam wasn't like that. You know he wasn't. He... he loved me.' Tilda buried her head in her hands. The sobbing shook her as if she was in a gale-force wind. 'Oh, God! Why has this happened?'

Tilda felt Haitch grasp her by the shoulders. 'Listen to me, you'll be fine. You'll get over it.'

Tilda couldn't believe she'd said that to her. *You'll be fine? You'll get over it?*

'I won't be fine, Haitch. I'm never going to be fine. My husband has left me. The man I thought I was going to spend the rest of my life with has fucking well left me. Over ten years of my life with him down the swanny. I thought I would be the mother of his children... I thought we'd grow old together and die in each other's arms. I'm not going to be fine, and I'm never going to get over it.'

Haitch sank back onto the floor. 'I'm sorry, I didn't mean to sound flippant. I only meant that you will survive this and I don't mean, get over it, but you will survive.'

'I'm sorry too. I feel ill. I don't know what to do. I don't know how to do it. Be someone who is not with Sam. I don't want to merely survive.'

'Maybe this is an aberration? Maybe he's had some sort of meltdown, and you'll get back together again.'

Tilda felt confused. Surely Haitch would grasp this? 'Why would I get back with the man who has had sex in my bed with someone else?' It was so simple. He'd cheated on her. End of.

'People make mistakes, Tilda.' Haitch's voice had been tiny, like a child's.

'Mistakes are putting the rubbish in the cupboard and chucking out the best plates. Those are mistakes. Not shagging another person in your wife's bed. That's stabbing her square between her shoulder blades.' Tilda looked at Haitch. 'You understand that don't you?'

'I... I...'

'What, Haitch? I know you love him too. He's been your brother for all these years. But what can you possibly say that would convince me to take the man back? And we seem to be forgetting the rather pertinent fact he has left me.' Tilda felt as though she'd been punctured. All the hope, happiness and love that had ever been in her life had seeped out and dribbled away. 'You know,' she said quietly, 'this happens every time with me. They leave me, and I don't know why. I really thought it would be different with Sam. I married him for God's sake. Surely that meant it would turn out differently. Why has this happened again?'

There had been a look on her sister's face she couldn't interpret. Rubbing at her eyes, she sipped at her tea. 'It's over, and I have to work out what that means. To be without Sam.'

'I'm so sorry.' Oh, the layering of emotion in Haitch's voice. She must have been feeling it too.

'You've got nothing to be sorry about. I'm just glad I have you. I don't know what I'd have done if I didn't. Also, please don't say anything to Mum yet. I can't face that now. I'll let her know what's going on soon but not right now.'

It was then that Haitch had broken down and cried. Tilda crawled across the carpet to pull Haitch into her arms. How strange that she had been the one to comfort her sister.

'I'm so sorry,' wailed Haitch. 'I'm so sorry. I'm so sorry.'

———

What had she got to be so sorry about?

SEVEN

Haitch

HAITCH REMEMBERED the conversation with Damian as if it'd happened yesterday. Already a strange morning that would be followed by a nasty little revelation. Lugging artwork from a hired van to a new gallery in the centre of Brighton, Damian had stumbled as though he'd been zapped with a cattle prod and tripped on the kerb.

Two years previously

'Fuck!'

He nearly dropped the piece of work he was carrying. She dived in and caught it.

'Butterfingers.' His voice was shaking, and a line of sweat beaded at his hairline, even though the day was autumnal crisp. 'Should look where I'm going, eh?' Making a grab back for the painting, he twisted his body crab-like as his eyes darted sideways. It seemed to Haitch that he was using the artwork as a shield.

What the hell was that all about? Haitch focused on him.

Face ashen and pupils dilated. She peered around him. A black cat, spiky and arched against the wall, fire bright eyes ablaze hissed at them. Holy shit! Was he scared of black cats?

'That pavement leapt out of nowhere.'

He stared at her in such a way that it felt a challenge. Should she have said something? *Hey Damian, are you scared of little old black cats?* She wanted to laugh, but the look on his face made her stop.

'They always do.'

Nodding at the gallery door, she walked back to the van to pick up a sculpture. By the time she wrestled it in, she was glad to place it on the floor. Stretching, she rubbed small circles in her back.

'My back is killing me.' Glancing over at him, she was relieved that his grin was easy. No trace of the frightened man she'd glimpsed.

Damian stepped up behind her and started to massage her back too. 'Don't strain anything. I need my best artist fit and healthy for the viewing.' His breath had tickled her ear. As Haitch twisted round, their mouths nearly touched. She leant towards him, believing for a moment, they were going to kiss. This was it. But he jerked away from her.

'Sorry,' he said and headed back out to the van.

What?

'Damian?' Haitch wanted to drag him back and smother him with kisses. 'I know you're my agent and all that—'

'Don't go there, Haitch.' Wow, the man did look miserable. What was coming?

'Is it me or—' How confusing was this?

'No, Haitch.' He sounded resigned. 'It's me. I know that's a cliché, but it's most definitely not you.'

'Then what is it?'

'I...' he stroked at his nose, 'I'm married, Haitch.'

Bombshell.

'Oh.' She swallowed. 'Right.' Her laugh was a little strained. 'Glad to know it's not me. I was starting to wonder, you know?'

'It's complicated.'

'It always is, Damian. Can we talk about it?'

'Now is not the time. As I said, I'm sorry.'

His shoulders slumped. If Haitch didn't know better, he looked like a man defeated, a man kicked. Someone who, quite frankly, didn't look at all like the Damian she knew. It had made her feel all wobbly inside, as if she'd suddenly got a massive dose of food poisoning.

Straightening his shoulders, there was Damian again. 'Come on. No time to hang about doing sod all. Haven't we got an exhibition to put up?'

Although Haitch carried on as if nothing had changed, she clung to one thing. He may be married, yet 'happily' hadn't sprung to mind. Maybe she could still be in with a chance? She had to have a taste of him. It wouldn't be forever. It never was.

EIGHT

Matilda

Thursday 16th June - Spain

'I'm Haitch, I'm Haitch, I'm Haitch,' Tilda mumbled under her breath.

'Hey, Haitch. Wasn't sure if you'd bunk out on me.' Damian air-kissed her on both cheeks but didn't make physical contact. 'Especially after what you said on the phone.'

'Yeah, well, you know...' said Tilda. What had Haitch said?

'I mean, you did sound rough, but you've bunked before.'

'What? Once a bunker, always a bunker?' Tilda handed him her suitcase and made a show of coughing. Normally, she'd never be that rude, though she knew that Haitch would. 'Which one is ours? I hope it's not that teeny tiny green Fiat. I know I love the colour green, but it doesn't look big enough to get one person in.'

'What do you take me for?' Damian pointed as he picked up the case. 'The Berlingo over there has been recommended for where we're going. So sadly, the limo's out.'

'Where are we going again?' Tilda followed him. The heat

made the skin on her cheeks taut, and she hoped she didn't have sweaty patches under her armpits. She was still dressed for the British summer, and that included leggings, long boots and three tops.

'Up in the mountains. I believe the villa is quite close to Granada.'

Tilda had briefly mugged up on the area. 'It's too bad we can't stay longer. I'd have loved to see the Alhambra Palace.' Breathing deeply, she tried to analyse the smells bombarding her. The rich, warm air smelled orange. The colour shone in her mind.

'You told me when I set this up, you didn't want to stay any longer than necessary. Remember?'

Leaning in close to her, his eyes, ordinarily a deep luminous gold, now looked black. If she stared into them too long, Tilda felt she'd fall in and never be able to climb out. Was that the effect he had on her sister? Could Haitch be in love with him? Not that it mattered as he was married. Yeah, as if that stopped some men!

She blinked. 'Of course I remember, although I'd still like to see it.'

Staring at Damian, Tilda realised the emotion she associated with him was more akin to fear, tinged with a soupçon of revulsion, but that could be explained; the story of how Haitch had got her first and only black eye. A man who could hit a woman wasn't someone to be trusted. Haitch had trivialised it, even seemed quite excited, but Tilda had been horrified. Maybe in hindsight this now wasn't such a good idea, as there were too many variables that might go horribly wrong.

Struggling out of a deep purple printed hoodie that she'd fancied at Haitch's, she climbed into the back of the car. Plush. And loads of space. The boot 'thunked' down. Damian slipped in via the other door, hanging his jacket on the hook and loosening the top button of his shirt. Boy, when the man cut loose, he did it in style. Tilda only knew what Haitch had told her. Damian never let anything get past him and was as proverbially as buttoned-up as his expensive silk shirt. She wondered if she'd see the real him over this next couple of days. Mind you, she had to be extra careful he didn't see the real her.

He slapped at the driver's seat, where a man in a dark top was waiting patiently. 'Okay?'

'Si, Señor.'

The car slid away from the kerb in a soft fluid motion. The windows in the back were tinted, which kept some of the blinding sun at bay. Tilda gazed out as the boisterous city gave way to the motorway. Cars passed them: fat men with cigarettes clamped in their mouths and sultry dark-eyed women; some with kids, seen only by arms and legs flailing in the back seats. The terrain changed. Rocky escarpments towered above the road and terraces covered in silver-leaved olive groves marched down their sides, embedded in tilled ochre earth. A vast expanse of turquoise could be spied as they swung round lazy arcs of road. It disappeared and appeared again. The Mediterranean. Bathed in sunshine, glittering and inviting. Colours so different from her own beloved English Channel. Everything intensified, bright, rich. She'd love to take some photos.

'Can we stop to look at the sea? Have a coffee?'

'You're like one of those kids in the back of the car. "I can see the sea." Come on, Haitch. We haven't got time. Maybe on the way back, if you clinch this deal.' He licked his lips and raised an eyebrow. 'What do you say?'

'Okay.' Ah! Is that what he did then? Carrots or sticks. You do what's expected, and you get to play on the beach, just like a kid. So that's how he viewed Haitch. Interesting.

The air conditioning wafted cool air over them. Tilda could see heat mirages shimmering on the tarmac ahead. They were driving through a great gash in the mountain, bare striated rock, and jagged peaks on either side.

'Now,' Damian turned to her. 'We need to talk business before we arrive at the villa. Riku Ishimoto has been the chairman and CEO of Burger King's Japanese franchise since 2010. Before that, he was CEO of Nokia Japan.'

'Does he speak English?'

'He went to Eton College, so yes, he speaks English better than most Brits.'

'What do I call him? Riku or Mr Ishimoto?'

'Mr Ishimoto unless he invites you to call him otherwise. Mr Ishimoto has emerged as one of the highest-profile and influential executives in Japan. He's sixty-three and still runs marathons, and most importantly, he keeps in touch with the younger generation's tastes. This is where you come in. He's seen your work and has hinted that he'd like to have your next piece. There's the eighty-thousand-pound bursary on top. Not to be sniffed at, eh?'

'What does he expect in return?' Please don't let it be sex...

'He's rich and I mean really rich. It's peanuts to a man like him. I think he's paying for a show. The fun of the hunt. So give him something to get his teeth into. The main thing is, he's a people collector. I think he views you all as if you are his menagerie.'

Tilda took off her cap and ran her fingers through her hair. 'I don't like to be referred to as part of a menagerie.' How much? Eighty thousand squids? No wonder Haitch didn't mention that. No pressure, then. The thought of these 'others' made her want to squirm.

'Suck it up, Haitch. He's renowned for watching people, sits on the side lines as his guests battle it out to be the top dog. He's obviously got a great deal of cash, and I get the feeling he's expecting you all to perform.'

'So, we're going to be in his own personal circus?'

'It could be that he'll choose who he will patronise based on what he sees tonight. Just be yourself, and you'll do fine.'

Tilda laughed, although she could hear a note of uncertainty in it. 'As if I could be anyone else.' Regretting coming wasn't an option. Haitch had asked for her help, and she'd said 'yes'.

Damian stared hard at her, reached out and fingered a lock of her hair. Tilda tried not to pull away. 'New colour? Hmm, I like it, not so punky.' Tilda nearly laughed. Not a good idea to mention she'd dyed it darker so she wouldn't be mistaken for Haitch.

His shirt sleeve slipped back to reveal his wrist.

'Thanks. The white blonde got a bit boring.' She gazed at his wrist and the tantalising glimpse of what looked like a posh watch. How much was that worth?

'What are you staring at? You're acting a bit weird.'

Tilda jerked her head up. 'Oh. Nothing. Sorry.'

He pulled his cuff down, and it was as if a shutter had slammed shut. 'Are you okay, Haitch?' He nodded slightly, while his eyes narrowed.

'I'm fine. Why wouldn't I be?' What was up with him?

'You enjoy your little games, don't you?'

Damian was rattled, but why? Oh no. Had Haitch bought it for him? Here she was seemingly pretending not to know about it.

'Only kidding,' she said. She tried a smile. 'Whoever got you that had great style.' She waited.

Looking puzzled, Damian cleared his throat. 'Yes. She has. Now back to business.'

Tilda felt as if she was one of those ghastly nodding dogs that people had in the back of their cars. Why hadn't Haitch warned her about the watch?

'Sure. Business is why we're here. This villa? We're all staying there?'

'Seemingly so. It's called *La Castilla Mori*. I gather that translates to the Moorish castle. Mr Ishimoto has rented it for his guests – you lot. Trust me, it costs hundreds for a room, let alone for the whole place.'

'All of us? I mean, you're staying there too, aren't you?'

'No, sweetheart. Except me, of course.'

'What?'

'I'm not part of the menagerie. I'm your agent, required to ensure you arrive safely.'

'Then what do you do?'

'I'm already booked into a nearby hotel. I'll pick you up tomorrow.'

'Now, I want to go home.'

'You'll be fine.'

Oh, Dear God! 'Here's hoping.'

If she'd known about any of this, she doubted that she would have agreed to do it. Mind you, Haitch hadn't been told either. Who in their right mind would agree to be in the same room as Mr Ishimoto's 'menagerie'? The thought of so much raw talent made her bilious. Was it too late to ask the driver to turn around and go back to Málaga? Sleeping on the airport floor sounded way more inviting than meeting that lot up close and personal. She knew Haitch would revel in it, but she wasn't Haitch. And what about Damian? He might scare her, but at least he had her back and now he wasn't even going to be there? Bad, bad idea.

Climbing higher and higher, the scenery changed. Orange groves were now intermingled with the olives, and dusty winding roads led past rocky dry riverbeds with exotic-sounding names. If they were translated, would they simply be 'big, dirty river' or 'river with a kink in it'? Brushy looking broom and prickly gorse clung to the steep sides of the mountains. Great fat-leaved cacti and oleander bushes grazed the car as they whizzed by, and crumbling, white-washed buildings scurfed the edges of the road as if they'd been trying to cross and had fallen exhausted at the side.

Finally, at a sign proclaiming 'Castilla Mori', the car swung right and glided along a narrow tarmac road. Along its edge, stones protruded like teeth from a gum, the only things between them and a terrible, vertigo-inducing drop on one side. Pebbles spat from under the tyres. Snaking upwards, Tilda stared resolutely out the front window. She prayed the driver knew what he was doing as he wrenched the wheel back and forth and stepped hard on the accelerator to push them around hairpin bends without sending them spinning off. Bloody hell! She had to do it all again tomorrow afternoon.

'Christ!' Damian looked quite grey, and he was gripping onto the handholds above the door. 'Didn't realise where it was. I wouldn't want to have to drive up and down here every day to get a pint of milk.'

Tilda was secretly relieved that he'd shown 'the fear' first. 'You must get used to it.'

Skidding to a stop, Tilda let her breath out in a 'woosh' and then she focused. 'Fuck me!'

'Not right now,' said Damian, 'I'm still feeling sick.'

Tilda flapped at him and pointed. 'Look at this place. It's unbelievable.'

They seemed to be at the edge of an immense semi-circle of gravel bordered by gigantic rocks pointing like standing stones at the sky. Plum coloured mountains loomed above them, dotted with clusters of tiny, white-washed villages like dropped confetti.

'Come on, I'll get your bag.' Damian grabbed his jacket, clambered out of the car, and opened the boot.

The driver walked round to open her door. Tilda slipped out. 'Gracias?'

The driver turned and grinned at her. 'De nada.'

A balding, rangy man in a black suit and tie and a younger man in black waistcoat and trousers had materialised in front of them. The older man stopped when he saw Damian.

'Good afternoon. Mr Montgomery, I presume and Miss Bee. I'm Jeremiah, and I'm the Concierge at Castilla Mori.' He turned and smiled down at Tilda. 'Miss Bee, Miguel here will take your bags and lead you to your room, where you can freshen up and then join Mr Ishimoto and the rest of the party. Someone will call for you at seven. You will all be summoned at the same time, so there will be no preferential treatment. I am here to facilitate your every need.'

'Have all the guests arrived then?' Damian looked worried.

'Not at all. We have a helipad below the villa and are expecting the next arrival as we speak.' Jeremiah raised an eyebrow at them. 'Very few of the guests elected to come by road.'

'Wow!' Tilda turned to Damian. 'Is that a fact?'

Damian sucked on his teeth and looked pointedly over her shoulder. 'Helicopters are not on my bucket list.'

'Well, they are on mine.'

Jeremiah took a step forward, gracefully waving his hand. 'This way, please, Miss Bee.' The older man cordially ushered her towards a band of trees.

'Call me tomorrow.' Damian started to walk towards the car but then doubled back. Leaning down, he kissed her cheek, his lips brushing her skin. 'Good luck, Haitch.'

NINE

Haitch

Blame.

It wasn't usually in Haitch's vocabulary. Along with guilt. She'd managed to erase blame after her father's death, or she'd have gone out and killed the drunk boy who'd murdered him. Placed both hands around his scrawny neck and throttled the life out of him. She'd re-run that image in her head a thousand times until she thought she'd go mad. She could've done it too, but she didn't, not to save her own skin but because she couldn't do that to her mum and especially not to Tilda.

As to guilt, well, she'd worked out at a young age that life held unexpected surprises, and most of them weren't pleasant, so why not live whatever time you had on Earth to the full? As long as she didn't actually cause harm to another human... no, let's re-phrase that, lasting harm to another human being, she was more than happy to turn a blind eye to all her own short-comings and appetites and expected the world to do the same.

Sex was always a game. She was not affected by Victorian ethics and prudishness, and if her mum or her sister had the faintest idea about her proclivities, then so be it. She wasn't under any moral obligation to either of them. At least, she hadn't been until 'that' day. It wasn't as though she'd set out with the intent to destroy her sister's life. It just sort of happened. Well, over quite a few times. It did just sort of happen, didn't it? Didn't it?

'Shite!' Haitch crawled from the bed, disentangling herself from Boo and the duvet as if they were lovers trying to pull her back. 'Gotta make a cup of tea.' Was she now talking to the bloody dog? As long as she wasn't answered, they'd be fine.

How long did it take a kettle to boil? Long enough that the memory hit her square between the temples, as if it was a physical blow and it had happened yesterday. She could remember every exquisitely painful detail, taste it, smell it all as it unfolded before her scrunched closed eyes. Sam.

Along with blame and guilt, she didn't do crying, yet hot, salty tasting tears dribbled under her nose and dripped off her chin.

'I'm so sorry,' she whispered.

When was the last time she'd seen Sam? Not just seen but to talk to. Haitch thought back. Her last exhibition. Three weeks ago. The Private View. It was back in the Brick Lane Gallery, although this time it was a solo show, only her work on display and definitely no sharing.

Saturday 28th May – Brick Lane Gallery

Pristine white walls perfectly offset her work. The invited guests, suited and booted and in posh frocks and bling, fluted glasses of champagne in hand, were milling around her installations and sculptures, all talking in low but authoritative voices on 'the meaning' of her art. It was all bollocks. She would've laughed if she could, although Damian was monitoring her alcohol intake with sharp hooded eyes, and anyway, these were the people who might buy her work. Not a good idea to shoot yourself in the foot there. Oh, but she could play 'the artist' so well, using all the in catchphrases, the memes, the necessary words that they understood meant she was on another plane of existence to their lowly selves. They lapped it all up.

Damian was never far from her, chatting eloquently and with passion about her work with potential patrons. It sounded so real, so from the heart. But was it?

'She's an amazing artist, as you can see. Haitch Bee is on a meteoric rise. I truly believe you'll have to be quick to snap up her work. If you do, you'll have made a wise investment for the future. I tell you; a day will come where none of us will be able to afford her.'

And every-so-often, she'd catch his eye, and he'd smile at her and raise his glass. She knew she had to be careful not to be the adoring puppy gazing up, all brown-eyed at her master. Sometimes it felt like that. She was a dachshund, and he was pulling her along on a sparkly lead. Did it matter? No, not yet. Not until he started to dress her up in costumes. If he ever gave her a cowgirl hat and a sequinned waistcoat, then it might. Knowing it was off-limits, she allowed herself to wonder if he did have feelings for her. Okay, he'd admitted to being married, but she was an old love. Surely it might be time for a new one. With her?

In the middle of telling an Arab, complete with the whole *sheikh* paraphernalia, about the hidden icon in the midst of one of her paintings, Haitch was jolted out of her theatrics by a loud voice coming from the entrance.

'I told you, I'm her brother-in-law. Just go and get her then, she'll tell you.'

Sam. Sam? Oh, shite!

'Please excuse me.' She'd practically sprinted across the gallery, aware of startled glances and exclamations. Sam was pushing against one of the guards whose sole purpose was to stop people from entering the show without an invitation, as he was trying to do.

'Sam?' He looked as if he'd been tossed around in a spindrier for a few days; he smelt heavily of whisky.

The guard had loosened his grip. 'Sorry, Miss Bee, but he doesn't seem to have an invitation.' He paused and cleared his throat. 'And I do believe he's been drinking.'

'Of course, I've got an invitation, haven't I, Haitch? I've just lost it somewhere on route.' Sam had grinned a lazy smile. 'As to drinking, I admit I've had a couple to oil the wheels, so to speak.' He'd swivelled to peer at the guard. 'You see, I haven't seen Haitch in quite a while. Have I?'

Haitch felt rather than saw Damian drift up beside her. 'Do we have a problem?'

Sam's smile hadn't extended to his eyes. 'Do we a problem, Haitch?'

Worst case scenario? Hell yes, and she wasn't prepared. At all. Never for a millionth of a second did she think he'd turn up at her private view. How would she get him out of there without causing a massive scene?

'Not at all.' Haitch'd lurched forward and pulled Sam into the foyer. 'It's lovely to see you, Sam.'

Damian had also moved a step towards them both. 'I'm sorry, but who are you again?'

'This is Sam,' said Haitch and then couldn't think of one more word to say.

'I'm her brother-in-law. Well, was.' His laugh had sounded derisive. Haitch nearly bit her lip in her anxiety. He turned to her. 'How is she? My beautiful ex-wife?'

Haitch had to suck in a breath; it felt as if her lungs were closing. 'She's as well as can be expected.' She hadn't wanted to say it, but he said it for her.

'In the circumstances.'

Haitch nodded. What would he say? Oh, man! Right in front of everyone who mattered.

'I didn't know that you had a sister,' Damian said slowly, looking intently at her.

Haitch blinked and hissed almost incoherently: *Sam, shut-up, shut-up, shut-up…*

'Oooh,' Sam said, 'I expect there are quite a few things you don't know about my wonderful sister-in-law.' He extended his hand towards Damian. 'And you are?'

'Damian Montgomery. I'm Haitch's agent.'

'Well, that's nice, isn't it?' It hadn't sounded that nice. In fact, it sounded like a threat.

'Come with me outside, and we can talk.' Haitch tugged on Sam's arm, but he twitched her off, a look on his face as if she was an annoying insect.

'I've only just got here, and I'd love to see your new work.' He waved at Damian. 'Used to see all the work before, well, before the fall and ultimate degradation. But I expect she hasn't told you about that now, have you, Haitch?'

Haitch willed the floor to crack open, so she could jump in. Him being drunk, there were so many things he could blurt out. She had to face it; none of them would be good, especially in front of Damian.

'Look,' Damian said, 'this sounds personal between the two of you, but I'm sorry to say, an exhibition is not the time or place to have this conversation. Either go outside or have this out another day.'

'Have this out?' Sam snorted. 'Oh, we've had some things out, haven't we Haitch.'

'Sam, please—' Things were now squirming in her stomach.

Squinting behind her, Haitch was mortified that some of the people who had come to see her work were now more interested in their little 'drama'.

'Sam, please, pretty please,' he mimicked. 'Pretty, pretty please.'

'Right.' Damian took hold of Sam's arm. 'I'm going to have to ask you to leave now. Pretty please.'

'Get your hands off me.' Sam stumbled back. 'This is assault, and I'll fucking do you.'

Damian indicated the guard. 'Call the police.'

'No.' Haitch wriggled between them both. 'There's no need to do that, is there Sam? You'll go now, won't you?' This was going to get much worse, and there was nothing she could do about it. Her so-called punters were edging closer, heads inclined, camera phones at the ready. She could practically read the headline: punch-up in a prestigious art gallery. YouTube hits galore.

'Do it. Call the police.' Damian tilted his head and stared at them both.

'Really?' Sam steadied himself against the wall. 'The police? I'm just saying hello to family, and you think it's alright to call the police, you fascist prick.'

'Sam. You need to go now.' Haitch felt her face burning, tears hanging off her lashes. 'Just go!' Shoving him hard through the door, he pitched down the steps. Struggling to his feet, he briefly rubbed at his knee then made a telephone shape with his free hand.

'Call me.' His laugh had made her hair stand up on end. 'And don't you worry, Haitch, you'll be seeing me again soon. That's a promise.' He walked off into the shadows.

Had he gone, or was he watching them still?

'What the fuck was all that about?' said Damian quietly

'Family stuff.' Haitch could feel something fluttering in her chest. Was this the start of a heart attack?

Damian gripped her elbow. 'Don't let it get messed up in our business.' His voice was low. 'I know you're a so-called "edgy" artist; nonetheless, patrons don't relish fisticuffs in the gallery when they're deliberating whether to pay out a great deal of wonga for your art.'

'I'm sorry if real life got in the way of our fleecing some rich twats.' It came out as a hiss.

'Fuck me, Haitch. If there wasn't so much riding on this, I'd give you a slap.'

Haitch winced. 'Been there, haven't we, Damian?'

She was gratified to see a hint of pink colour his alabaster cheeks. So, the man wasn't a statue, after all. Sometimes he let the facade of charm and sophistication slip and what was behind it was ugly and threatening. Today, she didn't find that at all sexy. Wrinkling her nose, she wrenched her arm from his grip.

'Get back in there, Haitch. Do your job, and I'll do mine. We might still be in with a chance tonight.'

Haitch glanced around, sniffed, and wiped carefully at her eyes. People were drifting back into the gallery. The guard was conspicuously not checking a lot by the door. As she turned, she saw a silhouette leaning up against a lamppost further up the road. She couldn't see for sure, but she knew it was Sam. Closing her eyes briefly, she counted to ten and then smiled. She'd been practising it in the mirror at home, so she knew the effect it had. Returning to the Arab, she launched straight in from where she'd left off.

'Is everything all right, Miss Bee?' He frowned and nodded towards the entrance. 'There seemed to be a little, oh how do you say it, fracas?'

'It's fine. Just a misunderstanding. Shall we continue?'

It was as if there were two commentaries rolling alongside each other that night. One was playing to the crowd, the other was going through all the scenarios that Sam could have in store for her. *And don't you worry, Haitch, you'll be seeing me again soon. That's a promise.* What was he going to do? How bad was it going to get?

Falling into bed that night, still dressed, with make-up uncleansed, Haitch watched all her thoughts as if they were films projected onto the ceiling.

TEN

Matilda

Thursday 16th June - Spain

OMG!

If Tilda died right now, she knew this was what Heaven would be like. Rustic buildings with terracotta tiled roofs, landscaped gardens with dark green leafy plants and tall shady trees, terraces with loungers covered in thick, white mattresses, wooden tables, and chairs, inviting turquoise pools. The cultivated areas drifted off into the wild Spanish countryside, with no borders, walls, or fences.

'Wow! It is so beautiful here.'

'It is indeed.' Jeremiah held out a steadying hand. 'Be careful of your step here. The *Castilla* is original, and that tends to come with quirky angles.'

Winding brick steps led them down towards the gardens.

'Are you from here?' Tilda had been surreptitiously observing him. With his complexion, he could be from any Mediterranean country or even as far as Northern Africa and the Middle East.

'I'm actually from Ipswich.' He raised a sardonic eyebrow. 'But I blend in. I speak seven languages fluently and have a master's degree in engineering.'

'I don't mean to be rude.' Tilda let go of his hand. 'But aren't you a little over-qualified to be a Concierge?'

'Not at all. We need to be the epitome of knowledge and good manners. We must accommodate the needs of every guest.'

'I hope the pay's good then.'

Jeremiah smiled. 'It's adequate for my needs, Miss Bee.'

'Are there any jobs going?' She smiled back at him. 'Only joking but...'

'I will keep you in mind.' Jeremiah inclined his head slightly.

Weaving through the gardens, following Miguel, Tilda could hear the drone of cicadas swelling and dying away as they passed. Small birds, like sparrows but subtly different, chirped loudly and fought in the shrubs, the branches shaking and tiny bodies erupting and then returning to the melee. A white butterfly fluttered past. The air was warm and smelt... it smelt of summer. Real summer.

'Sorry, hang on.' Tilda stopped and pulled out her phone. She had to capture all this for Haitch.

Placed on each white linen lounger was a neatly folded towel. The air was filled with the scent of shrubs that were in terracotta pots dotted around. Tilda recognised lavender, oregano, and rosemary. She imagined if you brushed past them, you would be enveloped in their scent. Bigger pots were home to young olive trees. Below a small rampart, she could see the slightly bowed roofs of the main building. A trellis woven with wisteria backed the porch area and aged, rusted lamps hung low. Now she understood why this place would cost so much. If only she could avoid this party altogether and simply lie on those fluffy white towels, soaking up the Spanish sun with a glass of red in her hand.

'Nearly there. We're in the main courtyard now. From here, you can access the whole of Castilla Mori.'

A rough stone floor, covered in patches of moss. Arches that led off in every direction.

'If you follow Miguel, your room is this way.' He bowed gracefully. 'I shall see you anon, Miss Bee.'

'This way, please, Miss Bee.' Miguel had a soft lisping accent. Through another archway, he led her past three doors and stopped at one with the number six on it. The door opened, and Tilda stepped into the room. 'Mr Ishimoto hopes that he has chosen well for you.'

'Yep. This will do nicely, thanks.' Turning about her, she stared at the beamed ceiling, the soft ochre paint, and the slightly uneven terracotta tiled floor. The cupboards were all simple wood, a chest with heavy hinges sat at the base of the bed, and a rustic set of drawers with a vase of dried flowers on top of it seated snugly in a recessed arch.

Miguel moved back towards the door after placing her bags on the pristine white bedspread. 'If you need anything at all, please ring this bell by the bed...' he indicated a switch, 'and someone will come immediately.'

'Thanks. Oh...' Tilda reached inside her bag, still slung over her shoulder, 'just a minute, er...'

'That's alright. Hasta luego.' Miguel closed the door quietly.

'Right then.' Tilda sat on the chest. Two boxy seats, covered in teal coloured jacquard print were positioned either side of a small round table, and a couple of books lay beautifully placed in the middle. Laid across the floor was a simple red rug. Tilda poked at it with the toe of her boot. Breathing in deeply, she strode across the room and pushed a door that was slightly ajar.

'Oh yeah! Come to mama.' The en-suite bathroom was

decorated in a 1930's style with a deep, claw-footed bathtub; a stepped sink on a boxy plinth; a loo and the ubiquitous bidet. A dark wood table groaned under the weight of yet more fluffy towels. Watercolour paintings of flamingos hung on the wall, and there was a spot-lamp above the simple glass mirror, ready she presumed, for them all to be able to pluck those unwanted hairs. Running her hand across the light duck-egg painted walls of the bathroom, she turned the taps on. Good. Lots of water. She'd been in places where you switched on the tap and had time to watch the World Cup before the sink filled halfway.

Taking more photos for Haitch, she was glad now she was here instead of her. Hurrah for flu!

Glancing at her watch, which she'd already moved on an hour, she knew she'd have time for a bath. There was no way she could come to such a place and not indulge in that. Examining the bottles left on a glass shelf by the side of the bath, she dribbled a bit of ylang-ylang and watched the bubbles creep up the side of the immensely gleaming tub.

After her bath, she dragged on her chosen clothes, which she'd neglected to hang up (as Haitch wasn't the ironed neatly type), and applied foundation, eyeliner and deep red lips. Smudging dark powder into her eyebrows, she stared at the face reflected in the mirror. There. She was Haitch incarnate. No one would guess. If she kept a tight rein on her mouth, she'd be fine.

Although she expected it, the tap on the door still made her jump. Grabbing Haitch's phone, she rammed it into her trouser pocket and then followed a young Spanish woman back the route they'd first come.

'We are meeting in the main living room,' said the woman. 'If there is anything that has not been provided, please ask one of the attendants, and we will try our very best to get it for you.' She ushered Tilda into the room through a stone-clad doorway.

The first thing that hit Tilda was the sheer size of the fireplace that faced her. White and ornately carved, with copper utensils that looked ancient along its ledge. She doubted she'd even have to duck to step into it. It rose towards the ceiling, which felt a hundred feet above her. A bookshelf to beat all bookshelves was positioned to the side, stuffed with sets of bound leather books, and facing it were two silver patterned deep, plump sofas. Lamps lit the room. A low table with fresh cut flowers was in front of the couches. To the left of the fireplace was a stone entrance, obviously original, with weathered and softened carved shapes crawling over it. The room was vast. A chipped gilt-framed mirror the size of one of her walls at home reflected dark paintings of men with beards, dressed in fur and ruffles. At the far end was a chandelier, but it was unlike any she had ever seen. Six foot in length, simple shaded lights were hung from a central point in the dark wood-beamed ceiling high above her. That was when she spotted the cameras. Scanning the room, she noted that an array of them was secured to various points, and to her horror, they weren't fixed but moving. One seemed to be trained on her. She felt light-headed that she was being watched; no, what was the word, oh yes, surveilled.

Holy crap! Right then. Slipping out her phone, she surreptitiously snapped around her. Was this allowed? Why not? If they were spying on her, then the least she could do was spy back.

There was so much to stare at that Tilda nearly missed the Japanese man of middle years leaning up against the far wall. She slipped the phone back into her pocket and hoped he hadn't seen.

'Miss Bee?' He walked over, hand outstretched. Was she meant to bow low or something? She shook his hand vigorously and kept her eyes level with his. She wasn't going to grovel or act subservient, not on Haitch's behalf. It was incredible how he looked rich as if wealth exuded from his pores. She noticed his nails were perfectly manicured, his light-coloured suit must have a designer label, and his teeth were flawless and brilliant. It wasn't just the watch, that was probably a Rolex or whatever, or the subtle scent that hung about him, that gave him that rich aura, it was all of it at once. He oozed money. And lots and lots of it.

'Mr Ishimoto?' Was her voice wavering? Get a grip, girl.

He nodded quickly.

'Very pleased to meet you.'

'I have watched your progress with great interest.' His accent was slight. 'Your work awakens something quite primal inside of me. I must admit, it takes a lot to do that.' His eyes hadn't left hers, and he seemingly didn't blink.

'I'm delighted to hear that.' Tilda also kept eye contact. 'If you'd said my work was "nice", I would be offended.' Such an Haitch thing to say.

'Of course, you would. Indeed, the word "nice" is an anathema to the true artist.' He turned to look behind him. 'Ah. More of my guests have arrived. Well, Miss Bee. I hope you have an enjoyable evening. I look forward to speaking with you more later on.' There was a look in his eye as he moved to greet the others now being led in. Was he aware of Haitch's terrible reputation of shagging anyone and everyone senseless? He'd said, 'It awakens something primal?' Blimey, she had to be careful tonight. She wasn't going to win this commission on easy sex no matter how desperately her sister wanted it. And if Damian kicked off, she'd suggest he waggle his arse at the man and do the deed himself.

Focusing on the other combatants either sidling in or stomping brazenly, Tilda wondered how she could ever compete against any of them.

'Hello, Haitch.'

Tilda visibly jerked. 'Er?'

The woman who had materialised at her shoulder had the sort of luminous blue eyes that made her feel she was falling headfirst into a bottomless lake. Tilda blinked.

'I'm Dawn.' At first, it seemed to Tilda that she was waiting for a response.

'Oh, hello!' Lame, but hey.

Dawn stared at Tilda intently, again as if expecting something, then she smiled, revealing slightly crooked white teeth beneath her sticky fuchsia lipstick. 'I saw your last exhibition before the delectable Damian got his grubby paws on you.'

Grubby paws? 'Oh, you've met him, have you?' But had she also met Haitch? Was this going to be tricky?

'I know of him, yes.' There was a curious light in her eyes as if she was reflecting some other room. Tilda resisted the urge to peer behind her.

'I don't mean to be rude, but have we met? I'm sorry, I've been introduced to so many people recently, I can't quite remember.' Tilda waited, hoping that would cover a minor faux pas.

'No, we've never met in person. You were busy talking to people, so I just looked at your artwork.' She smiled. 'Strangely enough.'

What would Haitch say now? 'Does that mean you liked my "before Damian" work and not my "after" stuff?' Tilda cleared her throat. 'Sorry, that's assuming you liked any of it.'

'Always like the original work before it gets corrupted. The real person shines through.' The woman sighed audibly. 'Then, well, the artist can quite literally change into someone else.'

Tilda tried not to swallow noisily. The real person? Change into someone else? Dear God, had she been sussed already?

Dawn continued. 'Anyone who gets an agent after struggling for so long often is altered by the experience; they must change or grow or conform to expectations. I find it quite sad that an artist such as yourself would need to have this other party who... um, not exactly controls you but seems to have free rein as to your direction.'

Tilda nodded. Haitch may be 'the artist', but she was an illustrator and a good one at that. Even before her marriage to Sam, they'd worked under different names to keep their identities separate. In her own life, she had to deal with editors, publishers and writers who kept changing their minds without a clue as to how much work it took to do one of her illustrations. Can you change the ears? Make the picture darker, lighter, red? But was Haitch controlled by Damian? Probably.

Tilda countered. 'You can either continue to struggle and remain true to your own artistic source or try for higher things and maybe lose a bit of your credibility along the way. It's never an easy decision, is it?'

'Seemingly not.' Dawn swept back an unruly tangle of honey blonde hair. Tilda glanced at her manicured nails, painted the same fuchsia as her lips. Two bangles with inter-twining rings clinked together on her wrist. At a guess, they were Indian silver, heavy and intricate. 'Enjoying the spectacle?' There was a long pause. 'Haitch?'

Why had she said her name in that way? So pronounced? Hold it together. She didn't know. How could she? 'Of course. Who wouldn't love all this?' Tilda motioned around the room, just as a short, stocky man with tied-back long chestnut brown hair, in tight-fitting dark attire strode into the room. He was either one of them or the lead singer in a Mariachi band. 'Do you know who that is?'

'I think that's Alejandro Moreno. He's a theoretical physi-cist.' Dawn nudged Tilda and winked. 'Pretty cute, eh?' Tilda didn't know if it was the way she said it, but it made her squirm.

'I suppose so. Look, do you know who else is coming tonight then?'

Dawn's eyes flicked across the room. 'Well, as far as I know, we have the physicist over there, an architect, a film director, an artist, presumably that's you, and a clairvoyant. I think that's all of us.'

It occurred to Tilda that none of them were supposed to know who was on the guest list tonight. Either this woman just happened to recognise all the people in the room, or she'd been primed about them beforehand. Which also meant she might have mugged up on them. Now, how much of an advantage would that be? And good God Almighty! She was up against these people. This was never going to work, and she wanted to go home right now!

Tilda took a slight step back. 'Sorry, but who are you again? I mean, what do you do?'

'I'm the clairvoyant.'

'Clairvoyant?' What?

'Don't worry. Your secret is safe with me.' Dawn winked again and walked towards the group now gathering in the centre of the room. Her strapless dress was funerary black, as were her kitten-heeled shoes and a thin black necklace encircled her throat. How they had all dressed for the part!

'Oh, crap!' whispered Tilda under her breath. She just had time to take a quick note of the others before a strange tinkling sound heralded a sudden hush in the room. Jeremiah was tapping a spoon on a glass.

'Mr Ishimoto would like to say a few words.' He stepped aside.

'I'd like to start,' Mr Ishimoto's voice was soft, 'by welcoming you to Castilla Mori. I have chosen all of you because of your...' He paused for a moment and tweaked something from his jacket. 'Merits. You are all reaching the pinnacle of your careers, and I would like to offer one of you a little help to get there. I want you all to be yourselves, of course, and although I know that this may be difficult,' he chuckled, 'the phrase "jumping through hoops" comes to mind. Remember, you are all in the same position. I relish honesty, and I will be put off if I think that any of you are staging a show for my benefit. I want to see the real you. We shall have dinner at nine. You will find your name on a card placed on the table. Drinks to complement all the dishes will be served at the table, and waiters with champagne will be serving you throughout the evening. But first I have a request: a photo of you all.'

Tilda turned to where he pointed and saw a camera on a tripod, with an anxious-looking young man fiddling with bits of tech, was to the left of them.

Mr Ishimoto beckoned to the group. 'I will email a copy to you all within the next few days. Also, I shall enclose the winner's name.' He twitched his fingers. 'Come, come. No need to be shy. Line up along here. Mr Orpheus Jackson to my right, with Miss Haitch Bee to his right.'

Tilda scuttled to stand next to a tall Black man.

'Group photo, eh?' he whispered down to her, looking as bemused as she felt.

'On my left,' continued Mr Ishimoto, 'I would like Miss Zaida Al-Nassar, then Mr Alejandro Moreno and finally Miss Dawn Rayne. Ladies and gentlemen, if you would fold your hands in front of you and put one leg slightly behind the other, bending your body into the centre. There now.' He took a step forward to peer up and down the line. 'We all look suitably formal for our photo.' He waved a finger at the photographer. 'When you are ready, Christopher.'

'Yes, Mr Ishimoto.' The young man seemed nervous. He coughed and then grinned. 'I will count down from three and then if you can all call out "cheese" and smile, that'd be great.' He squinted through the lens. 'Three, two, one – cheese!'

There was a rapid clicking of the shutter. Tilda shouted out with the others. Cheese? Really? What a truly 'cheesy' thing to do. They weren't having a school photo done, for crying out loud. If this was a herald of things to come, she wanted to go home. Now.

Mr Ishimoto was the first to break ranks. 'Well done, everyone. I'm sure you all look splendid.' He waved behind him. 'Last but certainly not least, and I do hate to be talking of mundane things such as money.' He raised a sardonic eyebrow. 'Would you all confirm an email address on the sheet on the table there. Whoever wins will then need to send me details of their bank account. I will also announce it online a day later.' He bowed. A quick jerk of his body. 'Now, please get to know the other guests here.'

Following the others, Tilda jotted down Haitch's email address.

She was also beginning to wonder if she should have dressed up more for the occasion, judging by everyone else. It'd all been Haitch's choice, so she'd had no alternative but to go with it.

Right. Get to know the other guests and be herself. Well, be Haitch. Tilda took a step back and found herself glued to the pristine white wall as if she was a barnacle on the underside of the pier back in Brighton. No. Don't think of that. Keep in the moment. A young waiter drifted past, carrying a tray laden with fluted glasses of something bubbly.

'Señorita?'

'Gracias.' Tilda reached for a glass. It was good stuff. She drained it in three gulps.

ELEVEN

Haitch

THIS WAS one of those points in her life where she could either go on pretending nothing had happened, the old head-in-the-sand scenario, or meet the issue head-on. Lots of heads here, although Haitch wondered if hers had gone walkabout.

Seven years ago

Sam and Tilda married two years after they graduated. They saved up for the white wedding Tilda had craved since a little girl. Not in a church but a register office. It didn't matter. The vows were said in front of the people who counted, and anyway, none of them had faith in God anymore, not since he'd taken their dad for no reason that they could discern, except to be bloody-minded. Who wanted to believe in a mean, cantankerous god? Tilda or Tilly, as Sam called her, had her bargain-basement fairy tale wedding with her handsome prince. What a picture they made. Tilda looked stunning in their granny's retro but beautifully stylish dress. He was smart in a borrowed frock coat and top hat. A lilac bridesmaid dress for her. Although Haitch personally hated lilac and honestly wondered what Tilda had been thinking when choosing her dress, she wore it without a murmur, and even thought she rocked it. It had all been done on a budget, yet they were adept at using what came to hand and turning nothing into something extraordinary.

'Wow, Tilda.' Haitch said, as Tilda stood in front of her dressed in her gown and veil. 'I don't mean to be all gushing, but you are the most beautiful bride I've ever seen.' And she meant it.

'This is the most amazing day of my life. I still can't believe it. I'm marrying the most incredible man I've ever met.' Tilda stopped and burst out laughing. 'Dear God, hark at us. We'll be crying in a minute.'

Haitch nodded and held her breath. 'Come on then, Soon-to-be-Mrs Green.'

'Mrs Green. Tilly Green. Nope, still not used to that but it's got a ring to it, hasn't it?'

'Possibly, although I still prefer Tilda Green. Now that sounds right.'

Sat at home in their mum's living room, the three of them made the decorations to be draped around their local pub where the evening party was to be held. All the wedding invitations were hand-drawn by Tilda and then printed at home. The cost had been negligible, as not many people were invited. Nearest and dearest. Haitch made the bouquets and headdresses, buying a variety of flowers and then copying tutorials she'd found on YouTube. Their mum slaved for days making the reception lunch they had in their mum's house and stashing it in the freezer. Borrowed chairs and extra tables groaning under the weight of plates of food. A simple buffet, everyone sat on miss-matched chairs, laughing and waving glasses of Cava.

Haitch stood; her toast had talked of their absent father, who would have been so proud of his beautiful daughter. More tears were shed.

———————

Seven years ago. Seven years of married bliss?

TWELVE

Matilda

—

'Hi, I'm Orpheus. Orpheus Jackson, and please don't mention *The Matrix.*' He had a rich, drawling American accent.

Tilda turned to look up at the tall, bearded man leaning against the wall by her side. He handed her another full glass, put his own on a low table placed against the wall where Tilda stood and wiped a pair of tortoiseshell glasses on his t-shirt. His shaved head was so shiny, Tilda swore she could see her reflection in it. When he put his glasses back on, his eyes looked twice their size.

'I'm Haitch. Haitch Bee.' They clumsily shook hands. Tilda grinned. 'Thanks for the drink. I think there was a hole in the bottom of the glass I had.'

'You're welcome. I've already had three from three different waiters, so it doesn't look so bad. Quells the nerves, it's a good strategy as long as you don't throw up in the ice bucket.'

'Good tip. Thanks.' She sipped the champagne, careful not to gulp it in case she choked. Tilda continued to stare up at him, feeling more confident. 'You probably know that people keep coming up to Samuel L. Jackson to tell him he was great in that film without realising that he wasn't even in it.'

'Yeah, I know. You wouldn't believe the number of people who think I'm named after Morpheus because they don't hear it right or have somehow related it to Samuel because of my surname, and as you say, he wasn't even in it. I'm Black, and you know, we all look the same.'

Tilda worried for a moment. Was that a joke?

Orpheus winked at her. Oh, thank goodness.

Tilda nodded towards the ceiling. 'You presumably know we're being filmed? I also presume there must be mics around the place too?'

'Yeah, I've spotted them. I suppose it's so Mr Ishimoto doesn't miss a thing.'

Tilda leant in a little closer. 'Do you think he'll watch them all later?'

'Why else have all this set up?' He squinted down at her. '"H.B.", are you named after an art pencil then?' His grin was wide and easy. And his teeth were very white, as were every American's in every movie she'd seen. There must be a lot of dentists whistling their merry way to the bank.

'Ha! It was because... my sister couldn't pronounce my name. It's her pet name for me, and it stuck.'

'So, what's your real name?' He picked up his glass and swigged it.

'If I tell you, I'd have to kill you.'

'Hmm, professional secret? What if I guess it? Helen? Hilary? Hermoan? I got that from Harry Potter, although I don't think you pronounce it like that, do you? I can tell by the fact you're smirking.'

'I'm sorry, I also read the whole book pronouncing it the way you did before someone enlightened me. Just keep away from Irish names. They'll do your head in.'

He scratched at his beard. 'Hettie? What about Heather? Hollie? Halle? Like in Halle Berry? She's an H.B. Hannah—'

'Harriet. I'm Harriet, or we could be here all night. I'm sorry, but I don't recognise you?'

'You mean which one of the menagerie am I? I'm the film director. Behind the lens, not in front of it.'

'American, or am I about to insult you?'

'New York, born and bred.' He cocked his head. 'You? London? Or again, is that what every American says?'

'Near enough.'

'And your part in this little charade?'

'I'm an artist. Would I have seen any of your films?'

'That depends on whether you're into African-American films that look at what it means to be a Black man in today's America.'

'Like Spike Lee?' Tilda closed her eyes for a second. 'Sorry, the first thing that came to mind. Note to self. Engage brain before opening mouth.'

Orpheus raised his glass. 'Let's say, if anyone compared my work to his in a favourable light, I would not be offended.'

'This is just a personal opinion, but I feel America is in a bit of a downward spiral.'

'When hasn't it been? It's changed only in the fact that we can now see what is happening because technology has allowed us to film it and, most importantly, post it online. I don't think it has ever really been different. Whereas before, it was hidden, now it's in our faces.'

'What do you think of "Fake News"? I mean, you're a film director, right? Stories are stories, except when it's put out as truth, that's when I have a problem.'

'As you say, that's a different ball-game altogether.' Orpheus frowned. 'Never before have the American people been so flagrantly lied to and cheated as they have over these last few years.'

'Yeah, well, we've got our fair share of that going on in Britain too.' Tilda drained the glass. She should slow down as her stomach was in knots.

'Never believed we'd start taking steps backwards. Thought we might stall a bit, but going back to the bad old days, well, that was a shocker. I suppose you could say that it's great material for film making.'

'Do you only deal with modern life or... what went before?'

'Before what? Before '45 got in and caused no end of havoc? Or do you mean before the Thirteenth Amendment led to the abolishment of slavery?'

'Yeah, before that.' Tilda could've kicked herself. Had she insulted him? Maybe you should never mention such a terrible subject to a Black person.

'Mostly inner-city life. I film in actual gang-run neighbour-hoods, which can be a little scary at times, though I have one thing going for me.'

'What's that?' She already knew.

'I'm Black.'

'Yes, you are.' Tilda nodded solemnly.

His laugh was throaty and warm. 'Ah, you noticed. And no, I don't deal with...' He stopped for a moment, and Tilda realised he was mimicking her own pause. '"...what went before". There are other people more qualified to do that than me. I think the film of *Ten Years a Slave* has shown that. I prefer to observe what the aftermath of slavery has done to us.'

'I read the book. Unbelievable.'

'His was only one story in so many. Yes, unbelievable.' Orpheus shifted to his other foot. 'What about you? An artist.'

'Fixated with repetition and pattern. I have themes of abstract expressionism, minimalism and surrealism, and I do truly believe that although my work is sexy and feminine, it has often made people run away from it.' Tilda reckoned that Haitch would be proud of her.

'Male people?'

'Mostly, but some women find my art hard to, how shall I put this, hard to come to terms with.'

'Note to self. Find Haitch Bee's work and try not to run. So, we have the arts covered with you and me. Do you know the guy over there, talking to that rather extraordinary Arabic woman?'

Tilda glanced over her shoulder. It was the Spanish looking bloke, and his face was sullen. Was it at something she'd said?

Tilda nodded towards where Dawn was making fluid gestures with her hands at Mr Ishimoto. 'Dawn, that woman over there, said he was a theoretical physicist. Whatever that entails.'

Orpheus' eyebrows rose as if pulled on invisible threads. 'That sounds a little unnerving. And what accomplishment can Dawn profess to?'

'She's a clairvoyant.'

'Communing with the other world?' Orpheus tilted his head to stare at Dawn. There was a look on his face that Tilda couldn't work out.

Tilda raised an eyebrow. 'Don't they talk to the dead? That sounds scary to me.'

'That's part of it.'

Orpheus finally focused back on her. 'Do you know who anyone else is then?'

'The other woman talking to the physicist must be, by default, the architect. I thought she might be an actress or a model, she's so beautiful. Her name was Arabic, though I didn't fully catch it.'

'How do you know all this? I thought none of us were meant to have any info beforehand?'

'Funny that because it was the clairvoyant who told me.'

'Seriously? Wow. So, we have the arts, which is us,' he said touching his chest briefly, 'the storytellers, the truth-benders, the eye-openers. Then we have the sciences of fact, maths and principles as embodied within architecture and physics, and finally, a dabbler in the occult. Interesting combination, don't you think?'

'Have we been picked because of what we do or because of who we are? Our, er—'

'Predilections?'

'Precisely.' Tilda was thinking of Haitch's reputation and was hoping that this had no bearing on why she was here. But what if that was the actual reason?

Orpheus stared at her. 'And have you any predilections then?'

Tilda felt a wave of heat rise up her neck. 'As much as anyone.' She motioned to him. 'You?'

'Much the same.' He shuffled his feet and pulled off his glasses to wipe them again.

Tilda looked across at the others. 'And how old are we, at a guess? I mean, I'm nearly thirty, but I don't think there's anyone here over thirty-five. Do you?'

'I'm thirty-three, and I thought I might be the eldest here. So, it's not just talent, it's age-related.'

'Excuse me.'

Tilda felt the shift in movement beside her. A round face came into view. The theoretical physicist had popped up at her shoulder. Maybe he'd discovered how to instantaneously teleport people from one place to another. *Beam me up, Scotty!*

'We were told to mingle, so I'm mingling,' he explained. 'I'm Alejandro Moreno. I caught the last thing you said just now. I'm twenty-seven, so yes, I think we are being picked at the start of our careers. This bursary or commission from Mr Ishimoto could be the thing that makes us.'

Tilda was the same height as Alejandro. His eyes were a spectacular green, dotted with flecks of gold. Tilda was as mesmerised as if a cobra was swaying in front of her.

'Eighty thousand English pounds.' Alejandro nodded. 'I like the sound of that.'

'And,' said Tilda, 'maybe a commission on top?'

'All of that sounds good,' said Orpheus. 'Hi, I'm Orpheus by the way.' His hand swept past Tilda to shake the other man's hand. Tilda pushed herself back against the wall. 'I'm a film director.'

'Orpheus? Not Morpheus, you know, the dude from *The Matrix*?'

Orpheus blinked rapidly and flashed a look at Tilda. 'No. Orpheus, as in the legendary musician and poet in ancient Greece, who could, according to some, charm all living things.'

'Wasn't he,' ventured Tilda, 'the bloke who went into the Underworld to get his wife back?' Whoops, this was probably something that Haitch wouldn't know.

Orpheus' eyebrows rose once again. 'Yeah, poor bastard was killed by those who couldn't hear his divine music for what it was. Boy, do I know that feeling.'

Alejandro turned to her. 'And may I ask who you are?'

'I'm Haitch Bee and I'm an artist. Alejandro,' said Tilda, 'we were reliably told you're a theoretical physicist. What's that when it's at home?'

'Hmm, how to explain it. Theoretical physics is a branch of physics that employs mathematical models and abstractions of physical objects and systems to rationalise, explain and predict natural phenomena.'

'Mathematical models?' Orpheus sucked on his teeth. 'Is that how we explain everything now?'

'Seems so,' said Tilda. 'What's the difference between theoretical physics and, you know, normal physics?'

'Good question,' said Alejandro. 'This is in contrast to experimental physics, which uses experimental tools to probe these phenomena. My field relates to consciousness, which most scientists don't like to talk about because you can't touch it and you can't see it.'

'Sentience?' said Orpheus. 'Having a sense of self?'

'Yeah,' said Tilda, 'like that gorilla who understood the idea of someone she'd never met giving her presents she'd never had.'

'That's my childhood summed up,' said Orpheus.

'Yes.' Alejandro nodded. 'The sense of selfhood or perhaps we should call it soul. Did you know that there's supposedly such a thing as a philosophical zombie? Someone whose behaviour and function are the same as ours, yet there is no one in there experiencing it.'

'I think I've met quite a few in my local pub,' said Tilda.

'Me too.' Orpheus grinned at her. 'That's a strange concept, though. A philosophical zombie? Wow.'

'So, what you're saying', said Tilda, 'is we need to be fully awake subjectively to experience our own awareness? Or something like that?'

Alejandro waved his hand at Orpheus and Tilda. 'You are a film director, and you, Haitch, are an artist. Yes? You have a sense of self.'

'Don't all humans have self-awareness?' said Orpheus. 'Of some degree?'

'Theoretically, yes. But we are beginning to feel that consciousness can be interpreted as a mathematical pattern.'

'Oh, dear. I'm crap at maths.' Tilda grinned up at Orpheus.

'Me, too. Excuse me?' Orpheus waved energetically at a young waiter standing with a tray of drinks in the middle of the room. He turned back to them. 'What about AI? This is something me and my friends talk about a lot in the States. Are we going to be taken over by sentient robots?'

'Terminator?' said Tilda. 'That Arnie cyborg scared the crap out of me.'

'Yeah. That dude was relentless.' Orpheus frowned. 'And is it possible to transfer human consciousness into an artificial body? Maybe that's more the question we should be asking. What's your view, Alejandro?'

The waiter nodded and came over. As Orpheus took a drink, so did Tilda.

'I have a question for you.' Alejandro looked from Orpheus to Tilda. 'Say we do manage to download a person's consciousness into a robot or cyborg, would you trust that new entity the way you did the real person?'

Orpheus held up a finger. They waited. 'If they looked the same and you felt they were the same, then yes.'

'And you, Haitch?'

'I think I would. Why? Wouldn't you?'

'I would wonder if they had lost their soul in the transference. I would fear that I was merely interacting with the husk that had been left behind.'

'I remember', said Tilda, 'an old film about that. The guy in question turned out to be a nutter because his soul was missing.'

Alejandro nodded. 'My point exactly.'

Motioning across the room, Tilda said, 'We seem to have divided into two groups. Should we go and join the others? Especially as Mr Ishimoto is in the other one.'

'You mean, with the women talking animatedly to him?' said Orpheus. 'Like their lives depended on it. Or rather a great deal of cash depends on it.'

'Let's go then.' Alejandro moved first. Tilda and Orpheus in tandem behind him.

Tilda only caught part of the conversation between Dawn

and the other woman in the group. Dawn seemed a little disquieted.

The woman coughed politely: '...as I was about to say that yes, today we struggle, though we do not give up easily.'

Tilda looked from one woman to the other. 'We don't mean to interrupt, but what were you talking about?'

The woman squinted at her. 'That my country and my religion have never been favourable towards women.'

'Where exactly are you from then?'

'Iraq. I'm sorry, I didn't catch your name?'

'I'm Haitch Bee.'

'Like in the pencil?'

'Just like the pencil.'

Mr Ishimoto stepped forward. 'I'd like to present Zaida Al-Nassar. A female Muslim architect in a male-dominated world.'

'I also have branched into architecturally inspired homeware, sculptural jewellery and limited-edition furniture.' Zaida looked down her long nose at each of them.

Tilda immediately took a dislike to her. Zaida seemed already eminently successful, and Tilda wondered what she was doing there.

'On that note...' Mr Ishimoto gestured through the stone entrance to the side of them. 'Let us be seated for supper, then we can all get to know each other much better.'

Tilda could have sworn he stared straight at her when he said it. Oh no.

Haitch

WOULD it be true to say she never meant to do it?

Maybe the only person she'd be lying to was herself, although self-deceit wasn't one of her things. Oh, but jealousy was a many-headed-beast. This wasn't even the first time, was it? Why did she get so resentful when Tilda found a new boyfriend? She knew she should have been ecstatic for her; anything that helped Tilda through those first years after their dad's death should only be rejoiced. But she'd acted as if she was a sulky teenager well after she climbed into her twenties. And what did she try to do each time that Tilda showed signs of happiness? Steal it from her, like the wicked sister she was. Suck it out as if she was an incubus sat on Tilda's chest at night. It was too damn easy. They'd mostly never twigged because men are pretty stupid and almost entirely blind when it comes to sex. She'd done things with them that made them all look sideways at her, or rather at Tilda. At that point, they had left. But she was always there with her bony shoulder for Tilda to sob her guts out on. Then she was a good sister.

Haitch tugged her knicker drawer open. Slipping her fingers

beneath the soft mound of lace and cotton, she fingered at the hidden trinkets. Why did she keep these things? Christ Almighty, if Tilda ever found them... but Tilda didn't rummage through other people's knickers, and that was a fact. There was also that tiny thrill of discovery. That moment. The fear aroused her. Would it ever come, and if it did, what would she do?

Maybe if Tilda had met Sam first, separately, it would have worked out differently. He'd been an artist on Haitch's course at The Slade. Not even her type, far too normal, and by that, she meant too close to what she was fleeing from. He was probably from a council estate, a scar on his lip testament to scrapping, intense eyes and twitchy. No, she'd met a load of these boys growing up. All grubby fumbling, fags, booze and then off like tick-infested dogs into the night to source their next lay.

Ten years previously

Tilda had been excelling in her own quiet way at Central Saint Martins. Friends were an uncertain quantity. Mostly because Haitch hadn't made any. Too busy being the 'it' girl. Had Tilda made new friends she didn't know about?

The end of the first year was always celebrated. A big bash. Tradition could not be usurped. Except they'd had a problem. The party for each college was usually held in the local bars.

'We can't meet in each other's places, or everyone will know we're twins.' Haitch had more to lose than Tilda on this point. She didn't want to share.

'Okay, then we'll either have to go to our own party or meet somewhere more obscure, so no one sees us together.' There had been a distinct tone of disappointment in Tilda's voice.

'Go to your one if you want to, Tilda. I'll understand.' Had Tilda struck up accords with people she didn't know? How did that make her feel? Though she wasn't up for halving her fame, she'd still felt a rankle of jealousy that Tilda might have new blood in her life. People that didn't include her.

Haitch could practically hear Tilda chewing on her bottom lip. 'No, I think we should honour getting through the first year together. It's been quite a haul.'

Good. 'I know. Listen, there's a bar near my school that's got a good rep, and it's not too close to where the others are going. Do you fancy going there?' Had that been mean? Manipulating Tilda in this way. 'Or would you prefer one closer to you?'

'I'm not that bothered. Yeah, why not go there. What's it called?'

'The Jeremy Bentham Bar. It's in Bloomsbury. Seems he, Jeremy, was the spiritual founder of the UCL. I Googled the place, and it does great burgers.'

'Got me hooked at burgers. Meet at eight then?'

'I'll be there.'

A heavy wooden bar, glass and backlit shelves of exotic bottles and everything painted either a cool sage green or white. Peering around her, the word 'traditional' lit up in her mind. The trouble was, when Haitch walked in, she was not the only one there. Hang on, who was that at the bar? Tall. Blonde. Familiar.

Sam? That was his name, wasn't it? Stood shoulder to shoulder with what could only be other students, although she didn't recognise any of them. She could've kicked herself. Perhaps choosing a bar this close to her art school hadn't been such a good idea. She'd have to leave fast without him recognising her. Turning, ready to sidle out, she spotted a mess of kids cluttering up the route back to the door. If she was quick, she could duck behind them... but she heard her name. Oh shite. Could she feign deafness?

'Haitch? What are you doing here?'

Haitch scrunched her eyes shut and spun back. 'Heya. Didn't see you there, er, Sam, isn't it?'

'Yeah, I'm Sam. Only been on the same course as you for like a whole year.' His eyes were such a deep green; they were almost black.

The other students stared at her for a moment and then their heads were hanging over their beers, disinterested. Sam disentangled himself. 'I'd have thought you'd be whooping it up with all the others at the Glenbury Arms.'

Haitch smiled. 'Just wanted a quiet drink, except it's pretty busy in here. On that note, I'll—'

She felt a body close behind her. Too close, but she'd sensed who it was.

From the look on Sam's face, she realised that he'd seen Tilda appear.

'Twins? Wow, who knew.'

'Well, no one.' Haitch made sure the smile didn't reach her eyes. 'Until now.'

'I'm Sam.' He stuck out his hand over Haitch, and Tilda reached for it. Was it then that it happened? Did sparks fly? Did they only see each other reflected in each other's eyes?

'I'm here for the burgers.' Sam looked at Tilda as if Haitch didn't exist. 'Do you want to join me?'

'Heard they're pretty good too.' Tilda's voice sounded a little breathless. 'Yes, we'd love to join you. Thanks.'

No, no, no! Haitch had felt a wave of irritation wash over her. The whole point was to keep them separate, ensure each group of their friends never knew about the other. 'I thought we were going to that other place?' She tried to catch Tilda's eye; but she was too busy gazing up at Sam all puppy-dog eyed.

'What other place? I thought we were meeting here 'cos the burgers are so good.'

Why was Tilda being so bloody obtuse? 'You remember that other place?' Surely Tilda understood they had to get out of there?

'No, I don't. We were meeting here because you said the burgers had a good rep. Job done.'

'Then it's decided,' said Sam. 'Look, that lot over there are about to move. Shall we grab their table?'

'Come on, be quick, or we'll lose it.' Tilda darted towards the table where students were gathering jackets and swilling down dregs of pints. Sam trailed her but glanced back over his shoulder.

'Are you coming, Haitch? I've been here before, and the burgers are really good.'

What else could she do? It was too late to do anything but damage limitation. They'd have to swear him to secrecy or threaten his dog or something.

Tilda had already tweaked three menus off the bar and was shoving the empties to one side of the table.

Sam's finger was glued to one of the pages. 'This burger is the best you'll get around here. I should know; I've sampled every one of the burger bars and restaurants in the area.'

'Your mum didn't teach you how to cook proper food then?' Haitch sat down at the proffered chair. This was something that was out of her control, and she didn't like it one bit.

'Haitch!' Tilda had that tone in her voice as if she was mimicking their mum. 'Don't be rude. You don't know anything about him.'

'She's right.' Sam turned towards Haitch. There was a strange look on his face. 'And your mum taught you how to cook then? If she did, count yourself lucky. Mine died of cancer when I was ten. My dad didn't have the time or the inclination for stuff like that, as he was too busy dragging up two boys by himself.'

Bollocks. Could the ground open up now? Haitch felt heat rush up her neck. 'Sorry. Feeling a little overwhelmed by it all at the moment. I didn't mean to be crass.'

'That's okay.' Sam leant forward. 'Unless your twin is called Mini Haitch or whatever, is it possible you could introduce us?'

Haitch glared at him and then rolled her eyes. 'Sam, this is my sister Tilda. Tilda, this is Sam.'

Tilda nodded. 'I'm very pleased to meet you. So, which one was the best ever?'

'This chorizo burger. It's got rocket, toasted sesame, caramelised onions, wheat berries, which are weird but nice. The tarragon creme-fraiche is to die for, and it's all on an arty-farty crusty roll. What more could you ask for?'

Haitch sighed. 'With the price tag to match.'

'Of course, but what do you expect around here?' He grinned, revealing perfect white teeth behind his scarred lips. Haitch wondered how he'd got it. His accent wasn't London, more northern, his voice crunchy like walking over gravel. A little frisson of anticipation shimmied over her skin. Perhaps he was more compelling that she'd first thought.

'For that price,' Haitch stared at him, 'I expect it to come on a gold-plated platter, carried on the shoulders of muscle-bound young men.'

'You can but ask,' said Sam.

'Hang on, Haitch,' said Tilda, 'you chose to come here. I just want it on a plate, and I'd like it now.'

'That too,' said Sam, 'can be arranged. So, three chorizo burgers? And can I recommend a pint of Punk IPA?'

'Sounds good,' said Haitch.

'Sounds amazing,' said Tilda.

Funny though, as the evening wore on, Haitch began to see something. Sam wasn't boring at all. He was reticent, yet when he started to talk, you listened. Boy, were his jokes funny, and his view of the world made her head spin. How had she missed seeing him? Looking closer, she now realised that he was cute, no, really good looking. Piercing eyes, a wide inviting mouth, puckered by the scar and just enough stubble that it would feel sexy to snog him but not sandpaper her skin off.

'Do you mind me asking,' said Haitch, reaching over to gently touch his mouth, 'how did this happen?' His head tilted, and he jerked back from her. Haitch felt a tickle of annoyance.

'This?' He fingered at the scar. 'When I was twelve, I got heinously pissed with my older brother. We were kind of off the rails at that point. Not dealing with our shit, or at least dealing with it in the only way we knew. In our drunken wisdom, we got on our bikes and cycled around town. It was our fault, no lights, wearing dark clothes, you know? Well, a car comes hacking out of a side street and doesn't see either of us. I go over the bonnet, but my brother...' Sam took a swig of his beer, '...my brother John goes under the wheels.' He shook his head. 'I'm pretty smashed up, but all I can think is that my brother is dead.'

Tilda brushed his arm. 'Was he alright?'

Haitch watched him smile at Tilda. A slow, lazy smile.

'Seems we were both so drunk, we must have been like ragdolls. We got off lightly, all things considered. I got cuts across my face and cracked ribs. John had quite a few broken bones as well. But we were okay. No charges pressed on either side. Our family, what was left of it, couldn't have coped with that. The poor driver, a young woman, was a bit of a wreck afterwards. Messy all round.'

'That's awful.' Haitch tried to show compassion as Tilda

had done. 'I mean for all of you.' Standing up suddenly, she'd leant over the table, kissed the tips of her fingers, and placed them on his lips. 'Poor, poor Sam.'

'We're both fine now,' said Sam, wiping his lips with the back of his hand before draining his pint.

Haitch ignored the slightly shocked look on her sister's face.

'Another drink?' Sam stood and tweaked a twenty out of his jeans back pocket. 'Same again?'

'Great,' said Tilda, gazing at the table.

'Yeah, why not,' said Haitch, grinning up at Sam.

Stories were swapped, laughter abounded, and much beer was imbibed. She'd sparkled and shone as if she was a bright and heavenly star. When last orders were called, Haitch hadn't been surprised that they were still there. She waited as they shrugged into jackets, but the invitation back to his place never transpired. Nor did he ask for her telephone number.

Ahh, it was so he didn't embarrass Tilda. He'd find her later at college and ask her then.

When Tilda phoned to say Sam had asked her out on a proper date, Haitch had been pretty taken aback. *What the fuck!*

It took a moment before she could reply. 'That's nice. When did he do that?'

'Yesterday. He called me up.' Again, Tilda had that girly, breathless quality to her voice. Haitch suddenly wanted to smack her.

'How did he get your number?'

'He asked for it when you were in the toilet,' Tilda explained. 'I mean, you've never been interested in him, so I thought it wouldn't matter.' Her voice was rising. '"That's nice?" Is that all you can say?'

When she was in the toilet? That meant he had been trying not to embarrass *her!* 'What do you expect me to say? I've shown great enthusiasm for all your boyfriends since we were fifteen, only to discover that they're all shits.' Whose fault had that been then?

'Well, thanks for the vote of confidence. Anyway, Sam is not a shit.'

'How do you know?' Haitch closed her eyes. Shut up now.

'Because you showed no interest in him for an entire year. Remember we both have a disastrous track record, and I do believe that yours is worse than mine.'

'Oh, right. I show no interest, so that must make him a nice guy?' Haitch had practically snorted. 'That's like saying all men with small dogs can never be serial killers.'

'He is a nice guy, and you know it.'

'Then that's brilliant. Go for it, Tilda. You know you don't need my permission.' How had this happened? How had Tilda managed to get the only bloke worth her time? Because she hadn't been paying attention.

Tilda's voice was small. 'You don't mind? He was your friend first?'

'Not really. I only just remembered his name that evening.'

She had known his name afterwards. Oh, yes, she had.

FOURTEEN

Matilda

Thursday 16th June - Spain

WHITE PAINTED walls only intensified the sense of deep reddish plum in the room. A large round table was in the middle, dressed in a pillar box red tablecloth and glossy white crockery, silver tableware and candles. Twisted red napkins nestled in the soup bowls and various glasses jostled for space around each placing.

There was a general movement towards the table. Heads bowed to read the little name cards. Tilda could feel her heart thumping as if her blood had become thicker, and her heart was having trouble pumping it around her body.

'Ah, Miss Bee.' Jeremiah stood at her elbow. 'You are here.' He pulled out a chair, and Tilda sat down with a nervous smile over her shoulder.

'Thanks, Jeremiah.'

Orpheus dragged a chair out to the right of her and sat down heavily.

'I think I need another drink.' He pushed his glasses up onto his head and wiped under his eyes. Dear God. Did he know how drunk he seemed?

To her left, Alejandro was tugging off his jacket and handing it to Jeremiah while a waiter guided his chair in. Having already chatted with them, Tilda felt a little calmer. Both men were clever and handsome: Orpheus in that quick-witted but slightly brooding and rather magnetic way, and Alejandro appeared cute but geeky. And boy, were his eyes beautiful. Now, what did Haitch say? The only person off-limits was Damian, and he wasn't even here. While her scruples forbad any hanky-panky with Mr Ishimoto, if the opportunity arose, not saying it would, but if it did, would she turn either of these two down? She had the right to have fun. Sod Sam. Especially as it wouldn't be her doing it.

Dawn was arranging herself on the other side of Orpheus, who was again rubbing his glasses with the edge of his t-shirt. Maybe this was his 'tell', his nervous tic. She knew hers, as Haitch had pointed it out so many times. Fiddling and tapping with things. Peering across, she saw Mr Ishimoto was pulling out a chair for himself next to Zaida. Was she the one to watch then?

Mr Ishimoto raised his glass, and everyone followed him. 'A toast. To a fascinating evening. I look forward to more stimulating and energetic discussions.'

Glasses were waved in a desultory fashion. Talk about damp squib. The fastest way to kill a conversation was to expect it to be entertaining. Who would be the one to break the silence that had descended on their little group? Not her, obviously.

Movement at her shoulder made her jump, as soup was ladled into her bowl. Tilda scooped up a spoonful of soup. Cold soup. *Cold soup?* It wasn't so much the taste; it was the shock of it not being hot.

'Mmm,' said Alejandro, 'Gazpacho. A traditional soup from

this area. Delicious, isn't it?' He pointed at a small dish of chopped onions, red and green peppers, and tiny cubes of cucumber. 'You need to throw all that in. Then sprinkle the croutons on top. Like this.' He showed them, and Tilda followed suit. Conversations stuttered into life.

'Alejandro, are you from here?' Tilda became aware of a considerable amount of garlic in her soup. At least if all of them ate this, no one should be able to complain.

'Colombia originally. Medellin.'

Orpheus leant over, and Tilda could feel his shoulder against hers. 'So, you're from the city that's even more dangerous than my own beloved New York.'

'Actually, San Pedro in Honduras is cited as the most dangerous city in the world. I lived there for a couple of years and was fine. Everything is relative. Do you mind me asking, is your city less dangerous or more dangerous because you are Black?'

Orpheus nodded. 'Good question. As you say, it's all relative. In certain quarters, I would be invisible. Still, if I walk into other less hospitable areas towards people of colour, I'd probably have the police called because I'm plainly a danger to that community. At least, nowadays.'

'Great options there.' Tilda shrugged.

Alejandro dabbed at his lips. 'And what about you, Haitch? Where are you from?'

'London.'

'A proper cockney?'

'Not everyone from London is a cockney. You have to be born within earshot of Bow Bells to be real. I originally hail from an estate in Hackney. Not the most salubrious place. Still, I've done okay for myself since then.'

'Ah,' said Orpheus, 'so not born into money, is what you mean.'

Tilda nodded. 'I hope I'm not presumptuous, but I don't think you were either?'

'Yep, definitely the wrong side of the tracks. Like you, I got out. I know it's a cliché, but it was either gangs or the police force, and sometimes you are hard-pressed to discern the difference.'

'Indeed.' Alejandro nodded. 'You forgot to mention the priesthood. That was my calling, but I believe I can serve God in better ways. Life can be very tricky if you are not rich in most countries. Could you pass the pepper, please, Orpheus?'

Tilda said to Alejandro, 'You're from Medellin. Isn't that where Pablo Escobar was from?'

Alejandro nodded. 'Yes. But just because he came from there does not mean he defines the place.'

Tilda said, 'It's a little tricky to disassociate ourselves from that point, though?'

'I've seen', said Orpheus, 'all the Pablo Escobar mini-series and documentaries. The people regarded him as a hero, even at the end. And as for his mother? Well, what can you say? She thought him a saint.'

Alejandro made a strange snorting sound. 'Maybe he was in certain areas of Medellin. He helped the people that didn't exist to anyone else. Not to the government, the police, the religious hierarchy.'

'He was a gangster, wasn't he?' Tilda thought she'd stick in her pennies worth. 'A drug-lord? Didn't he kill tons of people? Doesn't that make him by default a bad guy?'

'A really bad guy, yes. You could say he was evil.' Alejandro put his soup spoon down on the edge of the bowl and placed both elbows on the table. 'But if this man gave you enough money that you could send your child to a good school or so someone in your family could afford medical care that they couldn't before, what does that make him then?'

'Complicated,' said Orpheus, 'but still, shouldn't he be held accountable for all the terrible things he did?'

'He's dead. Shot by the police, so I think he's been "held accountable" already.' Alejandro twiddled his finger in the air. 'He will be judged by God, not man.'

'Okay,' said Orpheus. 'Can you simply wipe the slate clean by doing a couple of good things? I presume he was Catholic?'

'Yes, he was.'

'So, you can bung a bit of money to a local orphanage and say a few "hail Marys" and all is forgiven?'

'Maybe you can,' said Alejandro. 'You only need to ask God. He is the only one who can forgive you.'

'It's that easy?' Tilda shook her head. 'You get into Heaven because you said at the end, 'I'm sorry?' And God says, "hey, man, that's fine. No worries". Seriously? Is that how it works?'

'If you are truly sorry, then yes. It's called "absolution". The ecclesiastical declaration that a person's sins have been forgiven.'

'A release from guilt,' Orpheus wiped his mouth with his napkin. 'Rather handy, don't you think? Do what you want and no consequences.' Scrunching the napkin into a tight ball, he tossed it onto the table as if angry. But at what? Tilda noticed sweat beading on his upper lip. 'Murder, rape, sell drugs to kids. It doesn't matter, does it because of your "absolution" and your damn priests can hear every filthy bit of it, except they aren't allowed to tell the police.'

'This sounds personal, Orpheus.' Alejandro leant around Tilda to lay a hand on Orpheus' arm. He jerked away. 'I didn't mean to cause offence.'

'It is personal, and no, it's not you; it's more the belief system. It lets people down.' He picked up the ball of the napkin and dabbed at his mouth again.

Tilda looked up at him. 'Are you alright?'

'Yeah, sure.' He nodded around the table. 'We're missing what the others are saying.'

'But you were telling us something, and it sounded important.'

'Don't sweat it. I've drunk a little too much for my own good. Nerves, I guess. Maybe we should catch up on what the others are talking about.'

'Of course.' Tilda focused, aware that she could easily miss out on what was her primary function here. To get the prize for Haitch. But she felt as if they'd been teetering on a precipice and had only just pulled back in time. There was more to Orpheus' reaction than she'd understood.

'All I meant, Zaida,' Dawn was speaking, 'was that it must be challenging for a woman to have come so far in such a, as Mr Ishimoto has stated, male-dominated world. It was supposed to be a compliment.' She poked at the diced vegetables. Ah, the continuing conversation about Iraq and its view on women. Tilda needed to listen closely to this.

'I thank you for that.' Zaida gracefully fluttered her hand towards Dawn. 'Iraqi women have been affected by wars, sectarian and religious conflict, debates concerning Islamic Law and Iraq's constitution, cultural traditions, and modern secularism. Women's Rights organisations battle against harassment and intimidation while they work to improve our status in the law, in the workplace and in education.'

Tilda looked down at the pristine red tablecloth. Join in now or lose the initiative. 'Women's lib and feminists in the West are being ridiculed by many young women, who say they don't need feminism because they think we are already equal with men. They think all feminists are bullies and egotistical.'

'Haitch,' said Orpheus, 'some of them are. I think that there's a radical difference between the feminists that fought for equal rights through history and some of the feminists we have today.'

'These young women you speak of,' Zaida held her hand across her heart, 'they should realise that the world they live in has been fought for often with blood and death. If they think they are equal, then they have the feminist forerunner to thank for that. It was these women who achieved political, personal and social rights for these young women, who now believe they are equal to men. Sometimes at great cost.'

Tilda shook her head. 'Sorry to say this, but we're still not really equal even in the West. Not completely.'

An arm snaked around her right shoulder and whisked her bowl away. The table was cleared discreetly and in silence.

'You have,' said Zaida, 'the right to vote, to hold public office, to earn a fair wage, to own property, to receive an education. You have equal rights within marriage and protection from sexual harassment. This is what we are still fighting for in my country. I think your equality in the West is far more equal than you realise.'

'It was the sexual revolution that changed it for women,' said Orpheus, as he accepted a glass of red wine from a waiter. 'Societal changes.' He nodded, and half the liquid in the glass seemed to evaporate. 'Women's suffrage, reproductive rights including contraception and abortion.'

Zaida coughed. 'Equal rights have not reached most places in the world yet either, and those women who enjoy these rights in your countries should be thankful, although the great USA seems to be eradicating these rights as we speak.'

'I'm thankful we still have those rights in the UK,' said Tilda. 'Very thankful, in fact.'

'Me too.' Orpheus winked slyly at Tilda. 'Though, as Zaida said, we are now going backwards and that's a scary thought.'

Alejandro's spoon clattered down, making Tilda jump. 'I'm

from Medellin, the greatly impoverished part of Colombia. We are a devoutly Catholic country. This so-called sexual revolution is an offence to God. It has led to the murder of innocents.'

'I'm sorry,' said Tilda, 'did I miss something here? Again? Are we now talking about abortion?'

'Women sleep around, and when they get pregnant, they purge a child as if it was rubbish. This is a sin. Sex outside of marriage is a sin.' Alejandro picked up his spoon and tapped it on the table.

Tilda felt something balloon in her chest. There was a moment where she found it hard to breathe. 'I agree. When a woman's husband goes off and has sex with his bloody secretary or whoever, then yes, that's a sin in my book.'

There was a disconcerting sputter of laughter from Dawn. 'But it's a-okay to sleep with someone else's husband? Do you agree, Haitch?'

'What? I'm sorry, I don't get what you're driving at, Dawn'.

'It's fine to sleep with the husband of someone you know very well. And I do mean very well. Is that plain enough?'

Alejandro pointed at Tilda with his soup spoon. There was something quite aggressive about it. 'I wasn't talking about that. I meant when a woman has sex when she isn't married. When she is a whore.'

Tilda stopped moving. 'So that covers most of the women in the West. We're all whores then?' She leant across the table. 'Dawn? I'm still not sure what you mean?'

Alejandro continued, 'If you sleep with a man who is not your husband, then yes. Yes, you are.'

Dawn raised a perfectly plucked eyebrow. 'Alejandro seems to have seconded exactly what I was saying.'

Tilda thought she might pop. How could she have ever found this man even remotely attractive? Seduced by his pretty eyes. Or rather, not seduced. And what the hell was up with

Dawn? 'So that must go for men too. All those men who sleep with women when they're not married? Or sleep with other women when they are? That's okay then?'

'Men are men,' said Alejandro. 'We have appetites. Women do not.'

'You mean women should not,' said Dawn. 'Double standards here, folks.' She frowned across at Tilda. 'For some, I should say "fallen" standards.'

'Are you having a go at me about something?'

Dawn raised her glass and drank. Putting the glass down, she said: 'Am I? Why should I be doing that, do you think?' The way she said it made the tiny hairs rise on the back of Tilda's neck.

'I haven't a clue,' Tilda said as little waves of stress rolled over her.

'You are not married, are you Haitch?' Tilda swivelled at the sound of Mr Ishimoto's voice. The table had fallen quiet, and all eyes were on her.

'No, I'm not.'

'Have you slept with many men?' His voice was soft, though the words were clear.

Tilda dragged in a breath. *Holy crap!* 'Not that it's anyone's business but my own, but yes. I have. Quite a few.'

'Oh, to be so judged.' Dawn's voice was quiet.

'Yeah, right,' said Tilda. 'I kind of thought we'd got past the Middle Ages and their religious shit.'

'I'm with you there,' said Orpheus. 'Long live the sexual revolution.'

Tilda squirmed. It was Mr Ishimoto who'd actually asked the question. *Have you slept with many men?* What kind of question is that to ask someone at a dinner party?

'You don't think,' said Mr Ishimoto, 'that you should wait for the right man and only after marriage, then consummate your love? A group of Americans have the ideal that you save your virginity for your husband. After all, sexual purity is a commitment that is historically expected of, associated with and even demanded of women. Is that not precious?'

Tilda's appetite had slipped away. 'I'd like to ask if that goes both ways. Do the men follow the same rules?'

Mr Ishimoto shook his head slightly. 'Sexual abstinence is not something assumed of men.'

'Hey,' said Orpheus, 'then we are really stepping back in time and undoing what has been achieved with a great deal of hard work and often bloodshed. We are back to equality, and that doesn't sound like equality to me.'

Mr Ishimoto smiled, revealing tiny crinkles at the corners of his eyes. 'No, it does not.'

Next, a plate filled with little chunks of pale-coloured meat arrived. They were swimming in a clear but oily gravy. Tiny pieces of vegetables made it look more appetising. Tilda felt queasy. What did Orpheus say about throwing up in the ice bucket? A dressed green salad and a bowl of delicious smelling chips were placed before her.

'I do believe this is *choto*.' Mr Ishimoto stuck his fork in and chewed. 'Hmm, yes. Baby goat. Quite delicate.'

Alejandro continued. 'What about the rights of men? We are being attacked on every front.'

'Oh please,' said Dawn, holding her hand up, 'are you going down the route of a concerted campaign by furious feminists against poor persecuted little men?'

Good. The conversations were getting as meaty as the lumps of animal on Tilda's plate. And, more importantly, were veering away from her and her supposed rabid sex life. She needed to pull bits of herself back in as she felt she'd been peppered with a pellet gun.

Orpheus wagged a finger. 'I think you mean poor persecuted white, straight, middle-class men. These guys are raised to feel entitled and resent anyone who might get the same.'

'It's called,' said Mr Ishimoto, 'the PMS.'

'PMS? Sorry, but what does that stand for?' said Tilda.

'Persecuted male syndrome.' Mr Ishimoto smiled. 'And I think I agree with what Orpheus has just said. Gay men, Black men.' He nodded at Orpheus. 'Asian men.' He touched his own chest. 'Latino men.' He inclined his head at Alejandro. 'We do not seem to have the same platform as these angry, white men. They feel they are now victims of reverse discrimination. That there has been a transfer of rights from men to women. In everything from politics, economics and even in the social arena.'

'I agree with what you said,' Alejandro frowned, 'but that wasn't what I meant.'

'So, what did you mean?' Dawn's arms were held tight across her ample bosoms, pushing them up out of her figure-hugging black dress.

'Men feel as though they have been steamrollered into submission. They feel helpless. I think men are now the second sex, and they must stand up for their rights.'

'Seriously?' Tilda shook her head.

'Yes, seriously. What I'm trying to say is that men are now failed patriarchs and deposed kings, and women are to blame.' Alejandro's face was getting redder, and a vein was beginning to throb on his temple.

'Is this rhetorical, or do you believe this?' Zaida tilted her head to stare across at him.

'All men, whether Black, Asian, or Latino, and all the other men from every race and background, still all want and feel entitled to utter obedience from their children and subservience from their women. And don't get me going on gay men!'

'We won't,' said Tilda. 'That's a promise.'

'You believe that?' Dawn leant forward across the table and

stabbed the top with a manicured nail. 'You actually believe that in this day and age, women should be subservient to men?'

'It's in the Bible.' Alejandro practically snorted through his nose. 'Why do you think the marriage vows ask for obedience from the woman to her husband and only care from the husband to his wife to be?'

Tilda's mouth opened before her brain had time to clunk into gear. 'Because God is a twat?'

'What did you say?' Alejandro was now turning a truly frightening colour.

Dawn twiddled her fork around in the juices from the meat left on her plate. 'And if a man raises his fists to a woman? Is that acceptable too? In your world, Alejandro?'

'If she is not deferential towards her husband, if she speaks above her station, if she does not perform her wifely duties, then yes. Absolutely.'

Dawn rubbed at one eye, smudging a little mascara. 'And if she is all that and he still hits her?'

'Then she must have done something to deserve such punishment. Unbeknown to her.'

Tilda added, 'Wouldn't it be a good idea then to at least tell her what's pissed him off? Have a conversation? Not simply belt someone.'

'She should know without being told. A good wife should know.' Alejandro looked around the room, fixing them all with a stare. 'This is the natural order of things.'

'I don't mean to offend you, Alejandro...' Dawn leant across the table.

'Even though you have...'

'But what would happen if I hit my husband just because he annoyed me in some way? Would I get the same leniency of thought?' There was an underlying tone to Dawn's voice. Was this personal?

Alejandro's lips were thin. 'Don't be ridiculous.'

'No. Thought not.' Dawn's face twitched involuntarily, twisting her lovely features.

Had this woman been hit by a man? Her father? Brother? Husband? Not that Tilda could ask.

'Yes, but...' Tilda raised her hand. '...your religion has never been kind to women. Who do you blame original sin on? Eve. It seems to me that Adam must have been viewed as a stupid dolt then if he's not equally guilty for taking that bloody apple from her.'

'Which God or religion has ever been kind to women?' Orpheus looked about him. 'Just saying.'

Zaida cleared her throat. 'When have men in general been kind to women?'

'Touché.' Orpheus bowed slightly to her.

Tilda glanced around the table, catching Mr Ishimoto's eye. She blinked rapidly. He tilted his head, barely perceptibly, to stare back at her. Tilda felt as though she'd eaten something that was still alive and was using suckered feet to climb back out. She dragged in a breath. This was the show he was after.

Zaida peered round the bulk of Orpheus. 'I thought I heard you speaking of Pablo Escobar a while back. Didn't the man turn over more than twenty million dollars a year in personal income from drugs? And didn't he inflict misery on countless people? Yet, because he built a couple of football fields and some houses, he was popular amongst the locals. I wondered if they could ever comprehend his wealth compared to theirs.'

'He was nothing but a manipulative monster,' said Dawn. 'Anyone who could do such awful things and thinks by buying the people around him with gifts, that it cancels out all the atrocities he committed, then he's a monster in my book.'

'Ah,' said Orpheus, 'you must have missed the bit on absolution.'

Dawn sighed dramatically. 'A man who peddles drugs and preys on people's hopes and dreams is a devil in disguise. There should be no absolution. How could a so-called benign and loving god accept a man such as him into Heaven?'

'Oh, you people...' Alejandro leant back and stretched. 'You are like stuck records.'

'Yeah, whatever!' Orpheus shifted in his chair, and Tilda felt he was practically in her lap. 'I'm intrigued by what you do, Dawn. Clairvoyant, isn't it?'

Dawn nodded. 'It simply means clear vision. I'm a medium.'

'Ah,' sneered Alejandro, 'I don't mean to be rude or anything, but don't you, yourself, also peddle in dreams and hopes?'

What was that saying? You could hear a pin drop. Everyone stopped moving, frozen, as if they were participating in a mannequin challenge.

Dawn's face didn't change, not even a twitch of an eye, and Tilda was suitably impressed.

'I didn't think that allowing a person to say goodbye to a loved one was such a crime.'

'Is that what you do then?' Orpheus said quietly. 'I mean, there are several different strands to this, aren't there?'

'Yes. We can gain information about a person, an object, a location or a physical event through extra-sensory perception. There are three classes. There is precognition, which is the ability to perceive or predict future events. Then there is retrocognition, the ability to see past events. And remote viewing, the perception of contemporary events happening outside the range of normal perception.'

'And,' said Alejandro, 'you can do this? You can see into the void that is hidden from most mortals?'

'Yes, I can.'

'Really? You can peer through the veil into God's Kingdom?'

'You don't believe me. Well, you don't have to. A fact is a fact whether you believe it or not.' Dawn's plump lips were thinned.

'No, I don't.' Alejandro shook his head. 'Not at all.'

'Well, I do,' said Orpheus.

Dawn inclined her head at him. 'Thank you. Maybe it's easier for you, Orpheus, a film director, touching on imaginary stories that don't exist except in your mind or the mind of an author. Funny how most people can all relate to the physical world so easily. But if you can't see it, touch it, can you quantify it? When it comes down to the paranormal world, many baulk.'

'No,' said Zaida, 'I believe. We have always had oracles throughout history that were consulted for prophetic predictions. They were thought to be inspired by the Gods. It was a form of divination.'

'Seers too.' Dawn smiled a half-smile. 'They interpreted signs sent by the Gods.'

'Wasn't that through cat's entrails and old bones, though?' Tilda had thought Alejandro's eyes were luminous before, but now they seemed to be blazing

'The bones were heated,' said Dawn, 'and the resulting cracks were interpreted.'

Although her voice was neutral, Tilda thought there was an undercurrent of anger in it.

'So,' Alejandro couldn't hide his contempt, 'people went to war or made choices that could mean life or death over some burnt bones?'

'It was their way of life. I never said I did any of that. Correct me if I'm wrong, but didn't thousands of men go to war because their "God" decreed it? Even though it was obviously only a land grab by some greedy king.'

'Right,' Orpheus said, 'back to the original question. Which bits do you do?'

'All of it. I was also a psychic detective and have been consulted on several occasions by the police to use my paranormal abilities to help out on cases they were having difficulties with.'

'That's amazing,' said Tilda. 'Like what? Oh, I'm sorry, I'm not trying to test you. I'm simply fascinated by this.'

'I'm not at liberty to disclose details, but I have been consulted in finding the body of a murdered girl, a kidnap victim, a runaway and a number of other cases.' It was funny how Dawn looked less than enthusiastic telling of her accomplishments. She must have missed the memo saying they had to 'big themselves up'.

'How do you do it?'

'One time, for the murdered girl, I used a hair from her hairbrush, a plumb bob and a grid map. The police had exhausted every avenue they could think of. They too were sceptical until I located her, and she was brought back to her grieving parents to be buried properly.'

Alejandro had one hand lying flat on the table, although Tilda noticed the other was bunched and straining in his lap. 'As Haitch says, that's amazing. But I know for a fact that people such as you have diverted investigations and wasted police time. Frauds the lot of them.'

'Now hold on.' Orpheus was beginning to slur. 'These last few glasses must have caught up with him. 'Let the lady explain what she does.'

Mr Ishimoto suddenly joined in the conversation. 'You sound like you've had some experience of this. Please tell us.'

Orpheus' face sort of scrunched up, as though he'd smelt something ghastly. 'I'd rather not if you don't mind.' He reached for his glass, but his coordination was off, and the glass tipped over. The spilt wine spread, staining the tablecloth an even deeper blood red.

'Shit, sorry.' He fumbled to pick it up, but a waiter was ahead of him, the glass retrieved, and a clean napkin spread.

'Come, come,' said Mr Ishimoto, ignoring the interruption, 'Orpheus, don't be coy now.'

FIFTEEN

Haitch

Sam. Sam. Sam.

The forbidden fruit. Oh, how she longed for it, wanting to taste it, lick it, suck out all its juices until there were only a few dried pips left. It had to be good if it was no longer on the menu. Holy shit! Her sister's husband. As if her boyfriends hadn't been enough. Sam. Getting tastier and tastier each time she'd met him. Why couldn't she stop thinking about him? But he pervaded her thoughts as though she was enveloped in a Sam-scented perfume.

Saying she never knew where the idea had come from was a blatant lie. It had come from Tilda about a couple of months before. And the thought had wormed itself into her mind and was eating at her.

'I wonder if Sam would know if we swapped. You know, like we used to at work?'

Haitch hoped the look on her face didn't betray her. 'Why would you ever ask that?'

'Look, we're twins, theoretically identical in every way. So...' She frowned. 'So, what I'm trying to say is that would he know the difference between us? Would he know that you weren't me?'

'Der! Your hair is much shorter than mine for a start. I think he'd notice that.'

'No, I mean if we looked exactly the same, the same hair, clothes, perfume, you know?'

'You're not asking me to test this out, are you?'

'Of course not.' Tilda had rolled her eyes. 'I just wanted to know that whatever makes me, me, is not the same as what makes you, you.'

'Listen. I'm most definitely me, and you are you. This is getting weird. Can we move onto something simpler, please?'

The idea had stuck. Would Sam notice? Could he tell them apart?

SIXTEEN

Matilda

TILDA FELT IT THEN, the control that Mr Ishimoto had over the group. All of them jumping through those burning hoops, desperate for that prize that gleamed and glinted in the distance. She wondered if Dawn already knew which of them would get their grasping little hands on it. Dare she ask her? Undoubtedly having a superpower, a hotline to God, or whatever, was cheating. It was all getting a bit much.

Orpheus looked like a man being dragged, kicking and screaming to the edge of a cliff.

'As I said, I'd rather not.'

'Oh,' said Mr Ishimoto, 'I'd rather you did.' There was such an undercurrent of malice in his voice that Tilda shivered. 'Tell us now, Orpheus and don't keep us waiting.'

Orpheus laughed, although it didn't sound funny. 'Okay. There was a really sick guy in our neighbourhood, although we didn't know who it was at the time. After a spate of boys turned up horrifically abused and dismembered, a medium got involved. She went into all kinds of trances while holding objects that belonged to the kids. She was on all the local newscasts. I watched and didn't believe her. The same as Alejandro, I thought she was wasting police time, getting them to use resources that many of us in the community thought could be better used elsewhere. Then my kid brother disappeared.'

'Oh, that's terrible,' said Zaida, her hand fluttering over her mouth.

Orpheus swallowed loudly. 'She, I mean the medium, came to our house. She held my brother's favourite stuff, you know? His baseball bat; his old toy bear. I thought she was a fraud and begged my mom to throw her out. I mean, she looked like a fucking witch, all mumbling and eyes rolling.' Orpheus reached for a glass of water.

'Then what happened?' said Mr Ishimoto.

'She told us where to find him.'

Silence.

Dawn was the first to speak. 'Was he found alive, Orpheus?'

He nodded his head. 'Yes. Yes, he was. He was unharmed. Scared shitless but okay.'

'It is your belief then,' said Mr Ishimoto, 'that if the medium had not got involved, your brother would have been murdered in the same way as the others? Is that correct?'

'Yeah, that's about the long and the short of it.' His glasses were whipped off and polished.

Tilda let out her breath. 'I can see why you believe.'

'That's a terrible story.' Dawn looked genuinely upset. 'I'm glad that this woman was able to help you, yet I feel pity for the ones who were killed in such a horrific manner.'

'We were the lucky ones. The other families have had to bear the knowledge of what happened to their boys. We came so close to losing him.' His voice was rough as if he'd swallowed a handful of sand.

'Do you know...' Tilda didn't quite know how to word it. '...if the man who did this spoke to a priest? Is that why you seemed so upset earlier?'

'Yeah, he confessed his sins, but priests cannot break the seal of confession without being defrocked or excommunicated. They don't want that, now do they?'

'Listen, Orpheus,' said Alejandro. 'They have to live as if they haven't heard the confession. Most do urge the penitent to hand themselves in.'

'Well, our local priest couldn't have urged strongly enough.' *Ouch.* Such hatred was palpable.

Holy shite! Peering around the table, Tilda noted she was not the only one distressed by what Orpheus had said. There was a sullen feeling still in her gut. So, they were not here for their career merits. She was right; Mr Ishimoto was using their fears and passions against them.

Zaida was fighting for equality and was Muslim, and Alejandro was a medieval-style Catholic raging against equality of any sort. She, as Haitch, was a bolshy atheist and pro-sex, shown to be a bit of a slag. Orpheus' reaction to Dawn was crystal clear, as was his attitude towards the Catholic faith. Dawn was feminist and strong enough to hold her own (and scarily able to speak to the dead). Also, was she a domestic abuse survivor? Tilda thought of a reality show she remembered called 'Bet on your drunk' or something like that. In it, two drunks are told to fight, and you bet on the winner. Whoever is still standing gets a few measly bucks for beating the shit out of the other one. Was this Mr Ishimoto's version?

What was coming next? Hell! None of this was worth the humiliation. It was no good wondering what Haitch would do, as she wasn't the one mired up to her neck in this weird shit. She stood up as if someone else had commanded her legs to move.

'Just to say, it's been a lovely and enlightening evening, but if you don't mind, Mr Ishimoto, I'd like to turn in now.' She smiled as brightly as she could at him. What she meant was *before you turn us all inside out.*

Her chair squeaked across the tiles, and she had a momentary glimpse of her flat in Brighton. Why had she ever agreed to do this when she could've been back at home, painting quietly, listening to Beyoncé, and eating custard creams as if they'd gone out of manufacture and she had the last packet? And Boo. She wanted to be home with Boo.

'Why, Miss Bee. The evening has barely started.' Mr Ishimoto steepled his fingers and stared at her, not blinking, with his head slightly tilted. 'You've not even sampled the dessert, and I've been told it is truly delicious. A local treat.'

'Thank you, Mr Ishimoto, but my evening has ended. I wish you all a good night.' Tilda turned from the table to find Jeremiah again at her elbow.

'This way, Miss Bee.'

Tilda tottered after him. The air seemed thinner than when she'd first walked in at seven as if all that discourse had sucked the oxygen out. She could feel the eyes of the others on her back as she left the room.

'Are you alright, Miss Bee?' Jeremiah had a look on his face that she couldn't fathom.

'Have you been listening to all this?'

'We are expected not to hear anything that goes on here, but yes, I did catch a snippet or two.' His eyes were very dark in the soft lighting of the passageway.

'Do you think I'm all right then?'

He pursed his lips. 'Conceivably not.'

'Do you think I should have stayed and stuck it out in there, in that room full of piranhas?'

'Not if you want to come out unscathed.'

'You agree, then? It's a bit of a mess in there.'

'I can't comment on that, Miss Bee. But I must admit it has been an interesting evening so far.'

Tilda glanced back over her shoulder at the rectangle of light dwindling behind her. What were the others thinking? Most likely, *good, one down and only three to go*. Steadying herself against the rough stone wall, she also wondered if anyone had applauded her stance, or did they all believe her to be incredibly stupid by walking away from something that could change her future? She shook her head. Change Haitch's future. Oh hell, what was she going to say to Haitch? And as to Damian, she'd have to hurdle that when the time came. Her door was in front of her. Number six.

'Thank you, Jeremiah.'

'You are very welcome, Miss Bee. I hope you have a... restful night.'

Sat on the edge of the bed, she gazed at the phone in her hand. Haitch had wanted an update the moment she could. Tilda's head span, either from the amount she'd drunk, or more likely, from the fear and stress that was pumping adrenalin round her body at a rate of knots.

It was then she called Haitch.

SEVENTEEN

Haitch

WHAT WAS THAT TERRIBLE SOUND? The phone? God damn! She had to change that ringtone.

Haitch scrabbled around to find the bedside lamp, nearly pulling it off the small table. As she flicked the switch, the sudden glare made her eyes hurt. She winced and squinted at the name on the screen. Her name.

'Tilda?'

'Haitch, it's me.'

'I know that.' Haitch wiped at her eyes. It didn't seem to make much difference. 'Are you okay? Has something happened?'

'You could say that.' There was something very flat about her voice. 'I've blown it. I'm so sorry, Haitch. It all got too much.'

Haitch's stomach flipped. 'How do you know you have? Has Mr Watnot told you that?'

'Not in so many words but trust me on this.'

There was silence on the line for a moment. 'Tilda? Are you still there?'

'Sure.'

'Do you want to tell me about it?'

There was a deep inhalation. Then Haitch heard Tilda's breath whoosh out of her. 'I need to process everything that went on tonight. I'm sorry, maybe I shouldn't have phoned. It's just that it was all pretty horrible. You could've probably handled it better than me, but I had to walk away. God almighty, Haitch, it was like an episode of 'Black Mirror' in there.'

'Shame I missed it; you know I love those.'

'I know.' There was another pause. 'Are you mad at me?'

'Don't be stupid, Tilda. If you felt like that, then I'm glad you walked away. I wouldn't want you to do anything you don't want to, just for me. I'd hate myself if I ever thought that I'd forced you into something nasty.'

'Nasty. Yes, that's the word. I tried, I really did, but I couldn't go on with it. I suppose I'll have to brazen it out with Damian tomorrow.'

'Don't worry, say whatever you need to, and I'll get it sorted when you get back.'

'Thanks, Haitch. What a truly fucked-up evening.'

'I really should have been there then.'

'Yes, you should. Love you.'

'Love you too.'

What the hell had gone on there? She should've pushed for more details, as now Haitch's mind was crowded with images. An orgy, perhaps? Expected to run around that villa in animal costumes? Actually, that sounded fun. How about truth serum... hopefully not, given that Tilda wasn't who she was pretending to be. Was that it? Had she been found out?

The main thing was that Tilda had lost the commission. How did she feel about that? Dragging herself out of bed, Haitch patted her way along the wall to the kitchen. Still weak, she was glad to hear Boo's claws clip-clipping on the wooden floorboards behind her. If she collapsed, was Boo clever enough to call an ambulance?

What about Damian? Did he know they'd swapped? After rummaging for teabags, she leant her head against a cupboard door and envisioned his reaction. A nuclear blast of seismic proportions, probably. But if he didn't? They still might get through this.

She switched the kettle on. How did she feel? Was this karma? Probably not enough of it, all things considered, as she would come back from this, whereas Tilda didn't.

EIGHTEEN

Matilda

DOZING ON THE BED, as she hadn't the will power to climb under the pristine white duvet, Tilda was shocked into wakefulness. Had someone tapped on her door? What time was it anyway?

'Haitch?' A throaty whisper slid as if guided through the keyhole. 'Are you in here?'

A moment of disorientation. Why would Haitch be in her bedroom? Then she remembered. Tilda half fell off the bed and crept towards the door. 'Yes? Who is this?'

'It's me, Orpheus.'

Tilda put her hand on the door. What the hell was he doing here at... she peered down to see the tiny hands of her watch lit up. Half two in the morning?

Her voice sounded hoarse. 'Orpheus? It's pretty late.'

'I know. I'm sorry. I need to talk with someone.'

Tilda knuckled at her eyes. The door opened with the tiniest of creaks.

'Thanks, Haitch.' Orpheus pushed in. 'Just like to say, I

thought it was crazy audacious of you to leave the mêlée in that way. I should have followed you, except I wasn't that strong.'

Tilda flapped at the wall until she hit the light switch, which gently flooded the room with soft, ambient light. Orpheus crumpled into one of the boxy chairs and pulled out a bottle from within the folds of his jacket.

'One for the road?' said Tilda, still stood uncertainly by the door.

'Purloined from the drink's cabinet before I slunk out.' Orpheus unscrewed the cap. 'I expect it's all been filmed, so what the heck.'

'In for a penny, in for a pound.' Tilda sat opposite him, reached for the bottle, and took a hefty swig. 'What is this stuff?' She made a face and peered at the label. Limoncello? Sweet lemony syrup. Yeugh.

'It's not that bad, is it?' He tugged the bottle from her hand and took a swig. 'Ah! See what you mean.'

'I bet it cleans toilets well.'

'Sorry.' He grinned at her. 'What did you make of tonight's little charade?'

'Ghastly affair. You?'

'Same. I'm beginning to think we were right at the beginning. It was all to do with our predilections.'

'Uh-huh.' Tilda hoped that he wasn't here for that very reason. 'What happened after I left, or have you been sworn to secrecy?'

'No, but there was quite a bit of swearing. I think the term highwaypile-up would be apt here'.

Tilda had a sudden flash of her conversation with Haitch on the phone.

'I do believe that Mr Ishimoto is going to have fun sifting through all the shit of tonight.'

'Was it worth it? I mean, staying?'

'I think I'm a little drunk, and I probably said things that, in hindsight, I wouldn't normally have said. I wish I hadn't come.'

'Me too, and quite frankly, that baby goat could have been chicken.' Tilda yawned widely.

'Everything tastes of chicken.'

'Please, God. You're not now quoting *The Matrix* at me, are you?'

Orpheus closed his eyes, and for a moment, Tilda wondered if he'd fallen asleep. He opened his eyes suddenly and nodded towards her. 'Fancy a midnight walk around the place? Even if it's gone two now. Noticed you're still in your gear, so I don't feel guilty that I hauled you out of bed.'

'Yeah, well.' She shrugged. 'Kind of didn't feel like sleeping when I realised that I'd lost the commission.'

'You don't know that until the fat lady sings. Maybe Mr Ishimoto rates your honesty and integrity?'

'Maybe, although I don't think so. Okay, let's go and see what nighttime in the Castilla Mori is like.'

'Probably very dark. We'll need our phones for torches.'

'Never out of my back pocket.' Tilda waved Haitch's phone and yanked the door open. 'Which way, José?'

'Left,' said Orpheus. 'Oops, nearly forgot.' He swivelled and grabbed the bottle.

'Seriously?'

'Don't look a gift lemon alcoholic drink in the teeth.'

Tilda got the impression it was only the stability of the walls that was keeping him upright.

Most areas within the *Castilla* were lit by soft-coloured lamps, either centrally hanging or in sconces on the rough-hewn walls.

The walk back through to the dining room courtyard was bathed in warm bands and shadowed striations.

'This is a bit creepy.' Tilda looked back to where Orpheus was shrouded in darkness. That didn't make Her feel better until he tripped.

'Oopsy,' he sniggered. 'That Limonyello stuff is working its magic.'

Tilda raised an eyebrow at him as he lurched into the light. 'Nothing to do with the thirty or so glasses of champagne and wine you had before and during dinner?'

'And after. Mustn't forget them.' He waved the half-empty bottle at her. 'But I swear it's this stuff that's pushed me over the edge.'

Tilda peered in front of her. From here, the lights got few and far between, the odd coloured light glimmering fitfully. She didn't know Orpheus. And he was drunk. He might be at that funny stage now, but what if he slid into the belligerent frame of mind that happens when you drink. Sorry M'Lud! I never meant to do that. T'was the drink that made me do it. Could she trust him? In the dark?

'Are we going out there?' His was a stage whisper to die for. 'You're right. It does look creepy.'

Tilda laughed. 'Really? A great big bloke like you, from a city as scary as New York, frightened of some plant life?' A bird called out from the depth of the far trees. Orpheus jumped. 'And birds?'

'I thought all birds were asleep at night. What the hell was that?'

'It could well be a nightingale, and as the name suggests, it's up and about at night.'

'Well, I never.' He reached into all his pockets until he found his phone. 'Best to be on the safe side.' He tapped at it. 'Goddamn! Run out of battery.'

'Don't worry. I've got mine.'

Backtracking to the path that led to the gardens, Haitch's phone torch illuminated strange, twisted shapes as she swung it around. All those plants and garden furniture that'd seemed so natural in the warmth of the day, now loomed in unfamiliar poses, sending sharp contorted shadows fingering towards them.

'As I said, creepy.' Orpheus speeded up to walk by her side.

'From what I can remember when I arrived, we'd better be careful not to fall off any cliffs. Some looked lethal.'

'I'm up for not falling to my death.' He gripped hold of her arm. Tilda resisted the urge to shake him off.

Treading carefully, they wound past the lounging recliners, the waft of herbs redolent in the air as they brushed past. A large, covered terrace to their right looked too shadowy, so Tilda steered them towards a wall that snaked around the garden. Criss-crossing the garden, amber, green and blue bulbs lit up patches of vegetation or under-lit the leaves of the trees. Craning her head up, she searched for a moon. Yes, there it was, peeping out from behind a gently scudding cloud.

'It's a gibbous moon.' She doubted that Haitch would know that.

'What the hell is a gibbous moon?'

'When it's no longer full but not a crescent yet. Kind of half fat, I suppose.'

'So basically good for you?' He stared at her. 'You know, like half fat milk or cream?'

'Right. Ha, ha,' said Tilda. 'What a fantastic night. I mean, just look at how bright the stars are.'

'No light pollution,' nodded Orpheus. 'No nearby city to obscure it all.' He stopped and stared up. 'You're right. It's beautiful.'

Tilda saw moonlight gleam on the rims of his glasses. Then movement caught her eye. A darker shadow had detached itself and flitted across the roof of the squat building to the side of them. So, they were not the only ones taking the night air.

'We're not alone,' she hissed, trying not to laugh at her own staged whisper.

'Are we talking generally or specifically?'

'I mean, there's someone on that roof over there.'

'Oh! I thought we were about to discuss whether there might be alien life out in the vastness of the universe.' He pointed upwards.

'We can do that. But I wondered who was out here with us?'

'Judging by tonight, I think it could be any one of us. I don't think many people could sleep after experiencing all that.'

'Okay. 'Nuff said. We'll leave them be.' Tilda gripped onto the wall. Made of large stones, it felt cool and rough under her hand. Peering over, the edge fell away, the tiny globe of light further up barely grazing the darkness. How high were they? Picking up a pebble, she let it drop and counted. 'One pink elephant, two pink elephants, three pink elephants...' A soft thud as it hit the ground.

Tilda straightened. 'That's nearly a hundred feet.'

'How the hell do you know that?' Orpheus hunkered down to peer over the edge.

'Physics at school. An object falls about thirty foot every second. That's a really basic estimate, but I counted a good three seconds...'

'Pink elephants?'

'It works. So, best not topple off this wall backwards and ruin what has already been a ghastly evening.'

'Well, that'd be the cherry on top, wouldn't it?' He tugged on her arm. 'Let's get back to the villa.'

'Okay, except I didn't come all this way to not get at least a couple of shots out here. My camera's pretty modern so I might be able to get a few good nighttime pictures.' The screen lit up as she swiped and poked at icons. 'This should do it. I'm going for a burst.'

Tilda swung the camera around her, pressing the burst button down at intervals.

'What was that?' Orpheus turned. 'Voices?'

'I don't really want to talk to anyone else. Just one more, then we'll go back.'

'That sounds as if it's a bit of an altercation.'

'Best not to inquire then.' Her scalp prickled. She could swear she'd just heard a woman's voice call 'Sam!' Shaking her head, she peered up at the moon.

A sound drifted across as if born unwillingly on the night-time breeze. Mournful. It was as if cold fingers tickled down her back.

Orpheus bent down and squinted at her. 'Did you hear that?'

Tilda was waving the phone, the repeated flashes leaving residual images, making her blink. 'A fox? Or a ghost?'

Orpheus must have felt the same. 'I fucking hate the countryside. Let's get indoors where we'll be safe.'

The flash stuttered, and as Tilda lowered the phone, there was a heavy, dull thud below them.

'What the fuck was that?' Orpheus placed both hands flat on the wall and peered down.

'I don't know. Maybe someone else doing the pebble drop?

'Pebble? More like a boulder. Man, that sounded heavy.'

Tilda leant on the edge of the wall and tried to focus her eyes. Holding her phone out, she swept it across the darkness. Maybe she couldn't see anything in this dark, but perhaps the camera might pick something up.

'Come on,' said Orpheus, nodding over his shoulder. 'I've had enough of all this nighttime countryside fun. I prefer the vagaries of New York. Infinitely less scary. Maybe we can find someone who is still up to make us a cup of tea or whatever it is you Brits drink.'

'That would be nice. Which way did we come in?' Tilda turned and peered behind her. 'That way?'

'Not really.' Orpheus pointed in the other direction. 'No sense of direction? Come on, Haitch. Don't tell me you get lost in a shoebox?'

'Afraid so.' Funny thing was, Haitch could be blind-folded, spun a hundred times, put on a bus to the middle of nowhere, spun again and still be able to find her way home.

Friday 17th June

Tilda must have set the wrong time on the phone alarm. It couldn't be morning. She'd only just got to bed, had barely made a dent in the pillow. Peering at the screen, she stifled a yawn. Seven-thirty. *Seven-thirty?* Oh crap! Damian was coming at nine on the dot. He'd made that very clear. On the dot. Tilda needed a shower and hopefully have something decent to eat. What did the Spanish have for breakfast? Paella? Thinking about it, paella sounded quite appetising right now. Maybe finishing that horrible yellow liquor was not such a good idea after all. It wasn't as though she hadn't already drunk enough. Did pretending to be Haitch mean she had to down a skinful?

The shower was powered, hot, and so abrasive, it nearly took her skin off. Wonderful. Freshly scoured, Tilda dressed, applied her make-up as Haitch would do, sorely tempted to rub her hands over her face to get that final lived-in effect that Haitch was so good at. Her bag was packed and ready on the bed as she made her way back to the dining room. Initially, she thought it empty, but a movement by open French windows caught her interest. Dawn was leaning up against the frame, kind of clutching at it. Hiding behind dark glasses, her hair down and hanging low around her face. Maybe she'd had as good an evening as Tilda and was regretting that last mojito or whatever. Tilda stood, a little irresolute. Should she go over or pretend not to have seen her? There was something about the way she was standing, slightly hunched, that gave a warning sign. *Leave me alone*. Tilda wondered what her night had been like. Oooh! Had she communed with the ever-after and knew who had won?

Creeping across the tiled floor, Tilda peeked into the main kitchen just as a young man, obviously the waiter, scurried out.

'Ah, señorita.' He smiled. 'Please be seated.' He indicated a French bistro-style chair, pulled it out and waited for her to sit. The table had the scary red-hued cloth over it, which was a bit much after the night she'd had.

'Thank you. I mean, gracias.'

'De nada. May I take an order for your drink? We have fruit juices, teas and coffee. Fruit juices are orange, apple, grape—'

'I'll just have a coffee, thanks.'

'Coffee it is. For breakfast, we have a continental breakfast of croissants, jam and butter. We also have hams, cheeses, yoghurts, all manner of cereals, and finally, a full English cooked breakfast.' He stood expectantly.

Tilda had a sudden image of all the Brits on the coast, demanding their egg and bacon. In English. Would it be too stereotypical to have the full English? Yoghurt may be good for you, though after a night of drinking and little sleep, she needed cholesterol-inducing fat and carbs.

'The full English, please. And, thinking about it, can I have a glass of apple juice?'

'Of course, señorita.'

Looking over her shoulder towards the window, she noted Dawn had gone. Good. She didn't want a recap of last night. She wasn't sure what had happened there, as Dawn had been pretty heavy. Knowing she had been talking to someone who could see the future, the past and the bits in between was unnerving. Taking out her phone, she took photos so Haitch would have an idea of what she'd missed.

Breakfast was fast and delicious. Tilda wondered if any of the others were up yet. They probably didn't have a deadline, unlike her. They could get up at their leisure and have a helicopter whisk them away. Lucky bloody them.

'Mr Montgomery has arranged a car to pick you up at nine, is that correct?' Jeremiah had slipped quietly into the dining room as Tilda put her napkin on the table.

'That's the plan. I'm ready.' Tilda stood. 'Is anyone else up?'

'Miss Rayne breakfasted early, although I do believe she has gone back to her room. All guests have been asked to vacate the villa by two, so I presume they will be rising at their own pace.'

There was a little knot of apprehension in her stomach. Should she ask after Orpheus? Enquire what his room number was? Had they said goodbye last night? He'd walked her back to her room, taken hold of her hand and kissed it. That was it. Not even the proffered cup of tea.

'I've had a blast, Haitch.' Handing her the limoncello bottle, he ambled back down the corridor. 'Look me up if you're ever in New York, and we can talk about aliens.'

He waved a hand behind him. Tilda waited until he rounded the corner and then waited a few minutes more. What was she expecting? She didn't really know. The bottle was now empty and up ended in the wastepaper bin in her room. At the time, it seemed a sin to waste the last few mouthfuls. In the bright light of day, she regretted it.

Tilda turned to Jeremiah. 'Thanks for, you know, everything.'

'It's been a pleasure, Miss Bee. I'll walk you to the car park when you are ready.'

Five-to-nine and Tilda was waiting up on the ridge where

they'd parked the day before. Funny how that seemed weeks ago. The view was spectacular, and she wanted to imprint it on the back of her eyelids for as long as she could. The sun was cresting the top of the mountains in front of her, turning them from a deep mulberry to a salmon pink in minutes. Breathing deeply, she could taste the air, fresh and evocative. Such a shame that she couldn't stay longer. An image of Orpheus kissing her hand slid into her mind. Would he even remember seeing her last night? Sitting on a low stone wall, she wished to enjoy this and simply breathe. Nine o'clock passed, and then five past, then ten past. Where was Damian? Wasn't one of his pet hates people being late? Well, the bloke was taking the piss then. She'd have to have a go at him about tardiness when he arrived. Still, she waited, her bum going numb and the glare from the Spanish summer sun now hurting her eyes. She snapped a few more photos. But they were more for her now than for Haitch. Now Damian was seriously late, Tilda decided it was time to call him but it went straight to voicemail. Where was he?

At nine-thirty, the car arrived in a cloud of orange dust. The driver got out and shrugged.

'Mr Montgomery no arrive,' he said. 'I still take you to airport, no?'

'What do you mean? Where is he?'

'I not know. He not come. I wait half-hour. If I not go now, you miss plane.' He sucked noisily on his teeth. 'You want to miss plane?'

'No. I don't. But I can't really leave without Damian.' Tilda waved her hands around. 'Where the hell is he?'

'I not know. Phone him?'

'Yeah, right. Sorry.' Tilda rummaged in her bag and pressed his number. It went straight to voicemail again. 'Damian. Where are you? I'm at the villa, and if we don't leave soon and I mean very soon, we'll miss the flight.' She'd flown out by herself but Damian had promised to see her safely back. Was one of the others a client of his, too? That would explain it. Tilda ran her fingers through her hair and waved at the driver as she hung up. 'Do you know the hotel where Mr Montgomery was staying?'

'He not there this morning. Hotel say he leave at night. Not see him in morning.'

'Have we got time to go there now?'

'If quick.'

———

Using the combination of noisy hysterics and loud complaining, Tilda managed to get the hotel manager to open Damian's room for her. It was empty. The bed had been slept in, yet none of the freebies in the bathroom used. Towels neatly folded. He'd been there but where was he now? His travel case was zipped shut and tucked down the side of the bed.

'You have no idea where he might be?'

The manager shrugged. As the door was being locked, Tilda turned. A man was slipping into an adjacent room. The sight of him made her hair stand on end as if she'd been electrocuted. Sam! Same build. Same gold blonde hair. Same lithe way of moving.

'Sam?' It was a croak. Oh, dear God, on top of hearing his name last night, she was now seeing him all over the place. The door closed, and Tilda wiped an unsteady hand over her eyes. She had to purge him from her system, or she'd go mad.

'I call you if Mr Montgomery return, yes?' The manager ushered her to the front entrance, where her driver was waiting, perched on a small bench surrounded by pots of geraniums, and puffing heavily on a rank smelling black cheroot.

'Thank you.' Scribbling down her number on one of the

hotel's business cards, she handed it to him. 'I can be contacted on this number.'

The driver grinned gap-toothed at her. 'Hey, Missy? I take you to airport now? You lost man. No problem. Fare paid. Go now, and you get plane.'

'I just need to phone... someone. Please can you give me a minute?' The car was parked in the local square. Tilda leant up against an orange tree that was planted in the centre next to the largest rock she'd ever seen. An hour's difference meant she'd be waking Haitch at an ungodly time again, yet what else was she to do?

NINETEEN

Haitch

April 5th – two months previously

'How could you have done this to her?' There was a catch in
his voice. 'Your own sister.'

Haitch couldn't bear to look at Sam's face, see the betrayal
in the set of his mouth and the fear in his eyes. The slash across
his lips was white as if all the blood in his face had fled.

'Your own twin.' He pulled the bedclothes over his naked-
ness. 'I thought you were Tilly. Oh God, I really thought you
were Tilly.'

'I thought you'd be up for it. When we're alone, when
Tilda's in another room, you're always joking and mucking
about—' Had she misjudged it all so... wilfully?

'You're her sister, of course, I muck about.' Rubbing a
shaking hand across his face, he stared at her. 'What? Did you
think it was an invitation or something?'

'I... I...' Her heart felt as if it was trying to escape through
her ribcage. Had she been so blind and so vain that she eagerly
misinterpreted it? The thought that Sam had chosen Tilda over

her had always rankled. It must've been a mistake. It was, wasn't it?

'I'm your sister's husband, for Christ's sake! I stood in front of our families and swore to love her forever. Tilly. Not you. Which part of that didn't you get?'

'Oh, come on, Sam,' Haitch's voice trembled, 'you must have thought about it. What it'd be like?'

'Never. Why should I? I was happily in love with the woman of my dreams. I didn't need anyone else. I didn't need you.'

Haitch hauled herself out from under the covers. There was no point covering herself. 'When did you know it wasn't her?' Pulling on underwear, she kept her face hidden from him.

'When you... did stuff she doesn't normally do.'

Haitch stopped. 'Why didn't you think she was just being more adventurous?'

'I saw it in your eyes. I saw you.'

'You can't tell her, Sam.'

'I have to.' His voice cracked. 'I can't keep this from her. She'll know, anyway.'

'It'll destroy her.'

'You've destroyed her.' Sudden movement made her recoil. He had a hand around her throat and was squeezing. Her head throbbed. 'You fucking bitch! Why did you do this? Why, Haitch?'

Haitch sucked in a breath. This wasn't how this should end. Oh, God! He wouldn't kill her, would he?

'Because I could.' She forced the words out. 'This isn't just my fault. She wondered if you'd notice the difference?'

The blood drained from his face. 'Tilly spoke to you about this?'

'Yeah.' Haitch struggled to prise his hand from her neck. 'You're hurting me, Sam.'

'You think I care? I'd rip your head off if I could.' He pulled from her as if stung. 'What did she say?'

Haitch jerked away from him. 'That she didn't know if you could tell us apart.' She clung to what Tilda had said. 'She thought you wouldn't be able to.'

'Well, I did.' Dragging on jeans and shirt, he then slumped onto the bed.

'Eventually.'

'I was tired from work... then I saw you, all dressed up, and I thought how brilliant that my wife wants sex on a weekday. I wasn't going to question that in case you... she... thought better of it.' He raised his head. Christ Almighty! The look on his face. Rage. Did he have the capacity for murder? She'd never seen this Sam before. Terror fluttered in her chest.

He glared at her. 'You've even changed yourself to make you look the same as her. This was all premeditated. You did this to her, to us, on purpose.'

Haitch couldn't bear to see the shame and anger reflected in his eyes. 'I was testing you. She gave me the idea that she didn't trust that you could tell us apart. So, what does that say about you?'

'Trust? Don't ever say anything to me about trust. Why shouldn't I trust that the woman in my house is my wife? The woman who clearly looks like her, even smells like her.'

Haitch squirmed under his gaze. He was right. She'd dabbed Tilda's perfume on her wrists and neck. Having her own key meant this had been so easy to set up. She knew that Tilda was visiting their mum and wouldn't be back tonight. But what the hell was she to do now? If he told her, then all their lives would be devastated.

'I need you to get the hell out of my house, Haitch.' He made a move towards her. 'Right now.'

Haitch fumbled with her clothes and shoes. Or rather

Tilda's. 'I'm so sorry, Sam. I really thought you wanted this.' Half falling down the stairs, she clutched the front door handle.

Following her down, he swayed and reached out for the wall. 'Not in this lifetime.' His voice was hoarse. Was he crying?

'What are you going to do?' Did she want to know?

'I have no idea.'

'You can't tell her.' Her voice was tiny.

'Get out.'

'You can't tell her.' He moved so fast; he was a blur. The door was wrenched open, and she felt herself launched outside. Missing the front step, she crashed onto her knees on the gravel pathway that wound to the small gate and fence. Not quite a white picket fence but it was all that Tilda had ever wanted.

'Don't come back.' The snarl in his voice was frightening. 'Ever!' The door crashed shut so hard the living room windows rattled.

An image of Tilda slammed into her mind. Tilda wearing their granny's wedding dress, passed on through the generations. Simple but exquisite, made more exquisite by how happy she looked. Her smile was so wide, her eyes so alight with sheer joy. Looking to the future with assured hope. Because she had Sam by her side.

Crouching down, she hauled on the pretty dress she'd picked out of Tilda's wardrobe and struggled into the stilettos that matched the dress perfectly. Oh yes, she'd played the part of Tilda to perfection. Haitch lunged sideways and spattered vomit over the low hanging rhododendron leaves that fronted the property. It was always about the game: the rush of adrenaline, the fear of exposure, the need to do stuff with these men that she knew Tilda would never do. To prove a point. Tilda was the elder, but she was the better. At everything. That's what had always driven her. Until now.

'Fuck!' she whispered.

Clutching the bushes, she stood. Legs shaking and the sensation that she would throw up again, she crept slowly towards the gate. Had anyone seen her? Any nosey neighbour would be wondering what was going on at number twenty-two. Haitch hung onto the gate but didn't open it. Blustery April showers threatened, the sky roiling above her head and spatters of rain that stung her skin with ice. Fumbling, she did up the buttons on the dress. It wasn't enough. She'd left her... Tilda's jacket hanging on the hook by the front door.

Amazing. Haitch shook her head. Had she always been this selfish? So careless of the effects she might cause by an unthought through act? This wasn't going to go away in the morning. There was no way to ignore this. If Sam told Tilda, then her twin would hate her forever and a day. If he didn't, her skinny arse would be saved, but there would be a massive barrier between herself and Sam, and how would they account for that? Tilda would pick up on it in no time.

How could she have believed this was a good idea? She didn't ordinarily cry, but now the tears came hard and heavy. The gate latched behind her with a 'click'. Would she ever open it again? Who was she crying for? Herself or Tilda?

The ride home on the tube took far too long, curious faces peering at her silently asking if she was okay? Fumbling to get her key in the lock, Haitch pushed through and slumped back against the door. Home. What was that now? The place where you felt safe and loved. She'd stolen that from Tilda. From her own sister.

Going through the motions, one ear open for a phone call of screaming, the other for an enraged hammering on the door, Haitch microwaved a ready meal but left it cooling on the plate. Wrenching a cork from a bottle of red, the wine slopped as she poured. As her head nodded over the congealed mess in front of her, with the wine bottle down to the dregs, her phone 'pinged'.

You owe me.

It was from Sam.

Friday 17th June

That goddamn ringtone had to be changed. That was Haitch's first thought. The second popped into her mind like a Jack-in-the-box. The commission was lost.

Scrambling out from under the cover, she grabbed the phone. Yes, it was Tilda. And no, she didn't want to have to speak to her yet. It wasn't the commission; it was why she wasn't upset about it. How could she explain that? The phone blinked off, though Haitch knew it was only a matter of time before it rang again. A reprieve of sorts.

'Coffee, Boo?' She reached down to pet the dog. 'Not for you, silly. For me. You can have your delicious meaty chunks that smell so inviting.'

When the coffee pot was filled and gurgling on the stove, she jumped as the phone rang.

'Tilda? Are you on the plane yet?'

'No, listen. Damian hasn't turned up.'

'What do you mean?' It was as if someone with sharp, bony fingers had ruffled her hair.

'Exactly that. I'm on the way to Malaga airport, but there's no sign of Damian. He didn't pick me up at the villa when he was supposed to. We even went to check at his hotel. Have you got any idea where he might be?'

'Not a clue. He's meant to get you there and back. Has Mr Ishwotnot said anything?'

'No. I'll tell you, it's pretty weird. No one knows where Damian is. His hotel said he must have left late last night and hasn't been seen since. They're one of those latch ones, so they're not sure.'

'Are you okay? Who has the tickets?'

'I've got mine. I suppose if he doesn't get to the airport on time, I'll have to go without him.'

'You've tried calling him, haven't you?'

'Would you have tried calling him?' There was an icy tone down the phone.

'Of course—'

'Well, as your twin, I'm not stupid, am I? That was obviously the first thing I did.' Tilda let out a deep rasping sigh, and Haitch realised she must be quite stressed by now. 'It went straight to voicemail.'

'Okay. Sorry, Tilda. Keep me posted and if you need me to do anything, let me now.'

Where the hell was Damian? It was all well and good to lecture her on arriving promptly and then have the gall to not turn up. But there was more to it than that, wasn't there?

Where was he? *Sod him.*

———

Haitch knew that Damian had several clients whose talents were wide-ranging. She'd not bothered to do any research on them and hadn't been introduced or even seen one of them. He'd told her he preferred to keep all aspects of his business life separate, and she'd respected that. But now, if she'd had contact details, she could be ringing round to see if any of the others knew what might have occurred. Or could his absence be due to his elusive wife?

Served him right if something had happened and none of them knew of it.

TWENTY

Matilda

Privileged boarding had a lot going for it. It felt as if one moment she was settling into her wide and oh-so-comfy seat on the plane, slugging back a robust Bloody Mary and the next, she was ringing Haitch's doorbell. A relaxed taxi journey and not the usual bus ride topped the trip home off. After a certain amount of scuffling and bumping, the door was wrenched open, and Boo tumbled out, her tail wagging so hard she could barely keep her balance, pink tongue flapping and whining abjectly.

'Dear God, Boo. I've missed you.' Tilda buried her face in the thick fur.

'Thanks.' Haitch lounged up against the doorframe. This time she looked less like a plague victim and more like someone who was just a little poorly.

'I missed you too.' Tilda tentatively hugged her sister. 'I wish you'd made there it instead of me. You would have handled it better than I did.'

'Come in. We're not talking about this on the doorstep. We both need a cuppa and some chocolate digestives.'

Tilda focused. 'You've dyed your hair brown. Like mine.'

'I thought it would be better if we matched, even if it's not quite the same colour. Especially if we hear from Damian. It'd be tricky if I see him, and I've gone straight back to blonde. Ordered it online. You can't beat next day delivery.'

'Yeah, right. Especially as he seemed to like your new colour.'

'He did? He said that?'

'Yep.' Tilda nodded and hauled her travel bag in.

Haitch indicated the sofa. 'This time, I'll make you tea.'

Tilda curled herself up in the corner and watched in horror as Boo jumped up beside her. 'Oh, God! I'm so sorry.'

'No, that's my fault. I was lonely, and it was nice to have Boo with me.'

Tilda couldn't believe it. Haitch had allowed Boo on the sofa? Unheard of.

Haitch continued: 'I've phoned the hotel where he was staying, and they still have nothing more to tell us about it all. Don't worry, I said I was another client trying to catch up with him. I really can't think of any reason he would miss the flight and why he wouldn't contact us. Well, me.'

'You don't think he's been involved in an accident, do you?'

Haitch hesitated for a second but continued talking. 'If he has, surely someone would have reported it by now. There would be something.'

'Could be it was a hit and run?' Tilda shook her head. 'He went out late. Maybe something did happen, and whoever ran away scared.'

'That's terrible.'

Tilda heard Haitch's voice catch. Dear God, how insensitive of her. Even if she didn't or wouldn't recognise it herself, Tilda reckoned that Haitch was in love with Damian. This must have hit her hard. 'Sorry. Are you all right?'

'Sure.'

Tilda noted Haitch seemed in control as she put the mugs and packet of biscuits on the coffee table. She said, 'Who should we contact? The police?'

'Isn't there a certain amount of time you have to wait before you can say a person is missing?'

'Twenty-four hours. At least it's been that on every police show I've seen.' Tilda took a biscuit.

'That's what I thought.'

'This is crazy. I can't believe Damian has gone AWOL. It sounds ridiculous.' Tilda blew on her tea, Boo nuzzling under her arm. 'Listen, I'll get sorted with you here and then I'll take Boo home. We can call each other in the morning to see if anything has changed.'

'Sounds like a plan.'

'I also need to explain what happened at the party.'

'I don't care about that. I'm sorry I asked you to go.' Haitch reached over and patted Tilda on the knee the same way their mum always did. Reassurance. 'It sounded a complete nightmare.'

'I think the word "clusterfuck" springs to mind.'

'Tilda!' Haitch put her hand over her mouth in mock shock. 'You don't swear, so it must've been bad.'

'This Mr Ishimoto basically used all our fears and bigotry against us. We weren't picked for what we were doing. It was simply because of who we were or what we'd experienced. It was as if he got us to dissect each other.'

'That's horrible. Why would he do that?'

'Boredom? Because he can? Who can say what motivates a person to be a real dick? I mean, it was like he chose us all simply to watch us bicker and fight. As if he got some weird gratification out of it.'

Haitch frowned. 'Like what?'

'He mixed up people's religions, their belief systems, their past experiences and matched them to at least one of the others there, so they'd quarrel and get upset. And of course, we all did. Like we were all being choreographed by an unseen hand.'

'What was our part in this?' Haitch's voice was quiet. 'I mean mine.'

Tilda stared down at the floor. 'I guess he had you pegged as the whore in the story. The man actually asked if I'd, I mean you, had slept with many men, in front of everybody. It was shameful. Not for us.' She glanced at Haitch. 'For him.'

'Wow. Nice.'

Tilda noticed Hatch's hand was shaking as she took a sip of her tea.

'What about the others?'

'You're going to get a group photo sent through to you in the next few days. Mr Ishimoto said he'd let us know who the winner was then. I'll run you through them all when you can see them.'

'How kind of him. Was there any part of this clusterfuck that you enjoyed?'

'The actual villa was gorgeous, the concierge came from Ipswich, of all places, the food was great... and...'

'And?'

'Well, one of the guys was pretty nice.'

'Oh, you have to tell me now.'

'Nothing happened. But it might have. That's a big step, Haitch. Even allowing the thought in of someone else is huge for me.'

'I'm glad. One final thing,' Haitch held out a phone, 'remember to swap our phones back.'

'Look, can we do that tomorrow? I need to download all the photos I took so you have an idea of where you were supposed to be. I'd like to have a look at them first.'

'Incriminating pics, Tilda? Pray, do tell.'

'Haitch? Leave it out, will you?' It might be great to see Haitch, yet it often felt that she was more in her business than Tilda was herself. Wouldn't it be nice to have a little privacy, if even for a day or two?

It seemed strange to stride out Haitch's front door as Tilda again. But stepping into her own home made her stomach twist into knots. Retrieving tins of food for Boo and hoiking a ready meal out of the freezer occupied her for a while. Once she sat on the sofa, her lasagne gobbled, Boo dozing by her side, she allowed her thoughts to travel where they wanted to go.

Orpheus. Sam.

There had been only three or four real boyfriends before Sam. Each time she'd thought it was real. Each time they'd cut and run at the moment she'd been beginning to think it might be her 'forever' love, leaving her with an aching heart and many questions. In the end, they'd all seemed to have this look on their faces: disgust or fear, or something she couldn't identify. 'Why' was the question that never got answered. The one major boyfriend before Sam had moved town, so at least she had the satisfaction of knowing he didn't leave her willingly. At least, she hoped not. One less broken heart. Once Sam had appeared, she'd never envisioned her life without him. Marriage, kids in due course, getting old and creaky together until the end of their days. His betrayal had left a gaping hole that was Sam sized. There was no point shovelling shit into it. She had to make a well-built and anchored walkway over the top that wouldn't buckle under the weight of new emotions. If Orpheus had asked to stay last night, would she have let him? In a way, she was glad she never got to answer that.

Next, was the thorny issue of what had gone on at the party.

Hmmmm.

She decided to download all the photos and look at them properly in the morning. Were there any of Orpheus? Why couldn't she get him out of her mind? It was as if she was a teenager with a crush. She was nearly thirty, so surely, she'd grown out of stuff such as that by now? Maybe if she'd 'played the field' the way Haitch had done, then this wouldn't have been such a crippling event in her life. Wincing at the memory, Tilda opened her back door and felt the cool night air caress her hot cheeks.

Switching on the TV, she twiddled until she found SkyNews. Keeping up to date with the world was always a priority. There was the usual rattling of sabres from various political parties, details of an arson attack on a local business and an account of a man's body found near a small village in the south of Spain. She nearly missed it. Turning the volume up, she caught the last few sentences from the newscaster.

'Due to severe injuries, the body has not been identified, and there were no personal effects to be able to ascertain who this man might be.'

Tilda heard crackling, the same as when the telly went on the blink, but on this occasion, it was inside her head. What? The map behind him showed the region of Spain she'd just visited.

'If you have any information, please call the number below.'

Should she scribble it down? Hang on, she was making this huge assumption that this man might be Damian. But he had personal effects on him, didn't he? His phone? His posh watch? Even his wallet. A little voice whispered *unless he'd been robbed and murdered*. Had Haitch seen this yet? No, she didn't bother with the banalities of knowing what was happening in the world. She got her knowledge base from Facebook and Twitter. That was enough information for her to handle. If she called her now, and it wasn't Damian, then she would cause unnecessary angst. Until the local authorities knew more, she'd keep quiet.

Boo was banned from the bed. She was getting into far too many bad habits. Tilda wrapped her arms around her pillow and tried to push Damian's face from her mind. How he'd looked at her? How he'd looked at Haitch? Whatever Haitch might feel for him, it looked to Tilda as if it was reciprocated.

Please, God, he can't be dead.

TWENTY-ONE

Haitch

WHY DID it seem a lot colder now Boo and Tilda had gone? Haitch turned up the thermostat on all the radiators, not that they should even be on in June, for God's sake. Stupid British summertime. It didn't seem to make much difference.

Haitch contemplated calling Damian, but as her hand hovered over the phone, she realised that it wasn't her phone. He wouldn't recognise this new number, and it might complicate things. She'd have to explain why she suddenly had this new number.

Panic tapped at her, unnerving and incessant. Oh hell, what were these feelings that bubbled up? He couldn't be dead. Why? Because she hadn't had her fair share of time with him, she hadn't had the chance to come to terms with her emotional state. Thoughts of her father welled up, too, and intermingled in her mind. It was a terrible thing to never to be able to say 'goodbye' to someone you care about... someone you loved. Shut up! She didn't love him, couldn't love him. It wasn't going to happen. Ever. It kept coming back to the thought that she might never see him again. Her head felt light as if it'd floated off to the ceiling.

'Stupid bugger!'

Slipping the phone back into her jeans pocket, she paced the living room. Her stomach rumbled. Hunger. Yes, that was what was causing all this anxiety. A simple drop in blood sugar. Now she was on the mend; it was incredible how ravenous she felt. She'd been subsisting on instant soups and bread, and even if she'd been presented with roast chicken, she'd have gagged. But now, she could murder one. Was there anyone in the vicinity who could rustle a roast up at, well, two in the morning? Probably not. The open-all-night garage was about a twenty-minute walk up the high street. Blow that. Rummaging around in the fridge, she found wilting lettuce that was physically stuck to a patch of ice at the back and left-over basmati rice from when Tilda was here. Salad cream over it? Why the hell hadn't she asked Tilda to pick some food up for her? Not that she really knew what she wanted. Just food, really-bad-for-you food.

Hauling on jeans and a sweatshirt, she laced up her boots, grabbed her bag and, checking the front door was locked, started to walk down the street. There were always people about at this time of night. This was London. But something made her turn and stare back. Was that a person leaning against one of the plane trees that graced her road? She shook her head. God, she must've gone a little nutty having been cooped up indoors. What was that called? Cabin fever. Can you get that after only a few days? She marched forward.

Halfway there, she began to regret it. Her breath was stuttering, her legs were like rubber bands, and there was a pain in her chest that was alarming. Clutching at a lamppost, she steadied herself until she thought she could walk on. It took an inordinate amount of time until the welcoming, bright lights of the garage could be seen. Pushing in, she waved at the bored assistant who ignored her. He was intently looking at his phone and unaware of what was around him. She grabbed a basket and made her way slowly along every aisle. It would be so easy to stuff things up the front of her sweatshirt and then totter out, feigning pregnancy. Ready to pop. Glancing about, she noted the surveillance camera pointed at her. She smiled and did a little wave with the tips of her fingers. Was anyone there to see her?

A bag of Doritos, a bar of Galaxy and a can of Coke fell into the basket. Peering at the sad array of sandwiches, she picked cheese and tomato, slightly less suspect than the tuna or ham. Who wanted food poisoning right after having the flu? A carton of milk and a box of cornflakes followed. Best to have something for tomorrow, so she didn't have to come out again.

The assistant didn't even bother to look up at her as he scanned her goods. Glancing down the magazine racks, Haitch spotted the edition of *Vogue* with her face plastered on the front cover. She tweaked it out, where it landed in the basket. He scanned it through but still didn't look up. Good thing she wasn't wielding a knife as he probably wouldn't even notice.

'Hey,' said Haitch in her sweetest voice, 'look who's on the front of this magazine.'

'Yeah? Who?' he said.

'Me.' Haitch finally had the satisfaction of seeing his quizzical frown turn to incredulity as he stared at her and then peered intently at the cover.

'Wow,' he said, 'is that you? That woman's got blonde hair in the photo—'

'Of course, it's me. I've dyed my hair to be more, you know, incognito.' The last words were a conspiratorial whisper.

'If you want, to be incognito...' he whispered back doing the finger twiddling, '...then, why did you tell me it was you?'

Haitch felt heat scorch up her neck and across her cheeks. 'I thought you might be interested.'

'Yeah? What did you do to get on this then?'

He flapped the magazine at her, causing a crease across her perfectly photoshopped face. A niggle of annoyance rippled over her.

'I made it famous.' She handed over her card, expecting him to at least ask how.

'Good for you. I'm going to be famous too.' He keyed in the details. 'One day, I'll be on the front cover of something.'

Haitch wondered what he'd be famous for. Maybe slothfulness? Famous for not really giving a damn? 'Good luck with that.' Snatching her goods and stuffing them in her bag, she wanted to say it took a hell of a lot of hard work, then she caught herself. Oh, God! Did she just sound exactly the same as her mum? Even if she'd said it in her head. Was turning thirty the rapid dissolution of young being distilled into old? Overnight?

Shaking her head imperceptibly, she headed back out to the road, made pitch black by the brightness of the shop lights. Standing for a moment, she let her eyes adjust and then started to walk, thoughts swirling.

When she was back home, as she flicked the light switches and had the radio burbling quietly, Haitch felt a weird tingling down her spine. What had caused it? Aha, her computer was on. Normally, that wasn't unusual, but she knew she hadn't been on it for a couple of days. It had been turned off. Definitely off. She looked about her. She hadn't been burgled, if she had then stuff would be strewn everywhere, as most burglars are there to find your precious possessions and steal them as fast as possible. But as she stood looking around, she swore that things had been moved. It was only millimetres, but they were not where she'd left them. It was then she heard the sound. A teeny-tiny 'click'. The front door closing. Had someone been in her flat? Had someone just gone out?

Haitch froze, then ran to the hallway. It took a second to command her fingers to open the door. The street was illuminated by yellow lamps, but there was no one to be seen in either direction.

'Shit.'

Pulling the door shut behind her, Haitch rubbed at her eyes. Running around, brandishing a bread knife in front of her, she checked every room. Especially under the bed and in the closet. No one there. Too little sleep, on top of being ill, and now she was hallucinating. What? Had someone got into her house to look at the internet and move her pencils around? Get a grip. She was glad when the front door was locked behind her. Properly locked. Piling all her food onto a plate, she popped the can of Coke and went to sit on the sofa and watch *Game of Thrones*. She had the DVD boxset. A lovely bit of Jon Snow would do the trick to keep her mind off what could have happened to Damian. She had a vivid imagination and didn't wish to go where that might lead. So that left the other question nagging at the back of her mind. Doors don't make noises on their own account. Had there been a stranger in her place? No way. But if there had? Why? What did they want?

Saturday 18th June

'Haitch, great news.' Tilda sounded happy, considering it was still only about eight in the morning. 'I've just had a text from Damian saying he was caught up elsewhere, and he was sorry he couldn't pick me up. He said he wasn't able to contact me, well you, until now, so basically, we're not to worry, he'll catch up in a bit.'

'Finally!' Haitch struggled to sit up in bed. 'God, I had him pegged as dead or at least in a hospital somewhere with amnesia. After this, I'll tell you, he can never have a go at me for being late to something. He's not going to live this one down, the cheeky sod.' The relief she felt was like a deluge coursing through her.

'At least we know he's all right, and we don't have to go to the police.'

'It's brilliant news, Tilda. No awkward questions down the nick and all that.' No cracking of her fragile heart.

'Yeah, of course.'

'I know you've only just got back to Brighton, but do you fancy going to see a film tonight? There's an all-nighter showing five back-to-back Beatnik films. I think I've gone a bit stir-crazy.' She put on her best wheedling voice. 'You can stay over at mine tonight and go back tomorrow.'

'I'm working on my illustrations.'

'Then you'll need a break by then.'

'Maybe.'

'Meet me here? Say about seven? I'll get a bottle of red breathing and order a take-away. Will a Thai do?'

'Probably not what you should eat before going out to a confined space for hours, but when has that ever stopped me?'

'Will you bring Boo?'

'Are you getting attached to my dog, Haitch?'

'As if!'

TWENTY-TWO

Matilda

THE MOST IMPORTANT thing was that Damian was alive. Her night had been restless and full of fugues and phantoms that were just out of reach. Surfacing to the beep of a text, she'd woken as if she'd downed a double espresso. Grabbing the phone, she searched eagerly for the message.

Sorry for missing you. Had urgent business to attend to. Glad you got home okay. Will contact you soon. D.

That was all, yet it was enough for Tilda to dance around her room, waving her arms like she was Julie Andrews in *The Sound of Music*. Boo watched and then slunk on her belly out the bedroom door. She phoned Haitch, hearing the reassurance pouring out down the phone line.

The paintings for Walker Books were progressing. This was the eighth of ten watercolours in her Brother's Grimm's compilation of old German fairy tales. Commissioned by Walker Books, the deadline was hanging like the proverbial albatross around her shoulders. An enormous, dead and stinky albatross.

They weren't forgiving of overrunning time limits, and her jaunt in Spain had cost her a couple of days.

The phone rang, and Tilda nearly knocked over her water jar.

'Haitch?' she answered, expecting it to be her sister, then looked at the number. It wasn't Haitch's new mobile number. Or Damian's. What? No one else had this number.

'I hope it's you, or I've got someone else's number with your name.'

'Orpheus?' Tilda nearly dropped the phone.

'I hope you don't mind me having your number.'

'When did I give you my number?' Tilda could have metaphorically smacked her forehead. 'I'm sorry. That came out so rude.'

There was a gruff laugh on the other end of the phone. 'When I stole it from the hotel records.'

Tilda frowned. 'You did what?'

'Look, I'm not your normal day-to-day stalker. I needed to say a few things to you, and as you were a bit tipsy the last time we met, I reckoned that you would have given me your number if you were sober. Maybe not your address, though.'

'You're crazy. How did you manage to get into the hotel records?'

'Well, that could have been when all the commotion was going on. People all over the place, the staff running about, no one paying attention.'

'Commotion?'

'Yeah, about that. Really fuckin' weird.'

'Orpheus? What commotion?'

'Look. I don't have to be back in New York for a few days. I was wondering if I could visit you?'

Tilda's stomach did a backwards roll. 'Where are you now?'

'Well, truth be told, I'm already in London. I enquired about flights, you know, on the off-chance and luckily for me, someone refrained from turning up. I got their cancellation.'

'You're in London? Now? Right now?'

'Yep. Not angry, are you?'

'No, but a little shocked.'

'So, can we meet up?' There was a rustling. 'Do you want a bit of time to think about it? I can call you back in an hour or so?'

'Yes. If that's okay.'

What the hell? Apart from the fact that she was in Brighton, add to that was the fact she wasn't even who he thought she was, and more importantly, she really didn't know him from Adam. Tilda knew she should say 'no'. But she wasn't going to.

She called him back immediately.

TWENTY-THREE

Haitch

'HAITCH?' Tilda's voice sounded funny. 'Can I come over? I mean, like now? I need to talk to you.'

'I thought you had work to do?'

'I do, but something has come up.'

'Is everything okay?'

'Yeah, fine. It's just got a bit complicated, and I need to fill you in.'

'I'll be here. Use your spare key in case I'm in the bath or whatever.'

'Thanks. I've already sorted Boo. A neighbour's going to look after her. See you in a couple of hours.'

'Great.' What was this strange feeling? Disappointment? That the dog was going to stay with someone else? She should shape up and get back to being herself. If Tilda had been impersonating her in Spain, maybe she'd been impersonating Tilda here. That would explain her sudden and irrational attachment to Tilda's weirdo dog.

More importantly, what had Tilda been up to in Spain? She'd mentioned a bloke. Could that be it? Sometimes, Haitch feared any talks about prospective new boyfriends, in case they ended up talking about previous ones. She knew that it was only a matter of time before Tilda found out that she, her own flesh and blood, identical sister was the one who'd shattered Tilda's marriage and the prospect of 'forever'.

Sam's text had read: *you owe me.*

He'd faked some other liaison, said he had to leave, that Tilda was better off without him. There was no mention of shagging 'the sister'. Tilda's cosy world had collapsed around her. She'd argued, pleaded, raged and then accepted. All the while, Haitch had looked on with a false face, offering support, a shoulder to cry on while she knew that she was the one who'd plunged the knife in Tilda's back. Maybe it would come out soon, or when they were both silver-haired and prune-wrinkled. Either way, it would destroy them both. Forgiveness was not on the agenda, although retribution might be. For Tilda.

Tilda rang the bell but let herself in at the same time. The bell was an early warning in case she was up to no good. Well, wasn't she always? The front door had a distinctive sound when it opened and closed. Haitch shivered suddenly. It was the same sound she'd heard last night. No matter how she tried to ratio-nalise what had happened, it didn't make sense. Could someone have been in her flat? Nothing was missing; she'd rechecked this morning.

Haitch called out from the kitchen. 'I'm in here putting the kettle on.'

Tilda came to give her a hug. 'You're looking better.'

'I feel better, thank God. It's been pretty dismal.' She pointed. 'Got the last of the choccy bics in the cupboard there.

Popped out last night to get some supplies in. Quite frankly, I'm shattered from the effort. So not a hundred per cent yet.'

'Well, if it was flu, it'll take a while, then you can go back to drinking yourself stupid like normal.'

'Ha, bloody ha!' said Haitch. 'So? What's going on?'

'Apart from the horrible experience of being dissected at the party, there was one highlight.'

'And his name is?'

'Orpheus.' Tilda turned with her hands placed heavily on her hips. 'Don't laugh, and please don't mention *The Matrix*.'

Haitch pursed her lips, trying to control the fit of giggles that threatened to pop out. 'Orpheus? Sounds interesting. What's he like then?'

'He's Black and a very tall New Yorker. I think we hit it off, although he was really drunk, and I was probably only a stage behind him. That's why I'm here. He's already in London and has asked to meet up.' She arranged the biscuits on the plate.

Haitch paused to let this sink in. 'He's not on his way here now, is he?'

'No, of course not. I've arranged to meet him in a neutral place in the centre of town.'

Haitch warmed the teapot and slopped a little milk into each mug. 'Isn't this going to be a little tricky?'

'Tell me about it...'

'I am.'

'That's why I'm here. By the way, have you had anything through from Mr Ishimoto? I put your email down.'

'Why bother? Unless you think you didn't fuck it up?'

'No, that's for sure. I simply wanted you to see the others, so I can explain about them.'

'Okay. Won't meeting Orpheus put a cat amongst the pigeons, as they say? Won't he use that against you... us?'

'I don't know. Orpheus doesn't believe he's won it either, so maybe it won't bother him.'

'What people say to others and what they truly believe are two entirely different things.' Wasn't that the truth? Haitch nodded at the living room. Tilda trailed after her. 'How do you think he's going to react when you tell him you're not me?'

'That's just it. Do I tell Orpheus?'

'What?' Haitch held a biscuit an inch from her mouth but didn't bite into it. 'You have to tell him if you've any intention of seeing him again. How do you think this would pan out if you don't?'

'Sorry, you're right.' Tilda blew out the side of her mouth. 'It's not as if we've done anything. Not even a kiss.' A small smile played across her lips.

'What?' said Haitch.

'He did kiss my hand, but I don't think that counts.'

'Oooh, a gentleman. Not many of them still around.' She leant forward. 'Is he cute?'

'From my point of view, yes, although it's more that I really liked the way he thought. He was funny.'

'Okay. Looks as though I'm off to the cinema on my lonesome...'

'Oh! Yes. I'm sorry.'

'No worries, Tilda. Anything that makes you smile is alright by me.' She stirred her tea. 'Are you going to tell him today?'

'If you don't mind, I'll see how it goes first. If it fizzles out, then maybe I can leave it that he met you and that's that.'

'Sure.' Haitch stared at Tilda. 'If you're going to do that, then you probably need some of my clothes. Just enough that he won't wonder initially but not so much that it's not you at the same time. Give yourself leeway.'

'Thanks.' Tilda crunched through another biscuit. 'He also said something weird. He mentioned he'd nicked my telephone number from the hotel computer when, and I quote, "all this commotion was going on", but he didn't elaborate. Told me he'd fill me in when we met.'

'Sounds interesting. I wonder what that was?'

'Hopefully, I'll find out soon.' Tilda licked her fingers. 'Come on, make me a hybrid.'

'Yuck, that sounds terrible. A monster twin with two heads...'

'That's a hydra.'

'Oh. Yeah.' Haitch nodded. 'That's what you get for not paying attention in school.' Standing, she turned to Tilda. 'Were you me or you at the party?'

'I don't understand.'

'Were you clever Tilda or dumbed-down to be me?'

Tilda frowned. 'I think I was both. You're not dumb, Haitch; it's more like I can retain stupid bits of information better than you, but you're way more streetwise and savvier. If we were one person, we'd be perfect.'

'Lucky we're not then. Sounds boring. Am I going to get my phone back today, or do you need it?'

Tilda's eyes rounded. 'I can't give it back yet, can I? It's the one Orpheus is calling.' She frowned. 'Are you okay with that? Can you last another day with mine?'

'Looks as if I'll have to.'

'And I forgot to download the photos last night. I was just so tired.'

'Come on, let's get you looking like a... hybrid?' She raised her eyebrow.

Tilda followed Haitch into the bedroom. There was a momentary deja-vu as she opened her closet door and started to scrabble through the tightly packed clothes. 'How about this?' Tugging out a slim black dress with a slight ruffle at the bottom, she waved it at Tilda. It had the tiniest of patterns on it, barely visible. It was one of her favourites. 'Black leggings and my more fashionable buckle boots. I've even got some rather nice Indian silver jewellery that would suit you. In fact, if you want it, have it. I never wear it as it's too pretty. It'll look great on you.'

'Very kind and don't mind if I do.' Tilda slipped off her clothes and stepped into the dress. Then wriggled into the leggings. Haitch helped with the jewellery.

On the doorstep, Haitch pulled Tilda into a hug. 'Go get him, Tiger.'

'What? Shut up!' Tilda laughed and shook her head. 'I'll call you when I can.'

TWENTY-FOUR

Matilda

As she hovered under the impressive portico of the Saatchi Gallery, Tilda's stomach was doing somersaults to rival any Russian gymnast. As it was a stone's throw from Sloane Square tube, where she'd directed Orpheus, it felt fitting to meet there. Especially as she was to all intents and purposes, still Haitch. How the hell was she going to tackle this? *Hey, Orpheus, guess what? I'm not Haitch, I just kind of look like her. A lot.*

The leggings made her feel hot and sweaty, and she overrode the urge to hitch her knickers down. Not wishing to seem too eager, she was looking in the opposite direction to the station when a hand on her shoulder made her jump.

'Hi, Haitch.' Orpheus was grinning down at her. 'Against everything I've been told about English summers, it's pretty hot.' He shrugged off his jacket and laid it over a small rucksack at his feet.

'Hiya.' Tilda didn't know whether to stand on tiptoe to kiss him or to lunge out to shake his hand. He pre-emptied her by grabbing her into a firm hug. 'You have to remember,' she wheezed, 'we can have all four seasons in one day. Our motto is "be prepared". Bring sunscreen and a brolly. Gloves and a t-shirt.' He let go of her, and she sucked in a breath.

'It's lovely to see you again.' His grin wavered slightly. 'Pleased to see me?'

'Of course. Good flight?'

'Ooh, how polite. Yes, it's only a small hop compared to a flight to the US.' He took a step away from her.

'I'm sorry, just a little discombobulated by seeing you here.' She wondered what look she had on her face right now. Astonishment? Abject fear? Nothing that would make a nervous man feel confident.

'I can go if you want me to?'

Tilda opened her mouth to say 'no'.

'Like over there.' He pointed across the road. 'We can shout at each other.'

'Funny.' Tilda laughed. 'Did you say you hadn't been here before? I can't remember.'

'Correctomundo.'

'Okay, so we can go visit the gallery and get all arted-up? It has shows of up and coming and contemporary art, but the venue is a nineteenth-century building...'

'Did you read that off something?'

'Yeah. It's written on that plaque behind you.'

Orpheus turned to look. 'Oh, it is. Have you exhibited here?'

Tilda had to think about that. Had Haitch got this far? Surely, she'd know if she had. 'No. But it's a dream for most artists.' Or was it selling out? She wasn't sure.

'I get that.' He shrugged. 'What else is there to do?'

'We could have an amble around Hyde Park. Pop to a cafe for afternoon tea?' She looked down at her feet. 'Or a large beer?'

'Yes, please. All of it. But without the art bit. I know I should, but I don't want to be shut up indoors, no matter how beautiful the venue. I'd like to be able to chat and see pretty green things.'

'Trees? Bushes? Grass?'

'I may be from a big city, but we also have parks, you know. I have seen grass before.'

Tilda pulled on his arm. 'Let's get going. I seem to remember from somewhere that Central Park is a great deal bigger than Hyde Park. So, we might have to go round it twice.'

'Then that will call for double the coffee.' Picking up the rucksack, he stuffed the jacket inside and then slung it over one shoulder. 'Don't let me lose this as it has my laptop in it.'

'I'll try.'

'And you will succeed. You know you do seem to remember an awful lot of things.'

'An awful lot of useless things.'

This was precisely what Haitch had been talking about. Tilda loved facts, relished in history and recollected things precisely. Whereas Haitch hit life on a wing and a prayer, often made-up stuff and quite frankly, Tilda reckoned, she had her eyes shut most of the time in case she hit something hard.

'I'm following you,' said Orpheus, 'so which way are we going?'

'This way.' Tilda set off purposefully along Sloane Street. 'Have you heard from Mr Ishimoto?'

'No. Have you?'

Tilda shook her head. 'I hope you win it, especially as I'm not in the running.'

'You don't know that for sure. Not until that old fat lady sings.'

Tilda swung round to face him. 'You saw what he was doing. Do you really think he'd give the money to a person who cut his fun short?'

'Put that way, possibly not.'

'You told me that it was a train wreck or whatever after I'd left.'

'I can give you a blow-by-blow account or the highlights?'

'Highlights.'

'Dawn had a massive fight with Alejandro about what the Papacy might have hidden in the Vatican and the need for proper birth control condoned by the Catholic church. She stormed off not long after you. I might have said a few unsavoury things to Alejandro. I think Zaida managed to stay decorous throughout but did have a final dig at Alejandro and his Catholic dogma before she retired gracefully to her room. I really didn't want to be alone with Mr Ishimoto, so I beat a hasty retreat. That left Alejandro.'

'Not sure which of them I feel the sorriest for.'

Orpheus snorted with laughter. 'Do you think we'll all end up on YouTube?'

'Now that's a truly horrendous thought. What a waste of time and effort. If Mr I gets his jollies from all this, then great, that's what money can buy. For me, it was all a pile of steaming bullshit. That's my humble opinion.'

'Agreed.'

They carried on past Knightsbridge underground, where Tilda stopped. 'We can go to Hyde Park now, or if you want something to eat, there's The Hard Rock Cafe around the corner there.' She waved in the direction.

'Hard Rock? What, just 'cos I'm American you think I can't eat anything except our good ole American burgers?'

'Testing the water, Orpheus.'

'I thought you mentioned tea, you know, cream and scones and whatever.'

'Alright, then we can go to a wonderful cafe in the park and... chat.' The knots in her stomach were tying themselves up so tightly, she thought she might be sick. Being Haitch had been fun for a while, although now she could see the implications. Was she going to tell him or not? When would be the right time?

The park was soon in front of them, stretching away into the distance, an oasis of trees and birds amongst the city's concrete and tarmac.

Slowing her pace, she led Orpheus up the lane facing them and then turned right through a grove of trees. A white-painted ornate iron bandstand faced them. Columns held the octagonal roof up, and steps led up to the stage.

'I sometimes come here... with friends. It's a good place to survey the world passing. In winter, they have an ice rink here.' She realised she'd been about to say she came here with her husband. Now that would've been tricky to explain.

'It's nice,' said Orpheus, thumping up the steps behind her. 'Very olde-worlde.'

'You said you got my number when all this commotion was going on. What did you mean by that?'

'I came down pretty late, feeling a little bit hungover for some reason.' He raised an eyebrow at her. 'Not sure how that happened, but I'm never going to drink anything with lemon in it for the rest of my life.'

Tilda nodded her head. 'Yeah, I finished the bottle, so I'm with you on that one.'

'I went into the restaurant and noticed that no one seemed to be about. There were breakfast bits and pieces on the side, but when I went into the kitchen, still no one. I thought, okay, this is because I'm late. So, I grabbed a couple of croissants and butter pats. There was some leftover coffee in a jug, and I sat down to eat. I'd nearly finished and was on my way to see if there was more coffee when I heard a lot of voices out in the hallway.' He stopped talking and scratched at his beard.

'And?'

'And it was Jeremiah. He told me a body had been found

partway down the mountainside. Some poor fucker herding his goats had come across it.'

'A body?' Tilda's stomach lurched. 'I saw it on the news. They didn't say exactly where he'd been found, but they showed the map. I knew it must be close, though not that close. Blimey! Do they know who it is yet?'

'White male, that's all I know. So, while they were all milling about, I took the opportunity of sneaking a peek at their computer. I know I shouldn't have, and it's an invasion of privacy, but you'd gone before I'd even worked out that I was still alive.' He leant back on the metal railing. 'I kinda hoped you'd have given me your number if you'd still been there that morning.'

Tilda looked down. Would she have? It was only a number, after all, although now he was here, and she had to try to explain that he'd come all this way to see a completely different person to the one he thought he was meeting. Staring out across the swathe of green grass, the London skyline obscured by heavily leafed trees, Tilda smiled. 'Of course, I would have given you my number.'

'Phew,' he said. 'There was a bit of a delay there. You had me worried.'

'This body they found,' Tilda began, 'did you see it?'

'Hell no. I've seen stuff in the States that'd make your toes curl. I'm not gonna go hunting for it.' He paused. 'Why?'

'It'll sound a bit crackers, but that morning, my agent was meant to pick me up, although he never turned up.'

'You think it might be him?'

'No, no. He sent me a text message the next day saying he got delayed. It's just we... I mean, I wondered if he'd had an accident. The sort of accident that doesn't get reported as no one knows about it.'

'In other words, this sort of accident.'

'Yes. Damian, my agent, is okay, but this other man isn't. I expect he has friends and family who were wondering where he was, or when he was coming home...' Memories of her father surfaced, the police looking sombre on the doorstep, the disbelief and then the shock. Turning from him, she wiped her eyes quickly with the tips of her fingers and hoped he hadn't noticed. Clearing her throat, she looked up at him. 'Did he fall?'

'Seemingly so.' He chewed on his lip. 'The strange thing is, he must have fallen from somewhere in the villa. He was found just below it.'

'In the villa?' Tilda frowned. 'But surely that means that he either worked there or—'

'Was a guest? As far as I know, all us lot were accounted for. So, I presume he must be one of the waiters, or as you said, someone who was working there.'

'How sad. His poor family.' She knew what that felt like and wouldn't wish it on another living soul.

'Indeed. Look, I didn't come all this way to make you feel down. Shit happens, and for once, it hasn't happened to us. We should celebrate our continued existence in this world and remembering how we were wobbling about pissed above a massive drop; we should be celebrating in style. If you think about it, that could have been one of us.'

'Holy crap. You're right. One slip, and that's all it would've taken.' Tilda sat down heavily on the bandstand wall. 'Life is a funny old thing.'

'But death isn't. Come on, Haitch, let's go have a drink and something to eat. Forget the scones and cream. Know any good places around here?'

Tilda shook herself. 'If we go along this road, we'll get to the Serpentine Bar and Kitchen. I've been there a few times, and it's great.'

'That's good enough for me.'

It was as if she'd taken a dozen Temazepam as she walked along the edge of the river with Orpheus. Her feet hovered above the gravel of the road; voices were muted, the sun caressed her face. Spangles of light reflected off the water, becalmed, mostly, except when a gust shimmered over the surface. A memory of Brighton, the swelling waves rushing up and then being sucked back down the shingle in sibilant tones, filled her mind.

The phone beeped. A text message.

Meet me outside the Odeon in Leicester Square at 8.30. I'll explain everything then. D.

A message from Damian. And it wasn't for her now, was it. She stumbled, but Orpheus must have reached out fast to hold her up.

'Are you okay?'

'Could you give me a moment?' Clutching at him, she said, 'Sorry. There's a lot on my mind. But don't worry, I'm fine.' Reluctantly, she pulled away from him and re-sent the text to the phone she'd given to Haitch. That should cheer her up.

'Listen, Haitch, if you want me to go, I'll go. Not gladly, but I'll go.' There was such a look in his eyes that Tilda longed to pull his face down and kiss him.

'Let's get to the bar. We'll talk then. I need to explain something to you.' But would she?

'That sounds serious. Well, I can do serious too.'

They both seemed to be staring at different things as they walked. The Serpentine was beautiful, winding its way through the park but Tilda was now too preoccupied to really see it. She wondered what was going through Orpheus' mind. Did he have any inkling of what she might say? More to the point, what was Damian going to say to Haitch?

TWENTY-FIVE

Haitch

A MESSAGE BEEPED THROUGH. It was sent from her phone. Hang on? Oh yes, Tilda still had it. She must have just received it and sent it through.

Meet me outside the Odeon in Leicester Square at 8.30. I'll explain everything then. D.

Thank fuck for that! It was from Damian. The thought of losing him had forced Haitch to re-assess her feelings. It was like a hard and heavy blow to the stomach. What the hell had caused such a reaction? She didn't love him. That was a fact. He was nearly a stranger to her, but she'd felt bile rise up her throat when Tilda had called to say he was missing. Not presumed dead, although that's how she'd taken it. She'd presumed him dead. That message in the morning had made her feel light-headed, euphoric even. Not that she'd ever admit that to anyone. He was alive. A bloody selfish idiot: but alive nonetheless. Now she was getting ready to meet him this evening, her nerves jangling, her every movement making her clumsy.

Choosing the perfect outfit took a good part of the afternoon. She had to get it right. For him. Leaning her head against the full-length mirror in her bedroom, her breath huffed on the cold, shiny surface. Tempted to write her and Damian's initials on it, she laughed and shook her head. No one was there to see, yet she turned away, embarrassed.

'Dearest God!'

She pulled out her favourite skull and red roses dress. Very fifties with a goth edge. He'd appreciate that. Teamed with her skinny black jeans and biker boots, some spiky jewellery that would look good on a pit-bull terrier, she applied her make-up. While painting on her lipstick, she noticed her hair. Dark brown? Really? Dowdy mouse more like. But hadn't Tilda said that Damian preferred it to her usual white blonde? What exactly did that tell her?

'Shite.' It was too late to do anything about it anyway, so she might as well give it a chance. Tell him she would change it right back if he found the brown too dull. He'd accept that. Checking her phone for any more messages, she locked up. The journey to Leicester Square took longer than she'd anticipated. Tourists jostled and pushed as she was swept along with them. Announcements constantly told her that the train was *ten minutes late* and *sorry for the delay*.

Expecting to meet him outside the Odeon cinema at eight thirty, she was worried that with all the delays on the Tube, she'd arrive after him. Spotting the huge advert for the latest blockbuster against the black-hued building with its iconic block letters, she walked quickly up and scanned through the glass frontage. Groups of people and couples were milling around but no sign of Damian. Good, she wasn't late. Turning, she peered through the fluttering leaves on the trees that were ranged through the square. Lots of people scurrying; business people bearing cases that seemed to weigh them down and tourists licking ice creams and sucking on Coke cans. She glanced at her watch: eight thirty-five. Her head throbbed; her legs were weak. Maybe she should have asked him to come to her? She'd barely recovered from her illness and now had to feign being well, when she felt like shit. Maybe this was a bad idea.

Leaning against a tree, she imagined the lives of the people who passed her. That rotund man wearing a florid Hawaiian shirt with his arm around a much younger Asian woman was a high court judge. His fancy wig and gown had been left back at the courthouse. He'd obviously picked her up in Thailand, as he was too misogynistic to get a real girlfriend. That woman over there was a KGB spy, the children hanging onto her hand a ruse, microfilm in her sunglasses, ricin in her spiked stiletto heel. But, after a while, this game was boring her. How many deposed Eastern bloc leaders and bored runaway princesses could there be meandering through Leicester Square? Rechecking her watch, it read: nine twenty-five.

It was a warm evening in London, and myriad smells burst out: hot concrete, perfumes and after-shaves vying for attention; heavy sweat mixed with sun lotion. She smelled onions sizzling from tiny stalls, spices from nearby restaurants and the reek of alcohol from dull-eyed men waving glass bottles. She watched burgers being stuffed into mouths. She tottered to a bench and sat down, dabbing at the sweat that beaded her hairline. Not a good look.

Haitch didn't want to, but she scanned her watch again. He was over an hour late. Where was he this time? Was this his way of getting back at her? To teach her a lesson?

Right. She was off to the pub now. Damn him!

Busy was not the word that Haitch would use to describe

the pub she'd chosen. Packed from the floorboards to the rafters. Damn. She should've checked first that there was space. Hanging about by the door, she waited ten minutes, as she couldn't be bothered to fight her way to the bar. Her stomach rumbled loudly. A burger would sort her out. Sod Damian. If he turned up now, he'd find she was conspicuously missing. Touché!

Walking slowly down the street a few minutes later, with tomato ketchup dribbling down her hand and probably smeared across her face, she realised that something was happening. It was as if there was a slight time delay when everything slowed down. She could see what was coming, but she wasn't able to do anything about it. Her bag was being wrenched from her shoulder, her grab for it not fast enough as someone barged into her right side.

'Ouch! What the f—' The burger got thrown onto the pavement as she reached to grab the bag back, but they were too quick.

'Oy!' Haitch waved frantically at people circling around her. 'They've just nicked my bag! Someone, stop them.' There were glances, yet no one moved. 'I said "Help!"'

A swirl of kids, now a safe distance away, were rummaging in her bag. Haitch ran towards them, but they were young and sped away from her, dodging through the crowds.

'Someone? Please stop them!' But who was going to take on a gang of kids? They'd probably get done for bashing a minor. It was a crazy game, her running after them, a few elusive steps ahead.

Haitch turned too late as she was bumped hard in the back, her dress was lifted and then whoever it was shot past.

'Here it is,' a wiry mid-teen girl shouted, waving a dark object in her hand and then they were off like greyhounds after a rabbit.

Haitch fumbled at her back pocket. Now Tilda's phone was gone. 'Thieving little bastards!'

Her bag was chucked back at her amidst a great deal of laughing. Haitch scrabbled around to gather all the stuff that had fallen from it. Passers-by stared, although no one came to help her. She huddled in a shop doorway and went through the contents of the retrieved bag. Nothing else was missing. Her wallet, with credit/debit cards and all sorts of bits of information, was still in there, but minus the two twenties she'd tucked in. She'd snatched her set of keys from where they'd nearly skidded off the pavement into a drain. Her Ray-Ban sunglasses were in their case, her small bag of spare make-up untouched, and her stash of painkillers and indigestion tablets were nestled in their side compartment. Only Tilda's phone and some cash had been stolen. That now appeared pretty deliberate. However many times she'd been told not to have her phone in a back pocket, she always kept it there as it was the easiest place to stash it. Believing the dress would thwart potential thieves, she shook her head. Lesson learnt. Ensuring the bag was now tightly done up, she slung it over the other shoulder, so if anyone tried to grab it again, it would take her head with it. Should she phone the police? Well, obviously not on Tilda's phone. And to top it all, she'd lost the burger.

Haitch stopped walking, her legs rubbery. What the hell? Mugged? She leant against a section of wall between two shops, her breathing short and sharp. They may have been kids, but her heart was yammering in her chest.

It took far too long to get home. Key in the door, Haitch hesitated. Groping for the light switch, she slowly closed the door behind her. Imagination is a crazy thing, as she now thought she could smell a new scent. Not hers. She stood still and sniffed. What the hell was going on? It wasn't Tilda's perfume. Hang on? It couldn't be the same person as before, could it? Sneaking about in here while she was waiting like a wally for Damian to turn up.

Shrugging off her bag, she tip-toed into her living room. Again, there was that sense of another person having been there, as if just that moment, they'd moved into the kitchen. Haitch opened the door and peered in. Empty. Rattling at the back door proved that at least it was still locked. That left the two bedrooms and the bathroom. If someone was here, maybe creeping up on them with a large brass candleholder was the right way to go, except if it was Tilda, back early...

Haitch brandished the holder out in front and nudged her bedroom door. Nothing. The spare room, also nothing. That left the bathroom. Sucking in a deep breath, Haitch kicked it open. It hit the side of the bath so hard, it bounced back in her face.

'Ouch and double ouch.' Recoiling, she tentatively rubbed at her forehead. At least the bathroom was empty. 'Jesus. I think I'm losing my mind.' She closed her eyes and sniggered. 'Oh, really? And you're also talking to yourself.' Peering into the mirror, she tutted at the tiny mark that was blossoming on the left-hand side of her head. Please don't develop into a black eye.

Initially, she'd wondered why she kept the landline, it was so old fashioned, yet it was a sort of security for when she'd lost her phone on occasions. Should she phone the police? It was then she realised that it wasn't her phone that'd been nicked. It was Tilda's. Slumping on the sofa, she put her head in her hands and ground at her eyes with the heels of her palms. What a fiasco this whole thing had been, and she wished she'd never set it in motion. If she kicked the coffee table now, she knew it would probably break her toe. It'd been that kind of week. What should she do?

There were still the chocolate biscuits, some of the Galaxy bar and a few slightly bendy Doritos left on the worktop in the kitchen. That would have to suffice until she went shopping properly tomorrow. Returning to the kitchen, Haitch stopped. One of the cupboard doors was very slightly ajar. It'd always been a massive joke to Tilda that her sister had OCD about open doors. Leaving them open on purpose to annoy her was a particular delight when they were growing up. But she knew Tilda wouldn't do that to her now. In the privacy of her own place, Haitch indulged her preference, with no one to take the mick. Every door was always tightly closed. No exceptions. So how could one now be open? It was as if the ground had shifted, as if there'd been a mini earthquake in her flat. Haitch steadied herself. Scanning around, she searched for any other inconsistencies. Again, a drawer not entirely pushed in and the toaster at an angle she wouldn't contemplate. It may be a few degrees, but it was wrong.

Haitch's breathing fluttered. Back in the living room, she focused on every piece of furniture, the few objects on the table and side units, the stuff arranged on the oak shelving in the recesses on either side of the fireplace. It was as if the whole place had been bumped. Not one thing was where it should have been. Very nearly. But not exactly. Had she fallen down a rabbit hole? Maybe the bash on her forehead was more severe than she thought, and if it wasn't, then there had been a person in her house who had touched every single thing she owned. Racing to her bedroom, she placed a trembling hand over her mouth. The duvet was not tucked in the way it should be, the curtains were a little bit ajar, so the streetlight shone in, leaving a bar of light across the plush carpet. Yanking open the drawers in her dresser, she instinctively knew that another's fingers had trailed over her private things, her knickers and bras, her folded t-shirts and leggings.

'Oh, God!' Haitch half collapsed onto the big bed. Think. There was no forced entry, and only two people had a spare key. Tilda was out with that bloke from *The Matrix*. That only left Damian, 'What the fuck are you doing? You arsewipe!'

Tilda. She'd know what to do. Haitch wanted to scream, her control slipping away from her. Could she phone Tilda and beg for help? Was she over-reacting? Would she drag poor Tilda back from probably the only night in, like, forever that she might be having fun?

Bugger!

TWENTY-SIX

Matilda

'Is that the place?' Orpheus pointed. 'The Serpentine Bar and Kitchen?'

'Yep. Come on, I'm dying for a glass of something.'

Orpheus seemed suitably impressed as he gazed up at the building. 'Those are some crazy ass angles. Looking good, Miss Bee.'

Tilda winced at the name.

Glass walled; the diners could sit protected from the vagaries of the English weather but still see the landscape clearly. Today, the clement heat and soft, muted blue sky meant the tables outside were crammed, with chatter and laughter prevalent. Pulling Orpheus through the door, Tilda darted for a free table by one of the immense glass windows. Shaded from the brightness of the day by the tent-like canopy that shadowed the outside terrace, it still had a great view of the lake. The chunky, bare wooden counter was manned by students.

'They have a great selection of pizzas and salads here.' She waved at a board bolted to the left of the bar. 'The menu is chalked up on that blackboard over there. If you prefer, we can order a drink and then decide if we want to eat in a while?'

The young waitress arrived before he answered. 'Erm, a glass of beer and...?' He turned to Tilda.

'The same.'

The waitress reeled off the variety of beers, and Orpheus chose for them both. Again, an unwanted memory slid into her mind. Drinking pints of Punk IPA with Sam that first day she met him.

'Are you okay?' Orpheus leaned across the table and tentatively reached for her hand. 'You look as if you are miles away.'

Tilda gazed at the wall to their side, which was painted a light sage green and hung with paintings of local places and tapped her fingernails on the top of the blonde-wood table. 'I am, kind of. But it's not you, Orpheus. It's me.' Thinking about how that'd come out, she laughed. 'I didn't mean it like that, it's just there's a bunch of stuff I need to talk to you about, and quite frankly, I don't know where to start.'

A golden drink with a hearty head was placed in front of her.

'This is a good place to start.' Orpheus licked his lips and drank half the glass in one swallow. 'Nice.'

'Orpheus?' Tilda smiled. 'Listen, shall we get another drink and order some food? I'm starving. I usually go for the smoked salmon salad. Not too pricey, either. Oh, and this is on me, to say welcome and all that.'

'I appreciate that, but I was going to say it's my treat. For seeing me. I know I didn't give you much of a choice.'

'I could have said no and hidden. But I didn't. So, what does that tell you?'

'You're into stalkers?' He grinned. 'I'm going to look at the board. Be back in a moment.' Prodding his glasses further up his nose, he pushed out from the table to go to the counter. He walked like a large cat, all rolling shoulders and supple hips. Why was life so confusing? Did she like him? Yes. Was he funny? Hell, yes. Did she fancy him...?

'I've ordered another two beers.' The wooden chair creaked as he sat down. 'And I'm going for the Caesar salad. I get the feeling you want to tell me something. Just go for it, Haitch.'

Forcing air through her nose, Tilda said, 'I'm not Haitch.'

It wasn't so much a look of surprise, more of amusement that flitted over his face. 'We all have *nom de plumes*, monikers, handles or whatever you want to call them. You've already told me your name is Harriet.'

'My name is Tilda, well, Matilda. And I'm not saying Haitch is a moniker. I'm saying that she's my sister. In case you still don't get it, my twin sister. That is her name. I'm the one who called her that as I couldn't pronounce Harriet. I'm so sorry, Orpheus, I didn't mean to trick you.'

'Hang on; let me get this right. I met you in Spain, pretending to be your twin? Why?'

'She was sick, and she asked me to take her place at the party. Damian threatened her that if she wasn't at the party, he'd kill her, or whatever. Stupid really, considering I fluffed it for her anyway.'

'You don't know that for sure.'

'Maybe. I get the feeling you don't go against him. He blacked her eye once—'

'Her agent hit her?' Incredulity and anger infused his voice. 'What an asshole!'

'Yeah, but she had some sort of crush on the guy. My sister's weird at the best of times.'

A lithe young thing shimmied over with two more glasses of beer. Cutlery rolled neatly in napkins were laid down.

'Thanks,' said Tilda, grateful for the tiny interruption.

'Okay, then who were you when I met you? Her or you?'

Tilda wet her lips and then took a swallow of beer. 'A bit of both. She's the outgoing one who says what she feels. I'm the one who can remember stuff. You know, the useless stuff.' She sighed. 'Which one did you... like?'

'The one who tells me things I never knew. That one.'

It was as if she'd been wearing a scarf made of lead, that had now been lifted off her shoulders. That meant Orpheus liked her, for being herself, old clever clogs. She raised her head and stared at him.

'I'm not saying you have fluffed it, but what did the real Haitch say when you told her?'

'She was sorry she'd put me through it all. I did expand on how awful it was.'

'I looked up your... I mean her art. You're right. It is quite scary. But that's not what you do. Now, here's my question, what does Tilda do?'

'I'm a kid's book illustrator, classic fairy tales and new modern stories. I use watercolour and coloured pencils.'

'Conservative? Safe?'

'You mean the opposite of Haitch?'

He nodded. 'Married? Kids?' He didn't look like a man who wanted to know.

'Was married. No kids.' Funny how so few words could hurt so much.

'Amicably divorced, or is it pistols at dawn?'

'Not yet divorced and still pretty raw. I'm endeavouring to move on.' Had she said too much?

'Are you succeeding?' His smile was gentle.

'I hope so.'

Two plates of food were placed in front of them.

'Bon-appétit,' said the waiter.

Indicating his left hand, Tilda said, 'I didn't ask if you were married. No ring but that doesn't mean anything these days.'

'Amicably divorced. Amicably because she lives in another country. Moved to Sweden, where she repeatedly informs me, the Swedes have the best quality of life of anywhere in the world.'

'I get those posts on Facebook too. Good for them.' She snorted. 'Let them have their pickled herring and vodka.'

'And there's me thinking my diet needs to be improved.' Shovelling some of his salad into his mouth, he continued. 'My mum's Jamaican, and she does a mean goat curry with rice 'n' peas.'

'My mum's Scottish and does a horrible haggis.' Grinning, Tilda shook her head. 'I'm not being rude, and she knows it.'

They finished their meal in silence, yet it seemed as if it was a companionable silence, not strained and claustrophobic. Had he accepted what she'd told him, or was he mulling over the longer-term consequences of her 'confession'? It was too early to say.

The light was dimming outside, the sky melting from a deep Prussian blue to softest lilacs and pinks, the lake tipped with splashes of gold. A figure slipped between them, and with an oven lighter, lit the tea-light in the frosted glass jar in the centre of the table. It looked a bit incongruous, with the plastic bottles of ketchup and the cubed sugar in Kilner jars nudged to the far corner by their elbows.

'I hope you enjoyed your meals?' The smile from the waiter was genuine enough as he piled the plates onto his arm and took their empty glasses.

'Great, thanks,' said Tilda, watching him dance nimbly to the kitchen and return quickly to light the next couple's table. Tilda leant over and whispered: 'Might get a tip after all.'

'Fancy a coffee and maybe a liqueur that doesn't involve citrus fruit?'

Tilda leant back in her chair and patted her stomach. 'I've

already eaten too much, but I'm sure I could fit a bit more in. Cappuccino for me and I think a Bailey's.'

Orpheus caught the eye of a waiter and ordered. 'And I'll have an Americano and a brandy.'

'How cosmopolitan we are.' She raised an eyebrow. 'I'm being sardonic.'

'I'm American, so I don't even know what that means.' He tilted his head. 'Cosmopolitan, not sardonic.'

TWENTY-SEVEN

Matilda

TIME PASSED RIDICULOUSLY FAST. The nervous fluttering in her stomach was either to do with the strong coffee she'd had this late or, more likely, what would happen when they left the restaurant. Revelations aside, they'd had a friendly dinner together: had a laugh, passed information back and forth, so got a feel for the other person. What would come next? Tilda asked for the bill and paid it.

'At least let me leave the tip,' said Orpheus, laying a ten-pound note on the tray.

'That's a lot for what it cost,' said Tilda. 'Do you want me to break it for you?'

'Nah, they earned it.'

Gathering their belongings, they slipped out the main door. Lamps strung down the road shone with muted light across their faces, the still waters of the lake reflecting the lamps' soft glow. Having neglected to ask if he'd got anywhere to stay for tonight, she was searching for a way to inquire without it being too forced when the phone rang.

Tilda didn't recognise the number, but it might be important. 'Do you mind if I take this? I'll be quick.' He nodded.

'Tilda, you're not going to believe this. I've been brought in for questioning by the police. Damian. He's dead. He's fucking dead! I'm in the nick. I can't believe it. You've got to get me out of here.'

'Damian's dead?' She had to clutch hold of Orpheus.

'They found his body near the villa. They don't think it was an accident or suicide, and they're asking me all sorts of questions. Me! You've got to help me, Tilda.'

'That's horrible and unbelievable, but what's it got to do with you?' Tilda saw white lights spiralling at the edge of her vision. That man's body, on the mountainside below the villa. It was him! It was Damian. 'Did you say they've arrested you?'

'No but they're being pretty hard core.'

Holy shit! She'd only left a few hours ago, and now her sister was down the police station. None of this made sense.

Haitch's voice wavered. 'How can they think I had anything to do with it? I wasn't even fucking there! This is crazy. And to top it all, I got mugged in Leicester Square by kids. They nicked the phone you gave me. I don't understand what's going on.'

'They've got the wrong person.'

'I know. I can't stay here. I haven't done anything.' Her voice was muffled for a moment.

'Haitch? Are you there?'

'Listen, Tilda. When I got in tonight, it felt as if someone had been in my flat. Things have been moved about. You know I notice shit like that. When I told the police they waved it off like I was making it up. I need you to go back to my flat and have a nose about.'

'I'll get a lawyer for you if it becomes necessary. Did you bolt your back door?'

'I don't know, maybe.'

'I'm going to have a look at your flat. You said things had been moved about. I have an idea. I'll get back to you.'

'Don't leave me here.'

'I'll sort it, Haitch. Trust me. Hang on, where have they taken you?' Tilda's breathing was heavy, as if she'd been running, as she memorised the station Haitch had been taken to.

'I know,' said Orpheus, 'that I was eavesdropping, but do the cops think Haitch had something to do with what happened to Damian?'

'She said she thinks someone was in her flat. I think she's been set up.'

'Well, der! Unless you murdered him...' Orpheus cleared his throat. 'This isn't good, is it?'

'No.'

Orpheus frowned, 'Haitch wasn't there. You were with me most of the night, and I don't think you have reason to kill a man you barely knew. So why would anyone do this to her?'

'A vendetta? Some crazy sod she's pissed off?'

'Does she piss people off?'

'All the time.'

'Enough to frame her for murder?'

Tilda ground one heel into the floor and said quietly: 'That really depends on what she's done, doesn't it.'

'Think about it. Somebody sent those texts to you, well, Haitch, but it couldn't have been Damian due to...'

'Him being dead?'

'Yes. That.' Orpheus shook his head. 'You said you need to go to her flat?'

'I need to check something. I know you didn't come all this way to get caught up in shit like this, but would you come with me? Say no, and I'll understand.'

'Of course, I'm coming. It might be very dangerous. Whoever is doing this, they've already killed one man.'

Tilda chewed on her bottom lip. 'We can slip in via the fire escape. I don't want to be seen going in.'

'Okay. You think someone might be watching the flat?'

'Exactly.'

'That's pretty scary.' He stared at her. 'I'm still in, though.'

———————

Having told the taxi driver to stop two streets up, Tilda and Orpheus cut around the back and entered the garden through a high wooden gate. It was locked, but Tilda had a key. The neighbour's large basement flat had the main garden, though a narrow path, bordered by box trees, snaked up to the fire escape that led to Haitch's roof terrace on the first floor. It wasn't a large space, enough for a few potted plants that always looked a little uncared for, a lounger and the ubiquitous Ikea table and four chairs. Haitch wasn't one for entertaining at home. Using their cameras as torches, they crept up the metal staircase, careful not to make any noise.

'I've got her back door key but if she's left the bolt on,' said Tilda, 'then we'll have to go in the front door...' The back door opened, and she pushed inside. The kitchen didn't look any different from when she'd been there earlier. But she also sensed that everything had been opened and then closed again. Was that simply the police?

'What are you looking for?'

'I need to check one thing, then if I'm wrong, I have to rethink.' The laptop was nowhere to be seen but there appeared to be a small amount of water on the desk where it normally sat. 'The police must have taken her laptop. And look, there's water everywhere.'

'Is that what you were expecting?' Orpheus was hanging over her shoulder.

'Yes. Think about it, Orpheus. We know that whoever it is that's setting her up must also be the person who killed Damian.' She swallowed loudly. Those words shouldn't come out so easily. 'Haitch said she'd been mugged by kids. One of them grabbed her phone.'

'Her phone?' Orpheus nodded.

'The phone I'd given her, as I had to take her phone to Spain with me. What if they'd been specifically told to get it?' said Tilda. 'They wouldn't know that it wasn't hers, it was mine... so, that means there must be something incriminating on her phone.'

'The one you had at the villa—'

'The one I was taking pictures with that night. They think I might have pictures of them or whatever.'

'And you think they've also done the laptop?'

'They must think Haitch would have downloaded the images by now.'

'So, the phone and the laptop. They must really believe that Haitch had something on them.'

Orpheus rubbed at his mouth. There was a strange look on his face. 'Tilda? Remember when we were in the villa gardens? You dropped that stone and counted with your pink elephants.'

'We heard something...'

'Something heavy hit the ground a moment later.'

'Oh, my God! Do you think that was Damian? Were we there when he was murdered?'

Orpheus wrenched off his rucksack and undid it. 'Have you got your, or I mean, Haitch's phone on you?'

'Yes, why?'

'We can download the pictures right now onto my laptop and have a look at them.' Pulling out a laptop from the bag he'd been carrying, he unzipped the cover. The power cable followed. Tilda got out her phone. The download took forever. She turned away, her leg jiggling of its own accord.

'There we go.' Orpheus hummed something under his breath as Tilda turned back. 'Lots of shots out in the garden. Sit down, and we'll go through them.'

They sat down on the sofa and Tilda was aware of Orpheus leaning close to her as they pored over the laptop cockled on his knees. Clicking through, they examined each photo. The flash had illuminated the garden, revealing things that were hidden from their sight at the time. Giant urns and fountains were lit up.

'Wow! It was stunning, wasn't it?' Orpheus pointed at one. 'Shame I didn't see it for real.'

'Didn't you come through the garden?'

'No, I hopped off the helicopter and was led in through the lower main entrance. I saw the Olympic-sized swimming pool. That was enough for me.'

'I missed that. Damian...' She stopped. 'Damian said he hated flying. It wasn't on his bucket list.'

Orpheus gave her a twisted smile. 'Maybe it should have been, all things considered.'

'It's awful. I still can't believe it.'

'Hang on.' Orpheus pointed to the screen. 'What's that?'

'It's one of the bursts. I'll go through the images one by one. Now let's see...' It was as if someone had thrown a bucket of ice-filled water over her. Goosebumps shot up on her arms. 'Holy shit!' Tilda stared at the photo. The wall where they'd been chatting, shots where she had waved the phone around, something large and dark that got bigger as the photos progressed, that had plummeted from the building nearby.

'What? Let me see.' They were studying one of the final images. 'Is that an arm?'

'Look at the watch. It's Damian's. I'm sure of it.'

'Fuck! He must have fallen right past us, but we couldn't see.'

Tilda scanned through an earlier burst. 'Maybe there's something here.' She'd clicked at just the right moment. Two faces were illuminated. Tilda felt like the floor beneath her feet had turned to quicksand. 'Oh, no. No, no, no, no. No!'

TWENTY-EIGHT

Haitch

There was a heavy rapping on the front door.

'Coming.' Haitch was just about to get into bed. Dragging on a silk kimono, she yanked open the door to find two police officers standing on her doorstep.

'Are you Harriet Boswell?' The officer was tall and square-jawed. Eyes like shards of basalt. Shoulders that could barely fit through the doorframe.

'Er, yes. Can I help you?'

'I'm Detective Sergeant Durrant. We have a warrant to search your home. May we come in, please.' It wasn't a question as he produced some paperwork. He held it all out in front of him.

'What do you mean? Search my home?' Haitch grabbed at the papers but when she squinted down at it all, the words blurred.

'Can we come in, please Miss Boswell.' DS Durrant took a step forward, and it was as if she was facing off with a bulldozer. 'Please wait here with Detective Constable Lanscombe.' He indicated the slender uniformed female police officer stood at his shoulder. 'We have reason to believe that there may be incriminating evidence here that will help us with an inquiry we are currently dealing with.'

'Do what?' Haitch shook her head as another policemen followed them in. 'I'm sorry, but what are you doing here again? What inquiry? I don't understand what you're talking about.'

'We are not at liberty to disclose this information at present.' The officer squinted down at her, then gave a sideways glance to his female colleague.

'Please stay here,' said DC Lanscombe, 'and let them do their work.'

Haitch stared at her. She was about the same size as Haitch, but you wouldn't want to take this woman on. She was statue hard: a mini bulldozer. Stress curled around her like thick smoke. It was stifling, making her breathing catch. Haitch couldn't fault them. They were courteous and thorough. Each drawer they checked was put back, more or less how she wanted it. Every bowl upended was placed in its original position, kind of. All the packets and jars in her cupboards were stacked and in their own areas, sort of. Her breathing was speeding up. What were they doing here? They were going through her stuff as if they were touching her personally. DC Lanscombe, watched her intently.

'You appear to be a little perturbed. Is there anything you need to tell us, Miss Boswell?'

'I have OCD about things being moved.' Haitch dragged in a breath and pointed a shaking finger towards the living room. 'It's a bit of a running joke with my family, except it still upsets me. I've had it all my life.'

'I see.' The officer frowned. 'I'm sure this will be over soon.'

'What are you looking for?'

'I'm not at liberty to disclose that.'

Haitch wanted to shake this supercilious woman in front of her.

A deep voice came from beyond the living room. A man must be in her bedroom. 'Found something.'

Another voice responded: 'Take photos first. Then bag it for Forensics.'

Found something? Haitch pushed forward, the young officer hanging onto her elbow 'Forensics? What the hell is going on?' She pulled free of the officer. 'Get off me.'

'You need to remain calm.'

'I am calm, except there are strange men in my home rummaging through my things, and I don't know why.'

DS Durrant grunted, 'Take the computer, too.'

There were noises from inside the room. 'Ah!' said a voice. 'I think we might have a problem.'

Scuffling sounds ensued, until DS Durrant said, 'Okay, bag it and we'll do what we can with it.'

DS Durrant walked back into the hallway. 'Harriet Boswell, we'd like you to accompany us down to the station for questioning.'

'Sorry? What did you say?' She must've misheard. The words didn't make sense. 'What about?'

'We'd like to talk to you about the death of Damian Montgomery.' DS Durrant's face remained passive. You can't say something such as that and not show any emotion. Can you?

'Please tell me you're joking?' Haitch had to steady herself against the living room wall. 'Damian's not dead. I've just been to meet him...'

'Have you indeed? And did you meet him? Can you tell us where he is?' Durrant leant in. A peppermint aroma wafted over Haitch. Glancing down, she noted yellow stains on his fingers.

What the hell was happening?

'He didn't turn up. Listen, I can show you the texts he's sent me. I've got them on my phone.'

'We'll get to that in due course. Please can you hand me your phone and follow DC Lanscombe.'

Haitch stepped back and held out her hands. They were shaking. 'Is this a reality show? Is there a celebrity compère going to jump out and shout "surprise"?'

'No, Miss Boswell. This is as real as it gets. There's a police car outside, and we'll drive you to the station. You can make your phone call from there.'

'I'm not going to the police station as I haven't done anything. Damian is alive.' She backed into the wall. 'And I was just about to call you to say someone broke into my flat tonight—'

'I believe you have just returned from visiting Castilla Mori in southern Spain?'

'I, what, er... yes.' Haitch closed her eyes for a second. What could she say? No, sorry, that was my sister impersonating me. How could Damian be dead? 'It's not true. He's alive, I tell you. Look at the messages on my phone. A dead man couldn't have sent them. And did you hear what I said? There's been someone in my flat—'

'Rather convenient, wouldn't you say? Why didn't you call us immediately?'

'I was going to...'

'This way, Miss Boswell and again, please can you give me your phone.'

Haitch stopped. 'Oh shit!' She looked at the officer, who was staring at her with a flat, unsmiling face. 'It's been stolen.'

'Really. So, the phone you say has evidence that a dead man is still alive has been stolen from you. When was that, Miss Boswell?'

'This evening. I was going to meet him. Damian told me to meet him.' Her voice was rising.

'Again, rather convenient.'

What the fuck was going on here?

'No! No! My sister sent the message to me. It's on her phone.' Haitch saw the officer's expression. How did that sound to her? Guilty as charged. The floor was shifting under her feet. They were leading her out to a car with flashing blue lights. This couldn't be real. *Oh, God! Don't let this be real!*

'Please follow me, Miss Boswell.'

'Am I under arrest?'

'You are being brought in for questioning. That's all you need to know.'

PART II
The Bereaved

TWENTY-NINE

Sam

Tuesday April 5th – three months earlier

WORK HAD BEEN a right old nightmare. Renovating other people's either very expensive or most beloved artwork takes nerves or, as Old Gazza says, 'balls of steel'. Today had been one hell of a ride. They all had their specialism and passed work backwards and forwards, depending on who was best for the job, but Jeez! You know, sometimes the boss should turn stuff down. He wasn't stupid and knew what they could and couldn't deal with, but oh yeah, it was all to do with the 'readies'. The website explained carefully that they had to, 'assess the condition or damage' before assigning a specialist. Like fuck! Cleaning oil paintings. Tick. Tobacco stains. Tick. Water damage. Tick. Fire damage? Cross. Cue blarey old air horn.

'You might as well repaint the whole thing from scratch.' That's what Sam told him, Mr Finnegan, the esteemed proprietor of 'Fine Art Restoration'.

'Well, Sam. You could offer your services as a fine art copyist?' He steepled his fingers whilst leaning on the heavy oak table in his office. 'Or you could just do the sodding job.'

After the day from hell, he came home hot, bothered and pretty cranky. It felt good to close the door behind him. He vaguely remembered something Tilly had told him but couldn't recall what.

Dumping his bag by the hall table, as usual, Sam slung his jacket at the coat hook, but it missed. He didn't bother to pick it up. He was in that kind of mood. Somehow expecting to be alone, he was looking forward to cracking open a couple of tinnies, eating a microwaveable ready meal from the freezer and then diving into the rest of that bottle of Glenfiddich. There wasn't much left, so it needed to be drunk. He'd made sure the ice cube tray was filled last night.

Sam heard a noise upstairs.

'Tilly?' He could have sworn she was supposed to be out tonight.

'Come upstairs.'

'Okay.' Bugger. That whisky was sure calling to him. 'I'll be up in a mo.' She was on one a bit at the moment. He wasn't sure what was going on – cleaning out cupboards and ironing their knickers and pants. Weird. If she suggested they fill their evening hoovering, he was off down the pub pronto.

'Come up now,' she called. There was something in her voice.

His fingers twitched towards the living room and the drinks cabinet. Could he neck a hasty shot before going up? Would she notice? What was he? A man or a mouse? Sauntering into the living room, he quickly poured out a shot. The ice cubes would have to wait, as would Tilly. The golden liquid burned as it went down, and there was a loosening of the muscles across his shoulders. He stretched and felt a vertebra pop. That was great as long as he hadn't slipped a disc. All he needed was another twelve shots, and he might feel human again.

'There you are.'

Turning, he nearly dropped the glass when he saw her. 'Tilly?' Did his voice just squeak? 'Wow, Tilly,' he said again, lowering his voice. 'What's, er, what's the occasion?'

Christ Almighty! Had he missed their anniversary or her birthday or what? Hair softly curled, make-up provocative, her summer dress unbuttoned to show the lace of her bra. Was that a new bra? In her best shoes, the pointy ones with dagger heels. She never forced herself into those unless it was a high day or a holiday.

'Does there need to be an occasion for me to get a little dressed up?' Again, that little throaty sound. So sexy.

'No.' Was this a trick question? What had he forgotten? 'But there usually is.'

He watched suspiciously as she poured more whisky into his glass and then poured one for herself.

'I'll get some ice.' Her hips swayed away from him and into the kitchen, leaving him standing with his tongue hanging out. He tried to roll it back into his mouth. Returning with the glasses now clinking, she took a sip. She didn't drink whisky. What the hell was going on?

'Ugh.' Her nose wrinkled. 'Not nice. I don't know how you can drink this stuff, Sam.' The way she said his name made his hair stand on end. She tipped the rest of her glass into his. The drink splashed onto his hand.

'Ooopsy,' she said, bending down to lap it off with tiny motions of her tongue. It was as if he'd been buzzed with a cattle prod, electricity was shooting through him. There was so much blood thumping in his head and coursing through other places;

it was a wonder he didn't pass out. He had no other option but to gulp the drink in his shaking hand and hold it out for more. This was a game they hadn't played before, and he was unsure of the rules. Did she want him to throw his glass over his shoulder and grab her, thrusting his tongue into her mouth before thrusting something else? If that was the case, he'd better slow down on the booze. He needed to see some clear signals here.

Taking a step back, she undid more of the buttons on her dress and sort of caressed the top of one breast. Looking at him through her lashes, the tip of her tongue licked her bottom lip before she bit it a little. He wanted to jump on her now, rip off her clothes and smother her in kisses, but he held back. Christ! Had she been watching porn on the quiet then? Why hadn't she done that with him? Ah, it was a surprise. His beautiful but slightly naive wife had been mugging up on sex techniques for him. She reached for his trousers, which had gone quite tight, unzipped him and held him in her hand. Licking her forefinger, she slipped her other hand down the back of his boxers and rubbed at his anus. She'd never done that before.

'Mmmm.' An appreciative sound.

As she bent down, he stuttered: 'Tilly? You look fabulous, but you don't have to impress me, love.'

'Impress you?' She rose to stare at him. 'I don't want to impress you. I want you to feel like you've had the best sex ever.' Her eyes were reproachful as if he'd ruined the moment by quibbling. She yanked herself out of his trousers. What the fuck was he doing? Just shut up now and enjoy it.

'Sorry.' He shook his head. 'Didn't mean to be a damp squib. Just frazzled from work.' He grinned at her. 'Come on then, Mrs Green. Let's go.'

Her hands were on his shirt, tugging at the tie and flicking open the buttons. The shirt was off, thrown onto the living room floor, and her nails digging into his chest, tangling in his chest hair. Then she gripped the back of his head and pulled his mouth to hers. She tasted different. Something she'd eaten...

Up the stairs, tripping over each other, onto the bed. It was fantastic, so different, so dirty, so not like Tilly. He was not holding back. Full throttle. He heard himself, the grunting, wild noises. Lost in it. He didn't know the exact moment when he realised that she wasn't his Tilly. The animal senses had taken hold, and his dick was in control, overriding all conscious thought. But it filtered through slowly: drip, drip, drip. The twin's faces were identical, yet they each had expressions that were uniquely theirs. The way one raised an eyebrow, the other brushed her hair from her face. The way his Tilly looked at him, really looked at him – it was like a pail of writhing eels thrown over him. The woman undulating under him opened her eyes, and he saw a doppelganger with his wife's face gazing up at him in rapture.

Haitch? Sam froze, half pushing himself up from her perfumed and oily body.

'Sam. Oh, man, keep going. I'm nearly there.'

'Tilly?'

'Oh, don't stop, babe.'

'Oh, fuck!' He pulled out of her and rolled to the other side of the bed. 'Tilly never says, "oh man" and absolutely never calls me "babe". What the fuck is going on?'

Her eyebrows knitted together in one angry line across her forehead. 'What the hell are you doing? Come on, Sam.' She tried to reach for him, but he squirmed away from her. 'What's the matter? I called you babe, is that it? I'm trying out new things. If you don't like it, I won't say it again.'

His brain was sending messages, but his dick and hard balls were rioting against them. He was in bed with his wife, so what's not to love? Except now, he didn't think she was his wife.

'Give me a moment.' Holding his hand up against her, she ducked under it and slid across the bed to nuzzle his neck; soft licks felt against his throat.

'Don't you like it?' Her face was inches from his own. Haitch's face.

'Haitch?' If it wasn't her, his balls would be served with dinner that evening.

'What?' She scooted up to the headboard and leant against it. 'What did you say?' There was something in her eyes. Was it fear? It should be.

'I know you're Haitch.'

'That's a terrible thing to say. I'm your wife! I can't believe that you could ever think that my sister—'

'Prove it.'

'I don't need to prove—'

'I think you do. Show me the scar I gave you.'

'What?'

'Come on, you know the one.'

'When did you ever give me a scar?'

'When we went to Morocco, and I asked you to do a mountain walk with me. I knew you didn't want to, but you did it for me. You slipped and gashed the top of your leg. But then I shouldn't have to tell you that now, should I.'

The woman who wasn't his wife lounged against the headboard. 'You know I haven't got that scar.' She smiled so sweetly; a wave of nausea washed over him. 'But you enjoyed it, didn't you? With me.' Her smug face had that 'cat with the cream' look.

Shaking his head in disbelief, he couldn't even mouth the words that were pounding to be let out of his throat. *Fucking bitch.* He had betrayed his wife with the woman who looked the same as his wife. If it wasn't so awful, he'd be in stitches, rolling across the bed, holding his sides...

Finally, some words crawled out. 'How could you have done

this to Tilly? Your own sister?' He tugged the covers up over himself so she couldn't see his shrivelled dick. 'Your own twin. I thought you were Tilly.'

'I thought you'd be up for it. When we're alone, when Tilda's in another room, you're always joking and mucking about—'

She thought he'd be 'up for it' or some such shit? He wanted to smash her face in, but she looked so much like Tilly that all he could do was sob, wiping at the tears on his cheeks. He'd only ever cried in front of Tilly.

The words morphed and swirled around the room as if they were a toxic breach. Sam said something like: 'I'm your sister's husband, for Christ's sake.' Other words poured out.

That look on her face as if she was puzzled. Why should she be puzzled? He wiped the wetness from his face. A cold cramp crept across his chest. Had he ever given her cause to think he would want this? She told him that he must have thought about it. Had he? Why would he? He already had the most amazing woman he'd ever met in his life. It's already changed to 'had'. Past tense. Please, God! This can't be happening. Maybe if he bashed his head hard against the wall a few times, he might wake up.

Her voice was strangely calm. 'You can't tell her, Sam. It'll destroy her.'

He nearly laughed. 'You've destroyed her.'

In all this, he asked her why? Why did you do this? He focused. His hand was around her throat. Squeezing. How had it got there? She scrabbled at him, though his fingers remained clamped. Pupils widened. Voice rasping. She said that Tilly wondered if he'd notice the difference.

Her words came out of the mist: 'That she didn't know if you could tell us apart. She thought you wouldn't be able to.'

'Well, I did.'

'Eventually.'

That stung. Eventually. As Sam's grip loosened, she pulled from him. Red welts mottled her skin. Haitch's fingers tentatively touched where his had been.

'I was tired from work,' Sam said, 'but then I saw you, all dressed up, and I thought how brilliant that my wife wants sex on a weekday. I wasn't going to question that in case she thought better of it.' He stopped. Stared at her. 'You've even changed yourself to make you look like her. This was all planned. You did this to her, to us, on purpose.' This vile creature in front of him smelt the same as his wife, was dressed in his wife's clothes, even had the same hair colour. Now. Premeditated. Anger bubbled up from deep in his gut; his fingers itched to find that slender throat again and snap it. *Snap it as if it was a rotted twig.*

He couldn't think straight. 'I need you to get the hell out of my house, Haitch. Right now.'

'I'm so sorry, Sam. I really thought you wanted this.' Her face looked baffled and then worried.

Christ, she was getting into Tilly's clothes, walking across the landing, trailing her hand against the wall, as if she was unsteady. What would happen if he shoved her down the stairs, kicked her hard? But she'd half fallen down the stairs herself... Did that hurt? He hoped so. Clutching at the front door handle, she turned to look up at him.

His head was filled with Chinese crackers – popping, fizzling, and so bright. He scrabbled at the wall. Had she said that? *I really thought you wanted this.*

'Not in this lifetime.' It was barely a croak.

'What are you going to do?'

'I have no idea.' That was the God's honest truth. No fucking idea whatsoever.

'You can't tell her.' Was she whispering? Why? Who else was there to hear?

'Get out!' He was an animal, a wild beast; all his senses opened. Her nostrils flared like a frightened horse; he could smell her sweat, see her shaking, white-knuckled hands, her eyes were wide. Could he kill her now? Did he have that in him?

'You can't tell her.'

Had his head exploded? Ripping the door open, he pushed her out with the last strength he had. She missed the front step and fell. Blood on her knee. There should be blood everywhere.

'Don't come back. Ever.'

He had to slam the door before the rage clawing to get out made him do something he might regret for the rest of his life. Perhaps it'd be worth it.

Oh, God, Tilly! Slumping behind the door, he rocked, his arms tight about him, letting the tears fall. She wouldn't comfort him this time, would she?

What was he going to do? Somebody please tell him what to do.

THIRTY

Dawn

'SHOULD HAVE SEEN IT COMING.'

Amazing how many folk had uttered these droll words to her over the years.

'Ha, ha,' Dawn laughed, with a forced rictus of a smile. 'Maybe I did. Maybe, I have to let certain things just be. You know?'

Of course, they don't. People like her, 'they' told her, were all charlatans and swindlers: grifters and con artists. Preying on the exhausted and vulnerable, vampiric teeth plainly seen, imbibing like a fine-wine the last vestiges of humanity from the soul-dead by, God forbid, offering them 'hope'. How many conversations has she had with people who apprised her of the fact that she was 'disgusting and a bald-faced liar'? Too many to count on her fingers and toes alone. *This little piggy went to market.* Until they crept back to her, disguised with fear and a heavy heart to ask the questions they believed she couldn't answer. As if it were all a deception, though they had to try anyway....

Then there were the devotees, cramming themselves until

they were bloated with the paranormal, gorged full to the point where they would no doubt vomit ectoplasm all over the carpet. *Rings on my fingers and bells on my toes.*

It was no concern of hers if you gave credence to it or not. What is, is what is. The 'gift' didn't pop out of thin air when one was shopping in Marks & Spencer. No 'Saul on the road to Damascus' moment. They were born with it. Although, it might more easily be termed a 'curse'. There was no getting rid of it, no turning a blind eye, no ignoring it. Imagine that you wake up as a small child to see people clustered around your bed? Imploring you in reedy voices to do something for them? Freaked out? Hell, yes.

How did she meet Damian? Being a non-believer, he heard about her talents and came one day to test her out. Now Damian was never one to let 'the wool be pulled over his eyes'. Too much of a sceptic to be hoodwinked by a girl, precocious, to be sure, but still so young. Managing a boy band of pretty faces with monster egos but zero ability was beginning to pall. That's what he told her. It was obvious they would never make it past the car park, let alone the barriers at the 'Britain's Got Talent' shows. Casting his eye about to find a better source of income, it fell on her, Dawn Rayne. She'd been raised in Old London Town but with Basque blood running through her veins. Back in the early seventeenth century, she would undoubtedly have been burned as a witch. That area had a nasty bout of witch-hunts, which probably propelled her female forebears to seek a safer climate.

Although not in the public eye, he told her she was the 'real deal'. How did Damian know this? She told him incidents he couldn't refute, unable to wipe the incredulity from his face when she cast her eye to the other world and whispered details into his ear. Keeping her mouth shut wasn't an option when the channelling began, but she did have some semblance of control.

There she found the 'fear'. Not to be confronted. That was not asked for. Irrational, so never to be mentioned. A hark back to a medieval era and to his overly superstitious mother and not to be sanctioned in this modern world.

'You won't tell anyone, will you.' It was a statement.

'Who would care?'

Damian's eyes were fire-glow bright. 'Me, and I would not be happy.' Maybe there was a clue there, but she was blinkered by love or infatuation.

Married within six months, she loved him beyond endurance and truly believed that he loved her for a while: his exotic and other-worldly wife. The move to 'manager' was seamless. Negotiating gigs, venues, prices was instinctive to him.

'Your 'gift' is not a piece of merchandise,' said her mother. 'It's a special thing, a relationship with another existence and should not be treated as a commodity.'

'I've told him all this,' Dawn said. 'He thinks we should open it up to more people.'

'Please tell me you're not advertising on the internet?'

She had to turn her face away.

'Shame on you, Dawn. Well, I warn you now. Wherever your powers came from, they can be taken away, just as fast. You're not supposed to use them as if you're one of those fake American spiritualists who have hidden cameras, microphones and internet searches on all the poor folk who attend their rallies—'

'You know I don't do anything like that—'

'Maybe not, but I don't doubt that your precious Damian wants you to. He's more interested in what he can get out of you than you yourself. If you remember, I told you that before you went and married him.'

'I remember. I made my bed...' What else could she say?

Married to Damian for ten years, eight months and seven

days. He may have been ten years older in real life, but in terms that counted, she was the same as an ancient oak peering down at an acorn. And he knew it. The buzz he got from what she did faded over time, barely a 'blip' anymore, as far as she could see. Especially after the missing girl case. Poor little Emily. Only nine years old. Dead, dead, dead. He wanted her to do more such cases. She'd said 'no'. Damian wasn't a man you say 'no' to.

'After everything the police did,' he said, 'they had to turn to you, and you delivered the goods. Dawn, think about how many other poor sods are out there, with missing children, friends and family. They'd give their eye-teeth to have knowledge of what happened to them. You can give them closure. The same as you did with little Emily.'

Little Emily.

She'd already located Laura the teenage runaway, which wasn't hard as the girl had plainly bunked off with her boyfriend to his dad's place in Wales. Quite frankly, any idiot should have been able to work that one out by simple sleuthing and checking on the known facts. The whereabouts of the kidnap victim Megan was a trickier proposition. But she'd asked the right questions of her 'others' and was rewarded with an answer. Megan was discovered unharmed but severely disturbed and who wouldn't be? She was returned to the loving and somewhat gobsmacked bosom of her family and to the clutches of the mental health profession.

Little Emily was different. Believed dead. Presumed murdered. Remains not found. Family distraught. They procured her services after the police had hit the wall: no leads and no more clues. Sometimes the information Dawn received was fragmented, but this time it was as clear as watching a film in full colour. She wished it hadn't been. She pretended to use some of Emily's possessions as a focusing tool; it somehow made it look more authentic to the casual observer.

Seeing what had befallen little Emily as if she had been there. No one should ever experience that. Neither of them. Don't ask, she thought. Please don't ask how she died.

'I can't see the details of her death, although I know where she is.' Trying not to weep in front of the ashen-faced parents. Oh, how good a liar she'd become. At least they had the closure they sought.

How could Damian ask her to go through that again, not just once but over and over? The terror and suffering. The exquisite death that leads to the light and hopefully to peace. But not for her.

His fists came out of nowhere. Hitting where it did damage but not so much that others could see it. Practised. Like his remorse. All those 'sorry, sorry, sorry' and the great fat crocodile tears.

'I love you, Dawn. I love you so much.'

Trouble is, she loved him too.

THIRTY-ONE

Sam

Wednesday April 6th

SAM HEARD HER COME IN. His Tilly. He heard her come in and normally felt such joy, but this wasn't normal, was it? He felt a weight of lead heavy in his gut, as if he'd swallowed a cannonball. He had some semblance of a story, yet could he go through with it? Why should he? His word against her cheating bitch hearted sister's. But that was the point, wasn't it? Against the word of her twin. Her other half, if obviously not her better half. As Haitch said, it would destroy her. Hate is a word rarely used properly. He hated brussels sprouts. No, he disliked eating them; they tasted disgusting. He truly hated Haitch, though. Despised her. Was revolted by her and all those other words that could never convey this roiling storm in his heart. Now she was linked with his beautiful Tilly, and he was having trouble disassociating one from the other.

'Sam? Are you home?' Such innocence and lightness in her voice. That was about to come crashing down.

'Tilly?' Sam crept down the stairs, the holdall slung over his shoulder. She spotted that first. 'I need to talk to you.'

'Are you going somewhere?' A flicker in her eyes.

'Come into the living room, and I'll tell you.' Tell her what? One of the stories he'd planned during the night, while she'd been away? The night that'd changed their lives forever.

'Sam? Is there something wrong? You're kind of frightening me.' She shadowed him into the room on his heels. 'Sam?'

This she understood and was prepared for. That's what he'd told himself over and over again through the long, exhausting night. Her sister's betrayal wasn't. She'd be flayed and gutted, with no understanding why.

He hadn't given her his customary hug and kiss. Usually, he'd give her a quick touching of the lips or a brief encircling of arms. Of course, there was something wrong. Which story? Which story? Which of the people she loved the most will rip her apart? Him. It had to be him.

'Tilly, I don't know how to tell you this, so I'm going to say it fast. I've got to go, Tilly. I never meant to hurt you in any way but—' the lie was so big it physically hurt his throat to get the words out. 'I've found someone else. I've tried to make it work between us, but I can't. It's over, Tilly.'

She froze. Her breath stuttering in and out, yet there was no movement. As if she'd died and was still stood up. Sam shook that image from his mind.

'Did you hear me, Tilly?' Christ! He wished he could smash his head against the living room wall until it dripped with blood and the pain was gone. He'd worked it back, thought through how he'd feel if she told him this same story. His conclusion wasn't good, and he'd made sure this morning all sharp implements were tucked away. One sister has skewered his soul, and he didn't want the other stabbing him in his real, live, beating heart.

'What?' She dropped her bag and clutched at her temples as if he'd physically hit her. Don't break down. Don't tell her the truth. She'd never survive it. She'd told him when they'd first got together about the men who always left her. In the dark, early, drained hours of this morning, it occurred to him that this may be something that'd happened before. Had Haitch been the reason that all Tilly's boyfriends had fled? Had she had a piece of them and then spat them out, leaving them repelled or simply confused? Haitch did things Tilly wouldn't do, offered up bits that he knew would be too much for his sweet Tilly. Was Haitch the reason that Tilly was so insecure, so lost, so grateful for any love cast her way? It'd taken him years to build up her confidence, and now he was in front of her, willing to smash the core of her to shards.

'Sam? I don't understand what you're saying. What are you saying?' He could hear her heart cracking. As was his.

'I tried, Tilly, but I can't go on like this.' Sam stumbled towards the door. 'You're better off without me.'

That's when the fear hit. 'Don't do this, Sam!' A shriek erupted out of her. 'I don't know what I've done, but don't do this. Please, Sam. I'll make it work, please, please don't leave me.'

'I have to, Tilly. It's for the best.' What a truly weaselly thing to say. How hard it was not to cry, to show emotion. Steel batons strapped across his heart. There was still time to tell her the truth, wasn't there? Watch as her whole world crumbled and the solid ground under her feet gaped.

'I'll call you tomorrow to—' He had to swallow, though the spit got stuck in his throat, 'to arrange things.'

'Sam!' She whimpered noisily and hiccupped. 'Please, Sam, what have I done? Who is this other woman? Sam! Talk to me. Sam!'

Hearing her voice pleading and crying, he wove down the

path to the gate but didn't turn back. If he did, he would never leave. Looking down, Sam saw a patch of rust in the gravel. Blood. From Haitch's knee.

He should've smashed her fucking face in.

THIRTY-TWO

Dawn

DAMIAN WENT to see Haitch and her work at the Brick Lane Gallery. Dawn had visited the week before and been shocked by the raw vitality and oft sauciness, the grandeur and the microdots of mortality sprawled across the canvases and the crazy abstract pieces that Haitch had put up for her show. She must have enthused so much that it caught Damian's imagination. And she encouraged him. What a dolt.

She'd inadvertently put Damian on the scent of Haitch, and she wasn't at all happy about it. The fact was, she wasn't compliant anymore. This new girl would be. Damian's seeming ennui blasted by her work, and afterwards, Dawn realised, her beauty. So very him. Mind blown, he had the audacity to ask Dawn for a reading. About her. About this Haitch woman. So, she slipped into a light trance but kept hold of herself, not allowing herself to be overwhelmed by the information bombarding her consciousness. It was a mess. The cracked and broken imagery whirling in her mind, the sheer white noise of it all. She'd had readings like this before but not ones that were so disruptive, so neural pathway blasting. Truth be told, she was unable to grasp the significance of much of it, except how their lives would intertwine, their fortunes, too. Looking back, she asked herself why she did that reading for Damian? Why did she ask her 'others' his questions?

'Just can't lie, can you, my darling?' She loved it when he smiled at her that way. But what an insincere smile it was. And she kept her tears and her counsel to herself: *you're leaving me for her. And there will be death.* The message engraved on her soul, but it was like looking at the upside-down reflection in a wine glass. Distorted, yes, but still portraying the image it reflected. The refraction of understanding.

Was she, Dawn, already an 'artefact' to him? To be traded in for the 'next big thing'?

'We'll be made for life, my sweet darling,' said Damian, 'if Haitch Bee morphs from the caterpillar she is now, into the butterfly she could well become. Imagine what we'd earn if we market her right.'

'Like you tried to market me?'

'Yes, but you had a mind of your own. You didn't play ball with Daddy, did you.' He teased a stray lock of her honey blonde hair back behind her ear. Could he see the purpling bruises that she'd masked with dark-hued make-up, or did he choose not to?

Dawn tilted her head up. 'If I asked you to do something that would crush your soul, would you do it?'

'For you? In a heartbeat.' He cupped her under her chin. His nails pinched. Dawn resisted the urge to pull from him. 'You are the love of my life. I would do anything for you.'

Get those clichés. Such a predictable man. How could she reconcile that she was the catalyst that destroyed her own marriage? Happiness? Not so much now. Was it inevitable that he would find another muse? Perhaps. Then she'd be that beautiful butterfly, pinned to a board, to be viewed but never to be free to unfurl her wings again. He wouldn't allow it, could never let her go. A solid glass screen between her and the world. What was worse? She'd been so strong once. How had this happened to her?

Is this what it felt like to be buried alive? The enclosure of a still-breathing human into a tiny room with no escape. Dawn could see the final bricks being fitted, and in the last bit of space, Damian's grinning face with Haitch stood behind him.

THIRTY-THREE

Sam

Are they all such sorry specimens that when adversity hits, the first thing they do is turn to the bottle? Looks like it. Sam could see his brother John didn't need to say a word. His face said it all: *what have you done, you idiot?* He knew it could only be to do with Tilly, but John managed to glue his mouth shut while he went to sort out the box room, crammed with all the junk they wouldn't cart off to charity. His wife, Claire, made Sam a 'nice cup of tea' in the kitchen.

'So,' she said staring at the ceiling. She obviously didn't know what to say, either.

Sam didn't intend to break the silence in case he ended up a wailing mess on their floor. He couldn't ignore the fact that they'd opened their door to a wreck. He might be related, but he could barely stand and was clinging to their counter by the sink as if his life depended on it, which it did.

He'd gone straight out to the off-licence after leaving Tilly and bought a bottle of whisky. Down it went without touching the sides. Oh yeah. Good one, Sam. A bit of staggering about and calling anyone in his path a 'fucking dickhead' was closely followed by being picked up by the police. It seemed that he was a nuisance. He got that. He managed to impress them with his ability to get his brother's name and complete phone number out before throwing up across the station floor. Convinced that incarceration would have swiftly been put into effect if his brother hadn't gone into hyper-drive and arrived moments later, expounding on Sam's good nature and offering devout apologies. Spewing the remainder of the bottle he'd drunk over the station steps might have pushed it a bit far, but John had hauled him to the car and folded him into it. At least, that's what he remembered.

'Room's ready.' John came quietly through into the kitchen and eyed his wife. Sam thought he should say something, although he remained silent. Locked.

John continued: 'Do you need anything? We've got a spare toothbrush and flannel.'

'Thanks,' Sam nodded his head vigorously.

'Do you want to talk about it?'

'Not really.' Sam knew he was slurring.

'Okay.'

But out it came regardless. 'I fucked up.' He held his head in his hands. 'Right royally.'

'No, shit.' John tentatively put his arms around his shoulders. They'd never been the 'hug and kiss' type of family. It was understood they loved each other; they just didn't show it physically. So the touch meant a lot. Sam started to cry.

'It's all right, mate. You tell us when you're ready. You don't need to say anything now. Maybe you should get some shut eye, and we'll see you in the morning, eh?'

'Mnnph,' Sam said and crawled up the stairs. The offer of the flannel and toothbrush would be appreciated in the morning, but for now he needed sleep. If that was possible. Claire, who'd followed him up, carefully placed a large shallow bowl by the side of the bed on the floor.

'Just in case.' She patted his shoulder. 'Sleep tight, Sam.'

Sam didn't exactly remember his words, but late that next morning he managed to tell them about the terrible thing that had happened between him and Tilly. They could guess till the cows come home but 'sleeping with his wife's twin' wouldn't ever be one on their list. The probability was that they added two and two and came up with five: that one of them had done 'the dirty' on the other, and their once idyllic marriage was in ruins. Yeah, that was about right, wasn't it? But not in the way they thought.

Hanging upside down over the toilet bowl, he was liberally sick until there could be nothing left inside of him, including his soul. He'd sicked that up and left it stinking between home and here. They called in sick for him. Can't get sicker than this. Sick, sick, sick.

The saying was 'in the cold light of day', but for Sam, it was burning and feverish, with things swirling in his mind he longed to erase.

'We'll leave you alone for a bit, mate.' John had that expression on his face that showed, without words, he was at a complete and utter loss. He wasn't the only one. 'Give you a chance to sort yourself out. We'll get a takeaway tonight, then, if you want to talk, well, you know...'

'Thanks, bro.' Sam waved and smiled as cheerfully as he could in the circumstances. John appeared shocked as he backed out of the room. 'Give yourself time to sort yourself out' equals 'leave you alone with your thoughts'. Sam didn't want to be left alone with his thoughts, not that he wished anyone else was here either. Had they invented a time machine yet? Could he go back far enough to stop this? He mentally played through every scenario where he didn't have sex with Haitch.

If he told Tilly now what'd happened, would she take him back? If he begged forgiveness, grovelled and cried and pleaded? Around and around, he went. There was the small matter of Haitch. Not a friend, and that would have been so hard for Tilly to bear but her twin sister. It wasn't his fault. How many times could he say that? A million? A million and two? This thought kept recurring. Had Haitch done this before to Tilly? Was she the nemesis that Tilly never knew she had? Her very own Moriarty. Would she thank him if he exposed her sister's callous and selfish act? Or would she somehow blame him anyway and ruin all three lives in the process?

FUCK!

———

Endeavouring to compartmentalise his life and get on with the bits that weren't affected was proving tricky. Maybe others could switch off their emotions with ease. He couldn't. That was his opinion, and he was sticking to it. At work, his colleagues weren't fools. They could see there was a major rift in his life, but they didn't ask questions. Or they hadn't. Yet. Once the mistakes started happening, the unspoken question honed down to one: could he still do the job? Answer: no. Not when he'd drunk half a bottle of whisky for breakfast and gargled with a shot or two of vodka instead of cleaning his teeth. Obvious.

Sam hadn't been to see Tilly. He believed if he saw her face-to-face, he would break down and howl the truth to her. Then it would all be for nothing. He had to go through with this. It was a mad mantra, repeated over and over in his head. Should he speak to John? Or Claire, who might be able to put a feminine perspective on all this shit. No. Both John and Clare would advise him to tell Tilly the truth immediately, the whole truth and nothing but the truth.

What happened to his mates? Friends from school and art college? They'd slipped away. Missing in action, presumed lost. Married with kids usually does that. Too immersed in their own lives, jobs, and families to think about him. As he and Tilly had been. He tried not to think about the baby they'd been planning. They'd both agreed to wait until they were financially secure, except the old clock was tick-ticking. He knew Tilly was getting broody. Hormones kicking in. A year or two, max.

How long had it been? A few weeks since that afternoon in real time but a lifetime for him. There'd been a period of numbness, disbelief, followed by dilated hours stretched beyond their mortal limits, when the pain wouldn't cease. He'd hoped night after night that he might not wake up and even when asleep, he dreamt. No escape there.

What was that Hamlet line: 'To die, to sleep – to sleep, perchance to dream – ay, there's the rub, for in this sleep of death what dreams may come...'. He saw such terrible images of faces intertwined, leering, lewd, red-eyed and mouthing words he didn't want to hear. He blocked his dream ears.

A month down the line, Sam was called into the boss's office.

'You wanted to see me, Mr Finnegan.' He'd have to be brain-dead not to know what was coming.

'Sam, ah, yes.' The scratched mahogany desk was piled with contracts and card folders. The man was sceptical of technology. 'We've been reviewing your current progress. Hmm.'

'Yes?'

'Well, how do you think it's going?'

'Brilliantly.'

'Really?'

'No.'

'Sam...' Mr Finnegan shook his head. 'You haven't told us what has occurred, but we're not blind or stupid. Normally, you are an asset, your work is exemplary but...' He wiped at his nose and avoided looking directly at Sam. 'With the way things are going, Sam, you're currently a liability to this firm—'

'I've done bloody good work for you—'

'I know, Sam.' He tapped on the desk with a manicured fingernail. 'And if you let me finish, I'll explain what we are willing to do. You have nearly a month of paid leave that you can take to sort yourself out. We suggest you take it. If you need more, we will accommodate that, but it will be unpaid. You understand?'

'I—'

'No, Sam. You need to listen to me. If you make mistakes in our business, it not only costs us money, but our reputation is shot. There are certain things you don't recover from—'

'Talk to me about it—'

'I am!' Mr Finnegan practically snorted. 'There are obviously things you need to sort out, and you need to do this before we can continue with this conversation. Next time we meet, at a review in a month or so, I want, no, I expect you to say: "Mr Finnegan, everything is coming up roses, and all is fine with the world."'

'And if I don't?'

'You're fired.'

THIRTY-FOUR

Dawn

Friday 3rd June

THE FEAR that was engendered by the reading ebbed, though it had initially blasted her mind to jelly. It was still there but more like an old yellow-and-green bruise that only hurt if you prodded it hard. His version of the prophecy came true. Funny that. Haitch Bee was indeed a butterfly, and they were rich from her endeavours. Dawn hadn't been to any of her exhibitions since that one in the Brick Lane Gallery. She didn't care to see how Haitch had changed. How much of herself she had lost. Lost to him.

Damian still slept in her bed. They went through the motions of making love, but she was never quite 'there' as his neck muscles stuck out like rope and his body spasmed. Not since the day she'd lost the baby.

One punch too hard in the wrong place, that was all it took. Speeding her to hospital, as the blood ran down her legs, he silenced all the spiky and barbed words that could spew from her mouth.

'Say a word, and it will only be worse for you. You know that, don't you, Dawn?'

Only once before that time had he hospitalised her. The questions had been probing. He'd stood by her bed, the caring, devoted husband, as she'd consummately lied. They must have known. But Damian was a virtuoso when it came to 'selling', and he'd sold them the idea that she was a nervous neurotic who self-harmed. It was as though he had her on a rubber band; the harder she pulled against it, the worse the 'twang' was when she was catapulted back to him.

'This was all your fault, Dawn,' Damian said when the bleeding stopped, and she was allowed home. 'You shouldn't have made me angry. We lost our baby because you can't control yourself. You can't behave in a way that is fitting. This is on you.'

And what was her crime? Talking back to him. She'd lost her baby because she'd dared to have a differing opinion. If she'd had a carving knife to hand, she often wondered if she would have imbedded it where his heart should have been.

Why did she stay with him? The reading, of course. Their little 'play' wasn't over until the actors had flourished their last bow, strutting off the stage, the closing chords had been played in the orchestra pit, and the final clapping had abated. She was waiting for the silence.

After she'd lost the baby, she limited her readings to Tarot and Angel cards as they helped her to focus. They were less problematic than direct psychic links. They were always beguiling to the uninitiated. But if she was presented with a pack of playing cards, they would work as well. Of course, the crux was that the seeker wouldn't be so impressed when she'd turn up a King of Spades and told them about their impending change of lifestyle. It hadn't got the same kudos. But it did the job just as well as the beautifully illustrated and mysterious Tarot, with its fearsome 'Death or Devil cards' that, incidentally, never meant what most people assumed. The seekers only needed to listen. She offered glimpses into what was causing their problems, then suggested how to move past them, how to move forward. It's a shame that she couldn't seem to follow her own advice.

Nowadays, Dawn turned down all entreaties from parents with missing kids. 'I told you, I won't touch suspected murders again.' Damian's backhanders and punches showed her how he felt about that.

Whack, whack!

Her email box pinged with heart-wrenching pleas, day after day. She changed her email to a spectacularly unfathomable address, yet still it filled. Then the phone rang and rang, so she went ex-directory, but her number must have been sold on, and it rang again. Reliant on mobiles, there had still been times when she'd answered a random call to discover a sobbing parent on the line: please, just for me. Had Damian something to do with this relentless barrage? Probably. Dawn did a search on herself on the Internet and wished she hadn't. She'd got a moniker. The Hermit Medium. It could be worse, she supposed.

Did she trust Damian? She needed to think about that. Did she trust Haitch? Not in any lifetime. Damian didn't speak about her at their home, although outside of that, he was free with his words, mainly as he no longer talked about Dawn's achievements, which had been a source of entertainment for the previous years.

The amazing Haitch Bee. And weren't people interested,

especially at parties they attended. The 'curious' over cocktails and hors d'oeuvres. This was usually followed by a bout of raging heartburn.

Enjoying a respite, Dawn set herself up a night of special enjoyment. Damian had been called to a meeting in London and wouldn't be home until at least late afternoon the next day. Time for a bottle of Ribera del Duero, a Spanish wine that the Spanish generally kept for themselves and no wonder. Warm, soft, full of ripe flavours. Teamed with a focaccia loaf drizzled with virgin olive oil and rosemary, a large slab of Camembert and a bottle of Queen olives from Greece. A mixing of cultures, but what the heck. It was a Mediterranean blend.

The unexpected voice made her jolt. Wine spilt down her blouse. *What?*

'I've got something pretty big coming up, Dawn.'

A frisson of ice slid down her back. Why hadn't she heard the door opening? Her finger was pushed into the oozing cheese, and an olive bunched out her cheek. Only a quarter of the wine was drunk. She didn't wish to share the rest.

She swallowed noisily. 'That's good.' She watched him as he yanked off his coat and dropped the hold-all on the floor. 'I thought you were staying in London tonight.' Her stomach began to cramp.

'I've had an offer. Quite out of the blue. I mean, absolutely amazing.' He leant over to graze her cheek with a stubbly kiss. She saw him focus on the table. 'What's this?' He peered down at her, and Dawn stiffened. 'While the cat's away, eh?'

'I like this, and I thought I could have a treat.'

'A treat is two fingers of Kit-Kat. Not this heart attack

inducing mess.' He nudged the table hard, and it shifted sideways. The wine bottle teetered but didn't fall. 'If you put on weight because you can't control yourself, I won't be a happy bunny.'

She had to be careful here. 'It's the first time, Damian, and anyway, I missed you. I was comfort eating.'

'Missed me? Did you, darling? I'm sorry, I didn't mean to leave you alone.' He kissed the end of her nose. 'I promise I'll make it up to you. Now pour me a glass of wine. See how much I love you? I'm willing to eat and drink this crap for you to stop you turning into a fat porker.'

'Thanks. I appreciate it.' Dawn envisioned cracking him over the head with the wine bottle.

———

'It's a win-win situation.' They'd, or rather, he'd finished the sex part of their night. At least that was over. Tired from his day, she'd been worried he might not make it, but instead, he'd climaxed fast and seemed content to 'chat' to her.

She didn't like the sound of that. 'How so?' Cuddled into the crook of his shoulder, she nearly felt safe. A mirage for the night. So real, she could almost touch what it might be like to be in a loving, caring relationship. Equals, friends and lovers, companions, whatever. How she longed for that. She should have listened to her mother all those years ago.

'There's this Japanese CEO of a massive company. He's always on the look-out for talent. New talent, different talent—'

'So, he wants talent?'

'Hmmph.' Damian squinted down at her. 'He's compiled a list of people he'd like to attend a select party in Spain.'

'Good for him.' She was conscious of what was coming.

There was a klaxon going off in her head. She wriggled from his embrace and bumped back against the headboard.

'Dawn?' Damian gripped her elbow. 'What the hell is happening?'

'It's going to be in southern Spain, in a beautiful villa. There will be only five of us. Haitch will be there too.'

'I'm not going to ask how you know that. Especially as I don't even know that.' He was quite pale as he stared at her. 'All I know is that you and Haitch will be picked.'

She nodded. The imagery swirling was just out of reach as if it was an old heat burned movie that had been projected onto the ceiling. Scenes flickered and bubbled. There was the taste of metal in her mouth. Maybe she'd bitten her cheek? She poked her forefinger into her mouth and frowned at the blood daubed on the tip.

'There's a lot of money up for grabs.' Damian was breathless in his excitement. 'If Haitch wins, we get our usual cut, but if you win, we get the lot.'

Dawn was still staring at the blood on her finger. 'I think we're all going to lose.'

'Now, don't be like that. If you've got some inside info on how to clinch this deal, let me know now. If not, I don't want to hear it.'

'I can't go, Damian. I'm not that woman anymore. I can't perform party tricks.'

His body stiffened beside her. 'Party tricks? Back in the day, you were the real deal, Dawn. Until you threw it all away—'

Dawn rounded on him. 'It was going to rip out my soul, yet you seem to be okay with that.'

'Listen, my darling girl, you've already seen that you're there. As you said, with Haitch. It's written in the stars; it's your fate or whatever. You don't seem to have a choice, do you?'

There was always a choice. Dawn knew that. The old bruise in her mind was throbbing; images she'd managed to bury deep were re-surfacing. If she warned him, told him only bad things would come of it, would that stop him? No. The future wasn't malleable, and, unfortunately, neither was Damian.

THIRTY-FIVE

Sam

Okay. The 'F' word. Well, the other 'F' word. Fired? From the job he loved? Whose fault was that then? He had a month of paid leave. What was he going to do with it? Drink himself stupid?

Was this when his imagination started to morph into visions of revenge? This foul creature with his wife's beautiful face had not only destroyed his chance of happiness but had probably done it on more than one occasion to Tilly. The more he tried not to think about it, the more he couldn't let it go, like worrying at an ulcer beneath your tongue. It is painful, yet you keep on doing it. An eye for an eye, a tooth for a tooth. Biblical.

Poor John and Claire did their best by him, yet even he could see they were getting to the point where he might be directed to the front door, and the spare key requested back. Possibly, it was this mental picture of vengeance that snapped him out of it. It might be only a kernel at this point, but it was enough.

He'd been with Tilly for nearly ten years. The traditional gift for ten years was tin or aluminium, to show that your relationship was flexible, although they'd only been married for seven. That was copper and wool. He was aiming to get them a copper bowl fire-pit for the garden and a new wool rug for the living room from a designer shop. He'd already picked it out. Geometric and modern. That bitch had stolen all that from them. Stolen the years where they would have watched their faces cave in, grow crepey and wrinkled, wondered at the blue veins that marbled their skin, commiserated with each other at the aches in joints, the need for stronger glasses, the forgetting where the 'wotsit' was and finally what the 'wotsit' was in the first place. Looted. By a thief in the night. Or rather, afternoon.

Revenge. Hmm, Sam liked the taste of that on his lips, the look of it behind closed eyelids and the feel of it on his fingertips. As yet, he wasn't a revenge aficionado, but he'd read *The Count of Monte Cristo* and liked Dantès' style, which was meticulously plotted and executed. The ending hard-won, yet oh so pleasurable. Maybe he wasn't up for spending years of his life working out the details, but he could at least not go in waving guns as if he was a lunatic, missing his mark and probably shooting himself. Metaphorically. He would need to step back and adequately appraise the situation, and then, when the time was right, ensure that Haitch would never forget him. Never forget what she'd done. When planning a heist, it was best to know everything about the place you are holding up, daily timings, the people employed there, routines and the things that aren't routine. Also, work out all the things that could go wrong. It was the same with Haitch. Sam had to know his enemy.

THIRTY-SIX

Dawn

Saturday 4th June

THE SAME MORNING SOUNDS: sparrows forcefully arguing in the tree outside, branches shaking with their annoyance, next door's dog barking at their cat, sat slowly licking its paws, orange eyes sly, marginally out of reach of the snapping jaws, the revving of car engines as bleary-eyed neighbours closed garage doors, checked they'd not forgotten packed lunches, kids or themselves before driving off. But it wasn't a normal morning, was it?

Dawn longed to stay in the hidden place in her mind. Pull the shutters down, lock the door, switch off the light and then let her consciousness fly. Damian's not so gentle nudge in her ribs let her know this wasn't to be. The fact that she had been chosen to attend a prestigious party hosted by Mr Ishimoto, a wealthy and entrepreneurial businessman from Japan, obviously came as no surprise. What did come as a surprise was her reaction to it. Relief. Relief that it would soon be over. She had her part to play, as they all did, and she decided to play it to the hilt. Go down fighting, with a fixed smile on her face.

'Get the coffee brewing, my darling.' His next shove was more brutal, practically propelling her off the edge of the bed. Slipping her feet into slippers, she pushed the hair from her face, adjusted her knickers which had inched up her bum and straightened her t-shirt. She padded downstairs to sort out the percolator. Splashing her face under cold water streaming from the sink tap, she patted it dry with the tea towel and stared out the back door until the coffee pot was screaming. Damian's footfall down the stairs was heavy for such a loose-limbed man. It was like he was making sure she knew he was coming. Pouring two mugs out, she ladled a heaped teaspoon of sugar into one and a slosh of milk. It had to be just right. Not too much of anything but not too little either. Correct. She preferred her coffee black. Simple. Handing it to him as he walked in, Dawn motioned to the dining room next door.

'Shall we?'

They sat opposite each other down the length of the old refectory table they'd chosen together years ago. The space between them said it all.

Dawn started, 'Do you know who else will be there?'

'As yet only you and Haitch, as I'm both your agent.' He took a sip of coffee, his eyes never leaving her face. 'We're not supposed to know. I think Mr Ishimto wants it to remain that way, so no one has an advantage.'

'We could have an advantage.'

'How so?'

'If I describe the people I've seen, is there any way we might be able to find out who they are?'

'Wow.' Damian seemed suitably impressed for once. She hadn't seen that look for a long time. 'You can do that? You could see them that clearly?'

'It's as if some of them are moving but unbelievably slow. A sort of animated photo.'

Dawn sat with her eyes closed while Damian jotted down her descriptions and feelings. He then looked them up on the internet.

He appeared gleeful. 'This will make all the difference as we'll be forewarned about them.'

It wasn't until she got to one in particular that he stopped and stared hard at her.

'Tall, blonde short hair but floppy, greeny eyes. Comes across as fit. A scar through his lip—'

'Say that again?'

'Tall, blonde—'

'No, the bit about a scar...'

'He's got a scar through his lip. Here.' She pointed to her own mouth.

Damian sat back abruptly. 'That sounds like someone I met recently. But he can't be there. It doesn't make sense.'

'What? As much as I'm describing people I haven't met yet, and a party I haven't been to?'

'No, really. The others make sense. I think I know who they are but this, oh shit, what was he called now? Oh yeah. Sam. This Sam guy should not be there. Not in any timeline or future scenario.'

'Well, he is.' She paused. 'Who is he then?'

'Haitch's brother-in-law. Why on earth would he be there?'

'How should I know? I'm only telling you what I can see.'

'What else can you see about him?'

Dawn closed her eyes, letting the vision wash over her. A terrible wave of nausea hit her. Then she threw up across the kitchen floor.

'That good, huh?' Worry pinched at his eyes.

'Sorry,' Dawn wiped spittle from her mouth. 'I felt as if I

was on something like a Wurlitzer, spinning faster and faster until I hit something hard and black.' How could there be physical pain? Her head was in a vice that was being tightened, notch by notch.

'Have you seen this before?'

'No.' Her legs could barely carry her as she tottered to the kitchen for a towel to wipe up the sick, noting that Damian didn't bother to help her. As usual. The look on his face was a combination of disgust and eagerness.

'Do you know what it was about?'

A death. She was certain of it but unable to say it. Was it her own? Was that what she was seeing, and could that be why she was calm again?

'No. It might be simply a reaction to the vision.' She rubbed her forehead gingerly. The pain was excruciating.

'Your vision saying you've had enough for now? That sort of thing?'

'Damian? Could you get me a painkiller and a glass of water? Please?'

'Of course, my darling.' He skittered to the sink and Dawn could hear cupboards opening and water pouring from the tap unchecked. Such a waste. 'Here you are.' Amazing how tender he could be when it suited him. But obviously not today.

'Thanks.' Dawn swallowed the tablet. 'Now, can you work out who the others are before I go?'

'So, you are going. Good. I knew you would.'

Yes, but for reasons he'd never understand. And this man, this Sam, why was he there? All she knew was that he had an integral part to play.

THIRTY-SEVEN

Sam

Nearly two months later, after, now what should he call it, the 'deed that destroyed his life'?

'Listen, mate,' John had sat him down, as if he was a dad about to admonish his son. 'You need to sort yourself out sharpish. We can't carry on like this. It's not fair on Claire, and I can't bear to see you in this state. You still haven't told us what happened. We're going on guesses.'

Sam hung his head. What else could he do?

'So,' continued John, 'if this is your fault, then sort it. If it's not your fault, then also sort it. But get your life back, Sam. Please, if not for yourself, then for us.'

Whose fault was it? Sam sucked on his teeth and then dragged John to the box room. Pulling out the two bottles of whisky from under the bed, he led John to the bathroom and poured both down the sink. John watched in silence.

'Is that all of it?'

Sam nodded. 'I'll sort it, John. I promise.'

His review at work at the end of his month's paid leave didn't go quite to plan, yet he pulled it back from the brink. Just. Too valuable an asset to toss aside.

'You're still on probation,' said Mr Finnegan. 'Don't let us down, Sam.'

Sam had watched Haitch as she circled the Slade. Not so much social networking as search and destroy. Now here she was at Brick Lane Gallery. A solo exhibition. If Sam didn't hate her so much, he'd have said 'good for her', but that wasn't going to happen. He'd been doing his homework, and when motivated, he was a fast learner. There was no invitation, but he reckoned he'd earned a free entry. Hovering by the entrance for a while, he clocked who strutted in. A view through the front windows looked straight into the gallery, the easier to catch those passing by with money burning holes in their pockets. Not so much of the 'short arms and deep pockets' here. You could practically smell the wealth walking in through the door and staring appreciatively at the artwork. He remembered a repeated refrain from Haitch: *if people throw up over my art, then all the better. Job done.* He would gladly throw up, wipe faeces and blood, preferably her blood over every single one of the shit paintings now hanging on those walls and the godawful sculptures on plinths littering the floor space. He wasn't the jealous kind, had simply never been a fan. He could only guess at the bullshit belching from her lips, all the in-phrases, the catch lines, the hooks.

Shielding his eyes, he peered through the pane of glass and spotted something. Hey, look at that now. He might be wrong, but this could well be more than useful; it might be the game-changer.

His brother John had eventually been forced to point out

some truths. He wasn't drinking now but that didn't mean he couldn't act drunk. The tiny bottle of cheap whisky was hidden in his coat pocket. Swallowing a mouthful, he gargled with half the bottle and then liberally doused himself with the rest of it. A rich and inviting aftershave, eh? He was adept at the drunk-pretending-he's-not-drunk sketch. The walk that went with it, and let's not forget the overly loud voice. She might be doing the sales pitch to some turbaned Arab in the centre of the gallery, but he'd make sure she heard him. Only allowing one trip up the steps meant the security guard would initially have to give him the benefit of the doubt. He was alerted, although Sam got through the door easily, hanging onto the coattails of some posh urbanites heading in.

Now the guard was blocking his way. 'Your invitation, please, sir?' A slight uncertainty on his part but not on Sam's.

'Yeah, yeah.' Sam rooted around in his jacket. 'Got it here somewhere.' He flashed a lop-sided grin at him, for good measure.

'I do need to see it, sir.'

''Course.' Sam burped and waved a floppy hand in front of his face. ''Scuse me.'

'Sir? You're blocking the entrance. Other guests would like to get in.'

'Really?' Turning, he peered at the three men and a woman hanging back. They didn't want to push past. Well, who would?

'Listen, mate.' He could slur like a pro. 'I'm her brother-in-law. You know, whatsherface. In there.' He nodded.

'I think I'm going to have to ask that you leave.'

'Don't think so... mate.' Sam took a step forward.

The guard hesitated; probably aware a confrontation might ensue.

'Sir? I don't want to call the police, but unless you have an invitation, I'd like you to leave now.'

'Didn't you hear me, Sonny Jim?' Sam felt a tiny microdot of pity for doing this to this poor sod, but what the hell. He raised his voice. 'I told you, I'm her brother-in-law. Just go and get her, then she'll tell you.'

'Sonny Jim' took a step forward. They were pretty intimate right now, shoulder to shoulder, very macho. That's what he'd hoped Haitch would see as she skittered into the foyer.

'Sam?' There was a wonderful hint of hysteria in her voice. He wanted to crow 'surprise', but had to maintain the charade. That is, until he got what he wanted.

The guard backed away. 'Sorry, Miss Bee, but he doesn't seem to have an invitation.' He cleared his throat. 'And I do believe he's been drinking.'

Sam smiled oh-so-sweetly at Haitch, watched as her face did some gymnastics to cover her fear and confusion. 'Of course, I have an invitation, haven't I, Haitch? I've just lost it somewhere on route. As to drinking, I admit I've had a couple to oil the wheels, so to speak.' He turned to squint at the guard. 'You see, I haven't seen Haitch in quite a while. Have I?'

'Do we have a problem?' A slick male entered the fray. This must be her manager. Damian Montgomery. Could they have been friends in different circumstances? Sam doubted it. His whole demeanour was one of a jumped-up prick. So, no 'besties'.

Sam said, 'Do we have a problem, Haitch?

It was fantastic. Haitch was squirming as if she'd got fleas hopping about in her skanky knickers. 'Not at all.' She kind of stumbled forward, like an invisible hand shoved her. Latching onto him, she pulled him into a more secluded part of the gallery. 'It's lovely to see you, Sam.'

Damian followed as though he was on a short leash. 'I'm sorry, who are you again?'

'This is Sam,' said Haitch, her smile fixed like it'd been

painted onto her face. One of those godawful Victorian dolls with a ceramic head, and eyelids that moved.

'I'm her brother-in-law.' He had to blink a couple of times. 'Well, was.'

While Sam baited Haitch, he watched her reactions, saying just enough to rattle her but not so much that anyone listening would understand his insinuations. That delicious panic on her face. Would he blurt out something? How could she stop him? Between a rock and a hard place. Oh, and look at who else was listening in? Her adoring audience, eavesdropping, hungry for drama, for gossip.

Funny how the mention of an elusive sister made Damian frown. Ah, he didn't know then. That was useful.

'Right.' Damian grabbed hold of Sam's jacket. Woah! The man should keep his hands to himself.

Damian sneered into Sam's face. 'I'm going to have to ask you to leave now. Pretty please.'

There was something about the bloke that made the tiny hairs on Sam's neck rise. Haitch tried to intervene, tears in her eyes. It felt good. Should he say something now? Perhaps not.

Sam wasn't drunk, but she shoved him in such a way, he pitched through the entrance and crashed down the steps. Cracking his knee, the pain ricocheted out. It took a moment to be able to stand. He rubbed at his knee but didn't want her to know she'd hurt him. He made that little telephone symbol.

'Call me. And don't you worry, Haitch, you'll be seeing me again soon. That's a promise.'

What a picture. That dawning realisation that he wasn't going away. That Haitch couldn't sweep him under the rug or wish him gone. He wasn't bloody Tinkerbell and didn't care if she believed in him or not. He was going to make her pay. If he could've snapped a photo of her face at that point, it would have been something. He'd have stuck it on the front of the fridge or preferably on the wall to throw darts at.

What was she saying to Damian right now? What lies was she telling him, to cover up her true nature? Does he know her? More to the point, does he want to? Sam loitered outside, leaning against a lamppost, half to let the throbbing in his knee subside but also to let her know he was still here. Dantè's watching Fernand Mondego. And he had a plan.

Hang on, what did he see that was so interesting at Haitch's show? Damian. More like Haitch's reaction to him. Sort of fluttery lashes and simpering pout. Did she have the hots for the bloke? Because if she did, maybe he'd engender a lovely little surprise for them both. Tit for tat. Digging. Not flower beds, although he hoped to come up smelling of the proverbial rose. No, digging into Mr Montgomery's life.

It took Sam quite a bit of sleuthing to discover something useful. It seemed that Damian had a wife. But not an ordinary wife. She didn't have his surname, for starters. Dawn Rayne. Sam looked her up online and was astounded by what they said about her. Perhaps she needed a visit? Had Haitch met her, or was she locked in a turret somewhere, only letting her hair down for Damian to climb up? He came across as that sort of bloke, the one who hides his most precious possessions in vaults, so only he could enjoy them. But then again, Haitch had shown she wasn't bothered by any matrimonial ties. She'd probably cut off the wife's hair at the roots and abseil back down to the ground.

THIRTY-EIGHT

Dawn

Tuesday 7th June

Dawn, with her unique set of qualifications in the 'weird and unbelievable', thought she might at least be prepared for what life might throw at her. So, opening her front door, she should have already considered who might be stood with a quizzical look on their face on the doorstep. Sam wasn't anywhere on her list. It didn't matter.

'Sam?' Taking a step back into the hallway, she was rewarded with wide eyes and an open mouth.

'Have we met? I'm sorry but do I know you?'

'Not yet.' It was no good being coy; the man was already stamped indelibly on her mind. They all had their parts to play in the 'big game' to come. 'But you will.' Dawn beckoned him in.

Following slowly behind her, she could see he was taking everything in. Photos of her and Damian, ostensibly from happier times that she couldn't quite remember, adorned the walls, like trophies. There was one in particular. In this one, both of them smiling, although his hold on her waist was white knuckled.

'It's funny, don't you think?' Dawn turned to Sam, who was staring at the photos. 'You come to my house and then ask me if you know me?'

'I came to... talk to you.' His eyes swivelled to her for a second and then returned to the photos. 'Nice pictures of you both.' There was a timbre to his voice that could be construed to be threatening; it had many layers in it. Dawn heard pain. But it was personal and not directed at her.

'Would you like coffee or tea? I have plain chocolate digestives.'

'How did you know who I am?' He nodded as if a thought had occurred to him. 'Ah, Damian told you about a bloke with a scar through his lip.'

'Not quite. I told Damian about a bloke with a scar through his lip, though I wasn't expecting to see you here. Was that yes to a tea?'

'Coffee, please. Where were you expecting to see me?'

'Spain. Southern Spain, to be more exact. Come in.' She waved him towards a battered leather sofa. A wedding gift from Damian's mother. A Chesterfield, no less. A beautiful piece of furniture, for sure, although she loathed it. 'I'll get a coffee on.'

While she set up the Nespresso machine, she watched him watching her. 'You're Haitch Bee's brother-in-law.'

'And you're The Hermit Medium. Damian Montgomery's wife. According to the internet, you've done some crazy shit stuff. What, exactly, did you mean when you said you told Damian about me?'

'Over four years ago, Damian went to see a new, up-and-coming artist, at my behest.'

'Haitch?'

'Yes. Silly me.' Dawn shrugged. 'I set in motion something that has run away from me. Damian asked for a reading. About Haitch. I told him many things that have influenced our lives ever since. To my detriment. How do you like your coffee? White? No sugar?'

'Wow. How do you do that?'

'Most people have it white with no sugar.' Dawn handed a delicate cup and saucer to him. 'Your coffee.' Placing a plate of biscuits on the low-level table in front of him, she tucked herself into a big old easy chair. 'Why are you here, Sam?'

'Don't you know? You said you did a reading. Is that like having a vision? What did you see?'

'I saw all of us. In Spain.'

'All of whom?'

'You, me and Haitch Bee.'

Sam blinked a few times. Maybe this was his processing time. It must be a great deal to take in.

'I need to think about that.' Sam sipped his drink. 'How do you feel about Haitch, if you don't mind me asking?'

'I think we need to ascertain how you feel about her first.'

His gaze was unflinching. 'I hate the bitch. You?'

'Not that enamoured. Not quite up to hate yet, but I feel as if I'm getting there.' Nibbling at a biscuit, she made an expansive gesture with her hand. 'I presume you have a valid reason for such... hate?'

'I don't know why, yet I feel as though I can trust you. Did you know that Haitch has a twin sister? Does Damian know?'

Dawn stopped eating. 'If he did, he never mentioned her to me.' A twin? Two of them? God forbid.'

'I'm, at least I was, married to Tilly, Haitch's much nicer sister. That was until Haitch played a dirty trick on me. She pretended to be my wife and slept with me. I mean, she really pretended, went all out, dyed her hair, wore her clothes. You get the picture.' Sam was going to crush his cup if he gripped it any harder.

'She comes across as a nasty, manipulative young woman. I can see why you hate her. I presume she is the reason you're not with your wife anymore. Did, um, Tilly was it? Did she find out?'

'No.' Sam hung his head. 'I lied and said I'd met someone else. I couldn't let her be ripped apart by her own blood.'

'You took the fall for Haitch?' Dawn snorted. 'Why on earth didn't you tell her the truth? You were manipulated by her sister. You obviously, I hope, believed you were with your own wife.'

'As I said, Tilly would have accepted it from me, as this has happened throughout her life—'

'Sorry? What do you mean by that?'

'I think her previous boyfriends have left her, and she never knew why—'

'Ah!' Dawn interrupted. 'You think Haitch has done this before? To Tilly?'

Sam raised his head slowly. His eyes were such a startling green as if they were emeralds lit from behind. 'Yes. It makes sense.'

'Why have you come to me?'

'I went to Haitch's last exhibition.'

'Brick Lane. Where I saw her first work.' Dawn sucked on her lip. 'You saw them there? You saw Haitch and Damian.'

Sam raised his eyebrows, quickly peered around him and stood up. 'I clocked those photos on the wall as I came in. I'm sorry. I've intruded into your home, and I can't apologise enough.'

'You think those photos are of real life. You think we are happy. Look again.' Dawn pointed back to the hall. 'When you've looked properly, come back in and talk to me.'

Sam frowned but said nothing, walking out into the hall-way. He was gone for a few minutes. Time for her to finish her coffee and eat two more biscuits. What would he see? What was intimated, Damian's staged set or the underlying reality?

'Tell me what you saw,' she said when he came back into the room. From the expression on his face, she knew he'd spotted it.

'I might have got it wrong, and I don't want to upset or offend you.'

'You can't.'

'Okay. These photos appear to show a happy couple, except in some, you don't look that happy. It's as though you're wearing a mask. In one photo, I would say you were pregnant.' He had a fight or flight stance. 'You have a pronounced bump, and your face is lit up. Were you? Or have I put my big foot in my mouth?'

'I was. Go on.' Dawn made sure she didn't betray what was being screamed in her head.

'Then in the next, you're not, and Damian seems to have a tight grip on you.' He glanced around carefully. 'I can't see any baby paraphernalia, so I think you must have lost it. Sorry, not "it" but... the baby. Somehow.' He sat down heavily. 'I shouldn't be asking this.'

'Oh, do.' Dawn felt so calm with this stranger, setting free the secrets that had swarmed like ants in her soul. 'Ask away?'

'Dawn?' Sam's face betrayed what he must be wondering. His hands were held out in front of him.

'When my beloved Damian doesn't get his way, he's very free with his fists. I must have spoken out of turn, not done something to his liking, any little oversight could have triggered him. He was so miserable afterwards. Inconsolable.'

Dawn registered the look of disgust that flitted across Sam's face. 'He hit you? When you were pregnant?'

'He's hit me many times. But that day, it only took one blow. That's all. And my life changed forever.'

'Didn't you go to the police? Do him for battery and manslaughter?'

'That sounds like an accusation against me. You think I'm weak.'

Sam shook his head. 'No, I'm not saying that at all, but I gather it wasn't possible?'

'Not easily and no way I could guarantee my safety. Anyway, remember I said I did a reading for him? I knew I had to play it to the end. It finishes in Spain. It finishes with all of us.'

'You're beginning to freak me out, Dawn.'

'You should be freaked out. We should all be freaked out.'

'I didn't come here for this...'

'Then what did you come here for?'

'I... I...'

'Did you come for revenge?'

'Not against you. You were a blurry faceless person in my head.'

'And now I'm real?'

Sam nodded. 'Yes. I think I should go now. I didn't mean to involve you in this.'

'I've been involved for a very long time, Sam. My visions always tell a story that has or will come to pass.'

'I'm getting pretty weirded out right now, Dawn.'

'But you still want revenge?'

'Not at any price. Not if it might hurt another person. I mean, hurt you.'

'How do you think I feel about the man I loved beyond measure killing my baby? And then blaming me.' She watched his reaction to her words. 'Yes, he said it was my fault. I can't leave him; he would never allow that. At the same time, I don't want to stay with him.'

'Between a rock and a hard place?'

'Of sorts.' Dawn leant forward. 'Do you think you have a chance to win Tilly back?'

'I don't know. I think I had it in my head that if I mucked it up between Haitch and Damian... I'm not saying there's anything actually going on, but if there was, I had the idea it would hurt Haitch. That's kind of where I am. I'm trying not to think too much about Tilly right now.'

'So, you want Haitch to feel what you are feeling? Even if it's only a little bit?'

'Exactly. Sounds petty, doesn't it.' Sam wiped at his eyes. 'I don't think I'll ever get my Tilly back, so I want to hurt the person who I feel is responsible.'

'Doesn't sound petty to me; it sounds like real life.' She shifted in her chair. 'I'm not sure if I should say this, but I think you will get Tilly back.'

'And you think this will happen only if we all end up in Spain?'

'Yes. It's all blurred and muddy, though there's something...' Her voice trailed off.

'And you?' Sam tilted his head and stared at her with those emerald eyes. 'Do you want to hurt Damian?'

'I'd be happy for him to experience a modicum of the fear and betrayal he's inflicted on me.'

'Okay, then.' Sam clasped his hands. 'Are you saying what I think you're saying?'

'Oh, I think so.' Dawn tapped the table between them. 'Now, we need to plan. But not here. Damian will be home soon. Give me your phone number, and I'll contact you. We don't have a lot of time.'

THIRTY-NINE

Sam

His envisioning of every outcome of meeting Damian Montgomery's wife had never included that. First, she already knew him. From a vision? Never one to believe in all that hippy-dippy shit, his rule of thumb was if you could touch it, it was real. A person who could see into the future was far too scary for him, but someone who had seen him in a specific place and point in the future, now that was damn terrifying. Sure, he'd spilt his guts to this woman. Couldn't help himself. But did he believe her? Even if there was the remotest possibility that he could square it with Tilly without ripping them all apart, then it'd be worth it, surely? True, she had a reason to hate Damian, but was she simply using him for her own ends? Did it matter if their objectives were the same?

Second, how could he understand her acceptance of taking the blame for the loss of a baby caused by a person she should trust above all others? He'd thought Damian a prick when he'd met him at the gallery with Haitch, but a wife-beater? A murdering thug? Sam's initial misgivings had given way to a feeling of optimism. Whatever was coming, the man bloody well deserved it.

Bring it on!

Sam sprawled on the thin bed in the box room he now called home. The smell wafting along the landing made his stomach rumble. Two chocolate coated digestive biscuits this morning hadn't been enough to call lunch. Needing a drink desperately after seeing Dawn, he'd stopped off at the Ragged Fox on the High Street. A couple of shots. That was all, except 'guilt' must have been like an alcohol stinking stole draped around his neck as he crept down the stairs and entered the kitchen. He found John wrestling a large tray of roast potatoes out of the oven.

John turned the chunkily cut potatoes. 'Are you drinking again, Sam?'

'A couple. That's all. Listen, I've had the weirdest day in a long time and needed to steady my shattered nerves.'

John had that look on his face. The one he recognised as the 'we're rooting for you, Sam, so don't fuck it up now'.

'Care to tell me?'

'Quite frankly, John, if I told you, you wouldn't believe me. I don't even believe it.'

'Try me.'

'Okay. A medium told me this afternoon that I'd be getting on a plane to Spain in less than a week, and that by doing this, I might save my marriage to Tilly.' Was that what Dawn had implied?

'Oh, my good God.' John's hand froze above the steaming pan. 'Ouch.' He yanked open the oven door and clattered the roasts back in. 'You've been to a medium? Are you out of your mind? Oh, yes, sorry. You are probably. But really Sam...'

'I went about something else.' He couldn't mention she was

the wife of a man he was trying to poison against Haitch, who in turn, was the woman who had ruined his life. It was too complicated even for him to understand. 'I've never met her, but she knew me. This might be my chance, John.' To at least have the satisfaction of wrecking Haitch's life. How this could help him get Tilly back was beyond him, yet he was sure Dawn thought there was a chance.

'Well, maybe if you'd told us what the heck had happened to you both, we might have been able to help. Not some bloody dabbler in the bloody occult.'

'I couldn't tell you—'

'Did you tell her?'

'She's part of it. I swear I haven't the faintest idea of what is going on. All I know is, I need to be on a plane next Thursday. Can you help me?'

'You're bonkers, and no, I can't help you and neither will Claire.' John shoved him through into the living room and poured them both a hefty glass of whisky.

'I thought I'm not supposed to be drinking?'

'This is more for me than you.'

'Fine.' Sam drained the glass.

John poured them both another shot. 'You need to get a grip, Sam. Now, tell me what's brought this on.'

'You and Claire think I've been unfaithful to Tilly. Well, I haven't—' he saw the expression flit over John's face. 'And no, she hasn't been unfaithful to me either.' Not that he knew of, but he kicked that thought out. 'It's something else, and now I have the chance to put it right. I've got to take that chance. My life depends on it.' He swallowed. 'Maybe more.'

'You're playing stupid again. Looks like you're winning, too.'

'Ha, ha. Come on, John. Help me.' After everything, how was he going to get his brother on his side?

'Help you do what?' Claire stood with the doorway framing her, Sainsbury's shopping bags clutched in both hands.

'Get Tilly back.' And seek revenge on the woman who'd destroyed their lives in the first place. But they didn't need to know that.

'I'm fine with that.' Claire stared hard at her husband. 'Why are we both not fine with that?'

'You missed the mind-boggling bit that came first. That's probably why.' John rolled his eyes. 'Come on then. Let's get this mad party started.'

—

Dawn phoned late that night. 'There are still spaces on the Monarch flight, though you'll have to be quick. You don't want to arrive at the same time as Haitch but be aware that Damian and I will be in Málaga earlier to sort a few things out. There are even a few spaces left on my return flight. I don't know how you feel about it, but you could come back with me?'

'That'd sure piss him off, wouldn't it?'

'That's what I was thinking. A bit more 'sand in his face', so to speak. Book yourself into the same hotel as Damian; I would suggest room number 23. It's not near Damian's room but be careful.'

'Is that wise? What if he sees me?'

'Then it'll make him lose control even more.'

'Are you sure you want to go through with this?'

'I don't have a choice. I never did.'

'But to play it the way you've described. Surely that's dangerous? For us both?'

'Sam? If you don't want to go through with it, I understand. I've seen you there, but if you refuse to go, then perhaps the vision will change.'

'Can you change fate? I can't go back in time to fix what I did, but if you think by following your vision, I might have another go at it, then I'll do whatever you ask me to do.'

'Be there. Be there with me, and we'll get through this together.'

FORTY

Dawn

Thursday 16th June

WAS she the one setting all this in motion? You can't change fate. That's what she'd implied to Sam, but what if she could? Why be given a glimpse into the other side if there was nothing she could do about it all? Unless she was indeed the catalyst. No vision. No knowledge. That equalled no ending.

'Are you ready, darling?' Damian had that tone.

Of course, she was ready. Even if she hadn't been, he wouldn't risk a black eye or a limp just before this prestigious party. No bad press today.

'Let's go.' Sounding jaunty was anathema to her. Nerves. She'd suffered through years of anxious thoughts that had twisted her brain to mush.

The taxi to the station, the train ride to the airport, and even boarding the plane, swept past her as if she was watching a film. Not participating. Until the moment her seat belt clunked on.

'Dawn?' A tug on her sleeve. 'Mr Ishimoto loves intrigue and suspense. He adores science, religion. From what I've heard, he initiates debates that have been termed pub brawls in his time. Well-read, highly and expensively educated, he needs a show. Give him one, and you'll get the bursary, and if you don't,' his eyes narrowed, 'then we can fall back on Haitch winning it and at least we'll get the commission.'

An image of can-can dancers popped into her mind, frilly bloomers showing, black stockinged legs a-waggling. Was that the show she should offer this strange and demanding man? Or was it more a full-on punch-up? Snarling faces and heavy fists. Amazing what the sheer weight of money and power would allow a person to get away with.

'Don't you believe the other contenders might win it?'

'A film director and an Arab entrepreneur?'

'What about the physicist?'

'Maybe but that's why you've got to put on a good show. You know Haitch will be doing her utmost to razzle-dazzle the man.' Clearing his throat, he swigged half of the plastic cup of tomato juice sat in his tray. 'Once I've got you settled, I'll go and pick Haitch up.' He stared at her. 'I don't need to remind you that she doesn't know you're my wife.'

Dawn refrained from saying that she barely knew she was his wife. He continued: 'It's paramount she doesn't find out.'

'Yes, I know.'

He told her this every ten minutes. As if she was going to forget. But other things might slip out. Funny how he was sat next to Haitch when they returned to England, yet she had to take a later flight. Nice that. Very 'husbandly', wasn't it? And all because he believed that she, the great Haitch Bee, would win the bursary, not her. He'd make sure she knew who was responsible for her glory. Well, when he found out that she was booked on the same flight as Sam, she was looking forward to seeing the look on his face. Not so smug then.

Another taxi took them to the hotel where Damian was staying.

'You can freshen up first, in my room as you don't need to arrive all travel worn. We want you to make the best impression from the start.' He opened the hotel room door and ushered her in, 'I've ordered a taxi to take you to the villa in an hour. You'll arrive at the villa early, but then you've got time to get the lie of the land, so to speak. You'll have your own room in the villa, but you can call me anytime with updates. Okay?'

'That sounds good.' Turning with a half-smile, careful not to seem too eager for him to go, she kissed him lightly on the lips and gently pushed him back towards the door. 'Go get Haitch. I'll speak to you in the morning.'

'Make me proud, Dawn.' He blew her a kiss as he slowly shut the door. She pretended to catch it, but the moment the door clicked shut, she threw the imaginary kiss away with an 'Urgh!'

Her ear against the door, she listened for a full minute for the sound of returning footsteps. Opening it, she peered out, careful to ensure she had the key. No one around. Tiptoeing, she rounded the corner of the hallway and tapped lightly three times on the number 23 door. It opened a crack, and an eye peered at her before an arm snaked out and pulled her in.

'Has he left?' Sam nodded over her shoulder.

'Yep. Gone to pick up the delectable Haitch and leave his wife to get to the place by herself.'

'Nice. Have you got the map of the villa?'

'Here.' Dawn pulled a crumpled A4 sheet of paper from her handbag. 'This is the route to where I'll be. There are steps here and here. Both get you to the roof terrace—'

'Is that where we're supposed to be? You know this? I mean, it was in your vision?'

'It's where I feel we should be. It's as simple as that.'

Sam nodded, but his face betrayed his strain. A muscle twitched under his left eye.

Dawn continued. 'I'll call you half an hour before I call him. That should give you time to be in position. If you get lost or whatever, call me back.'

'Do you think this will work?'

'I don't know. It should certainly piss him off, and that's all I can hope for right now.'

'But you still can't see what happens clearly?'

'No. A jumble of images, but we're definitely on that roof.'

'Written in the stars. Weird.'

'I'm going to get a quick shower, then the taxi will take me up there. Keep out of sight. I want Damian to be incredibly shocked when he sees you. I know what he's like. All the while he thinks he has me at home, the compliant little wife, he'll pursue Haitch, but if he feels threatened, if he thinks he might lose me and worse, to another man he knows, he'll forget all about her.'

'More to the point, she'll know she's lost him. That's what I want to see.'

'It might get dangerous. Are you sure you're prepared for that?'

'I can hold my own. Go now. I'll see you up there. And don't worry, I'll be quiet. I want to savour that moment when he thinks I've beaten him, and you're mine.'

Dawn carefully let herself out and sidled back to her room. A quick shower, a change of clothes, and she was waiting in the foyer with her small overnight bag when the taxi drew up. The journey would have been spectacular, but Dawn was locked inside her mind, rehearsing what she would say to Damian. Getting the subtle nuances right was going to be crucial if this was going to work.

'Miss Rayne.' A tall, distinguished man helped her from the car, while a younger man took her bag from her. 'I'm Jeremiah. I'm the concierge here. Welcome to Castilla Mori. We do hope your experience here will vastly exceed your expectations.' He raised an eyebrow at her. 'And if they don't, we'd like to know why.'

Dawn smiled as she thought she was expected to. Walking through countless courtyards and Mediterranean gardens, she could barely listen as this man told her about the history of the old Moorish castle. Scents bombarded her nose; noises assaulted her ears. The intense colours ran and swam before her eyes. Then they stopped at door number 10.

'Your room.' Jeremiah swept in before her and waved his hand. 'An assistant will be here for you at seven, and they will lead you to where the party will commence. Please ring for anything you need, Miss Rayne.'

The room was sublimely tranquil. Muted colours, the half-lowered shutters a defence against the shimmering heat outside, soft furnishings. Marvelling at the air conditioning that blew sweet, cool air around, she shouldn't have bothered changing back at the hotel as she was as sticky and chafed as when she'd landed in Málaga. So, the meeting was at seven. The walk-in shower was welcome, though she avoided the bath as she was sure she'd fall asleep in it. Knowing she had to be careful, she composed sentences in her head that she thought she might be able to slip into the conversation. Things she hoped would only cause consternation to Haitch, and that would be meaningless to anyone else.

There was a list of services offered by the villa on a tall table by the bedroom window. Steam ironing. Yes, that'd do nicely. She phoned and asked for her little black dress to be ironed before the party started and was satisfied when it was taken and delivered back to her within half an hour, wrinkle-free and encased in a plastic sheath, for a tidy sum of fifty euros. Ker-ching. Charged to Damian's account.

The next step was her make-up. It must be perfect, a painted mask behind which to hide. The tap on the door came as she was slipping on her black kitten heels.

'One moment.' Opening the door, the young man from earlier was waiting in a deferential stance. Obviously, no lounging allowed here.

Dawn followed him through a maze of alleys, walkways and arches until they stepped into a room with the most immense fireplace she had ever seen. In fact, the whole room would be the ideal backdrop to a Latin version of Downton Abbey. It was plush, gilded, neutrally decorated and enormous. Gazing upwards, something caught her eye. Was that a camera? Dearest Lord! In every corner and at other convenient positions, cameras peered down, their lenses trained on the lab test rats in the room. Of which, she was one. Blinking rapidly, she saw the Japanese man walk across the room... and there she was. Haitch. Something lurched inside. Was she going to chunder? Projectile vomit her barely edible aeroplane lunch across the richly patterned rug? Her fingers twitched, anticipating the feel of skin beneath her fuchsia painted nails. Now, now. She must retain control and have no thoughts of scratching faces. At this point, she was unsure if she'd be doing it for herself or Sam. What a self-centred, selfish, egotistical jumped-up little Madam that girl was! There. That felt better.

She waited. Having spotted Mr Ishimoto now heading towards a man who'd walked in, Dawn hauled in a breath and sauntered over to Haitch.

'Hello, Haitch.' She scanned the other woman's face. Even under all that heavy make-up, she was gorgeous.

Haitch jerked. 'Er?'

Not an auspicious start.

'I'm Dawn.'

'Oh, hello!'

She smiled at Haitch. The woman in front of her was beautiful, no doubt about that. Dawn had expected a trace of the debauched character to be visible on her face. She must be the same as Dorian Gray and have a painting hung in a dark closet stuffed with grungy clothes that showed the twisted and repulsive creature within. This woman had innocent eyes; a vulnerability that belied what Dawn knew of her. How strange. But she mustn't be fooled, for that's what tricksters do. But it still unnerved her.

Dawn's hair was tumbling over her face. She swept it back, and her bangles clanked. They were gifts from Damian from when he'd travelled to India in his youth. Silver. Heavy and beautiful. About the only objects she'd try to save if her house was on fire, even if Damian was still inside. What did that say about her? Oh yes, she had her priorities right.

As they chatted, Dawn endeavoured to see what made Haitch tick. Everyone had buttons to press. She merely had to find what would annoy this young woman and then use it against her.

'Enjoying the spectacle?' She waited for two seconds longer than she should. 'Haitch?'

'Sorry,' Haitch stepped backwards, 'but who are you again? I mean, what do you do?'

'I'm the clairvoyant.'

'Clairvoyant?'

Oh, the look of disquiet that flitted over Haitch's attractive features. Did she think Dawn could see all her dirty little underhand romps as if they were lingerie on sale displayed in a shop window? As if it were as easy as that.

'Don't worry. Your secret is safe with me.' Dawn winked

again. Surely, that must be provoking, whatever the reason for doing it? And as yet, Haitch had shown that she had no idea who she was, but she'd understood that she'd been baited.

———

What was their bounteous host saying now?

A group photo? As if any of them would be happy to hang that on their wall when they got home, especially as only one was going to win. Unless it was to gloat. But it was ironic that the Japanese use the word 'cheezu' to make people smile when taking photos. Dawn wondered if someone like Haitch would know such a thing as that. The camera clicked. Thank goodness that was over.

Mr Ishimoto was smarm personified. 'Well done, everyone. I'm sure you all look splendid.' Pointing behind him, 'Last but certainly not least, and I do hate to be talking of mundane things such as money, would you all confirm an email address on the sheet on the table there. Whoever wins can then send me details of their bank account.' Mr Ishimoto bowed, so very oriental in his mannerisms that he was practically a caricature.

Should she even bother, as it was doubtful that she'd win? Well, just in case. Dawn wrote her email on the sheet in a neat hand.

Right, now to keep tabs on Haitch, and try her best to ensure she had a truly rotten time. The thought made her all warm and fuzzy inside.

The evening was all about the chit-chat, which she realised was being recorded with tiny mikes set up at strategic points. Wasn't this illegal? What on earth was wrong with the man, that he had to eavesdrop on all their conversations? Why didn't he simply try talking to them, one on one and listen? It wasn't that it was boring. Far from it. It was the duality of it. Here to ostensibly win the coveted prize, and yet her prize was something else entirely. Striking up a conversation with a woman who introduced herself as Zaida Al-Nassar, Dawn lamented this meeting would be so brief. Here was a woman who was not only artistic but had fought to get into a man's world within a man's world. She was highly educated, outspoken and seemingly as tough as the soles on army boots. Glancing surreptitiously across the room to keep track of Haitch, Dawn was fascinated by Zaida's response to her rather flippant remark 'that your country and your religion have never been favourable towards women'. Eventually, she glimpsed Haitch and two men walking towards them.

As Zaida spoke to the group, Dawn wanted to shout 'bravo' but thought it might be inopportune at that point. What an incredible woman. She also noted the look that Haitch gave her. Utter disdain. Good grief, was she so vain and needy that she couldn't allow someone else to have a little glory?

Mr Ishimoto finally gestured through the stone entrance to the side of them. 'On that note, let us be seated for supper, and we can all get to know each other much better.'

The small group shuffled towards the table with their bijou name tags beautifully hand-written in a copperplate script. A deep-red tablecloth and simple white crockery waited for them.

As napkins were deployed and glasses half-filled with white wine, Mr Ishimoto raised his glass. 'A toast. To a fascinating evening. I look forward to more stimulating and energetic discussions.'

Dawn sipped, aware that Orpheus was not the only one who'd imbibed a little too much. Haitch had packed away a few glasses. That old adage that champagne didn't get you drunk would not work here. Anything with alcohol in had alcohol in. Do the maths.

Was the fluttering in her stomach merely hunger, or was it nerves? Soup was ladled into her bowl. Gazpacho. It was good

they were being served the cuisine of the area. The face that
Haitch made when she slurped in a spoonful nearly made
Dawn laugh out loud. Wasn't expecting it to be cold then?

Between the heated discussions on her right, where Zaida
and Mr Ishimoto battled out their viewpoints on each other,
Dawn heard snippets from Haitch and her little adoring
entourage. Dawn swallowed bile as well as the cold soup. That
jumped up girl couldn't help herself. Like a she-cat in heat,
waggling her arse at any male who stopped to sniff at it. There
was mention of Medellin and London and New York. Pablo
Escobar. Who hasn't seen any of the series on the ghastly man?
She caught the tone of Orpheus' voice when he spoke of the
Catholic church and Alejandro's corresponding anger. Why were
they here exactly? Damian had implied that Mr Ishimoto might
like a good discussion but preferred a quarrel, a proper dispute.

When the conversation turned to equality and the role of
feminism, Dawn squirmed. What could she say about her own
life? Held captive by the man she loved and loathed in equal
measure, unable to be the woman she always believed herself to
be because of fear of retribution. Nowhere to hide. He would
always find her and drag her back. She could never get away
from him while either of them was alive. Was this why her
vision had been so important? She instinctively knew that there
would be an end to it all, yet how that would play out, well, that
was the question.

Dawn shook her head. What had Alejandro said? 'Women
sleep around, and when they get pregnant, they purge a child as
if it were rubbish. This is a sin. Sex outside of marriage is a sin.

Haitch's face changed. It didn't look like Haitch's face
anymore, more a facsimile, a copy of her face. 'I agree. When a
woman's husband goes off and has sex with his bloody secretary
or whoever, then yes, that's a sin in my book.'

Dawn couldn't help herself. A laugh sputtered out. What the heck was going on here? Who was she to have the gall to moan about sex with a married person? The words leapt out of her mouth before she'd thought them through. 'But it's a-ok to sleep with someone else's husband? Do you agree, Haitch?'

'What? I'm sorry, I don't get what you're driving at, Dawn'. What was so strange was that she genuinely looked as though she didn't know. Face all blank, not a quiver of a muscle, a widening of the eyes or a speeding up of breath. What a consummate liar, she'd most likely pass a lie detector with a smile.

Dawn couldn't let it go. 'It's absolutely fine to sleep with the husband of someone you know very well. And I do mean very well. Is that plain enough?' She hadn't mentioned 'brother-in-law', but it must be clear what she was alluding to?

'I wasn't talking about that.' Alejandro waved his spoon at Haitch. 'I meant when a woman has sex when she isn't married. When she is a whore.'

Haitch's voice rose. 'So that covers most of the women in the West. We're all whores then?' She leant across the table. 'Dawn? I'm still not sure what you mean?'

Alejandro continued. 'If you sleep with a man who is not your husband, then yes. Yes, you are.'

Dawn was enjoying this. 'Alejandro seems to have seconded exactly what I was saying.' Haitch was getting agitated. This was working out better than she'd hoped.

Haitch shook her head. 'So that must go for men too. All those men who sleep with women when they're not married? Or sleep with women when they are? That's okay, then?'

'Men are men,' said Alejandro. 'We have appetites. Women do not.'

'You mean women should not,' said Dawn. 'Double standards here, folks.' She stared at Haitch. 'For some, I should say fallen standards.' Oooh, dig the knife in deeper.

'Are you having a go at me about something?'

Sweet Lord! Was the girl an imbecile or what? Dawn decided to string this out. Raising her glass, she sipped and then put it down slowly. 'Am I? Why on earth should I be doing that, do you think?' She allowed a slither of contempt to taint her remark

'I haven't got a clue.'

There it was. The stress rolling jaggedly over Haitch's words.

'You are not married, are you Haitch?' said Mr Ishimoto. All the table was listening.

'No, I'm not.'

'Have you slept with many men?' His voice was soft, although the words were clear.

Haitch looked as if she'd been whacked round the face with a dead mackerel. 'Not that it's anyone's business but my own, but yes. I have. Quite a few.'

'Oh, to be so judged.' Dawn smiled at Haitch. What a thing to say to a guest. Her distaste for Mr Ishimoto was increasing exponentially with every comment he spoke. What a despicable little man. Money. That said it all and meant he could say whatever he liked with seeming impunity.

'Yeah, right,' said Haitch. 'I kind of thought we'd got past the Middle Ages and their religious shit.'

Although Dawn did agree with her, she couldn't show it. She'd lose the initiative, and yet the evening was moving in directions she hadn't dreamt of. It was apparent that Mr Ishimoto was orchestrating his own pocket-sized drama based on their personal viewpoints. Were any of them here due to their own merits and achievements? The evening would tell.

FORTY-ONE

Dawn

ALEJANDRO CONTINUED to froth at the mouth. If only she could say all the raging words that bubbled up here without punishment. Damian was elsewhere and would never hear what she might say and be offended, letting his fists fly, whittling down her sense of self until there was barely a matchstick of a woman left. But she kept her silence.

Alejandro was gaining momentum and was being encouraged by Mr Ishimoto, a lion trainer prodding at a bad-tempered lion with his whip. Dawn focused on the last thing he said.

'They feel they are now victims of reverse discrimination, that there has been a transfer of rights from men to women. In everything from politics, economics and even in the social arena.'

A 'pub brawl' was precisely what Mr Ishimoto was looking for. Transfer of rights from men to women? Not in her little enclosed world.

Alejandro ploughed on. 'I think men are now the second sex, and they have to stand up for their rights.'

Sweetest Lord! Dawn shook her head. Men now the second

sex? What did the idiot boy know of such things? Was the thought of even slight equality creeping up on them enough to make them cack in their pants?

And yet more drivel was belching from his mouth. 'All men, whether black, Asian or Latino and all the other men from every race and background still all want and feel entitled to utter obedience from their children and subservience from their women. And don't get me going on gay men!'

'You believe that?' She knew who else believed that too. Damian. Dawn tapped the tabletop with her nail. 'You actually believe that in this day and age, women should be subservient to men?' All that fighting for equality had whizzed over this Neanderthal's head as it had bypassed her beloved husband. Was that being rude to Neanderthals? But he was a relic of a bygone age that should have been stopped by now. Down with the patriarchy!

'It's in the Bible.' Alejandro practically snorted through his nose. 'Why do you think the marriage vows ask for obedience from the woman to her husband and only care from the husband to his wife to be?'

Haitch shouted: 'Because God is a twat?'

Oh goody. Pub punch-up here they all come.

'What did you say?' Alejandro had turned a deep ruby red, nearly the same colour as the wine. He'd surely go 'pop' soon and leave a sticky mess all over the room.

Dawn knew she should keep her mouth shut tight, but she wanted to hear the answer. 'And if a man raises his fists to a woman? Is that acceptable too. In your world, Alejandro?'

'If she is not deferential towards her husband. If she speaks above her station. If she does not perform her wifely duties, then yes. Absolutely.'

Dawn rubbed at one eye. She knew the rationality behind it all. 'And if she is all that and he still hits her?'

'Then she must have done something to deserve such punishment. Unbeknown to her.'

'Wouldn't it be a good idea then to at least tell her what's pissed him off? Have a conversation? Not simply belt someone,' Haitch added.

Dawn glanced across the table at this woman she detested. So, she did have a thought separate from her almighty ego in that pretty little head of hers.

'She should know without being told. A good wife should know.'

It was that easy, then. *A good wife should know.* So that's where she'd been going wrong.

'This is the natural order of things.'

'I don't mean to offend you, Alejandro—' Dawn turned to look at Alejandro.

'Even though you have—'

'But what would happen if I hit my husband just because he annoyed me in some way? Would I get the same leniency of thought?'

Alejandro's lips were thin. 'Don't be ridiculous.'

'No. Thought not.' Leaning back in her chair, Dawn wondered if Damian worked using the same logic. How many red-edged daydreams had she had of cracking a broom handle around the back of his head? Not once either, but over and over again, till the red bled from her thoughts and stained the ground instead. Too many to count.

The combatants fought on. Her heart wasn't in it when asked about how her 'powers' worked. It was too painful. Haitch seemed to be quite entranced by her words. How strange.

Orpheus then told them of his brother, painful memories clouding his face, making his eyes wet. What a truly terrible story. Poor Orpheus. She'd had her fair share of those.

Dawn found her voice. 'Was he found alive, Orpheus?' This

was too close: why she didn't care to do this anymore, the horror of it.

He nodded his head. 'Yes. Yes, he was. He was unharmed. Scared shitless but okay.'

Tears prickled at the corners of her eyes. Alive. How good that must have felt for that other medium. A rarity.

'It is your belief then,' said Mr Ishimoto, 'that if the medium had not got involved, your brother would have been murdered in the same way as the others? Is that correct?'

'Yeah, that's about the long and the short of it.' Dawn noticed that Orpheus polished his glasses a lot, especially when he appeared stressed. Like now.

Haitch looked as if she might cry too. 'I can see why you believe.'

'That's a terrible story,' said Dawn. 'I'm glad that this woman was able to help you, yet I feel pity for the ones who were killed in such a horrific manner.' She'd known one of them. Experienced a child's horrific death and faced her deepest fears. Not once but twice.

'We were the lucky ones,' said Orpheus. 'The other families have had to bear the knowledge of what happened to their boys. We came so close.' She'd been on the other side of that. Not so lucky. The death of a child, anyone's child, was dreadful. The death of her own, unbearable. The voices around her became a burble, saying nothing words, strange sounds only.

Haitch stood suddenly and smiled at them all. 'Well, it's been a lovely and enlightening evening, but if you don't mind, Mr Ishimoto, I need to turn in now.'

Dawn watched an array of emotions flit across the other woman's face. It was odd because, for a moment, she didn't look at all like Haitch. As if someone else was inhabiting her body. It couldn't be. Could it?

'Why, Miss Bee. The evening has barely started.' Mr Ishimoto stared at Haitch as if down the barrel of a shotgun. Hairs stood proud on the back of Dawn's neck. 'You've not even sampled the dessert, and I've been reliably informed it is truly delicious. A local treat.'

'Thank you, Mr Ishimoto, but my evening has ended. I wish you all a good night.'

Jeremiah emerged behind her. 'This way, Miss Bee.'

Dawn watched as Haitch practically tottered from the table. Sweet Lord, was she jealous? How had Haitch, so needy and grabbing, showed more fortitude of character than she had? She'd missed her own chance of getting out a lady, with all integrity intact. Now she had to continue to play 'battle' with the ones left standing until an opportunity arose, where she could bow out of the fray with some dignity. What was going to come from all this?

———

Dawn had that numbing realisation as she closed her bedroom door in the villa, that she'd given Mr Ishimoto what he'd wanted in every respect. Alejandro's next rant was enough to turn a saint into a raging, knife-wielding, foamy-mouthed maniac. Wiping surreptitiously at her mouth, Dawn kicked off her kitten shoes.

'What a prick!' Rolling her eyes, she held her head in her hands. It was all on film, and she hoped it wasn't for sale to the lowest bidder, so to speak.

Dialling Sam's number, she waited, an ache spreading out from behind her eyes. Not a migraine, please? Not now, when the next few hours would be so crucial.

'It's me.' Holding the phone to her ear, she wondered why she was whispering. Or was the room bugged as well?

'Are we on?' Sam also seemed to be whispering. An automatic response to subterfuge.

'Yes. I'll call... him, in thirty minutes. Does that give you time to be in position?'

'I'll be there.' The phone clicked off. Dawn was left staring at her stockinged feet. A thread was hanging. Thirty minutes could stretch to infinity.

After a few deep breaths, she touched Damian's number. 'Damian? I need you to come up here.'

'It's late, Dawn.' There was a pause. 'Have you blown the commission then? Is that why you're calling?'

'I think I've found something out—'

'Tell me.' His voice had gone from sleepy to eager.

She whispered, 'I can't. I think the room is bugged.'

'Then come down here. I can send a taxi up to you now.'

Still whispering, she said, 'I need to show you. It's up here. It's important, darling. I need you to see it and tell me what you think. You'll know what it means much better than I do.'

'I'm coming up.'

'It'll be worth it, Damian. Trust me. I'll meet you on top of the main building. It's more private as only the restaurant and living rooms are under it. There's a pathway that leads directly to the roof terrace.' Apprehension vied with excitement.

'I'll be there.'

Slipping into flat shoes and winding a dark scarf around her shoulders, Dawn crept through the slumbering building and wound her way up to the roof terrace.

'Pssht?' They'd agreed not to use their own names as much as possible.

Sam stepped out of the gloom. 'I thought it a good idea to keep really hidden. As I was sneaking up here, I caught a glimpse of Haitch and some big Black bloke in the gardens over there. We don't want uninvited guests.'

'Haitch is with Orpheus then? That looked like it was on the cards from the go. She just can't help herself, can she?'

'Yep. That's Haitch for you.' He shuffled his feet. 'How did it go with Mr D.?'

'As planned.'

'If he goes for you, I will step in. You know that, don't you?'

'I understand, but you must be careful. Damian may be a city man, but he knows how to fight.'

'Yeah? Against women—'

'I mean it. Don't be too nonchalant, or he'll get you.' Gently pushing him back, she nodded over her shoulder. 'He'll be here in a moment. Get into position.'

Sam melted into the darkness behind a set of squat trees in terracotta pots. One warm-hued light lit up the area where Dawn waited. Sporadic pockets of light marched across the roof terrace. It felt like an hour, yet it could only have been minutes until a figure appeared and disappeared as if it was strobing. Damian.

'Hello, darling.' He was smiling and it looked real. 'What information have you got for me.' Reaching out, he looked like he was going to enfold her in his arms but Dawn stepped back from him.

'I'm glad you're here, Damian. Something like this should always be face-to-face.'

'Something like what?' Suspicion curled around his words. 'What game are you playing, Dawn? You know I don't like games.' He rummaged in his pockets.

'I'm not coming back to you. In fact, I'm leaving you.' The words slipped out as if oiled. How easy it was.

'Not in this lifetime,' he growled at her.

'Yes, in this lifetime. Right now. You can't touch me. All I wanted to do was say goodbye to you.'

'You seem to have forgotten that I'm your husband.'

'Not for long. I'm going to file for divorce, and you know what I'll be citing as the reason. There was such a long pause. 'Damian? Did you hear me?'

His voice betrayed his doubt. 'You won't divorce me. You love me too much.'

'I used to love you, Damian, but not anymore.' She exhaled loudly. 'Not after what you did.'

'And what did I do?'

'You know what you did. At least, if there's still the last vestiges of a decent human being inside of you.'

Damian laughed. 'No one else will want you. Not the same as I do.' He was moving his hands and Dawn realised that he was slipping on gloves. Oh, this couldn't be good.

She moved back from him. 'Is that a fact? Maybe I've already found a man who loves me more than you do.'

'What? What did you say?' There it was. That edge to his voice telling her she'd hit her mark squarely. He only wore the gloves when he was about to beat her. Was that coming next?

'You'll get the papers soon. I know you're picking Haitch up in the morning, and you're on her flight. As my flight is later than hers, I'll make my own way to the airport. Then I'm going to stay with him until I get a lawyer sorted.' She didn't have to wait long. The emphasised 'him' would be the red rag to the bull.

Dawn saw his eyes were practically slits. Light glinted off his teeth. That smile, a beast baring its fangs. So horribly familiar.

Damian cocked his head. 'Now tell me again. I want you to look me in the eye and say all that again.'

'I'm glad you came. I didn't want to do this by post, a "Dear John" letter or worse an email—'

'Just say it. I want to see you mouth these words.' The gloved hands twitched.

'I'm leaving you. That's it, Damian. We had our time together, and now that time has passed.'

Damian took a step towards her. 'You said something about another man?'

'Yes. I did.'

'Who is this cock-sucker when he's at home?'

'Why,' said Sam, striding out into the light, 'that'll be me.'

'What the fuck? You?' Damian turned to Dawn. 'You are kidding me! You're leaving me for him? Haitch's brother-in-law?'

'In a nutshell.' Dawn grinned up at him although her heart was beating fit to bust. 'Funny how things turn out, eh, Damian?'

'Yeah,' said Sam, moving up to put his arm around Dawn, 'if Haitch hadn't ruined my life with my own wife, I'd never be here with yours.'

'What the hell are you talking about?' Damian's fists were bunched by his side.

Sam sighed and shook his head. 'Haitch pretended to be my wife and slept with me. I couldn't tell my wife, or it'd kill her. So, I found your wife instead. We never expected to hit it off as much as we did. I mean, we're soul mates. She saw it in her vision. Us. Together.'

There was a movement across Damian's face like shifting tectonic plates before a volcano erupts. Dawn pulled back from him, tugging on Sam's arm. Sam must have looked down because he didn't see the punch that slammed both of them to the ground. Sam lay still. Oh, sweet Lord! Had he been knocked out? Disentangling herself from him, Dawn tried to stand but Damian's foot connected with her hip. Pain ricocheted down her leg.

'You fucking bitch! You don't leave me. I leave you! I was

going to leave you for Haitch. She's what you used to be. You don't get to do this first, and you don't do it with him!'

There was a groan. Sam heaved himself over, leaning on his elbows, something dark dribbling down his chin. Damian's fists lashed out as Sam struggled upright. Countering, Sam managed to deflect the punch but was again pushed back. At a disadvantage, he defended himself against the blows falling on him. Damian was a possessed man, spittle flying from his mouth.

'Listen, mate.' Sam wiped a stream of bloody froth across his arm. 'You're welcome to Haitch. The slut. Haitch of the big, wide-open—' Skidding sideways, Sam got to his feet. 'You won't be her first, and you certainly won't be her last. Oh, she's good, trust me—' Sam dodged a swing, 'in a porn star kind of way, so you'll have fun for a while.' He held his hands up. 'But it won't last. Me an' Dawn now.' Sam pointed at where Dawn was gripping the trunk of one of the small trees. 'We're forever. So just get over yourself, you ignorant prick!'

Dawn should have seen it coming. Damian turned fast and came at her, one fist connected with her shoulder, the other smashed her round the side of her head. Swizzled, as if she was a rag doll, she fell, an ankle twisting beneath her. Sam was over in a leap, and the two men grappled. Snatches of swearing and grunts were muted by the deep ringing in her ear. Damian landed a thump that sent Sam stumbling back to the edge of the terrace. Teetering for a moment, his body crashed through the light-weight reed fencing and hung over the edge, his arms flailing to get a purchase on the stone wall beneath him. Damian approached him with his hands outstretched.

'Sam!' Dawn could see it all happening in her mind. 'Get up!'

Scrabbling, she hauled herself upright, pain spreading across her whole body. Her vision flashed, the beginning of a full-on migraine. The side of her face was on fire.

Damian reached out to Sam, but Sam hoisted himself up and slid down, his back to the small wall. Dawn tried to clear her eyesight. Damian, kneeling on Sam's chest, now had both hands around Sam's throat. The sounds were terrible, such gurgling. Sam's legs were kicking out less and less. Oh, God! Damian was killing him. Was this what she saw in her vision? Dawn crawled across the ground and wrapped one arm around his neck, the other arm useless. Pulling him back was like grappling a bear. His neck muscles hardened as if he was in the throes of orgasm. The thought of someone else's death. Was the excitement that great?

'Get off me, you stupid bitch.' Damian shrugged her off like she was a child. He must have thought that Sam was done as he focused on Dawn.

Dragging herself back to the wall, Dawn put her knees up to her chest. A small protection against what she knew would come. Sam was lying prone and twisted. No movement to show he was still alive. Flares of light lit up the sky from below in the gardens.

'So, you're leaving me for him, eh?' Damian rubbed a smear of blood from his nose. 'Have fun with that, my darling.' He hit her, sending reverberations through her. There was nowhere to go. Another blow and another. Then she caught something from the corner of her eye. It was her only hope.

'Damian.'

'Sweetheart?' It was like he ran icy fingers down her back. He was going to kill her. She knew it.

'Damian!' She motioned with her chin. 'Look.'

At first, Damian ignored her, then he turned. A black cat was walking towards them. A black cat?

Damian reared up and tried to get away from it, but as he went to pass it, it hissed and arched its back. Dawn knew how scared he was of them. All he had to do was dodge sideways.

'Dawn! Get it away from me!' Flailing his arms, he stumbled backwards and crashed into the fencing. She heard the canes cracking through the humming in her ears. He was gone. Then only a strange low moan. Flashes lit up the sky again. Dawn sat and waited, unable to move. Where was he? Clinging to the wall? Hanging by one hand from a branch or something? How high were they?

'Uuugh!' Sam shook his head and rolled to peer up at her. 'Fuck me. I don't think that went to plan. Christ, are you okay, Dawn? I saw what he did to you.'

'I'm alive. I think.' Dawn shifted and winced. 'Oh God, Sam, I thought he'd killed you.'

'That's funny,' Sam coughed, 'I thought he'd killed me too.' He slowly turned and looked about him. 'Where is he? Did he leg it?'

'He went over the wall, Sam. I can't hear anything. I got hit on the side of my head. Can you?'

'Nothing. Shit! We're only on a roof terrace, aren't we? He hasn't fallen far.'

Dawn closed her eyes for a moment. 'Three sides overlook the gardens but...' She swallowed, '...one side goes down a cliff face.'

Sam got to his knees, hands splayed before him, head hanging low. 'Which side did he go over?'

Where was he? Which side did he go over? *Humpty Dumpty sat on a wall...* 'I have no idea. What's that?' There went the flashes again.

Sam pulled himself to the wall and looked over. 'It's Haitch and that bloke. She's taking photos...'

'I saw that earlier.' Dawn wiped at the wetness around her eyes. Now was the time to clear her head and start thinking clearly. She unwound and gingerly stretched arms, legs, prodded at her torso and touched the side of her head. Damage?

Yes, most definitely, although she'd endured worse. 'Sam? We need to work out where Damian is and… how he is.'

Sidling around the edge of the wall, Dawn heard him groan. 'I think we're all fucked.'

'It's the cliff edge, isn't it?' *Humpty Dumpty had a great fall…*

'Yep.'

'And you can't hear him shouting?' *All the king's horse's and all the king's men…*

'Nope.'

'We have to call for help, tell someone that…'

…couldn't put Humpty together again…

'No, first,' said Sam, 'we've got to get you to a doctor—'

'No way. Not for me at least.' Dawn indicated his injuries.

'We need to think this through,' said Sam, looming close to her as another flash of light lit up his face. 'Before we alert the authorities, especially the police. Dawn, we could be done for murder. You know what I'm saying.'

'We have to find out if Damian is alive…' *Done for murder?*

'He's not alive. You know it. More than any of us, you know that's the truth.'

'We should find out. He may be injured but not able to call for help.'

'Okay. Listen, I'll get you to your room and then I'll go look for him.'

Dawn nodded. It was about as much as she could do.

It seemed a long way back. Easing her onto her bed, Sam stroked her hair from her face. 'It's going to be all right. I don't know how but we'll make it all right.'

'It's my fault, Sam. I think I've killed him. I set all this in motion from that stupid vision I had. If it wasn't for me, you wouldn't be here, and all this wouldn't have happened.'

'Yes, it would. One way or another, maybe some part would

be different, but the end would be the same. I'll find him. I need you to be calm and don't call through to anyone. Please? Until I get back to you?'

Dawn put her head in her hands. 'Yes.' Her voice was muffled, yet he heard. The door closed softly.

FORTY-TWO

Sam

IF DAMIAN WAS DEAD, then they were truly screwed. They'd
planned to piss him off, send him off on one, not send him over
the edge of a cliff. Dead? Christ Almighty. Sam could barely
walk for shaking. Had they inadvertently killed a man? He was
a complete shit, for sure, but he didn't deserve this. What the
fuck were they going to do? Maybe he was still alive.

Orientation in the dark was tricky, although he'd always had
a head for directions. Poor Tilly once got lost in the ladies' toilets
at Gatwick airport and freaked right out. Stop! Don't think
about her. Not now.

Mule trails crisscrossed the mountainside. In daylight, this
would be a lovely walk but lit only by starlight and a moon beset
by scudding clouds, it was hard going. Brambles snaked round
his ankles, scratching and threatening to pitch him down the
scree and gorse covered slope below the villa. There were noises
in the dark that made him shudder. Aided only by the torch on
his phone, Sam shone it upwards and located two breaks in the
fencing that circled the roof terrace they'd been on. Weaving
downwards, there seemed to be smashed vegetation. Following

the most likely route down, Sam slipped and stumbled until there was a fork in the track. Which way?

'Damian?' Why was his voice so hoarse? He gingerly touched his neck. 'Ouch.' Oh yes, Damian had been strangling him.

Taking the right-hand path, Sam skidded on pebbles below a rock he was clambering across. Half keeling over, he put out a hand to catch himself and felt something soft. Turning his head, he shone the torch. The hairs on the back of his neck stood up as Damian was staring straight at him.

'Damian?' It was a squeak. Sam crashed back into the gnarly bushes that dotted the track, his hand trembling so much, the light wavered.

One eye remained open, and he had a look of puzzled surprise on half his face. The other half was smashed and raw. Sam gulped in air and waved the torch around. Damian's head was facing towards him, yet his torso seemed to be the other way around. As if he'd been twisted in half.

'You alright, mate?'

Sam blinked. What the fuck was he doing? Of course, Damian wasn't alright. He was dead. Completely and utterly dead. Lunging, Sam retched loudly. He waited, nausea washing over him, his eyes blurring in and out of focus. What were they going to do? How could he keep Dawn out of this? His life had been over the moment that Haitch had duped him. Haitch. It was her fault, not his, not Dawn's and possibly not even Damian's.

'I'm so sorry, mate. I really am.'

He couldn't bear to look round. Christ Almighty. He was dead, and this was a disaster. What were they going to do now?

Rocking back on his heels, Sam switched off the torch. No good wasting power and drawing attention to himself. He had to work out a plan. What time was it? When did the sun come up here? Same time as England? Shining the torch back over the body, Sam saw the pinky-coloured watch on Damian's limp wrist poking from under a glove. Why had he put gloves on... oh, he was preparing himself for a fight. He was getting set up to beat the shit out of Dawn. The bastard deserved all he'd got!

Without thinking, he ripped off his t-shirt and wrapping it around his hand, pulled off the gloves. They would have his and Dawn's DNA all over them. He carefully unclipped the watch and slid it off, then searched through his pockets until he found what he was looking for: Damian's phone, wallet and keys. Would that make it look like he'd been robbed or rather grave-robbed after he'd fallen? A passing light-fingered goat herder? Oh God, he didn't want to get some poor sod grilled by the police here. If this was a used path, then the body would be found easily. Should he move him? Sam dragged in a breath. No, the less he mucked about with it all, it might still come across as an accident. A horrible, bizarre accident but an accident none-the-less. Maybe?

'Fuck!' Sweat stung the many cuts across his face. Shining the torchlight, he stared at the bruises and ragged grazes across his knuckles. 'Fuck, fuck, fuck!'

He was drenched in sweat as he pulled the t-shirt back on. Clutching Damian's phone in his other hand, he returned the way he'd come. He'd need Dawn's cooperation if his idea, flimsy as it was, would work.

Stood irresolute near the villa, Sam resisted the urge to creep to Dawn's room. They were running out of time. Backtracking to the hire car, he drove as carefully down the winding road as he could. Getting stopped by the local cops and having to explain what he'd been doing and why his knuckles were shredded would be a catastrophe. So, back to the hotel. It was one of those that gave you a latch key. All that meant was that the guests could come and go as they pleased without waking the happily snoring staff. Thank Christ for that.

Back in his room, he stared at himself in the mirror. He could practically see red handprints circling his throat, and every bit of him ached. Lifting his t-shirt, he recoiled at the lesions that were already mottling his skin. After splashing tepid water on his face, he retrieved his phone.

Would she answer? 'Dawn?'

'Yes? Did... did you... find him... him?'

'He's dead, Dawn. I'm so sorry. I never meant it to be like this. I need to talk to you. Can you do that?'

'Are you going to tell me how we can sort this out?' There was a muffled sobbing sound as if she had her mouth covered. 'I hated him for what he did to me and my baby, but I never wanted him dead. Do you believe that, Sam? You have to believe me.'

'He attacked us, beat the crap out of us. Anyway, neither one of us shoved him. I didn't really see what happened, did you?'

Dawn made a strange sound. 'It was a black cat. He's always been terrified of them. He must have been so pumped with adrenaline that he couldn't think straight. He ran backwards, to get away from the cat and then he wasn't there anymore. I didn't even hear a scream.'

'A fucking cat killed him?' Sam wanted to laugh, it was the shock kicking in. 'Dawn. I took his watch and his phone.'

'Why?' He could hear she was fading.

'I'm going to set Haitch up. I need you to help me.'

'What? Set her up for what? Murder?'

'Think about it, Dawn. Whose fault is all this?'

'Haitch's, mine, oh I don't know.'

'Yes, Haitch's. We're not going down for murder. She is.'

'We didn't murder him. It was an accident.'

'It was, except then we need to explain why I'm here at something I wasn't invited to. That could be tricky.'

Dawn was silent. Sam wondered if she'd passed out.

'Sam? Those flashes? If they were Haitch and Orpheus taking photos, they might have inadvertently snapped one of us. With Damian.'

'Then we need to get that phone back and delete everything.'

'This is too much, Sam. We should call the police and tell them what happened.'

'Tell them a black cat killed him? Is that what you're saying, Dawn? They'll go for that, won't they? You've heard that foreign police forces can be a little hard on us Brits?'

Silence. Was she now thinking this through? His mind was going supernova. He'd wanted revenge, and maybe now he could get it for real. Except she'd be punished for what she hadn't done instead of all the things she had. Tit for tat.

'Have you a proposition?'

She was in.

'Yes.'

What had he got to play with? Sam clutched the toilet bowl tighter, aware that there could be nothing left in his stomach. But he was loath to leave the sanctuary of the bathroom. He'd specifically taken the phone, wallet, watch and keys. Sifting through the wallet, he pulled out business cards, pounds and euros, credit cards and some receipts. One card advertised a 'Gentleman's Club'. That translated to strip joint with expensive drinks. Nice. Did Dawn know her hubby visited such places? Did she care, as long as she wasn't being beaten up by the sick bastard? Phone. Keys. Had he made a mistake by taking them? Boy, his head hurt.

Keys. Yes, the keys. Hands shaking, Sam examined each one in turn. There it was. A key with H on a separate ring. It must be Haitch's spare.

Lurching from the bathroom, he fell onto the bed. The last thing he remembered was Dawn's warning: Haitch might have photos of them. An image of Tilly's face swam before him as he blacked out.

Help me.

FORTY-THREE

Dawn

DAMIAN WAS DEAD. No matter how many times she repeated this, it didn't feel real. What kind of people would leave him alone down there? People who were sick in soul and damaged. Damian was dead, and she and Sam would probably be imprisoned for murder or manslaughter. She had got Sam involved. She must take responsibility. How had the vision led them to here? Was it solely that she'd read into it exactly what she wanted and not what was there? She'd seen a death because she'd engineered it herself. Believing it might be her own was a sorry excuse now.

Examining her injuries, she let out a deep sigh. With a bit of luck, she might be able to get through the next day unnoticed. Dark-glasses and deft use of make-up had served her well in the past. Her hearing had returned, although the left-hand side of her face was swollen. Bruises were blooming down her leg and discolouring her arms. She could keep these hidden, although any movement of her shoulder made her want to scream. Her leg and hip were stiffening up, making walking hard. Poking about in her bag, she found the painkillers she always carried.

Downing a double dose, she hoped it might at least dull the agony for a while.

Should she call the manager? Was he called Jeremiah? He'd have to help, if even to save the reputation of the villa. No. Sam said he'd got a plan. She had to trust him.

'Damian?' It was a whisper. 'I never intended this to happen. You were meant to be my forever love. I loved you with my whole being…' The words stuttered, 'but you killed our baby and blamed me for it. I couldn't forgive you, so I don't expect you to forgive me either.'

An alarm. That's what that sound was. Groggy from the tablets she'd taken, Dawn heaved herself out of bed, a toe touching the cool tiles. The phone was ringing. Grabbing it quickly, she mumbled: 'Yes? Dawn here.'

'It's me.' Sam sounded old as if the experiences of last night had aged him fifty years. 'Meet me at the airport at two in departures.'

'Have you worked something out?' *Are we going to spend the last viable years of our lives in a Spanish prison?*

'I'll tell you when I see you. Are you okay?'

'What do you think? It doesn't take a medium to tell you what I might be feeling right now.' Were her words harsh?

'I'm sorry. Call me when you get there.'

Breakfast. It should've been a delight. Able to order anything on the menu, her stomach was now twisting in knots, and her lips were puffed. As she sat at a table near a window, a young waiter approached with a list.

'Orange juice. Thank you.'

Dawn, her make-up applied carefully, avoided making eye contact, hiding behind blocky-shaped sunglasses. Thank goodness they were the fashion now. She'd never get away with a skinny pair. Wearing a long-sleeved top and linen trousers, she hoped she looked stylish instead of someone concealing something. It was beginning to heat up outside and the cicadas were bursting into a rhythm, even though it was still early. Focusing on the sun's rays spreading out as it rose, she repressed the sobs rising from her gut.

The juice stung her lips, yet she swallowed gratefully, aware that tears trickled down her cheeks. She mustn't show emotion. Wiping at her eyes, she finished her glass as Jeremiah slipped up to her.

'Can I get you anything else, Miss Rayne?'

'No, thanks. I'm going to my room. I'll send for a taxi when I'm ready. I presume that we don't have to say goodbye to the rest of the group. Is that correct?'

'That is quite so. The party finished last night. You are all free to go when you are ready. May I call a taxi for you? You can phone down to reception when you need one.' Peering at her, he looked as if he was about to say something but changed his mind.

'Thank you.' Dawn turned to the French windows. 'If you don't mind, I'd like a few more moments to enjoy this amazing view.'

'Of course.'

Dawn waited until he'd returned to the reception area and then levered herself up from the table. Even if Jeremiah had seen her swollen face, he was trained not to ask questions. It wasn't his business, was it? The tablets were wearing off, and the pains in her hip and shoulder were excruciating. Not wanting to draw attention, she decided to exit via the French windows.

Grabbing hold of the frame, she steadied herself, aware of someone entering the room behind her. Pretending not to hear the soft footsteps, she stood quietly, but whoever it was, turned at the last moment, moving to another part of the room. Hearing low voices, Dawn took her chance and hobbled back to her bedroom.

After an hour sat on the bed staring vacantly into space, she roused herself and asked Jeremiah to call the taxi for her. Then she was heading from the villa along the scary, barely tarmacked road. Damian was somewhere down there, lying in the heat and the dirt. Had his death been quick? Had he realised as he fell, if only for a split-second, that he was going to die? She'd done all this.

The journey to Málaga airport was a blur of pain, nausea and flitting images. All she knew was that she had to get home. She'd be able to think straight then. Calling Sam, she waited by a yellow *Correos* post box. Their chosen meeting place. They were on the same flight but not near to each other.

'Dawn?'

Sam's face was scrunched, and he had the appearance of someone who hadn't slept for a week. It was meant to be a 'kick in the teeth scenario' for Damian, but now he wouldn't be able to appreciate the gesture.

'I still can't believe it. Is this wise, Sam? To leave without notifying anyone?'

'Probably not.'

'Surely, if we go now, there is no turning back. We still have time to tell the truth, haven't we?'

Sam knuckled at his eyes. 'I don't know. Do you want to throw our lives to the mercies of a foreign court? I'm really not up for that, Dawn. I read that, only sixty years ago, the Spanish were still publicly flogging women who'd been caught wearing no-sleeve tops on a Sunday. That's the mindset we'd be up against.'

'If we own up, the most they can do is try us for manslaughter. It was an accident. If we leave, they will most likely say we murdered... him.'

'Or we work out an alternative story.'

Dawn shook her head. 'I don't like this.'

'Dawn,' Sam hunkered down and took hold of her hands. Leaning in closer, he whispered, 'We can't change what's happened. But we could change the outcome, the end of the story.'

'The one where we imply that Haitch killed him?'

Tugging her by the arm, Sam pulled her to an unoccupied bench. 'We won't be able to talk on the plane, and we should be careful not to be seen together too much.'

'What, exactly, are we going to do?'

'If and when you are contacted, you tell the police that you got back as expected, but Damian didn't come home. You knew he was picking up one of his clients, Haitch Bee, in the morning. In fact, you'd seen them arguing on one of the roof terraces the night of the party.'

'Arguing? Will anyone believe that?' It hurt so much to speak.

'You say that Damian had told you it might be a bit rocky, that he was going to tell her that he was letting her go, as she was... let's say getting too needy, and that he was going to concentrate on your career.' Sam had to swallow and drag in a breath. 'You tell them she'd bought an expensive watch for him and that he was going to return it to her as it was getting too much.' He paused as if thinking. 'You tell them he was wearing it at the party, ready to hand it back to her. They'll be wondering where it went...'

'And what happened when he didn't come home?'

'You say you phoned him, but it went to answerphone. You assumed he was sorting loose ends or whatever.'

'This is never going to work.'

'How many people knew what kind of relationship you had? What I'm trying to say is that, to the outside world, you had a loving, caring relationship. Right?'

'Yes. All a sham.'

'Precisely. No one else knows that do they?'

'So, I saw them arguing. Then what?'

'I'm working on it.'

'That sounds a bit flimsy to me. What about any pictures Haitch might have?'

'I'm working on that, too. I'll let you know once I get a semblance of a plan. You have to trust me, Dawn. We'll get through this.'

Glad that too many seats separated them on the plane for any more conversation, Dawn downed more painkillers and dozed, slipping in and out of a sleep filled with shadows and bloodied faces. Finally opening her front door, she was bombarded by the smell of furniture polish and potpourri. Firmly shutting it behind her, she allowed herself one sob. She phoned Damian, terrified that he'd answer it and relieved when it went to voicemail where she left a concerned message. The devoted worried wife. Facing away from the photos on the wall, she crept to the bathroom. It took the last of her strength to run a hot bath. What would it take to simply sink below the water and sleep? But then she might meet Damian. Alive, he'd scared her. Dead, he would terrify her.

FORTY-FOUR

Sam

IF HE WANTED to implicate Haitch, then he had to work this all through. Damian's phone was unlocked. Who in their right mind had an unlocked phone? At least he didn't have to take it somewhere. There were a couple of voicemails from Haitch querying where he was. Then he heard the one from Dawn. It sounded normal, which was all he could hope for right now. He'd had a near miss back at the hotel, just managing to get into his room and close the door as Haitch rounded the corner. He didn't think she'd seen him. As long as no one knew he'd been there, the police wouldn't be looking for him as a possible suspect. Why should they?

Seeing how frail and vulnerable Dawn was at the airport, he worried that they wouldn't be able to pull this off. Deciding to check into a Travelodge for a night, he went to a McDonald's and punched down a burger and fries. Gone were the days of fresh fruit and salads. Thoughts swarmed inside his head like angry wasps. What if Haitch downloaded her photos and there were incriminating ones of them? Slurping the rest of his coke, Sam took out Haitch's spare key. Ten minutes tops, he could be slipping into her flat. It took longer than ten minutes to get to her flat, and Sam could see that she was still in. What had she thought when Damian hadn't picked her up that morning?

Loitering beneath a fat-trunked tree opposite, he knew he could quickly duck behind it if she came out. He waited. And waited. Just as he was contemplating leaving, Haitch slammed her front door and jogged purposefully down the road, her sweatshirt hoodie pulled up, but Sam knew it was her. Where the hell was she going at this time of night? How long did he have? Go. Go now.

Dropping the key twice made him more jittery. He managed to get the door open and pushed inside, his heart yammering in his chest and his breathing fast. It took only a moment to locate the computer and switch it on. Going straight to her photos, Sam flicked through the most recent and noted with relief that they were dated more than a week ago. Cocking his head to listen, he moved around the flat as fast as he could, carefully searching under or behind things for her phone. Where was it? Knowing Haitch, probably in her back pocket.

Footsteps thumped up the front steps. Fuck it! She was coming back. Where could he hide? There was nowhere to hide. The spare bedroom off the hallway? Diving into it, he tucked behind the door.

Haitch came in noisily and headed into the living room. The radio blared, making him jump, then she turned the volume down. Creeping out, Sam peered up the hallway. She was poking at the computer. He'd forgotten to switch it off. Stupid mistake. She was moving across the room, her back to him. Sam tip-toed down the hallway and gently opened the door. It made a sound, a 'click'. Whipping out, he hunkered down in the communal bin area, making himself as small as he could. Her front door opened, and he heard her feet padding down the steps. From his position, he could easily see her looking up and down the road. If she turned to her left, she'd spot him. Fate was on his side that night. Turning to her right, she mumbled 'Shit!' and strode up the steps. Sam waited for another couple of minutes before he crawled out. Had she called the police? Scanning around him, Sam scooted down the road, not quite running but at a steady pace. There was no wail of sirens or flashing lights. Another near miss. How many lives did he have left?

———

The bed in the Travelodge was large and comfy; still, he felt small and uncomfortable, thrashing from one side to the other, up and down for most of the night. Waking early, he had a cold shower and then texted from Damian's phone to Haitch's: *Sorry for missing you. Had urgent business to attend to. Glad you got home okay. D.* Did that sound like the sort of text Damian would send or was it missing lots of smiley faces and kisses? No. He wasn't that kind of man. So, how was he going to get the phone off Haitch?

Knowing he had to be out of the lodge soon, Sam toyed with the puzzle pieces that he had to lock together. Watch. Phone. Wallet. Keys. He'd tried to find Haitch's phone, but it must be on her. What did he expect? Tilly always had that sexy bulge in her back pocket, and how many times had he grabbed it out? Come on. Think this through. Yes. This might work. Dangerous? Most definitely. Stupid? Absolutely. Could it work? Maybe. That was all he had.

He searched for a locksmith and got Haitch's key replicated. Boy, was he on a time limit here.

The subsequent text to Haitch's phone read: *Meet me outside the Odeon in Leicester Square at 8.30. I'll explain everything then. D.*

He intended for her to wait for hours, then at least she'd be away from her flat. That's where Dawn's part in the plan came in.

He phoned Dawn. 'Meet me as soon as you can.' He gave directions.

'I'm literally heading out the door now.' He heard the door slam; the swish of material and the faint click of heels.

'Are you okay? Have you heard anything yet?'

'I've been contracted by the police.' Dawn's voice was breathless, as if walking fast. 'They've found him, found Damian. Two officers turned up at my door. The hotel had contacted the local Spanish police to report that Damian was missing and hadn't paid his bill. After he was discovered, and they'd linked him to Mr Ishimoto's party at the villa, it was Jeremiah who identified him. He told them h'd met Damian briefly when he arrived with Haitch.'

'Shit! Are you alright?'

'I think I handled it very well. Played the shocked and grieving widow perfectly.' Familiar muffled noises were in the background. The sound of cars, people in the distance. 'That's probably because I am a shocked and grieving widow!'

The sarcasm was not lost on Sam. 'Did you say what we planned before?'

'Just enough.'

'You mentioned the watch?'

'Yes. I told them Damian had been wearing it when he left me in the hotel. I told them it was a gift from another client and that she was getting quite pushy.'

'What else did they ask you?'

'If I saw anything else that night?'

'And you said?'

'I saw Haitch and Damian arguing in the villa on a roof terrace. I was walking in the garden and saw them.'

'What did they say to that?'

'They asked me if I thought that was strange? My husband with this other woman.'

'How did you reply to that?'

'I said no because she was always calling him and trying to get him to come over. I also said he was going to try to talk to her about her constant pestering, as it was putting a strain on our marriage.'

'And then what?'

'I told them about the watch, and I added I believed that Haitch wasn't capable of murder. That if something had happened, then it must have been an accident.'

'You defended her? That was a good touch. After that?'

'I didn't say much else, just cried a lot.'

'Okay. Do you think the officers saw your... er, bruises?'

'No. I'm extremely adept at my make-up now. I took enough painkillers this morning; I'm practically numb.' There was a bib of a horn and some muffled noises. 'I don't know how much time I've got, Sam.'

'I'll give you the key when we meet.'

'I need to get over to her place before she or the police get there.'

'I'll try and keep her hanging on for as long as I can.'

'Hopefully, I won't need long. Thanks for getting me a key cut.'

———

It'd be risky, but then this whole thing was a house of cards, ready to tip and tumble at any moment. After seeing Dawn and passing her the key, Sam ensured he was in Leicester Square ahead of Haitch. He'd mapped out numerous escape routes. If he couldn't find what he was looking for, he'd have to do it himself. He fingered the balaclava he'd bought. If he was fast, it might work?

She arrived looking flustered and was obviously searching for Damian in the crowd. Luckily, she was easily recognisable. A skull and red roses dress and skinny black jeans and biker boots. Scary spiky jewellery. Sam had forgotten how punky she was. Her look fitted his plan perfectly. Sam squinted. Her hair was now dark, and for a moment, she looked more like Tilly. He shook his head.

Sam had to be vigilant. Money in his pocket. Damian's phone. Haitch's spare key. If he was collared by the police for any misdemeanour, they'd have him for murder. The watch he'd passed to Dawn.

Wow. Haitch would sure wait a long time for the man. It was closer to ten now.

They were rag-tagging through the crowd. Kids, five, maybe six of them. Disparate ages and sexes but street kids none-the-less. Sam managed to get in front of them and be loitering at the mouth of an alley when they raced past.

'Oy!' Sam waved a wad of notes and nodded for them to come over. They were as wary as feral cats offered a saucer of milk.

'Watcha want, mister?'

Was this the leader? A scrawny boy of about thirteen. Didn't look as if he'd been house trained.

'I have a hundred pounds here if you do a job for me.'

'You a copper?'

'Do I look like a copper?'

'Nah. Boots ain't big enuff.'

The kids sniggered and took a step forward. They were all grubby around the edges.

The leader put his hands on his hips and slouched. 'So, watcha want?'

'There's a woman... she's my ex-wife, and she's got some of my stuff—'

'You want us to get it back, eh?'

'That's right. I'm looking for a phone. You can take anything else she has. I only want the phone. Do you think you can do that?'

'For a hundred? Nah.'

'It's all I've got,' said Sam. He shrugged his shoulders. 'Take it or leave it.'

'I don't think that's all you've got.' The boy shrugged his shoulders too. 'Two hundred. Mugging someone, especially a woman is pretty hard-core. We'd get into a lot of trouble for that. Gotta make it worth our while. Take it or leave it, mister.'

Sam raised an eyebrow. The boy mimicked him again. 'Okay. You get fifty now and the rest when it's done.'

'Show us you got the money in the first place.'

Sam held onto the money belt around his waist and eyed the kids. Tugging the zip open, the wedge of notes was visible. 'Now, you think of doing me, and I'll fucking kill you. Understood?'

The idea must have crossed at least one of their minds by the collective swallowing.

'Awright.' The boy nodded. 'Who's the mark then?'

Sam nearly laughed. Such little thugs and gangsters in the making. 'She's in the pub over there. I want her phone. That's it. Just her phone. She's wearing a gothic horror of a dress, all skulls and red roses over tight black jeans. She's also got great big biker boots on. Dark hair, skinny. Think you got all that?'

'Yeah, we got that.' The boy turned to the others. 'Don't do nuffink stupid.'

'One last thing. Check the back pocket of her jeans. She sometimes has her phone in there. I'll be here when you've done it.'

'It's as good as done.' The boy grinned up at him.

———

It might be warm, that sort of humid city warmth that sucked the energy out of you, yet Sam came out in a cold sweat that soaked his back and left sweaty patches under his armpits. Would the kids do it or run with the cash they had? Or an alternative he hadn't thought through. What if they called the cops on him? Finally, there was a hard pelting of feet.

'Here you go, mister.' The boy waved the phone at him.

'Did it go okay?'

'Easy. Now give us our money.'

Sam inched forward, keeping a tight grip on the money. The boy did the same with the phone. When it was in his hand, Sam released the cash. The kids ran off down the street, shouting and laughing. Maybe they'd stitched him up, and this was one of theirs, a cheap old Chinese copy. Relief poured through him. It was a Samsung Galaxy. She always had one.

'Dawn? I've got it.'

'And I've done what you asked me to.'

'Are you out now? Haitch will be on her way back.'

'Heading out the door now. I'll throw the rubber gloves when I get further away. Shall I meet you?'

'I think we'd better get back to our respective places and keep our heads down for a bit. See what happens...' Sam stared at the phone. 'Hang on, there's something wrong. I'll call you back in a minute.'

This wasn't the phone that had sent the texts yesterday. The number didn't match. This wasn't the phone from Spain.

'Fuck!'

It came out as a strangled cry, and a woman and child veered from him. Sam turned his head sideways, so she couldn't see his face. Why did Haitch have this second phone and more to the bleeding point, *where was the other fucking phone?* Sam clutched at the wall, his hand bunched, nails digging into the softness of his palms. Was Dawn right? Should they have gone straight to the Spanish police with the tale of the murdering black cat? Now he wanted to cry.

FORTY-FIVE

Dawn

KNOWING that Sam had literally escaped from Haitch's the day before by the skin of his teeth didn't make Dawn feel good about this. The newly cut key slipped in and turned easily, but she hesitated. No one was about, yet that didn't mean the nets upstairs weren't twitching. Wearing horrendously old-fashioned dark glasses, a floppy hat and some sort of kaftan she'd found at the back of the closet, she might be taken for an elderly aunt come to visit. Better get in quick or turn around and go home now.

The hallway was long and decorated white, with some of Haitch's own work, although there were a couple of paintings in stark contrast. Subtle and tightly drawn watercolours depicting, amongst other things, some of the fairy tales that she'd known as a child. Were these done by Haitch's sister? The poor, lied to, cheated upon sister? The woman Sam loved.

Rousing herself, Dawn ventured further in, overwhelmed by being in the lair of the beast, this woman who was endeavouring to steal everything from her and had already done the same to Sam. Not that she wished to keep Damian for herself. Far from it. If he'd simply said he wanted a divorce, that he had found another woman, she'd have been fine with that... no, she'd have been ecstatic. But there was no way he would have set her free.

Rubber gloves on, she poked through drawers, opening cupboards and fingering Haitch's things. Each time she put it all back as carefully and precisely as she found it. Hmm, where should she put it? This inconspicuous thing that could tip the balance against Haitch. She listened? What was that sound? Voices? Oh, thank goodness, it was only people out in the street. Clutching at her chest, she backtracked to the bedroom and slid open a drawer full of knickers. Lacy ones, thongs, ones with patterns and some plain, but underneath them was an odd assortment of objects. Dawn pulled her hand out fast. It looked the sort of drawer a serial killer might have. Mementoes. No, trophies. Thinking about it, this was the perfect place to stash the watch. From Haitch to her husband Damian, and now it was being returned to her. Oh, the irony of it. She tucked it in, but not so hidden that someone searching might miss seeing it.

Was she really doing this? Stopping for a moment, she closed her eyes. Damian was dead. There was no bringing him back, but to point the finger at an innocent woman? Innocent of this, at least. Could she do that? But she'd already lied to the police. Laid a trail of breadcrumbs to follow. It led here. If she didn't follow through, then it was her word against Haitch's, who could say she'd been the jealous wife and killed Damian. Now, that was not too far from the truth now, was it? Who else knew about her true relationship with Damian? No one. He'd made sure of that.

The next thing to sort out was the laptop. Opening the lid gently, Dawn poured a glassful of water over the keys and dribbled it into as many ports as she could find. Then carefully mopped up any excess.

Checking one last time that she hadn't moved anything too much, she walked quickly from the flat, without turning back. If anyone had watched her, she hoped they'd still see the elderly aunt.

When the phone went, Dawn slowed. Sam. Had something gone wrong?

'There's a big pub down the road from Haitch's place called The Red Ferret. Can you meet me there? I'll be as quick as I can. We have a problem.'

A wave of cold air swept over Dawn. Problem? 'Should I go and get the, um, thingy back out? Do I have time?'

'No. Haitch is on her way home now. Get in the pub and wait for me at the back if that's possible. I'll find you.'

———————

The waiting game. Was she sick of it, or what? It took him ages to arrive.

When Sam pushed his way through the punters to where she was sat on a bench, Dawn didn't know whether to scream at him or burst into tears. Probably both. He squeezed in beside her.

'It's not the same phone.' His voice was low. 'She's swapped the one she was using in Spain for this new one.'

'Why?'

'I wish I knew.'

'No photos then?'

'No. It's like a new phone. Nothing at all.'

'That means the one she was using at the party is still out there?' Dawn drank the rest of her wine in two gulps. 'Does that mean she's already downloaded the pictures and knows we were part of it?'

'We have no idea what's in those photos. We might be doing all this for nothing.'

'Unless the police are now looking for us.'

'Unless that.' Sam shook his head slowly. 'I'm so sorry, Dawn. I thought I could get us out of this. Looks as if I've failed badly.'

What were they going to do now?

'Why on Earth would Haitch have this other phone? Listen, if she took this phone out with her, maybe that means she left the one from Spain back in her flat?'

'But we've both searched for it there.'

Dawn tap-tapped on the side of her empty glass with her fingernail. 'Doesn't matter. It must be somewhere we didn't think of looking. We go back to her flat—'

'Again?'

'Yes. Again. And we really look for that phone.'

'This is getting out of hand.' Sam peered around the pub. 'Maybe we should now turn ourselves in.'

'One last chance, then we deal with whatever is coming our way.'

Sam ground at his eyes with the palms of his hands. A small moan escaped him. 'She must be back by now. I'll see if she's in the flat. If she is, I'll say I'm looking for Tilly, that I thought she was there.'

'That's a gamble.'

'It's all we have.'

'I found something when I was looking for a place to hide the watch.' She touched him briefly on the shoulder. 'I think she keeps souvenirs of everyone she's slept with. Did you lose anything after, well, you know?'

Sam cocked his head to one side. 'Now you mention it, I haven't been able to find the cuff links my brother gave me a couple of Christmas's ago. I'm sure I had them not long before... You think she might have them?'

'It's worth a look.'

FORTY-SIX

Sam

What was he going to do if Haitch answered the door?

Ringing on the doorbell, he banged a couple of times for good measure. Waiting for a few minutes, he motioned Dawn up the steps and quickly opened the door. Standing in the hall, he listened. Nothing. What were the chances that she'd popped out again? Not high and she might be back any second. Or, most likely, she was home and calling the police.

Dawn mouthed: 'Are we okay?'

Sam shrugged. Not really, sprang to mind. There was no excuse he could ever come up with to cover why he and Dawn would be stood in Haitch's flat without her permission.

Wiping at the sweat on his top lip, Sam pushed into the living room.

'Haitch?' Oh shit. She was in. Stood gaping at him with some huge Black bloke at her shoulder. That's why she hadn't answered the door.

'Sam?' Haitch waved her hands. 'What are you—' Her eyes swivelled. 'Dawn?'

'Hello, Haitch.' Dawn came to stand beside Sam. 'Hello Orpheus.'

'Dawn. Sam.' The other man nodded as if this was all perfectly normal. He turned to Haitch. 'What the hell is going on?'

'Sam?' Haitch's face looked wretched. 'We've seen the photos. You were there. With Damian. He's dead, you know.'

Seen the photos? Oh, God! There was evidence, concrete, hard, glossy full-colour evidence that placed them there, at the scene of the crime. A crime that didn't actually happen until they'd left the scene. A paradox, really. Had his legs turned to jelly? They weren't doing a good job of holding him up.

'We know.' Sam pointed at the sofa. 'Do you mind?' He slumped into it. Now what? Had they already called the police?

'It was an accident, Haitch.' Dawn took a step forward.

'I'm not Haitch. I'm Tilda…Tilly.'

Sam looked up. 'What?' What did she just say?

'I'm Tilda. I was the one who went to Spain. Haitch was ill. She asked me to cover for her.' She peered down at Sam. 'What I want to know is why you were there? With Dawn? Ah!' Something darted across her face. 'Now, I get it. She's your new love.' Tilda's voice cracked.

'No, she's not.' Sam lurched to his feet, hands out. 'Tilly? It's really you? You were the one we saw in Spain? What the hell is going on?'

'That's kind of what we'd like to know?' Orpheus nodded. 'You know?'

'Christ.' Sam shook his head. 'You wouldn't believe us if we told you. Where's Haitch?'

'At the police station.' Tilda's face was slick with tears. 'She's being questioned about Damian's death, except I think we can all say she couldn't have had anything to do with it?' The look in her eyes pinned him to the carpet.

'We didn't kill him,' said Dawn. 'He tried to kill us.'

'Hell,' said Orpheus, 'has this got batshit crazy or what?'

'I think you have to tell us, and then let us decide if we believe you.' Tilda moved Orpheus' laptop round to show them the photos. 'We have one of Damian falling past us, and then one of you two lit up. Very recognisable, as you can see. My sister is in the nick, possibly accused of a murder when she wasn't even in the country at the time. Now, as I was, and I know for certain that I didn't kill him that night, that leaves you two. My husband... my soon-to-be-ex-husband and you, Dawn. I don't know what your connection is in all this.'

'Damian's my husband.' Dawn blinked rapidly. 'Was my husband.'

'Your husband?' said Orpheus. 'Pray, tell us what the fuck is going on?'

Sam pointed at Orpheus. 'I know I don't have the right as yet to say this, but who are you again? And what are you doing with my wife?'

'I think with your track record,' Orpheus said quietly, 'she might now be your ex-wife? Just saying.'

Sam itched to punch him as hard as he could in the face, although that probably wouldn't help much.

'Sam.' Dawn's voice was gentle. 'You must tell her the truth. In fact, if you don't, I will.'

'What truth might that be?' Tilda eyed Dawn.

'At the party,' Dawn continued, 'I thought you were Haitch. I made barbed remarks at you to rattle your cage, as they say. But of course, you had no idea what I was alluding to, did you?'

'I remember you were pretty weird towards me. Not exactly friendly or supportive. So, all that was for Haitch's benefit. Why?'

'Sam? Tell her. Tell her all of it.' Dawn gestured towards the kitchen. 'Any chance I can make a pot of tea?'

'Why not?' Tilda laughed a little hysterically. 'Why not have a lovely cup of tea while we discuss why you've framed my sister for murder.'

Sam wanted to run from the room. 'We need to sit down. This is a long story, and most of it's not nice.'

FORTY-SEVEN

Matilda

THAT NIGHT, Tilda listened to every word Sam and Dawn told her. Or rather heard the words; they were so incredible. And they hurt as if she'd been sliced a thousand times. Sam hadn't cheated on her. There was no other woman… there was just a woman who looked exactly like her who had torn out her own sister's heart and thrown it away. Tilda knew Sam was telling the truth. How he had been fooled by Haitch. The fact that Haitch had purposely made herself look, even smell the same as her. How could she have done that to her?

'We need to see what's in that drawer.' Sam stood and made his way slowly to the bedroom. 'Where is it, Dawn?'

Tilda followed Dawn in, watched as Sam pulled the knickers out of the drawer and upended the rest of the contents onto the bed. Tilda didn't want to see this. They were violating Haitch's private space. But it was more that she knew she was about to be violated more.

'You shouldn't be doing this. It's wrong.' Something tightened in her chest. 'Is this about the watch?' Tilda couldn't work it out. 'Why plant the watch?'

Sam frowned. 'To incriminate her? Listen, Tilly. The main thing here is I think she keeps trophies of the people she's shagged.'

'More like preyed upon,' said Dawn.

'What's that got to do with anything?' Tilda was going to burst. 'It's none of our business. I can't let you do this.'

'This is more to do with you, Tilly,' said Sam. 'You need to look.'

'No. I don't. Get out. Get out all of you now!'

'Here.' Sam grabbed something and then brandished them at her. What were they? Tilda moved further in. Leaning down, she recognised the cuff links that Sam's brother John had given him the year before. What were they doing in here? What had Sam called them? Trophies? These things were here because Haitch had fooled her husband into sleeping with her and she needed a keepsake. Proof. Her eyes slid over the other items spread over the duvet. She focused. Memories bubbled up. Most of these she recognised. Trinkets only, although weren't these things that had belonged to her ex-boyfriends? How had Haitch ended up with them? No, no. It couldn't be. She looked up to find Sam staring at her.

'Anything you recognise here, Tilly?' he asked.

'What does this mean?' She sounded like a child.

'All your lost boyfriends? They're here, Tilly. All stolen by Haitch.'

'No, no, no!'

Tilda crumpled onto her knees. Both Sam and Dawn got an arm about her and walked her carefully back into the living room.

Now it all made sense. The way Haitch had always patronised and manipulated her. If she was the weaker twin, she didn't want to be reminded of that every time they met. *Life isn't fair. You should grab what you can with both hands*. That's what

Haitch had told her time and time again. Which was funny, in retrospect, considering that Haitch had made Tilda's whole life unfair and had grabbed what she wanted, including her husband and, by all accounts, Dawn's too. It was too much to take in.

Sam and Dawn continued to talk. Breathless, prompting each other if one faltered, the words spewing out. Piling up around her until she couldn't breathe.

Oh, God! This was her twin they were talking about. Her other half, her blood and flesh. Flawed beyond belief. Amoral. A fucking bitch! But, she was still her sister. The one whom she'd shared a womb with from the day they were conceived to the day when they were born. Tilda rubbed at her eyes.

'I wish I could say it another way.' Sam's voice splintered. 'But I can't.'

Her beloved sister was the same woman who had gone out of her way to sleep with Tilda's husband. Identical hair colour? Used her perfume? Wore her clothes? Then did things she would never consent to.

Tilly's voice was flat; all emotion crushed out of her. 'She's done the same to me with every boyfriend?'

'That's what it looks like,' said Sam. 'I'm so sorry, Tilly.'

'And you never intended to kill Damian? It was an accident?'

'It was his fear of cats,' said Dawn, 'he was terrified of them. Simply put, he ran the wrong way. He would have killed us. Look...' She undid her trousers and pulled down the waistband. Huge purple mottled bruises spread across her hip and down her leg. 'I have more, except decorum prevents me from showing you. Sam?'

Sam closed his eyes briefly and then pulled up his t-shirt. His stomach was covered in discoloured marks and swelling lumps. Pulling down the neck of the shirt, Tilda saw the ruddy marks around his neck. Handprints?

'We really were fighting for our lives.'

'That's fucking bad,' said Orpheus. 'Why didn't you tell the authorities what you've just told us. Haven't you made it worse now?'

Dawn said, 'We had no way of explaining why Sam was there, except to say we were planning revenge on Haitch and Damian. And if you look at it that way, it appears we got it.'

'But you planted the watch here.' Tilda raised her head and glared at Sam. 'You're saying that Haitch argued with Damian on that roof and somehow managed to shove him off. To his death. She then found his body and stole his stuff, including the watch she'd bought him. And then she hid the watch back here in her home.' Tilda sniffed. 'As a keepsake, along with all the other bits she's stolen over the years.'

'Yep,' said Sam. 'That's about it.'

'Why would they be arguing? I got the impression they were in love.'

'I'd say,' Sam cleared his throat, 'that she was getting too much for him. I mean, he was happily married.' He cleared his throat again. 'She was embarrassing him and threatening his idyllic home life. Or something like that. Maybe they were grappling over the watch, and he skidded...'

'Hmm.'

Could Tilda condone punishment, which would include prison, for something Haitch hadn't done, in recompense for all the things she had? An eye for an eye. Tenfold. How biblical. Could she do what they were asking of her? She was all for punishment if you'd done the crime, except in this case, Haitch hadn't. No one had. A black cat? *That's who dunnit, m'Lord!* What was that quote? 'One may smile, and smile and be a villain.'

'Orpheus?' Maybe he could help her decide. 'You were with me. You're probably going to be called as a witness. What are you going to do?'

Orpheus leant back in his chair. 'Man. This is some weird-ass shit. I'm still processing. I mean, you couldn't make this up if you tried.'

Sam nodded. 'I did say you wouldn't believe us.'

'I'm not saying I don't believe you,' said Orpheus slowly, 'but you're asking us to implicate an innocent woman in a murder case. You're asking us to lie to the police. That's heavy. You should not do anything like that with no conscious thought. A man is dead. That's pretty final. It sounds as if he brought it all on himself, but he's still dead. I can cope with that. If the cat did it, then that's between him and the cat. But,' he paused and looked fixedly at Tilda, 'we're not saying the cat did it. We're saying Haitch did it. We are the jury, judge and executioner right here in this room.'

'Sam. You should've come to me,' said Tilda. 'You should have been honest. You should have told me the truth.'

'I thought it would break you.'

'And this hasn't?' Her voice cracked.

'I'm so sorry.' Sam knelt down in front of Tilda. 'I can only say for myself, but whatever you decide to do, I won't contest it.'

'Nor will I,' said Dawn.

Orpheus cleared his throat noisily. 'Okay. I'll go with whatever Tilda wants. I'll tell the truth if that's the case, or I'll say I saw Haitch and Damian arguing on the roof terrace. Truth is, I'm about as confused as a person can get. I can understand Sam's thirst for revenge, and I clearly like clairvoyants because of past deeds. Both Damian and your sister sound as if they were a match made in hell, and as I said, he's dead, not murdered as such but dead all the same. If we're going to lay it at the door of your good-for-nothing sister, I need a drink. Has she got any bottles of high-alcohol booze?'

'There's a bottle of brandy in the cupboard here.'

Tilda pulled out the bottle and four small glasses. Her mind was rolling around inside a tumble drier. If only she could find the 'off' button.

'Do you know what you will do?' asked Dawn.

'I'm going to have a drink,' said Tilda, 'and then try not to scream the place down.'

'Good plan,' said Orpheus.

FORTY-EIGHT

Sam

____

THEY TOOK a taxi to Sam and Tilda's old house in Haywards Heath. The 'For Sale' sign made Sam flinch. Had it also affected Tilda? Squinting sideways at her, her face was a blank. Too much information tonight had made her shut down.

They'd all decided to stay together so they could talk through their options in the morning.

Opening the door and ushering them in, Sam said, 'We only have one spare bedroom, so would Dawn like to have it? Orpheus, we can offer you the sofa bed in the living room.' Sam showed Dawn and Orpheus the way. 'I'll sort out towels and whatever you need.'

'I'm beat,' said Orpheus. 'If you don't mind, then the offer of the sofa is great.'

'Me too,' said Dawn. 'This has been a terrible few days. I'm hoping I might actually sleep tonight as I am so tired.'

Exhausted, he and Tilda cleaned their teeth and climbed into bed but not like old times. Curled into a tight ball, the bed shook with her crying.

'Tilly? Do you want me to sleep in one of the armchairs?'

'No. Please stay.'

He ached to put his arm around her. 'I'm so sorry, Tilly.'

'I know.' Rolling over, she propped herself on her elbow. 'Sam? Do you still love me?'

'That's the dumbest thing I've ever heard. Of course, I still love you. The thing is, do you love me? After all this?'

'I'll never stop loving you. It's just the way I love you might be different. I need to get my head around all this.'

'I get that.' His heart was cracking oh-so-slowly.

'I feel as if I've been hit head-on by a juggernaut. You've been living with this for months, but it's so raw for me. How can I trust anyone again if my own twin could do all this to me? I think what hurts the most is that I never knew. I didn't pick up on any of it. There must have been signs? Why didn't I see anything? I'm so unbelievably stupid—'

'No. No.' He gently pulled her onto his shoulder. 'You trusted someone who you should have had blind faith in, who should have protected you, not stabbed you in the back.'

'But I believed that's what you'd done? What does that say about me?'

Her hair was pooling over his chest. 'I didn't give you the option. I felt I had to make sure you didn't find out about Haitch. I thought you'd understand it better if it was me. If I'd told you the truth then, which in hindsight I should have done, I thought you'd take it so much harder. Then it all ran away from me.'

'What should I do?' Her voice was childlike. She traced a finger through the hair on his chest and sniffed loudly. Sam longed to cry too.

'I can't and won't tell you what to do. That has to be your decision and yours alone.'

'So many lives are mixed up in this. How do I know I'll make the right choice?'

'You don't. You do what you think is best and then live with it.'

'That's shit,' Tilda said and turned over, her back now to him.

Sam woke with a start. For a second, he remembered nothing, a blissful state where none of this had happened. Where was he? Then it all came flooding back. Lying in their old marital bed, Sam tilted his head to see if Tilda was beside him. Her side of the bed was empty. Reaching over, he felt that it was cold. She must have been up for a while. Soft voices from downstairs told him that either Orpheus or Dawn was up.

How did he feel about Orpheus? Not too wrung out for jealousy, but he understood. He could never ask the question: had she slept with him? If she had, it was because she'd been under the impression that he was a cheating piece of filth that had shagged another woman. Left her for another woman. Was in love with another woman.

Pushing himself quickly out of bed, he dressed in jogging bottoms and a t-shirt. A shower would have to wait. He could discern voices emanating from the kitchen.

'Hi,' Sam said, 'hope you all slept well.'

Dawn smiled over at him. She was filling a percolator with coffee. 'Well enough for someone who might be going to prison for a long time.' Screwing on the lid, she placed the coffee pot on the hob. 'It'll have to be black, as there's no milk.'

'Black's good,' said Orpheus. He held out his hand towards

Sam. 'Hey, no hard feelings, man. Having heard your stories, I need to say,' he lowered his voice to a whisper, 'that nothing untoward has occurred between your wife and myself.'

Sam shook his outstretched hand. 'Orpheus? If it had, at that point, it wasn't any of my business. I'm glad I'm no longer viewed as the cheating shit. Maybe that's now been upgraded? I have no idea at this point.' Turning, he peered into the living room. 'Is Tilly in there?'

'Yeah, she's looking for anything posted from Mr Ishimoto. If you think about it, quite a few of the competitors are here.'

Sam pushed into the living room to find Tilly staring at the computer screen. There was such a peculiar look on her face that he stopped.

'Tilly? Is everything all right?'

'Not sure.' She looked up and waved him over. 'Sam. This is crazy. Read this.'

Sam bent over her shoulder. An evocative smell of freshly washed hair and body lotion enveloped him. He closed his eyes.

'Sam?' She was looking up at him. 'I knew I wouldn't get the email from Mr Ishimoto, so I looked at his website. Look.'

A photo, stiff poses and forced smiles. There were Orpheus and Dawn. He stared at Haitch.

'God, Tilly. You look so like her. I'd never believe it was you.'

'It wasn't. Read the notice.'

Sam scanned the words.

It is with the greatest pleasure that I can now inform you that the artist Haitch Bee has won the commission. Well done, Haitch Bee. I was impressed with her integrity. I saw a woman who was faithful to her nature. I wish her well and look forward to seeing her new work in the future. Heartfelt condolences to the other competitors. It was an enlightening evening.

———

'Seriously?' Sam stood up quickly. 'Haitch won? I mean, you won. One of you won...' How was that possible? Because although she'd been playing Haitch, this Mr Ishimoto had seen the real Tilly, she couldn't help but be herself.

'Orpheus? Dawn?' Tilda shouted towards the kitchen. 'You've got to see this.'

Orpheus and Dawn came in slowly.

'I won the commission. How about that.'

'Congratulations.' Orpheus spread his hands wide. 'Then you need to give him your bank details.'

'But I can't give my bank details. I'm not Haitch.'

Dawn tutted. 'You won that money because of who you were. Tilda. Not Haitch. I very much doubt that Haitch would have won by herself.'

'I have to let him know that it wasn't m—' She fluttered a hand over her mouth. 'Oh. No.'

'If you do that,' Sam said slowly, 'that will definitely let the authorities know that something is very wrong. Dawn has already said she saw Haitch and Damian arguing on the roof terrace...'

'They'll think it was me.' Tilda frowned. 'They'll think he found out that we'd swapped, we argued, and then I shoved him over the cliff.' She shook her head. 'I'll be done for manslaughter or worse. I never thought of that.'

'Well, neither did we,' said Dawn, 'as we didn't know you were pretending to be your sister at that time.' A strange look played across her face.

'What's the matter?' said Sam.

Dawn sighed. 'There was a moment when I wondered if it might be you. Then I disregarded that idea.'

Sam took a step forward. 'You never thought to mention that to me?'

'I really didn't think there would be any reason for Haitch not to be Haitch.'

Sam nodded. 'I know that one.' He glanced at Tilda, who twisted her face away.

A gurgling came from the kitchen.

'Coffee's brewed.'

Dawn hurried back. They could hear the clack of mugs and cutlery.

'Here we go.'

The smell of freshly percolated coffee was wonderful. Sam took his mug last. No one made eye contact, staring at the floor, gazing out the window. It was as if they'd all been put through the wrong cycle on the drier and come out crumpled, baggy, ill-fitting.

'I've made a decision.' Tilda thumped her mug on the table. 'And I've got to do it now.'

FORTY-NINE

Matilda

'ARE YOU SURE ABOUT THIS?' Sam stood in the living room doorway, one hand on the door. He looked as though he wanted to bolt out of there as fast as he could. Dawn was lurking in the hallway, and Orpheus was making himself busy in the kitchen. 'We can go down the shops – pick up a pint of milk? You know? Give yourself more time to think. Some... privacy?'

'If I have more time, I might change my mind.' Tilda tapped the phone on her leg. Sat curled into the arm of the sofa, she shivered, although it wasn't cold. 'Anyway, I'd have thought you'd want to hear this. After everything that's happened. Isn't this what it was all about?'

Sam shook his head slightly. 'It's more complicated than that, isn't it?'

'It always is.'

'We never meant to involve you.'

'No. You wanted to implicate my twin for a murder that she didn't commit. Of course, that wouldn't involve me, would it?' Did she want to cry? Laugh hysterically? Roar her pain out until her lungs bled?

Sam's grip on the door tightened. 'I wanted, well, we wanted to punish her. I thought I'd already lost you. I didn't think further than that.'

'No. I can see that. Stay, Sam. I need you here.'

'What about me?' Dawn poked her head in over his shoulder. 'Shall I go?'

'No, I think you should all hear this.' She raised her voice. 'Orpheus?'

'Coming.'

'Okay.' Sam walked in, head down and perched at the other end of the sofa. 'Are you ready for this? Do you know what you're going to say to her?'

Dawn followed him in and sat on the facing seat and Orpheus on the other.

Tilda shrugged. 'Kind of. I think I'll go where she leads.'

Sam wiped an unsteady hand across his face as Tilda keyed in the number. Tilda stared over at him, resisting the urge to chew on a fingernail, twiddle at her top or do any number of things she knew she did when nervous. Who was in control now?

'Hello, Haitch.' She put the phone on speaker.

They'd been allowed a phone call. Tilda could practically hear her own heartbeat thumping in her chest.

'Tilda!' Haitch's voice was jubilant. 'Finally! Thank fuck! I knew you wouldn't let me down. I've been going mad here, wondering what was going on. Hope you've got the champers in. When are they going to let me out?'

'I don't know.'

'Really? You've told the police that it was you in Spain? That I had nothing to do with Damian's death because I was at home with the flu?' There was a long wait. 'Tilda? Are you still there?'

'Yes, Haitch?'

'You have told them, haven't you.' It was a statement, not a question. 'Tilda? Answer me.'

Tilda wet her lips. It was amazing how dry they were. 'You know, I've got a question for you. You remember that day when I called you to say that Sam had left me?'

Tilda swivelled sideways and studied Sam. His skin was grey tinged, and dark circles ringed his eyes. This last week had taken its toll.

There was an intake of breath. 'Yes, of course I do. Why?'

'And do you remember you asked if I knew who she was?' Sam's hands were clasped white-knuckled in his lap.

'Yes.' Was that a hesitation? Did she realise what was coming next?

'And I said I asked him, but he said I didn't know her, which was good as I also said I'd smash her fucking face in if I did.' A drawn-out pause. 'Do you remember that?'

'Yes.'

'And do you remember how you kept saying "I'm so sorry", but I didn't understand why you should be sorry, then I thought you were sorry for me...'

'Yes.' Tilda heard her swallow noisily. 'I remember.'

'Well, certain things have come to light. You know, cufflinks and lots of other little things that I seem to remember. I found them in your undies drawer when I was in your flat trying to help you.'

'You went through my knickers drawer?'

'Yes. As I said when I was trying to get you off the hook for murder. That was when.'

'Tilda?'

What was wrong with Haitch's voice? Sounded as if she was half-strangled.

'Yes, Haitch?'

'I... I...'

'Yes, Haitch? Is there something you'd like to tell me?'

It was amazing. Such self-restraint when she could be shouting obscenities and hurling the phone across the room.

'I never... I never meant to hurt you. You must believe that.'

'You never meant to hurt me, repeatedly? Is that what you're saying?'

'Yes.' Tilda heard another deep intake of breath. 'I'm so sorry, Tilda.'

'Well, if you mean it and you're sorry, that makes it okay then, doesn't it.'

'Really? Am I forgiven?' Such hope in her voice.

'No. Dear God, Haitch. It doesn't work that way.' There would be no absolution here. 'You destroyed my life. Not once but many times. You purposefully wrecked my happiness with the man I wanted to spend the rest of my days with. So, back to your original question. Have I told the police that I was in Spain instead of you? Well, quite frankly, Haitch, no, I haven't.'

'What? But you were—'

'Was I? No, I think you've got muddled up. You went to Spain, using your passport, wearing your clothes. I was at home, finishing my commission for Walker Books.'

'Tilda... what are you doing? Please don't do this.' There was a scrunching sound. 'What did Sam tell you? He's lying to you, Tilda. Oh, the man's a snake. He was the one who came onto me. He seduced me! It wasn't my fault.'

'It's never your fault, is it? Here's the thing, Sam has only ever loved me. Yes, you heard that right. So, tell me, Haitch. What were you wearing that afternoon? Because I distinctly remember I couldn't find one of my dresses and a pair of shoes. Had no idea where they had gone. Do you?'

'I might have borrowed them at some point. That means nothing. You know we've always shared.'

'Hmm. Yes, I think we have always shared. At least I have.

You don't wear anything like me. Not for years. Too boring and house wifey. So, Sam seduced you, eh?'

'You have to believe me. Sam said he loved you, but he wanted more. He told me he'd always had a thing for me. Knew I could give him what he wanted. It's his fault, Tilda. Not mine.'

'I'm sorry, weren't you there then? I mean, whatever happened to saying, "no". If he tried it on with you, why didn't you tell him to fuck off, or even let me know that my husband was a piece of shit?'

'I didn't think you'd believe me.'

'But you still had sex with my husband. That's the bit I have trouble with, Haitch. Wearing my clothes, smelling the same as me. You even had your hair coloured like mine. I remember thinking that was odd at the time. Different style when I saw you later, although I think you looked just like me that day.'

'Tilda, this isn't funny. You can rage at me all you want later. I swear I'll make it up to you but get me out of here. Please?'

'Pretty please?'

'I didn't kill Damian, and you know it. I don't know who did, but you can't leave me here. You have to tell them the truth. You must.'

Was Haitch beginning to cry? Big, fat crocodile tears or real tears of fear? She should be frightened.

'No, what I have to do is try to sort out my marriage to my husband. You know we missed our wedding anniversary? Seven years, with a little hiccup in between. But I truly believe we're going to make it. Yes, I feel very positive right now.'

Glancing at Sam, she noted he now had his eyes closed. His face looked wet. Dawn had her hands clamped over her mouth. Her eyes were wide. Orpheus, bless him, grinned and gave her a thumbs up.

'Tilda? Don't do this to me. You're the only one who can save me. You know I didn't kill Damian, and I know you didn't

do it either. There's a killer out there! You can't let them go free.'
She laughed too loudly. 'I know you're punishing me and
getting me all wound up. That's okay. I understand, but you've
got do what's right. You have to. You just have to.'

'Don't worry, Haitch. I'll do what's right. You'll be fine.'

Did Haitch even understand the connotation of what she'd
just said? *You'll be fine, Tilda. You'll get over it.*

'You will tell them it was you in Spain?'

'No, Haitch. I won't. But as you've said to me so many times,
"you'll get over it".' She swiped across the phone, hearing a wail
that was cut off. It was done.

Sam reached across and brushed her lightly on the shoulder.
Tilda squeezed her eyes shut.

'I know you're not okay,' he said, 'but you can still change
your mind. This might be enough of a lesson for Haitch.'

'Dawn's already implicated by saying she saw Haitch and
Damian arguing on the roof.' Tilda snorted. 'Then, if I say I was
impersonating my sister, I'd be dropped right in it.'

Dawn stirred. 'We were the ones who started all this. We
should be the ones to end it.'

Tilda leant back into the sofa and gazed up at the ceiling.
'This is the hardest thing I've ever had to do. I love my sister, but
I also hate her guts. She was happy to steal my whole life. To
steal Dawn's, too. And Damian, he killed his own unborn child
and didn't show one speck of remorse.' Peering across at Dawn,
Tilda mumbled: 'Sorry, Dawn. I felt something was off with him
when I met him in Spain. He scared me, and I believe that was
what Haitch found so attractive in him. I wonder what she'd
think if she knew what he'd done and how he'd blamed you.'

'I don't know if she'd care,' said Sam, 'as long as she got what
she wanted.'

Dawn smiled. 'Whatever the outcome, if I go to prison, at
least I'll be free of him.'

'You won't go to prison.' Tilda straightened her shoulders. 'The police have your statement, and Orpheus…' She nodded at him. 'You said you'll say the same? Is that still true?'

'If that's what you all want. It doesn't feel good, I must admit, but we're kind of stuck here.'

'See?' Tilda continued breathlessly. 'Two witnesses, totally unconnected. Three, if you count me. I'm going to say she was addicted to Damian, that he was like a bad drug she couldn't shake free from.'

'I'll second that.' Dawn raised an eyebrow. 'I should've listened to my mother.'

'So,' said Sam, 'we're all really doing this?'

'I think,' said Dawn, 'that Mr Ishimoto might even let you have the money if he feels you've entertained him enough. Although that would drop us all in it.'

'Well, if Haitch is in prison,' said Sam, 'it might be a bit tricky spending it. And I'd be pretty pissed off if he does still give it to her, all things considered. Tilly won it. Haitch doesn't deserve a penny.'

Tilda frowned. 'I doubt his entertainment would extend to someone who might be convicted of manslaughter. He's a businessman, after all.'

'True.' Sam nodded. 'His business affiliations probably wouldn't be best pleased if he's seen giving money to a criminal, no matter what he gets up to in his spare time.'

Tilda said softly, 'I think we're all going to need a holiday after this—'

'But please not Spain.' Dawn shrugged. 'How about Norway? The Fjords?'

'I still can't believe any of this has happened.' Putting her head in her hands, Tilda started to cry and then felt Sam's arms encircle her. As he'd always done. She scrabbled to pull him closer and whispered, 'I love you, Sam,' into his ear.

Epilogue

'MRS GREEN.' DS Durrant looked kindly at Tilda. 'Thanks for coming in at such short notice to answer a few questions for us. Do you mind if I record this?'

'No. That's fine. Anything to help.'

He placed a recording device on the table between them.

'Would you like a cup of tea or coffee?'

He waved behind him. They were in an interview room. It was similar to all the interview rooms she'd seen on every police procedural show: grey, bland and unwelcoming.

'No. I'm fine thanks. What is this all about, please?'

'Can you tell me what the relationship between your sister Harriet and Damian Montgomery was like?'

'Her agent?' Tilda sucked on her teeth. 'That's a very personal question and I'm not sure I want to answer it.'

'It would help us greatly with our enquiries if you could answer now.'

Tilda flinched. 'Okay.' She flapped her hands around. 'Haitch is a very intense person...'

'So I gather. And?'

'It was like Damian was a drug and she was addicted.'

'Did she ever give him any gifts? Outside of his agent's commission?'

'I...' Tilda hung her head. 'There was this watch...'

'Can you describe it?'

'It was posh. And I think it was pink, you know, that rose gold that everyone drools over. Personally. I don't like it. It reminds me of something that's come out of a cheap Christmas cracker.'

'And you're sure it was a gift for Mr Montgomery?'

'That's what she told me.'

'Your sister Harriet has made some serious allegations.' He sat in the chair facing her.

Tilda rolled her eyes. 'What now?'

'Can you tell us where you were from Thursday the sixteenth of June to Friday the seventeenth of June this year?'

Tilda looked away as if she was trying to remember. 'I was with my husband. We'd been having some problems, and we decided to take a bit of time off to try and sort them out.'

Would God strike her down? Could a bolt of lightning hurtle in through the police station roof to blast her to ash?

'Are you sure about that? You weren't in Spain at that time?'

Keep control. They'd discussed what she was going to say. 'Why would I be in Spain? I had a deadline for work the following week, so there'd be no time for a jolly to Spain.' She waited a moment only. 'My sister Harriet was in Spain that week.'

'You're telling me you didn't impersonate your sister at a party held by a Mr Ishimoto?'

'Impersonate her? Is that what she's said? Have you met her? We might look similar, yet we're poles apart in personality. Anyone who'd met her would know if I'd tried to pretend to be her.' She swept her hand down the length of her body. Knee-length skirt, buttoned-up blouse and pretty sandals. A touch of make-up. 'I could never pull it off.'

The officer's eyebrows rose as he also looked her up and down. 'I see, though you must concede that it is possible? Being identical twins?'

'I suppose anything's possible. As I said, I was at home with my husband, Sam.' Shaking her head, Tilda rose to her feet. 'Is she trying to implicate me in this? I can't believe it.'

'She does seem to think that you are the key to this. That you were there and not her.'

'And what's her evidence? That we look alike?'

'Quite frankly, Mrs Green, there's no evidence that anyone else was involved in Mr Montgomery's death. Forensics have confirmed the DNA on the watch matches the deceased and your sister. The watch was found in her drawer at home after his death and there was no other DNA on the body except from his wife. This appears to be an open and shut case.' He switched off the recorder. 'Thank you for your time. I'm sure all this has been a terrible shock to you.'

'It's awful. I don't think I can ever forgive her for trying to pin this on me.'

'I bet.' He motioned at the door. 'Thanks again for your time and we'll be in touch if we need anything more from you.'

Acknowledgments

I would like to thank my publisher, Hobeck Books, for believing in me and my work. So many, many thanks to Rebecca and Adrian. And thanks to Jayne for her fabulous cover.

Many thanks to all my readers. I love to get pictures of readers with my books while on holiday or curled up in front of the fire at home. It's special. I love chatting with you all, so get in contact with me.

Thanks to Brian Price for being the go-to man for all police and procedural authenticity. Without him, we would just make stuff up!

Thanks also to the wonderful authors, indie and traditionally published, who have read and reviewed my books.

So, again, thanks to everyone who has helped me on my journey to here.

And, lastly, if you have enjoyed this book, please can you leave a rating or review. It makes an immense difference to a new author.

Thanks

HILLY BARMBY

About the Author

Hilly attended Rochester College of Art to experience an excellent Foundation Course, which led to a degree course in Graphic Design at Central School of Art and Design in London. Here, she led a colourful life, which she has woven into many of her stories.

After her degree course, she went on a woodworking course to make furniture. Combining her art and woodworking skills, she got a stall at Covent Garden Craft Market to sell hand-made chess and backgammon sets.

She moved to Brighton, a fabulous city and this is where Best Served Cold is set. After teaching Design Technology for fifteen years, she gave it all up to relocate to Órgiva in southern Spain. She has been here for the last seven years, living happily in an old farmhouse on an organic fruit farm in the mountains, with her partner and two rescue dogs.

Hilly is also part of Artists' Network Alpujarra (ANA), a community of artists who have exhibited extensively in the region of the Alpujarra. She also makes ceramics, jewellery, and up-cycles anything not nailed down.

To connect with Hilly you can find her on a variety of platforms.

Website: www.hillybarmbyauthor.com
Instagram: www.instagram.com/hillyollie

Twitter: https://twitter.com/Hilly_Barmby
TikTok: www.tiktok.com/@hillybarmby387
Facebook: www.facebook.com/HillyOllieBarmby
BlueSky: https://bsky.app/profile/hilliebillie.bsky.social

Hobeck Books – the home of great stories

We hope you've enjoyed reading this novel by Hilly Barmby. To keep up to date on Hilly's fiction writing please do follow her on Twitter.

Hobeck Books offers a number of short stories and novellas, free for subscribers in the compilation *Crime Bites*.

- *Echo Rock* by Robert Daws
- *Old Dogs, Old Tricks* by AB Morgan
- *The Silence of the Rabbit* by Wendy Turbin
- *Never Mind the Baubles: An Anthology of Twisted Winter Tales* by the Hobeck Team (including many of the Hobeck authors and Hobeck's two publishers)
- *The Clarice Cliff Vase* by Linda Huber
- *Here She Lies* by Kerena Swan
- *The Macnab Principle* by R.D. Nixon
- *Fatal Beginnings* by Brian Price
- *A Defining Moment* by Lin Le Versha
- *Saviour* by Jennie Ensor

- *You Can't Trust Anyone These Days* by Maureen Myant

Also please visit the Hobeck Books website for details of our other superb authors and their books, and if you would like to get in touch, we would love to hear from you.

Hobeck Books also presents a weekly podcast, the Hobcast, where founders Adrian Hobart and Rebecca Collins discuss all things book related, key issues from each week, including the ups and downs of running a creative business. Each episode includes an interview with one of the people who make Hobeck possible: the editors, the authors, the cover designers. These are the people who help Hobeck bring great stories to life. Without them, Hobeck wouldn't exist. The Hobcast can be listened to from all the usual platforms but it can also be found on the Hobeck website: **www.hobeck.net/hobcast**.